# Meet Me at Apple Blossom Lane

## ANITA FAULKNER

ONE PLACE. MANY STORIES

HQ
An imprint of HarperCollins*Publishers* Ltd
1 London Bridge Street
London SE1 9GF

www.harpercollins.co.uk

HarperCollins*Publishers*
Macken House, 39/40 Mayor Street Upper,
Dublin 1 D01 C9W8
This edition 2026

1
First published in Great Britain by HQ,
an imprint of HarperCollins*Publishers* Ltd 2026

Copyright © Anita Faulkner 2026

Anita Faulkner asserts the moral right to be identified as the author of this work.
A catalogue record for this book is available from the British Library.

ISBN: 9780008781644

This novel is entirely a work of fiction. The names, characters and incidents portrayed in it are the work of the author's imagination. Any resemblance to actual persons, living or dead, events or localities is entirely coincidental.

All rights reserved. No part of this publication may be reproduced, stored in a retrieval system, or transmitted, in any form or by any means, electronic, mechanical, photocopying, recording or otherwise, without the prior permission of the publishers.

Without limiting the exclusive rights of any author, contributor or the publisher of this publication, any unauthorized use of this publication to train generative artificial intelligence (AI) technologies is expressly prohibited. HarperCollins also exercise their rights under Article 4(3) of the Digital Single Market Directive 2019/790 and expressly reserve this publication from the text and data mining exception.

Printed and bound in the UK using 100% Renewable
Electricity by CPI Group (UK) Ltd

# Praise for Anita Faulkner

'Utterly charming! I adored every page of this sweet, funny, feel-good story' **Sandy Barker**

'Hilarious, sexy and romantic. I was rooting for Rosie from page one' **Susan Buchanan**

'Anita serves heart, soul – and a generous helping of pumpkin spice, I adored it' **Nicola May**

'*You Had Me at Pumpkin Patch* will make you laugh, make you swoon and above all leave you feeling cosy and warm. The perfect autumn read! **Helga Jensen**

'Warm, witty, and completely wonderful! My favourite read of the year so far' **Jaimie Admans**

'Cosy, charming and utterly captivating' **Heidi Swain**

'Full of fun and colour **Bella Osborne**

'Endlessly joy-lit. Bursting with character and warmth' **Christie Barlow**

'A heart-warming and uplifting romance!' **Holly Martin**

'Such a fun ride! Faulkner brings colour and humour to every line' **Pernille Hughes**

'I absolutely adored this book. Fresh, funny and upbeat' **Kitty Wilson**

'A vibrant, charming book. Makes me quite want to take a colourful adventure of my own, especially after these rather beige past couple of years!' **Isla Gordon**

**ANITA FAULKNER** writes warm and witty romcoms from her upcycled bureau near the Cotswolds. Described by her agent Kate Nash as 'a sparkling new voice', Anita loves dreaming up quirky characters and extremely awkward dates.

Her debut novel, *A Colourful Country Escape*, was shortlisted for two Romantic Novelists' Association awards. It was followed by *The Gingerbread Café* – which is too delicious to be missed. Anita is thrilled to be writing for HQ Digital. Her autumn romcom, *You Had Me at Pumpkin Patch*, is packed with her usual warmth and wit – and a whole lot of pumpkins. And *Meet Me at Apple Blossom Lane* is set to bloom as the next small-town spring romance.

When Anita's not writing, she's busy coaching other writers, running her fiction writers' membership, Writers' Dream House, celebrating books in her Facebook group, Chick Lit and Prosecco. If you're a fan of books and stories, Anita would love to stay in touch! Join her mailing list for backstage news, offers and her exclusive monthly LOVE letters … www.anitafaulkner.co.uk

## Also by Anita Faulkner
*You Had Me at Pumpkin Patch*

*To Mumsie*
*Thank you for giving me life, love, and a lifelong fascination with books and stories. You have been my one constant thing. Xx*

# Chapter 1

New Year ... same old ridiculousness. Actually, no. Much worse ridiculousness. But as a renowned professional love coach, Alyssa wasn't about to type that into Instagram.

*Deep breaths. Just smile.* She forced a grin, moved her phone screen to where the disco lights made her look a little less garish, and snapped a few selfies. Surely one of them would do.

It wasn't that she didn't enjoy a New Year's Eve party, exactly. She just wished they were a bit earlier in the day, so she wasn't tempted to wedge her eyelids open with crispy breadsticks or try not to yawn into her sleeves. And they'd be better if everyone wasn't dribbling drunk, yelling songs about not forgetting *auld* acquaintances (who were probably better off disremembered) and slurring nonsense about how much they 'loved' each other. (They honestly didn't.) Oh, and she couldn't deal with fancy dress. Though she did have a *really* good reason for that. Nor karaoke – which was an awkwardly touchy subject. And now she thought about it, those popper things were a tad frustrating. She pulled a clump of stringy paper from her hair.

OK, so in fairness, she probably *didn't* love a New Year's Eve party. But nobody liked a fun sponge – so she'd learned to pull up her positive pants and play her part. Her boyfriend, Arnaud, deserved that much. He'd put so much into planning the party for his family and friends, in his gorgeous Chelsea house where they both lived. He'd forked out for a grand marquee with proper heating and twinkly lights. A dance floor. A band, a stage, flowing cocktails. Objectively speaking, he was a sweet guy. She almost felt guilty that she'd politely declined to get down with the quirky creature costumes. Her pink chiffon could arguably pass as a jellyfish, if you squinted a bit and you weren't at all familiar with marine life.

'*Ma petite puce*.' Arnaud arrived at her side and planted a kiss on her cheek, even if it was a tad drooly after his umpteenth French martini. She'd become used to being called his little flea, which was apparently a term of endearment.

Music boomed around them, the band playing something by The Killers. Guests chatted loudly, a few still bopping around, dressed as everything from bumblebees to monkeys. The air smelt of expensive perfume and the remnants of quail egg blinis.

She smiled at Arnaud, put down her drink, and rearranged the wonky ears on his giraffe outfit. He was tall, blond and good-looking, and always had a twinkle in his eye. They'd been together for nearly two years, and he was definitely a catch. Noticing the phone she was still clutching in one hand, he slipped into place beside her, ready for a joint photo. He was great like that too. He knew it looked good for her brand if she was in a stable relationship, just like it was handy for him to have a girlfriend with him for work schmoozing and those slightly dull golf dinners. As much as she cared for him, she chose her relationships for convenience, and she'd always been honest about that. It wasn't her fault if she was a love coach who didn't believe in love – even if she didn't dare let that catastrophic truth out of the bag.

'You've thrown a brilliant party,' Alyssa said kindly, as she uploaded something sparkly and upbeat to social media, wishing her heaps of Instagram followers a happy new year. Was it rude to ask him if people might be leaving soon so she could peel off her scratchy false eyelashes and get to bed?

'It's only just beginning,' said Arnaud, pulling her into a hug. He was particularly clingy this evening.

Alyssa felt her heart sink. It was nearly one a.m., and most of the canapés had been scoffed hours ago. Hadn't they done their hosting duties?

'Will you dance with me?' His big brown eyes looked hopeful.

Oh God. He meant smoochy dancing, didn't he? The band was moving on to the slow songs, and she hated all that stuff. He knew that about her, Though with the drinks and general revelry, perhaps he'd forgotten. He'd been busy all night, mingling, dancing, bringing people together. She'd fluctuated from being politely on his arm, overseeing logistics, to hiding in a quiet corner to check in with her social media. Some might say the latter was superficial, but it was her work. And it didn't hurt to have a pocketful of online acquaintances for when real life wasn't your cup of tea.

'Need to powder my nose!' she said quickly, even though she wasn't actually having a T-zone crisis. She pointed towards the nearest bathroom and shrugged apologetically, trying not to feel too bad about those puppy-dog eyes.

Though when she got back from the bathroom, things had gone from inconvenient to mildly disturbing. Arnaud was up on the stage where the band had been, only now the karaoke machine was back on and he was bellowing love songs and scanning the room, presumably for her. Which was fine if you were into that sort of thing. But if drunken love songs gave you flashbacks to the worst night of your life, they could make the room spin. She made to turn away, but he spotted her.

'Alyssa! *Ma chérie. Mon coeur.*'

His heart? This did not sound good.

'Come onto the stage. Let me sing to you.'

About what? She was perfectly fine down here. And suddenly the faces in the room were looking at her expectantly. Several safari animals began cheering. Somebody kicked off one of those unhelpful rhythmic claps. What was this all about? Arnaud had paid for perfectly good entertainment. He didn't need to start singing badly or to drag her into his merriment.

'I'm fine. Thank you.' She held up a hand, trying to look breezy, even if she felt more like she was being whipped by a strong wind. What had they put in her sparkling water?

'Awww, she doesn't like too much affection,' Arnaud crooned to the crowd. 'But sometimes, I cannot help it. She is my everything.'

Alyssa blinked a few times and arranged her face into a smile, though she could already sense it cracking. What was he doing? Had he lost the memo? Was his right mind on a mini break? She knew that for most people, public displays of affection – and private ones – were entirely normal, rather than moments that instigated an internal meltdown. But perhaps most people hadn't been publicly and irrevocably stung before.

And now Arnaud was holding out a hand to her, willing her to join him, and someone dressed as a hairy black tarantula was trying to jostle her towards the stage. As a coach, she had coping mechanisms for times like this. But as a frustratingly flawed human, most of them flew out of the window when it came to herself.

Instead, it was as though her world was spiralling, sucking her back to that awful night. The night, twelve years ago, when she'd been standing on a stage in front of almost *everyone* from her hometown, dressed as a big sponge turtle. She clapped a hand over her mouth, as though her current actions might change history. But back then, the words had already been said. She still felt the scar of them. Because she'd declared what she'd naively thought was her *true love* to her childhood sweetheart, when he'd been secretly making offspring with her so-called best friend. A double kick in the soul. It was a night she never spoke of and did her best to block out.

She reached out to steady herself, her hand landing in a plate of congealed cod's roe.

Arnaud was laughing gently into the microphone, like her sudden clumsiness was the most adorable thing. Which was what made it so much worse when he told the room he loved her, and he wanted to make her his wife.

*His wife?* Her stomach churned.

She'd always been clear that love and marriage were not part of her package deal. If he'd known about that fateful night when she'd made a massive fool of herself, he wouldn't be doing this. As for marriage. From everything she'd seen, it could be as precarious as a cheap wedding cake topper with sickly icing. But now wasn't the time to start thinking about cake.

'I said I love you, *ma chérie*. Do you love me too? Will we get married?'

She'd get married when pigs grew wings.

Alyssa tried to straighten herself, assessing the situation. As proposals went, this seemed impromptu. No ring, no getting down on one knee. Arnaud would probably regret it when his hangover slid in. But she knew how rejection felt. How could she do this with minimum destruction?

'Fish finger disaster!' she blurted out, holding up her food-smeared hand as she backed away from the crowds, her belly still lurching. 'Actually, I feel a bit ...' She pulled her best *queasy* face and darted back in the direction of the bathroom.

It didn't take long before Arnaud was knocking on the door, asking if she was OK and how long she'd been feeling sick. She could hear him telling one of the hired waiters to start clearing the marquee and handing out coats. Well, that much was a relief.

She could have stayed hidden in the toilet, pretending she was too ill to come out. Or she could have said: '*Yes, yes, I love you too, my feathery little duckling.*' But it wasn't fair to lie to him. And she'd been in enough relationships of convenience to know when it was time to conveniently end it. For all of her many faults, she wasn't cruel. So, taking a breath she opened the bathroom door.

# Chapter 2

It didn't take long for Arnaud to establish Alyssa wasn't ill. She did *a lot* of pretending to the outside world, but she drew the line at stringing her boyfriends along. Fair was fair.

'You can't just say you love me?' Arnaud asked, his body slumped against the bathroom tiles, his giraffe ears once again wonky.

'No,' she said simply, from her spot on top of the toilet seat lid. Her tone was gentle, but her words honest. She'd ended a good few relationships when they'd started to look too serious, but preparing to dump someone with a charming view of a Villeroy and Boch bidet was a new one. 'And I'm sorry. It's really not you.' She winced at the cliché, but it was true.

'Don't you even have a heart?'

'Of course I do.'

Nobody could live without such a vital organ, and she'd definitely felt it beating as she'd rushed from the crowds to lock herself in the loo. Though she knew what he meant. Their relationship had been heading towards the commit-or-run stage – especially with her being thirty-one, and him a decade older. And if he was suddenly becoming the *commit* sort, he deserved to find someone who could give him more.

'I'm sorry,' she repeated, standing to straighten his costume for the very last time. 'I'll be out of your hair in the morning.' She knew she had to make it easy on both of them, even though she had literally no clue where she would go.

There went the end of yet another era. Exactly how many eras was one person allowed? Alyssa snapped a few last shots of herself with Arnaud's big house in the background. Not that she lived there anymore – but people didn't need to know *all* of her business. She sighed at the photos, opting for one where her choppy pink waves looked decidedly more carefree than she felt, and where enough of her gym top was showing to imply she was popping out for a bracing, New Year's Day run. Which she absolutely wasn't, because real exercise was hard, sweaty work.

With a few prods, Alyssa uploaded the photo to social media, typing, *'New Year, New Me!'* with as many joyful emojis as she could muster.

Well, it wasn't exactly a lie. Things *were* about to change, in a huge, nose-diving-without-a-parachute kind of way. She tried to stop her insides from plummeting. Oh, Arnaud. He'd picked his moment to start kidding himself he was falling for her. And whilst he'd half-heartedly said she could stay on for a few days in one of the spare rooms, she knew from past experience it wasn't wise to stick around. He'd only start getting sentimental again and make it even more embarrassing for them both. It was safer to get out of there.

She blinked a few times, trying to ignore the strange stinging sensation at the backs of her eyes, which was probably just the cold weather. It was flipping freezing in London in January. She shoved her phone into her bag and wrestled herself into her pink-and-black parka, and a black beanie hat. She did *not* want to be recognised on this next, humiliating leg of her journey. It was a side effect of her large online following that people often spotted her – and appearances were everything. Like umbrellas on a wet day, it paid to keep them up.

Alyssa trudged along the quiet suburban streets, dragging her fake Lulu Guinness suitcase through the grey sleet. Even though the affluent area of Chelsea was postcard perfect, fluffy white festive snow was reserved for Christmas cards and those cheesy romcoms she could no longer bear to watch. Real life was never that glossy, even with an Instagram filter. She kept her gaze down, not wanting to see the glowing lights from other people's vast and beautiful homes. At least their windows would be shut in this weather, so she didn't have to hear jolly voices or laughter, even if most of it would surely be exaggerated. Didn't everyone feel a bit miserable, with another long year stretching out in front of them?

She shook her head and lifted her chin, remembering what she would say if she was coaching someone. *Reasons to be cheerful.* She had seven whole days to get back on top of life, before she ran out of money and might have to start busking or selling her body to old men. And the place she'd managed to bag at extremely short notice hadn't *actually* been listed as 'The World's Grottiest Flat'. There might be all sorts of reasons the rent was as cheap as itchy knock-off perfume, and the landlord had declined to share photos.

Her eyes flicked to her watch. Just a few more minutes. A few more imposing streets. Alyssa had arranged for the Uber to pick her up somewhere other than Arnaud's house, and to drop her off a few streets from her dreaded destination. She didn't want anyone putting two and two together and spreading unfortunate gossip online.

Was it too late to wish she was the sort of person who saved money instead of splurged it on things that temporarily cheered her up? Not that she'd earned much of it lately. As for financial planning – that was for people who thought about their future or had dependants to worry about. She had none. Which was *fine*. But she was innovative, wasn't she? With her primal fear of commitment, she was always having to start afresh. Sometimes with drastically different hair and a brand-new name. Because *Alyssa Heart* certainly wasn't her real one.

Spotting the Uber, she waved at the driver and when he popped the lid of the boot, she crammed her luggage in. Then she pulled her hat down as far as she could, folded herself into the back seat, and gave the man a muffled greeting.

The car reeked of stale takeaway and pine-scented Magic Tree, and it was just her luck that the driver was the sort to tape photos of his wife and kids to the dashboard, like a montage of his lovely life. She looked away.

'Hackney, is it?' he asked, giving her a quick glance in the mirror.

She'd already typed the exact destination into the app, hadn't she? 'Yes. Thank you.'

'Bit of a comedown. From here, I mean.' The driver chuckled.

Didn't he know it was rude to make conversation in London? That was what she liked most about this place. Not like the nosy Cotswold town where she'd been born. She managed a polite 'mmm hmm'.

'Been staying with family?'

She didn't *mean* to grit her teeth. 'No.' Perhaps if she kept her answers short, he'd get the hint, as harmless as he was.

'Friends?'

Alyssa felt herself bristle. She had plenty of them, of course she did. It was just they were all online, and she'd never met most of them. That was perfectly normal these days. Real-life friends, like men, could trash your heart, if you let them.

'No,' she concluded. He didn't need the full story.

He paused for a second, eyeing her in the mirror again. When was he going to start this forest-smelling car?

'Do I know you?'

Used to people sort of recognising her, she was running out of patience. 'I'm kind of late, so …'

'Right, yes.' He started the engine. 'Let's get you home.'

'It's not my ...' Her voice trailed off. Because it was about to become the closest thing she had.

If she didn't know better, she might wonder if that weird, hollow feeling in her chest was because no one was expecting her. She'd made a quick bank transfer for a week's rent, and there would be a key shoved under the doormat. No one would care what time she arrived, or even if she didn't. But smiley taxi driver and his two-dimensional, slightly fading family didn't have to know that.

Alyssa must have fallen asleep on the journey, which was probably just as well. She didn't need to dwell on what she was leaving behind, nor where exactly she'd be landing. Anyway, Hackney definitely had its desirable parts, even if World's Grottiest Flat might not be one of them. Having waved her driver off with a tip she couldn't really afford, to account for her bad mood and exhausted snoring, she dragged her stuff up the sticky-carpeted flights of stairs and arrived at her new front door. One hundred and thirteen. It was a myth that numbers could be unlucky.

'Right, well. Let's crack on.'

There was only herself to hear – which was probably for the best. In fact, the whole tower block had seemed deserted, like one of those vacated places, earmarked for destruction. As long as the wrecking ball didn't arrive too soon, what could go wrong? Like a person who'd resolved to tear off a plaster, she whipped the key from under the mat, turned it in the lock and stepped inside.

'Urgh.' Her hand flew to cover her nose and mouth, wishing for the simpler times when her senses were being assaulted by pine fresh. What was that stench? Was her landlord harbouring *dead people*?

She grabbed some spray from her bag and moved around, throwing windows open and performing a vanilla-scented fumigation. At least she didn't have a year-start hangover, or she would have felt even more nauseous. She was now strictly a one-drink kind of girl, because too much wine time could lead to utter humiliation. Although maybe New Year's Eve would have gone quicker with a wine glass stem to strangle. How could you be in a room packed with people and feel completely alone? She'd been doing much the same for at least a decade, albeit different partners, different parties. Though perhaps the loneliness was to be expected when she only chose men who were unlikely to get emotionally attached, and she swiftly moved on if they did. They were always decent guys, and definitely not married. She had morals. But she opted for men who were too busy focusing on other things to dote on her, like Boardroom Bradley, who'd relished a good meeting and had rarely been home before nine p.m. Or Vincenzo with the nice holiday villa, who travelled a lot to see family so didn't get under her feet. Or were divorced and done, like laid-back Lionel, who had no desire for further romantic gestures, wedding bells or bearing crotch fruit.

She sighed. Much like the state of this flat, Arnaud had finally seen the cracks she couldn't paper over.

Alyssa reached up and swiped a cobweb, grateful at least that it didn't have a spider attached to it. This place wasn't *completely* terrible, was it? She took a moment to look around her. OK, so the flat was a bit pongy, and the furniture had seen better days – but she was the queen of plastering on a smile and pretending everything was bloody brilliant. There was a cupboard full of cleaning stuff, and she could leg it to a launderette with the bedding. There *probably* wouldn't be rats, even if she had seen some traps and a scribbled note saying: 'Kill the vermin. They're anyone's for a piece of cheese'. This was just a stopgap until … well, something.

But what? It had been far too long since she'd had a paying coaching client. No income. Zero enquiries. That was a problem she'd now be forced to stop ignoring. She had a talent agent who was meant to bring her PR and media gigs to boost her visibility and income, but lately, Rufus had been worse than useless. Perhaps she hadn't been pushing herself either. Had she got complacent, living with Arnaud and not needing to contribute much? Or, more worryingly, was she becoming jaded when it came to her unlikely, love-themed career?

Was she giving off some kind of bad-luck energy? She used to find it a breeze to help couples to stay together and put on an affectionate show, even though she'd never believed in the 'L' word. Her no-nonsense, dispassionate outlook had been what set her apart. But as time moved on, she was finding it hard to be bothered about other people's relationships – or her own. Why was that? She had avoided anything 'meaningful' since she'd fled to London twelve years ago. It had been easier to pick someone 'reasonable' and play her superficial, non-heart-wrenching part.

And now it was time to play a new one. This wasn't exactly how she would have chosen to embark on a journey of change. In fairness, nobody liked change, but when it was flung at them like a wet sponge, they had no option but to duck or fight. Which would she choose? And who did she even have to talk it through with?

She dropped onto the single bed, with its flowery sheets that looked like they belonged in the Eighties, feeling worn out again. Her hand twitched to her phone. She had at least a hundred and twenty thousand followers. She only had to post a pic of her toenail polish or an uplifting quote about something or other, and she'd have an onslaught of people to chat to, even if it was trivial natter.

As she went to click onto social media, she froze. There was something small and furry in the corner of the room – and it was staring at her. If there had been anyone around to listen, she might have screamed.

# Chapter 3

'Ask the universe for someone to talk to, and it sends you a mouse,' said Alyssa, through nervously clenched teeth.

At that point, she would usually have leapt up onto the bed for safety or yelled for the mouse police, if they were even a thing. Though with the day she was having, being accosted by a real-life Pikachu felt like the least of her problems. So she sat perfectly still on the Eighties flowery bed, racking her brains for a plan. Before she could make a list of people she definitely wouldn't call, the creature moved towards her, scritch-scratching across the bare floorboards with a boldness she had to admire.

She remembered the brutal-looking traps in the cupboard, and not for the first time, wondered where on earth she'd landed. She wasn't one to get sentimental, but the tiny thing was defenceless. Did it just make a little '*hello*' squeak?

'Hi there,' she heard herself saying.

Trying to make friends with a rodent. It was a rock-bottom kind of day.

The small thing sat on its furry behind, cleaning its nose with its petite pink paws. It was reddish brown, in a shade her hairdresser might have called a rosewood balayage, and it didn't *look* like it was the ringleader of a small mouse army – though she didn't know much.

'Look, you can't live here. It's probably not hygienic – for you or me.' She pointed to the bedroom door. 'If you leave now, we'll say no more about it. Agreed?'

But the mouse just stared at her. She sighed and reached for her bag. 'I'm trusting you. Do not tell people I keep strawberry muffins in my second-hand Birkin. *Or* that I speak to mice.'

Alyssa took a deep breath and stood, careful to keep her distance from the uninvited guest. She backed towards the bedroom door, dropping a careful trail of muffin crumbs and trying not to lament her last sugary snack.

'People think I live on tofu and quinoa. Though tofu tastes like SpongeBob's armpits. Have you tried it?' The mouse cocked its head. 'Well, don't.'

A love coach was essentially a life coach who had specialised. She'd long since decided it didn't look inspirational or disciplined if she couldn't even coach herself to keep her hands off the cake cupboard. The healthy-lifestyle persona was something she'd taken on when she'd reinvented herself as Alyssa Heart. It had made her and her brand popular. *Liked.* Everyone deserved to feel that way, didn't they?

She continued the trail towards the flat's entrance, and at last, the mouse followed, taking the odd nibble and filling its cheeks. Alyssa opened the front door, placed the rest of the muffin down, and pointed.

'Yum yum. Now off you go. Have a lovely life.'

With a few sniffs of the air, the mouse took the hint and scurried into the hallway. She locked the door behind it. She'd done Pikachu a favour. Who said she didn't have a heart?

Alyssa tried to ignore the strange worry about whether her unexpected roommate would be all right. She was *not* so lonesome that she needed to start befriending small creatures, like something out of a Disney movie. She was a brave, independent woman who could deal with life's crap. So she strode back to the

Eighties bedspread, sank down, and grabbed her phone.

Arnaud had called her phone usage an obsession. *'Be present in the moment'*, he'd warned, like something from her own Instagram grid. That was all very well if your present moment didn't involve a high risk of bedbugs. She preferred to think of her social media as a comfort. A place where she could be accepted with hundreds of likes and hearts, even if the online persona she'd created wasn't *exactly* her. She knew it was superficial. But strangers had embraced her when so-called *loved ones* hadn't.

And if she was going to find work to scrape her way out of here, she had to get back to her social media. That was where her potential love coaching clients would be, if she could just sprinkle a few virtual muffin crumbs to encourage them.

She clicked onto her 'New Year, New Me' post, her insides filling with relief to see people were liking and chatting to her. Her eyes scanned the comments.

**@tinatinyharris** – *You're smashing it! You always do. Happy New Year, you gorgeous thing. X*

There, that was nice – even if she was excelling at precisely nothing right then. People *thought* she was, and that was a start.

**@lovedupbuttercup** – *Thanks to you I feel like a New Me every day! I'm so in love. Joshi and I spent New Year in Paris, overlooking La Tour Eiffel. Fireworks! You're incredible. My heart feels ALIIIIIIVE!!!!!! Xxxxxxxxxxxx*

Alyssa felt an impulse to roll her eyes. She'd coached *lovedupbuttercup* two years ago. She was a sweet thing, but she was convinced Alyssa had helped her to fall in love with her husband Josh all over again, after his affair with their nanny. Alyssa was pleased she'd been of use, but how could love possibly exist when your dearly beloved couldn't keep his todger in his trousers?

Alyssa had simply used self-belief and strategy to pull them back together. It wasn't magic.

She sensed a churn in her gut, which was probably just hunger. When she'd been cheated on by what some might call her *childhood sweetheart*, she'd been just nineteen. It irked her that she still thought of him, with his messy deep-brown hair with flecks of auburn and eyes the colour of twilight. That had been the only time she'd dared to believe something deeper could exist – and look how dreadfully it had ended.

Still hunting for potential clients, she spotted a comment from @garypratt that made her jaw tense. Gary was the only person whose coaching contract she'd had to terminate, nearly five years ago, because he'd *'fallen in love with her'*. She made a point of not telling her clients love was a fantasy, as that was bad for business. But *really*.

> **@garypratt** – *Anytime you decide your 'new me' involves ME, I'm right here for ya. Just saying. Looking good, Alyssa. Twit twoo. ;-)*

What was with the owl noises? She gave his comment a heart to be polite. He wasn't *always* trollish.

After pinging out a few messages and a positive post that she hoped might lead to at least a sniff of work enquiries, she started to scroll the *interesting news articles* her phone's algorithm had suggested. Sharing useful things with her followers kept her looking relevant and professional – even when she didn't feel it.

She pulled a face at a story about a woman who'd smuggled a boa constrictor in her leggings. How did these algorithms decide what a person liked to see? She understood there was code involved, like little tech goblins spying on your online behaviour and feeding you more of what you liked, with the aim of getting you hooked. It was sort of creepy.

Then her gaze landed on the word *Hartglove*.

Her chest tightened. The algorithm was way off course, because she did *not* want to see that. It was the name of the Cotswold town where she'd been born. The place she'd escaped from as soon as she could, with what she'd stupidly thought was a broken heart, but now knew better. That stifling town that held memories of gawping locals, an embarrassing night in a turtle costume, and a pair of twilight blue eyes …

She stood quickly, hoping to break free from the spell but failing. She was still gripping her phone, and the algorithm goblins were winning. As much as she didn't want to click onto the article, she couldn't not look.

*No Love in Hartglove* was its title. 'Well, they've got that right.' Her mind brought up an image of her parents, who were still there – and apparently still together – even after the shocking revelations about their relationship that had left her sure love was a lie. A horrible memory slid into her mind, and she promptly shook it away. That ugly scene was another good reason she'd packed her bags and run.

'The title should be: *No Love Anywhere*.'

Though now she'd opened the article, she may as well read it, in the interests of her occupation. It sounded like they could do with a love coach in town. She shuddered. Well, it wouldn't be her. Not even if hell froze over and turned into a particularly lovely ice hotel. Her eyes scanned, picking out the juicy bits.

*Statistics show the quaint Cotswold town has the fewest number of couples in the country …*

Quaint or out of the Dark Ages?

*Hartglove was presented with the Most Loveless Town of the Year award …*

Had there been a ceremony? That must have been awkward.

*Residents were shocked. The tongue-in-cheek award comes only a year after Hartglove was voted Least Cheerful Town Around. One occupant grumbled it was rotten for people's spirits, not to mention tourism. Another resident vowed they'd make a comeback.*

*There are even rumours that a surprising plan is underway. We'll keep you posted.*

'Please don't.' She pressed to close the article, a strange shiver running through her. She must shut the flat's windows.

Alyssa only half wondered if the grumbling occupant might be someone she knew, like Mrs Halfpenny from the convenience shop, who'd always had her nose in everyone's business, between dishing out fizzy sweets and making pyramids out of toilet rolls. Or perhaps most people were long gone.

And she only vaguely let her thoughts wander to what on earth their '*surprising plan*' could be. Because nothing that happened in Hartglove was any of her business – and she would make sure it stayed that way.

# Chapter 4

All Washed Up. Well, she wasn't going to take the name of the launderette as a sign, even if it quite literally *was* a sign, complete with dodgy flashing electrics and a wonky letter A.

Alyssa leaned against the industrial washing machine, letting its slow rumble calm her as the Eighties duvet cover went round and round on 'scorch the stains' hot. The place smelt of cheap fabric softener and the air was stifling, though at least she was the only one desperate enough to be in there boil-washing sheets on the first day of the year.

Her hand edged towards the phone in her bag. *Must find clients. Must not get sucked into reading anything about hideous Hartglove.* Her fingers found the familiar glow of the Instagram logo and she pressed to enter its aura. The app's algorithm would hit her with love-related content in the same way her phone's news section had – but here, she was @alyssaheart_thelovecoach – and 'love' was her business. She was expected to pass judgement on things related to her topic. It worked well that she was often on the blunt side, because controversial views grabbed attention.

'Wow, what's this tripe?'

She spotted a post from a new account called @appytogether. It reminded her, with a jolt, of a song she could no longer stand.

'Happy Together'. *That humiliating Hartglove night.* She screwed her eyes shut to try to block out the image that was appearing, but it was going nowhere. A stage. A love song. A humiliating rejection. And those truths she'd heard shouted across the room. Sweat broke out on her top lip, and she opened her eyes quickly, swiping it away. That was years ago. The past was done. She took a few deep, fabric-softener-infused breaths. *I am here.* Rolling her shoulders, she got back to her phone screen.

Her common sense told her to keep scrolling, because more than enough had gone wrong for one day. But whoever was behind the account had tagged her name, which meant it would be rude not to reply. She sighed. Rude wouldn't get her any clients.

Could she get away with dropping a couple of heart emojis and moving on? But the more she scanned the post, the more she couldn't help getting pulled in. The concept sounded more ridiculous than the woman smuggling a boa constrictor in her leggings.

'An app that makes people fall in love?' Alyssa scoffed. Not even she could bring about *that* sort of miracle. How could anyone claim a bunch of computer code could do the trick?

When people kidded themselves they were in love, it was simply a cocktail of brain chemicals. Cortisol to make your heart race. Dopamine for euphoria. Oxytocin that made you feel attached. Just like taking a pill, all of that could – and did – wear off. It was tomfoolery of the mind, for the undisciplined. When it came to emotions, it paid to stay teetotal and avoid the 'love' hangover. Although she'd be ruined if she ever admitted *that* publicly.

She scratched her head, which was covered with a hat to hide her distinctive pink hair. How did anyone think a phone app – which was essentially a computer programme hiding behind a pretty user interface – was capable of anything even close to the brain's own hocus-pocus?

If nothing else, she was intrigued.

So she read on …

*Our brand-new app will soon be ready for its trial run! (You are going to LOVE this. Seriously.)*

*'Appy Together has been years in the making. And even if we say so ourselves – it's about to whip the world up into a love-induced whirlwind.*

*Imagine a phone app that can take two willing participants … and make them fall in love!*

*The app promises that after a series of seven carefully selected 'love tasks' the participants (who will first pass a basic compatibility test and will be geographically close – because nobody wants to accidentally fall in love with a porcupine on another continent!) will be head over heels in love.*

*'Appy Together has been designed to work for people who are completely new to each other – and get this – for couples who have had a shot at love together before but have missed the target. (Just call us Cupid!)*

*Our app is fully in control of deciding the seven tasks, and each new task will be dependent on the couple's individual feedback on the task that came before. Isn't that clever? We think so too! And we're about to prove it.*

*Seven bespoke tasks. One love that's built to last.*

*Are you game?*

*Make sure you're on our exclusive mailing list if you want to be invited. (Click on the link in our bio.) This is one hook-up you can't afford to miss …*

Alyssa gawped at her screen. Well, she wouldn't be joining *that* mailing list. An app that thought it was Cupid and made you believe you were falling for whoever they matched you with – as long as they weren't a porcupine? She'd heard it all now. Who was behind it? There weren't any photos of people on 'Appy Together's Instagram grid. Probably some tech geeks, with an excessively chirpy helper to write their social media posts. Alyssa pushed herself away from the rumbling washing machine, suddenly clammy. Not only were these claims ludicrous, they essentially said: 'Hey, Love Coach, don't bother getting out of bed tomorrow. Our app can do your job automatically.'

She exhaled sharply and began to type.

*@alyssaheart_thelovecoach – Congratulations on the new app and thank you for tagging me. It all sounds fascinating. Though wouldn't you say 'relationships built to last' should be based on strong foundations of trust, communication and teamwork?*

*'Love' takes the hard work and commitment of two dedicated people – and if they somehow miss the target, they can seek the services of a professional – human – Love Coach. I play 'Cupid' for people who are single but ready to mingle, and for struggling couples too.*

*Sorry to burst your bubble, but an app couldn't possibly replicate this. Relationships can't be measured or massaged by codes in an algorithm. Though thanks again for tagging me. Such a pretty logo. X*

She smiled to herself. Bad news should always be delivered like a dog poo sandwich. Place the unpalatable part in the middle, with something more pleasant either side. She'd started with congrats and ended with a positive thought on their logo – even though the orange heart was actually kind of garish.

If she was lucky, that would be the end of it. Although

something told her it wouldn't. If they'd caught her on another day, she might have given them less of a sting – but she was tired and fed up, and she had enough on her plate, without some unidentified app nerd piling on extra peas.

Alyssa began scrolling again, though it wasn't long before a notification popped up to say @appytogether had replied. Didn't these people take New Year's Day off?

*@appytogether* – *Thank you for your feedback, Miss Heart. We really are grateful that you took time out of your busy evening to respond. It sounds like you have the same beliefs about love and relationships as us. (Though we'd sprinkle in fun, adventure and intimacy, for good measure!)*

*Our app has been programmed to take the things you mentioned into account – and more. If you don't believe 'Appy Together could bring two potentially compatible people together, resulting in love and romance, you're welcome to be one of the first to give it a whirl. We challenge you to prove us wrong! (And if you don't believe it can work, you surely have nothing to lose.)*

*P.S. We love your logo too.*

Had they just dog-poo-sandwiched her right back? Alyssa felt her skin prickle. As if she had nothing better to do than swan about, proving an app couldn't be some sort of algorithm fairy godmother.

*@alyssaheart_thelovecoach* – *I'm already in a committed relationship. Thank you though. Good luck with your endeavours.*

There. They didn't know she'd just been dumped.

**@garypratt** – *That bloke you were with (guy with the funny name) changed his Facebook relationship status to 'single' earlier. Sounds like you're free. I'll be your ultimate match. ;-)*

Trust Gary bloody Pratt to know more than she did about Arnaud's Facebook status. Urgh. He deserved a spiky comment for that.

**@alyssaheart_thelovecoach** – *Sure you wouldn't be the porcupine?*

Gary didn't even warrant the dog poo sandwich.

**@appytogether** – *She doesn't sound keen on you, Gary. Alyssa – sorry to hear you're newly single. Any time you're ready for the challenge, we can hook you up. We might have just the person …*

No, they did not – because such a person did not exist.

She threw her phone back into her bag. As soon as she was done in All Washed Up, she was going back to bed. The best way to get away from everything you couldn't be bothered to deal with was to sleep. By tomorrow, this nonsense would have been buried by the next wave of social media posts and trends, and she would never have to think about it again.

# Chapter 5

'Oh, Beryl, you're so beautiful. I just want to …'

He pulled his mouth away from hers, his voice deep and breathy. So much deeper than when they'd first become friends. She couldn't believe they were doing this. It was a good job his parents were out all night, because that kiss was *hot*.

His twilight eyes settled on her, the amber glow of the lamplight almost turning them the shade of midnight. One was a touch darker than the other, which made them all the more mesmerising. Every smooth, semi-naked part of him was fascinating in this light. She lay on his bed in her white underwear, the evening sticky with heat. He was on his side next to her, leaning on one elbow, her body almost on fire in the places where their skin touched. She reached up a hand to his chest and ran her fingers down it, noticing the slight dips and knots where he'd been using the college gym. His nipples hardened. He closed his eyes and whispered her name again. It was a name she'd never liked and had always wanted to change. Until she began falling in love with the way he said it – like it was the one word that meant everything.

'You can.' She answered the question she thought he'd been about to ask. 'I want it too.'

The next sound he made was more of a groan, as though words

had escaped him. Her fingers continued their slow descent until they reached the bulge in his underwear. His hardness pulled the stretchy material taut and thin, so she could feel every ridge and undulation. She massaged gently, feeling him throb. She wanted more and she didn't want to wait.

She pulled him on top of her, his weight folding as though his feelings for her made him powerless. Their warm bodies writhed as they kissed more deeply, his mouth almost becoming hers. He tasted of the rum and Coke they'd been drinking in the student bar, sweet and spicy. She fantasised about his tongue exploring her in other places, hot and firm, filling her with his longing. The thought was almost too much. She groaned her fantasy into his ear, and after one more deep kiss his mouth moved to her neck and his tongue began trailing a sensuously slow line between her breasts and down her stomach, those dark blue eyes pinning her as she nodded furiously. A giggle escaped her, and she pushed his head downwards.

Her whole body shuddered as his mouth reached the place between her legs. She pulled her underwear aside for him and his face sank into her, his mouth moving against her as though he instinctively knew her rhythm. She rocked herself against him, her groans mixing with his, the warmth of his mouth and his breathy sighs making an orchestra of pleasure that rippled upwards. His hand reached out and found a breast. She clamped her hand onto his and encouraged him to grip harder. His fingers thrummed against her nipple, and she thought she might burst with the thrill. As his mouth moved between her legs, she heard herself gasping for more. And suddenly there was a kaleidoscope of colours, exploding like fireworks as her whole body shuddered uncontrollably.

'Devan, Devan, Devan …' She couldn't stop repeating his name. She'd never felt such pleasure and she didn't want it to end.

When she finally stopped shaking, she pulled him back up to her.

'Let's do *everything*,' she breathed. It wasn't her first time, but it would be her first time with him. And the first time with anyone who had meant something. She *loved* him. She was sure of it now.

And then he was putting on protection and they were kissing again, their hands exploring, his body on top of her, his hardness inside her. She felt *complete*.

She murmured in pleasure as they moved together, him gasping her name as his face nestled into her. His skin smelled like amber and the aftermath of sunshine.

The moment seemed to go on, as though they were stuck in a delicious loop. Him saying her name, more gasping, more kaleidoscopes. And she was yelping something that sounded like '*I love you*' – but she couldn't be sure.

And there was so much dampness. Her pyjama top was soaked through. But wait. She hadn't been wearing a pyjama top. Had she? Then there was a strange sort of buzzing, and some scratching, and …

Beryl felt herself jump, her eyes snapping open. Her hand flew to her chest, where she *was* wearing a pyjama top, and it *was* soaked through. Although she wasn't Beryl anymore. She was Alyssa.

'Argh!' Alyssa sat up quickly and flicked on the bedside lamp. It made a crackling sound, and she hoped it wouldn't electrocute her. It didn't give out a soft amber glow and there was no sexy man in the bed next to her or on top of her. In fact, that guy had never even been inside her. 'That stupid damned dream.'

She called it '*the single dream*' because although she'd had it often over the years since that night – which hadn't quite ended as intimately as her sleepy imagination would have her believe – the dream only arrived when she was single. Even her dreams had firm principles. Though that was another reason it was easier to bounce from one empty relationship to another. When she was in one, she didn't have to endure pointless teenage fantasies. They were irksome and embarrassing, and she surely hadn't liked him *that much*. His tongue *might* have caused her to think she'd seen weird kaleidoscopes, though they'd both been a bit drunk. And the next night it had all gone wrong.

Thank goodness she never had to go anywhere near him these days. Devan Shaw was probably still married to his real teenage sweetheart – her once best friend of a lifetime, Sylvie – likely living in a charming cottage in Hartglove like a pair of monogamous beavers. She had no idea, though presumably they'd be one of the few, if the place had *love problems*. And as much as it had broken her at the time to be betrayed by what felt like everyone, she'd patched herself up and had learned not to care – even if her make-believe dreams hadn't quite got the memo. Dreams were unruly like that.

Alyssa jumped out of bed, pulling off her pyjama top and searching for another in her suitcase. She hadn't bothered to unpack, seeing as she only had seven days before she'd be evicted. And, unless she made some money, seven days until she was homeless and begging for scraps. What a comedown from that lovely big house. If only she'd been more focused on her career and less complacent. Hindsight was a wonderfully annoying thing.

Her phone was glowing, so she guessed that's what the buzzing had been. More social media notifications. So what was the scratching sound? Her eyes scanned the floor. On second thoughts, it was better not to know.

She pulled on a fresh top and launched herself back onto the bed, bringing her phone with her. It wasn't great for anyone's sanity to start scrolling social media at stupid o'clock, but she needed the distraction. *Tomorrow would be better.*

She clicked onto Instagram, praying for anything to help her block out visions of a certain semi-naked person with a bulge in his briefs.

'Oh hell.'

This was possibly worse. She'd all but forgotten about the inane banter with @appytogether and how ridiculous their concept was.

So ludicrous that every human and their pet Yorkiepoo had

added replies to the comment she'd written. Her notifications were flooded. At that point, she should have saved herself by reading a trashy magazine or making a cuppa. Or even going mouse hunting … Anything that didn't involve getting dragged back into *this*. Yet her eyes couldn't resist. The post was going viral – with everyone clamouring for the same outrageous outcome.

They wanted @alyssaheart_thelovecoach to take up the challenge and put the app to the ultimate love test.

All parts of her sank into the sagging bed, her head spinning. She would normally brush this off or laugh about it. Her usual self would come up with another witty put-down that would bring her even more followers and make her feel good. But right then, she was exhausted. And she had enough problems, without adding this circus of an app to her list. Her thumb found the option to unfollow the post. In the morning, she'd get on with making her love coaching business popular again, so she could regain her income and scrape back some self-respect. And it wouldn't involve being *'Appy Together* with anyone.

# Chapter 6

Day five of living in the World's Grottiest Flat. The thought reverberated around Alyssa's brain like the voiceover from *Big Brother*. Just two days until she'd be evicted, and she still had no cash or coaching clients to help pay for anything else.

Right then she was pacing around London's Victoria Park, taking smiley snaps of herself for social media and pretending to the world that everything was fan-sparkly-tastic. She was trying to ignore the fact that everyone else seemed to be in twos, as though there'd been an announcement she hadn't been informed about. Couples ambled around the lake, pointing at the fountains and grinning. Others sat on benches, cuddling up against the cold. Even the solo walkers had a dog to fuss or a friend to stop and chat to. Well, at least she could take some discreet, long-distance shots of smoochy couples for her love coaching promo. She was in the business of selling the togetherness 'dream', after all.

Alyssa had spent the past few days frantically trying to attract some love coach clients, in all the ways she knew. She'd emailed and messaged and posted everywhere online. She'd even phoned past clients to see if they needed any help or had friends who were struggling.

Then there had been the copious number of selfies she'd

been taking around the trendier parts of her new area, from the Shoreditch street art to the Camden markets, making out she was creating an attractive new life for herself now she was temporarily single. She'd even snuck to the top of an exclusive apartment block and made a video of the London skyline, pretending she was recording from the balcony of her new penthouse suite.

The fakery wasn't making her feel good, but she had to do something to help her look like a desirable person to work with. Though *none* of it was bringing her any clients or enquiries. Could people see through it? Was she giving off *desperate* vibes? The most attention she'd had was from Pikachu the reappearing mouse guest. Well, that and a whole lot of online nagging about a certain love app. She preferred the rodent.

Just as she was trying to pull yet another forced smile at her phone screen, it buzzed. It was a message from her monumentally useless talent agent, Rufus Diamond, whose name was probably as false as his dayglow veneers.

**Rufus:** *Got a job for you. This one's a blinder. Meet at the usual café? 3pm? We'll have to move fast.*

Much like a diamond, Rufus *had* shown moments of brilliance when she'd first become his client, all those years ago. He'd hooked her up with a few TV interviews and speaking gigs that had helped to kick-start her career and explode her Instagram following. For that reason, she felt a strange sense of loyalty to him, even if these days his dwindling list of clients called him *Ruthless Rufus*, and he only dished out dregs of questionable work.

He pretended to favour his usual dingy café, so they didn't get 'spotted'. She knew the real reason was that he was a total cheaparse. But who wouldn't love a free packet mix *crappuccino* when they had nothing else going for them?

**Alyssa:** *Today? Quite busy, but I'll see what I can do.*

He didn't need to know her only other options to chat would be with a bunch of randoms on Instagram, or a mouse.

**Rufus:** *See you later, Hot Lips. Prepare to be amazed.*

**Alyssa:** *FYI, calling me Hot Lips is not acceptable.*

If there was a 'dickhead' emoji, she'd be using it.

**Rufus:** *Noted. Though you WILL want to kiss me when you hear this. Just saying.*

She doubted that very much.

# Chapter 7

'No way. I'm absolutely not doing that.' Alyssa pursed her lips. Rufus ruddy Diamond had surpassed himself this time. On the scale of potential dream jobs, this was the stuff of *teeth falling out* nightmares.

'Why not? It's a bloody brilliant offer.' He shifted himself, making the legs of his chair creak.

They were in the sweaty bosom of The Pitts Café, which always reminded Alyssa of that grim place they visited in the TV show *The Apprentice*, before someone got fired. It was ringing true right then, and it wouldn't be her for the high jump.

Alyssa clopped her rank-tasting cappuccino down on the chipped Formica table, not caring that half of it spilled out.

It turned out the people at 'Appy Together had reached out to Rufus when she'd stopped responding online. Yes, they were offering a lucrative deal for a relatively easy publicity campaign – but she had her reputation to consider. As if an app could make people *fall in love*. Alyssa glared at her agent.

Rufus waved his phone screen, using his stumpy finger to point out just how viral the social media post had become. Was that why she'd had the unexplained burst of new followers over the past week? At least it hadn't been *bad* for her brand. Yet.

'Love is big business, Miss Heart. And it's *your* business. These people are asking for *you*.'

Her agent was probably one of the few people who'd known her long enough to suss out she was a non-believer where love was concerned. But like her, he knew which side the bread was buttered. 'Love is ...'

'All around. In the air. All you need.' Alyssa read the comments from the screen in front of her. 'No more than a collection of clichés and a load of bullshit.' She pulled her woollen hat down further, wishing she could hide from all of this.

The previously bored-looking waitress Princess Trudy's ears appeared to prick up under her plastic tiara and Alyssa chided herself. She wasn't usually so unprofessional or grouchy – at least not in public, where people might recognise her. But this offer had got her riled. The whole idea made her skin crawl. The worst thing was that it was the best and only option she had going for her. What on earth did that say?

'And you wonder why I haven't got job offers lined up for you?' said Rufus, running a hand over his greying blond goatee. 'You need to drop the attitude.'

She pursed her lips again – because perhaps he had a point about that bit.

'Anyway, Hartglove needs you.'

Alyssa spluttered. 'Hartglove?' she repeated.

'Yes, this is the clever bit. The town was voted most loveless place, or some such, and 'Appy Together has latched on to the idea of running a media campaign to change the town's fate before next year's awards, linking in with the launch of their app.' Rufus beamed. 'You and 'Appy Together in Hartglove – a match made in heaven! Aren't you from there?'

A match made in *hell*. Was this some kind of desperately cruel joke?

'I am not going back to that place, for a lot of very good reasons' She had no idea if her main reason for staying away still even lived there. Though Devan Shaw certainly still existed in her dreams, even if he was uninvited.

'But they're hot for you.'

'They don't even know me.' Alyssa doubted anyone really did. On the plus side, she'd been the boringly named Beryl Bagnor when she'd grown up there. If she went back with pink hair, a completely different persona, and a new name, people might not even recognise her. *Not* that she was going back there. 'Anyway, I'm not looking for a new relationship, because I've been single for less than a week. And I'm not even geographically close, which I seem to remember them saying was important for a *match*.'

'It's a publicity stunt. Just go with it.'

'Well, I'm not interested in completing seven pointless tasks.'

'That's the beauty of it,' said Rufus, leaning across the table. Alyssa made a point of leaning backwards, trying not to wince as she banged her head on the window. Princess Trudy, who'd been busy tapping on her phone, looked up and glared. 'If you don't believe it will work, you just have to go through the motions. Smile for the cameras, play nice. Seven harmless projects. Job done. Think of all the potential media coverage and the TV opportunities that might spin off from it.'

'Wait, what? The tasks are like projects?' Alyssa tried to keep her voice down. 'How long could this thing drag on for? What if one of the tasks is to trek to Kathmandu in matching underwear?'

Rufus raised his eyebrows. 'Then I would pay to see that.'

She added another reason to her *no* list.

'I'm joking. Look, the tasks will be in Hartglove, if they're planning to give the place a boost. It's likely you'll be in and out in an hour each time. And seriously, the money they're offering.' He rubbed his belly, no doubt thinking of his healthy cut of the cash and the slap-up steaks he could treat himself to. Perhaps the joy of depriving him should be another reason not to.

'I don't even know who's masterminding this thing, do you?' Alyssa politely shooed away Princess Trudy, who seemed to be edging nearer with her cleaning cloth. 'It's like *The Wizard of Oz*, when nobody knows who's behind the curtain, because you can only see some bloke's backside.' The thought gave Alyssa the creeps.

Rufus scratched his head, even though his hair was covered by his back-to-front baseball cap. He'd clearly never played baseball. 'Isn't the point with *The Wizard of Oz* that he's just a normal guy with a few neat tricks? Maybe the magic is in the true love.'

A shudder ran through her. 'I doubt it.'

'Anyway, yes, I'm sure I saw a name.' Rufus pulled his phone from his pocket and wiped the screen on his trouser leg. 'Let me check this email. Someone who lives locally, I think. That's why it's tied in with this Save Hartglove thing.'

Alyssa froze, her *crappuccino* halfway to her mouth. *No.* Though she knew she was being stupid. The chances of it being a person she knew – or a *certain* person she knew – were slimmer than a gnat's bum hole. And yet ...

Rufus was scrolling his screen with the excruciating slowness of a sloth.

'Let me just check this other message from ...'

'Rufus! The name.'

He looked up at her. 'Snappy, aren't you? You on edge? Or avoiding someone in that hometown of yours?' His eyes shifted to her hand, which was drumming an agitated beat on the table.

'No. I couldn't actually care less. In fact, don't bother checking.' She glugged the rest of her drink and clonked the mug onto the table. 'I'm already out.'

Rufus eyeballed her. 'You making any money right now?'

She shifted uncomfortably in her seat.

"Cus you're certainly not making me any money. I haven't had any decent commission from you in a long while. You're drinking my free coffee and taking up valuable space on my books. There are young, energetic hopefuls who'd kill for an agent like me.' He waved his arms around himself as though she should be impressed with his Nineties rapper look. 'If you don't take this job, you might end up needing to find yourself another agent. And with your recent track record in bringing in no cash, good luck with that.'

Alyssa's stomach cramped a little tighter. There were plenty of things she wanted to say in response. Retorts like 'Get stuffed, you pillock' or 'Put your hat on properly – you're not eleven'. But her brain wasn't completely stupid. Getting dumped by her boyfriend and then her agent would be career kamikaze. She already felt like she had fewer options than Pikachu the mouse. It was too wild to go burning bridges. And Rufus wasn't all bad, under the dodgy outfits and bravado.

'Oh, here we go.' He waved his phone screen. 'Knew I'd seen it somewhere. The name of the contact for this publicity campaign.'

Alyssa took a deep breath, avoiding the urge to snatch.

He squinted at the screen. 'Teijo Yoshida. You heard of him?'

She finally allowed herself to exhale. 'No.' Thank goodness. Not that there was any reason to think Devan would be involved, other than he kept inexplicably hijacking her thoughts. Why would he be? The last time she'd seen him they'd both been studying psychology – not computer apps. She'd never got the chance to finish the course. He'd probably passed with knobs on, in the annoying way he always did.

'Most people you knew have probably moved on, if the town is that rubbish.'

'Maybe. Can you check the paperwork for a name?' she heard herself asking. Damn it. It didn't even matter. There was no way she was doing this. 'Devan Shaw.' She clapped a hand over her forehead. Had she said that out loud? And why was *The Single Dream* now appearing in her head, in full technicolour? She grabbed a menu to fan her face.

'Old flame?' Rufus asked, noticing her getting flustered.

'No.' She pursed her lips.

'*Devan Shaw*. Never heard of him. And I would have remembered a funny name like that. A bit like Devon, the place. And sea*shore*. Get it? Don't tell me, he's got blue eyes and sandy hair, body like a surfer.'

'He's not a surfer,' Alyssa managed to puff. 'And his eyes are …' She shook her head. It didn't matter that they were the colour of twilight, or that his hair was dark brown with hints of auburn, or his body …

Alyssa stood up sharply, though her legs began wobbling. 'Like I said, I can't do this.'

Because what if Devan was still in town? And what if he was still with Sylvie? She never asked her parents about either of them during their infrequent, awkward phone calls – which was what her relationship with her parents had amounted to, other than the odd time when her mum was in London and insisted on meeting for a stilted brunch. Alyssa didn't want to seem interested in her past peers, and she did not want to hear about how great other people's lives were.

'How could I possibly go back to Hartglove, fresh out of another failed relationship and desperate enough to get paid to be matched with *anybody* but a porcupine?'

'It could be the start of incredible things. Both professionally and personally,' said Rufus.

'I doubt it.'

Alyssa grabbed her parka and pushed her way out from the table, crockery shaking and chair legs screeching like violins. It was time to leave.

'It's not like they're asking you to bone this stranger, or anything,' Rufus yelled after her as she moved towards the café's exit. 'I mean, not unless you want to. We'd definitely need a bigger fee for that.'

## Chapter 8

Just ten minutes left before Alyssa had to be out of the World's Grottiest Flat, and the clock was ticking. Reasons to be cheerful – her landlord had offered her a downgrade to the World's Grottiest Basement, which was surely one up from living under a park bench in her wheelie suitcase? She just wasn't sure how she was going to fund it, what on earth her landlord meant by a 'special arrangement', or if she could live with *'no windows and a slight issue with rising damp'*.

She refolded her clothes for the eleventy-billionth time that morning, rearranging things in her case as though having her socks in colour order was going to vastly improve her messy life. Since her chat with Rufus two days before, she'd been frantically trying to come up with other options, like her brain was on a treadmill. Was accepting the offer to publicly road-test the 'Appy Together love match app the only way to get out of this musty armpit of a building and back to work? Not to mention that if she didn't take it, her agent had hinted he'd consider throwing her off his books. Dumped *again* was not a good look.

Despite her best efforts, she'd gained no new love coaching clients. It was as though the harder she tried, the more people sensed her desperation. She couldn't run to her parents as her relationship with them was stunted, and they still lived in the one town she was determined to avoid. There were no real-life friends to call on, because she'd obstinately avoided meaningful friendships since Sylvie. Acquaintances came and went with boyfriends, and online friends could never know her real predicament. That was just too mortifying.

She held up a pink T-shirt. Could she sell some stuff? But she only travelled light as she was often moving on, and most of her clothes looked good but were secretly bought from Vinted. As for trying to get a simple bar job, she'd soon be spotted and snapped for social media, then everyone would know her love coach business was failing – and she'd never get another client. She pushed the T-shirt back into her case and zipped it shut.

Coaching was all she knew, and she missed being good at it. Whether she believed in love or not, fantastic results had brought her money and grateful praise. Everybody needed to be needed. To have purpose. Her logical brain told her this seven-love-tasks charade might give her some of that, even if it would mostly be for the cameras – and getting paid to be there *might* reduce some of the sting. But her logical brain could just naff off.

'I cannot go back there,' she announced to the flat's bare walls. The lack of décor made her words bounce back at her. She hadn't returned to her hometown of Hartglove since she'd left it and there was nothing to go back for. Going backwards was humiliating, especially when you weren't in much of a better place than when you'd fled.

And then there was Devan. Her heart pounded every time she thought about bumping into him – and not in a good way. If he was still there, there was surely no way she could dodge him forever, unless she could manage to hide behind her pink hair and new name. Though if he was still happily married to Sylvie and they were bringing up their child – or perhaps children – maybe neither of them would care what superficial single loser shenanigans she was involved in.

She sighed and wheeled her suitcase to the front door, standing it next to her fake handbag. When she'd lost Devan, she'd lost both of them, like the worst kind of two-for-one deal. Sylvie had been her best friend since they could walk – like sisters. They'd grown up sharing Furby toys, Britney CDs and secrets. Their friendship had later become a three with Devan, but they were never meant to share *him*. The betrayal had stung and had left her not trusting anyone. *Still*. Boyfriends came and went, but Sylvie was meant to be her person.

Her phone screen flashed with a call. It was Rufus. Well, he'd have to wait, because there was somebody at the door.

'Hurry up, Miss ... whatever your name is,' a voice bellowed. 'It's go time.'

Judging by the sound of jangling keys, it was Lennie the landlord. 'The new people are waiting, and I hope you've cleaned. This penthouse is in high demand.'

Alyssa groaned. This guy had as much spin as her agent. It was more like a jailhouse than a penthouse – though he couldn't put that on the advert. She just prayed the basement he was about to show her was liveable, because she couldn't afford any of the options she'd investigated, and at least Lennie didn't ask for references or care what her real name was. And he'd offered her a *deal*, whatever that meant. She hoped it would involve her paying some rent from her deposit money, as she didn't have spare cash. She swung the door open.

Lennie was short and greying and carried an actual clipboard. He sniffed the air and pulled a face, which was a damned cheek. Alyssa pinched her mouth shut.

'Greetings. I'll give the place a once-over to see how much of your deposit I need to keep,' said Lennie, tapping his clipboard.

Alyssa gulped.

'Though if you take the basement flat, I'm sure we can overlook any minor issues.'

He winked at her, in a way that made her want to go and have a wash. What was all that about?

'You've attracted those filthy mice back!' Lennie pointed an angry arm at the skirting board.

Alyssa turned quickly and saw Pikachu scuttle across the floor. 'It's just the one mouse, and he's actually not that bad.' As sad as it was, the fluffy thing had kept her company.

'I'm setting the traps.' Lennie marched past her to the cleaning cupboard.

'No!'

Pikachu was tiny, and no creature deserved to have its bones crushed. Before she could think better of it, she bent down and opened one of her shoeboxes, tipping in the remains of the packet of mini cookies she'd stashed in her handbag.

'Psssst. Hop in.' She slid the box across the floor.

The mouse froze, other than a twitch of his nose as he assessed the situation.

'Look, I'm not one for trusting people either. But sometimes we're all out of options.'

Then seeming to decide Alyssa was the lesser of two evils, the mouse scrambled up the side of the shoebox and jumped in.

'In it together,' Alyssa whispered as she hurriedly replaced the lid, not remembering when she'd last said anything quite so conspiratorial.

Maybe following the crumbs to stay alive was the only plan.

# Chapter 9

Alyssa used her sleeve to mask her nose and mouth as the stench of Lennie's basement flat assaulted her. They hadn't even stepped over the threshold yet, and she could already see mould patches creeping up the walls and suspicious stains on the threadbare carpets. Perhaps she'd been naive to think she could deal with this pitiful downgrade.

'Get in and make yourself at home,' said Lennie, giving her an unwelcome shove from behind.

'Oi!' Alyssa spun around and glared at him, trying to keep the shoebox steady under her arm. 'Less of the manhandling.'

Lennie huffed. 'Sorry, miss, but I've got a busy morning. You've already told me you have no more money. Isn't manhandling ... well, part of the deal?' He laughed at his own joke. 'If you're going to be a snob about it ...'

So that's what he'd meant by a 'special arrangement'. *Gah.* She had wondered but had generously given him the benefit of the doubt.

'No, it is *not* part of the bloody deal, and I'm not a snob. I'm just a human being. *With standards.*' They did not include living somewhere that should probably be reported or condemned as unfit.

Lennie shrugged. 'Got any other options?'

'Plenty,' she lied. 'And being fondled by a gropey landlord will never be one of them.' That much was true.

Then she swiftly barged past Lennie, waved goodbye to her deposit – because legal action would risk revelations that she'd lived in this dive of a building – and pulled her wheelie suitcase out of there.

When she hit the street, dark grey clouds were rolling in and she could smell the metallic threat of rain. The air was heavy.

'Nowhere to go. Well, this is becoming a thing,' she muttered, before squaring her shoulders and dragging her belongings away from the tower block of doom.

At least this time she wasn't *completely* alone. As well as her pocketful of social media followers, she now had a mouse. She ought to do right by him, so that was something to focus on, wasn't it?

Suddenly tired with the weight of everything, Alyssa plonked down onto a bench, letting her suitcase clatter to the ground. She set Pikachu's shoebox down next to her.

'Rufus!' she said to herself, remembering his missed call from earlier.

Checking her phone, she saw there were now several more, so she called him back.

'Where have you been?' he barked. 'Have you seen the stuff on social media this morning?'

'No, I've been ... busy.' She wasn't in the mood to explain.

'Still slobbing around in Hackney?' He made a noise that sounded doubtful. 'Well, it looks like that waitress from the café – plastic tiara and the Princess something-or-other name badge – has been telling tales.'

Alyssa wound her brain back to The Pitts Café, with its chipped Formica tables and dreadful coffee. 'Princess ... Trudy? What tales?'

'You're not going to like it.'

Alyssa blew out a long stream of air, her breath making fog. There wasn't much she liked about this day so far. 'Try me.'

Rufus cleared his throat and read. '*Alyssa Heart, that love coach with the pink hair and stingy agent, says love is a load of clichés and bullshit.*'

'*Arghhhhhh.*' Alyssa clapped a hand over her forehead, screwing her eyes shut and wishing that when she opened them this whole crappy year would turn out to be a bad dream.

Though in truth, she *had* spat out something scathing like that. And as somebody who'd built their whole occupation on supporting people's love lives, that kind of truth bomb was like career self-annihilation. Her insides clenched.

She was usually so measured. So professional. She knew not to say stupid things where people might overhear them, or let her feelings spill out. She was a coach, for Christ's sake. Alyssa heard her own sob before she felt it. It reverberated through the backstreet, hitting her ears and bringing her back to the spinning present. Were there actual tears snaking down her cheeks? She swiped them away.

'You crying?' Rufus asked. 'I mean it's shit that she called me stingy, but I'll get over it.'

'Great for you.' Alyssa sniffed. 'Anyway, why has it taken two days for this to come out?'

'Looks like she posted it on Instagram straight away, but the kid's only got forty-three followers. It took a while for anyone to notice. But now they have …' He sucked in his breath like a mechanic who was about to tell you your car's knackered. 'Various news sites are all over it. It's being shared far and wide, and it's turning into a right old scandal. People are calling you jaded and out of touch. They're saying you've spent your career faking it and ripping people off.'

'What the hell?' Just because she secretly believed relationships were about strategy more than swooning, it didn't take away from her positive results and the fact she made a difference. And she would *never* rip people off.

'*Is Miss Heart no more than a heartless con woman?*' Rufus read.

Alyssa's jaw tightened. 'How dare they.' She felt anger bubbling up inside her. Anger at being talked about, metaphorically pushed around, and even physically manhandled by a stumpy landlord called Lennie. Fury at spending a whole week doing her level best to find work yet being forced to choose between a basement with rising damp or a backstreet bench. And rage at feeling so ridiculously out of control with *everything*.

Well, she was going to make a stand.

Maybe she had started this potential career suicide with her wayward words. But if she was going to stay current and claw her way back to being a successful coach and an expert who people listened to, she knew how to end it. She had a point to prove. Because yes, she was damned well good at her job, when she had the chance to be.

'Is the offer from 'Appy Together still on the table? And what do we need to do?'

# Chapter 10

If a person had too long to think about something scary, they would talk themselves out of it. It was human nature. Alyssa knew that much from her years of being a love coach.

That was probably why this whole 'Appy Together charade had been thrown together at warp speed, without her having a cat in hell's chance of stopping to see sense. Though in her more suspicious moments, she wondered whether it was less 'thrown together' than she was being led to believe. Perhaps it was more contrived – and less generated by the mystical powers of a phone app algorithm – than everyone was making out.

It had been barely forty-eight hours since she'd walked out of the World's Grottiest Flat with her worldly possessions and a stolen mouse in a shoebox – the box now safely stowed near her feet. And here she was, pulling up in her agent's car in her old hometown, with him muttering something about the weather staying *clement*. He'd been checking his weather app all morning, even though he claimed to know nothing about what Love Task One was. Rufus was a terrible liar.

With the wild rush of everything, Alyssa hadn't yet seen the converted barn she was meant to be living in or met any of the love app people. In fact, Rufus had said she'd probably never bump into them, because they were surely a bunch of tech nerds who didn't get out much. Their contact was a person named Teijo, who worked for a specialist media agency which 'Appy Together had recruited to deal with the publicity campaign. Rufus had wafted huge wadges of contracts in front of her and had got her to sign everything. *'No need to read all the boring small print,'* he'd reassured her. *'That's what you pay me for.'* She guessed he ought to do something to earn his cut. She'd been too busy rushing out to buy a new outfit and get her pink roots sorted, once Rufus had dished out her advance money.

The cash had even paid for a two-star hotel for the past two nights, which had felt like luxury compared to that dive with the stained Eighties bedspread. And the dizzy heights of free instant coffee had taken the sting off the copious numbers of questions she'd had to complete on the love app, to help it to select an *appropriate* first love task and pair her with her *Budding Ultimate Match*. She rolled her eyes at the thought of it. If they didn't realise that shortened to BUM, they were as stupid as some of their inane questions. Did she prefer clouds or grass? Spiders or snakes? What were her feelings about mud? By that point, she'd wondered if she was about to be matched with Ranger Hamza. Although he was rather nice. 'It's showtime,' Rufus announced, waking her from her ranger-related daydream. 'We're here.'

*Showtime.* Her body tensed. But no, she could do this. She was only on show here as Alyssa Heart. *Not* Beryl Bagnor – the town's biggest love fool. That person had been deleted and upgraded a long time ago, both physically and online. The press release had gone out – she'd insisted on Rufus arranging that much, and she'd triple-checked the wording. In the statement, she'd 'divulged' that she'd never visited Hartglove – but having been headhunted as the go-to love coach, she was keen to help the town with their alleged *#loveproblems*. She just prayed the statement – and the fact she had a whole new pink-haired look since her teen years – would keep the press and public from finding out about her unfortunate past here. She'd called her parents with a firm warning not to talk about her connection to them or the town, for 'professional reasons'. They surely owed her that much.

Rufus jumped out of the car and rushed around to her door – which was not at all like selfish Rufus. As he swung the recently waxed black door open and a camera flashed, she realised Rufus was playing his part in the PR spectacle. Of course he was. If this project was a media hit it would be great for his profile too and could definitely lead to more opportunities for them both. No wonder he'd binned off his backwards baseball cap and brushed his hair.

Alyssa took a deep breath and stepped out of the car, trying to look poised and on top of life. In truth, she hated having her photo taken by other people and the lack of control over what images they could share of her – even if she still had toast crumbs in her teeth or the light made her look like the devil's bride.

The muddy ground felt soft underfoot from the previous night's rain, but she'd been sure to wear her flat army-style boots with the pink roses. She had no intention of being caught off balance, and every intention of being able to kick arse and run.

She'd done her best to dress confidently, with her bright waves looking bouncy and her glossy lips ready for ginormous fake smiles, even though her insides were churning like a cement mixer at the thought of being *here*. And of having to pretend she did believe in love, albeit that there was no way she'd be falling for it – or *in it*, as the saying went.

'Smile,' Rufus hissed at her. 'Your career depends on you doing a bloody good job of this. Local media people are here. Don't cock it up.'

Alyssa gave herself a quick shake and flashed her teeth in what she hoped would pass as a beam of joy, as cameras clicked, and a crowd began closing in on her. As irritating as Rufus was, he was right. She did need to belt up and do her job. She was a capable, professional woman who could play along for the publicity and collect her healthy pay cheques. Her aim was simple. To prove relationships required human connection, not algorithms – and when people needed help on their journey, they could reach out to another human, not a phone app. Preferably Alyssa Heart, The Love Coach. And yes, she was pleased that shortened to TLC. The creator of BUM should probably come to her for a few lessons in acronyms.

In fact, if this app company was willing to take the risk in paying her to potentially prove their love app was pointless, whoever was behind it probably was a bird brain. She'd agreed to do the tasks. She hadn't agreed to be kind about them. Though from 'Appy Together's social media, they seemed to enjoy the controversy.

'Miss Heart – are you keen to find out who your new love match is today?'

The voice came from one of the journalists who had gathered around the car, some holding microphones, others with fancy-lensed cameras. With the low sun glare that was dazzling her view, Alyssa couldn't tell exactly who had asked, but to her relief, she didn't recognise anyone.

She shielded her eyes. 'It doesn't matter who they are. An app can't possibly make me fall in love with them.'

'But what if you do? I mean, 'Appy Together reckons it's on for a one hundred per cent success rate,' another voice chimed in.

'I don't see how it can be,' Alyssa replied, doing her best to keep up her carefree smile. It was just one question at a time. Think, smile, respond. No need to get flustered. 'Love is a very personal thing, isn't it?'

'So you *do* believe in love then? Because you've been quoted as calling it a "*load of clichés and bullshit*". And yet you reckon you're a professional love coach?'

Alyssa took a deep breath. 'You'll see from my comments in the press release that I was quoted out of context, during a private conversation. Yes, clichés may be best-placed in greetings cards – but feelings are very real.' She placed a hand on her heart, as she'd practised, then gave a quick look over her shoulder. But Rufus was busy pretending to tie up his shoelaces, even though she was pretty sure he wore slip-ons. He often harped on about no publicity being bad publicity, so he was probably loving this. Well, she didn't need him swooping in to save things, even if he should probably pull his weight for talking her into this.

She held on to the car door, which was thankfully still open. She was a woman in flat boots, and she was not going to wobble.

'Are you worried about what the seven love tasks might be? Or having to spend months with someone you might not even like?'

'It won't be months.' Alyssa waved her free hand. 'Just seven short tasks.' Well, her lease on the barn was for six months, but Rufus assured her she'd barely have to spend much time with this stranger as part of the PR stuff, even if 'real' matched couples would surely need more *quality time*.

'What if one of the tasks is living together?'

'Or sleeping in the same bed?'

'Or walking up the aisle in a big meringue dress, with fourteen flower girls and an owl for a ring bearer?'

'How far are you willing to take it, Miss Heart? Will you go *all the way* to prove the app can't make you fall in love?'

Alyssa steadied herself and stepped forwards, closing the car door behind her. The media had had their share of banter. It was time she took charge and got on with the first task – whatever that was.

'OK, OK. That's enough,' she told them, trying to look calm and collected. It was also important the media didn't get a rise from her. 'Work to do!' Her love coach persona wasn't easily fazed, and on good days she managed to convince herself she was that person – even if so far this year it had been a struggle.

But she was here, in her brand colours of black and bright pink – from her black skinny jeans to her fluffy-hooded parka – and she could do this.

'Miss Heart? I'm Teijo from Lucky Seven media agency. We're

working for 'Appy Together on this campaign and I'll be your contact. I'm dealing with promotion, publicity, logistics ... Oh yes. And making sure these seven tasks go off with a bang! Let's step this way, if you're ready?'

Alyssa squinted against the sun to get a good look at him. He was tall and friendly-looking with floppy black hair, and he was easy on the eye once the sunbeams got out of the way. She liked that he was an outsider like her too, not an actual employee of 'Appy Together. Shame she wasn't being paired with him, really. She wasn't in the market for a new partner, but if she had to spend time with an unknown quantity, it may as well be someone agreeable. He held out his arm for her. There, *very* agreeable. She took it, noting it was warm but spark-free. Exactly how she liked things.

'Ready as I'll ever be.' She matched his stride as he walked towards a gated entry to the main field. It was a field she had once known well.

# Chapter 11

Alyssa remembered the field from her years of messing around here as a teenager, lounging in the long grass with friends, sipping apple cider and making wild plans they'd never see through. Most had dispersed and gone to uni and had probably never come back here. Other than Devan and Sylvie, who'd been at the local college with her. She'd once heard on the grapevine they'd stayed here after she'd left, got married and had their child. She didn't know if they'd stuck around after that, because she hadn't so much as google-stalked them. Other than for the purposes of never bumping into them, ever, ever again, she didn't want to know.

She kept her gaze forward, knowing if she let it stray to the right, she'd see a big old apple tree with a twisted, mossy trunk. Sitting under that tree, which had been heavy with spring blossom in a way she'd once thought romantic, she'd had her first kiss with Devan, while a *certain song* had played on his phone. She'd expected it to be an awkward clash of teeth and tongues. But it had stirred her in ways that still came to her in dreams, where her heart escaped from her chest and twisted with the tree's roots, which wrapped around them, binding them …

Alyssa felt herself stumble and she gripped Teijo's arm. Just being here was stirring her.

'I'm not a bloody soup,' she muttered to herself. Anyway, it wasn't yet spring, and the town's apple trees would all be barren. Nothing whimsical to see here.

She straightened up and tried to focus. There was a noisy crowd ahead, and she guessed that was where they were heading.

'Are you all right, Miss Heart?'

'Hmm?' She shook her head free from its thoughts and looked at Teijo, the winter sun still dazzling her.

'You seem tense, and you were mumbling something. You've gone a bit pale. Are you worried about the flight? It's safe enough, as long as the weather behaves. And I'm sure your BUM will.' He was winking at her. Why was he doing that? What flight? And where was this *BUM* hiding?

Alyssa pulled away from Teijo, squinting into the distance and pulling her sunglasses from her bag to lessen the glare.

She was acutely aware of Rufus cursing behind her, as though Teijo had said too much too soon. As her vision became clearer, she scrutinised the crowd of people ahead. They'd been huddled around something, but they were backing off now, as a noise roared to life. The thing they'd been gathered around was a wicker basket, and the noise was coming from a fan, which was filling a ginormous red balloon with air. A hot air balloon. For a *flight*.

Her stomach dropped.

So this was why Rufus had been obsessively checking the forecast. Well, he could stick his *clement* weather up his backside. She whipped her head around, but he was now conveniently out of prodding distance. Alyssa did not like flying, unless it was on an aeroplane with decent seatbelts and a snack bar on wheels. Heights made her feel nauseous and out of control, and she could not embrace them one bit, unless she was safely enclosed and couldn't see the ground disappearing. Swinging around the sky in a picnic basket did not pass that test.

What was more, she wasn't keen on small spaces. Or people. Or being stuck in small spaces with people. Which she guessed was exactly what flying around in a picnic basket was all about.

The roar from the fan filled her ears and made her head oscillate. As a coach, she knew she ought to be in better command of her mindset. But sometimes deep breaths and visualising yourself not plummeting to a torturous end were not enough.

Somehow, she'd arrived at the edge of the crowd, even though she could barely feel her legs and her mind was racing. So this was Love Task One. No wonder she'd been kept in the dark until it was too damned late to scurry. Would the tasks get worse from here? Noticing her presence, the huddle parted. Even Teijo had dropped her arm and disappeared, and Rufus had shouted something about going back to the car to check on the mouse. Rodent duties were about all he was good for. She might see fit to compare him to one if that wouldn't be wildly unfair on Pikachu.

Suddenly, it seemed like it was just her and the incessant roaring, and the back of someone who seemed all too familiar. *It couldn't be.*

The back turned until it was a front. One she hadn't seen for twelve years, other than in particularly embarrassing dreams. If she believed in such things, she might have said her heart almost stopped. Though that was probably just shock. What was he doing here? The last time she'd seen him she'd been in the throes of some ridiculous grand gesture of her affections. Only it hadn't ended like it did in those big-screen love stories.

Devan Shaw.

He was almost a foot taller than her now and had definitely been getting busy with his dumbbells. She usually liked a tall man, but right then she did *not* appreciate feeling like a hobbit. His dark hair was blowing from the blast of the fan, allowing glimpses of the auburn he'd often been shy about – or had he been pretending about that too? Her fingers twitched as she noticed the tiny vertical dimple on the tip of his nose that she'd once loved to trace. Her fist probably just wanted to bop him. And since when did he start wearing thick-rimmed cool geek-guy glasses, which accentuated his night-sky eyes – one darker than the other?

*What the actual?* She shook herself down and ripped off her sunglasses, because she preferred it when the sun was blinding her.

Why the hell was he here? What was he some kind of hot air balloon specialist? One of those bloody journalists? Or just one of the crowd, smugly married and coming to gloat at her single loser antics? If he'd brought Sylvie, the lying, scheming pair of them could just sod off.

'Beryl?' he asked, looking into her eyes. One eyebrow quirked in question, making his glasses go wonky. It was criminal how much they suited him, sitting neatly on his good cheekbones that she absolutely wasn't jealous of.

She stepped backwards, so she didn't have to see his *I'm so wonkily perfect* features. No wonder she'd once fallen for his lies.

'My name's Alyssa. Alyssa Heart.'

Maybe it was nonsensical, coming back to her hometown, hoping not to bump into people she didn't want to see and trying to pretend she was a whole new person. But they'd issued that carefully worded press release distancing her from any connection to the town. And she *had* changed, other than the kinky Devan dreams she was trying her best not to think about in case her face flamed red. New life, new look, completely different name. She was not that soppy teen with smudged eyeliner and glitter ballet pumps, who'd almost believed in love.

'Beryl, it's Devan. Maybe you don't remember me? I mean, it was ages ago, and …'

At least no one else was close enough to hear him. He took off his glasses, as though it might jog her memory. What was with his innocent, lost-boy look? Clearly, she wasn't the only one around here with a questionable persona.

When was this two-timing shag bag going to bugger off and leave her to this task? She had a BUM to meet, and she hoped he was less annoying than this guy.

'Can we start again?' Devan asked.

Alyssa's jaw tightened. As though being dragged into his tangled web once wasn't enough.

'Like I said, it's Alyssa. I've got work to do, so if you'll please excuse me.'

'Yes, work. With me. I'm the creator of 'Appy Together. It's my business. I designed the app.'

Alyssa felt like she was in one of those moments where the world screeched to a halt. He'd designed the app? What the *hell*? Her head darted around for her agent, but it looked like he was long gone. Rufus *must* have known about this. And he'd kept it from her, even when she'd specifically mentioned Devan's name. So much for *'You'll probably never see the tech nerds.'* Well, that was a steaming load of crap. She should have read the paperwork herself.

Clearly Devan was back to his usual underhanded behaviour too. Was *everyone* playing her? Had he tagged her in the social media posts on purpose? Had he engineered things to get her here, for cruel kicks? Well, she wasn't going to show she was on the back foot.

'Great,' she said, in the most upbeat way she could manage. 'Nice to meet you.' It was about as nice as having her nipples eaten by rabid raccoons, but perhaps it didn't even matter who was behind the app. Teijo was her contact and at least he couldn't possibly be her *love* match.

'Ooh, is that Beryl Bagnor? Percy and Pearl's daughter?'

Did anyone else want a pop at her today? Alyssa winced as she heard an older lady's voice from the crowd. Was that Mrs Halfpenny, who used to serve them sweets in the corner shop? She'd surely been close to retirement back then, so how was she now looking so sprightly? Perhaps it was the 'Save Hartglove – Love at First Flight' T-shirt she'd squeezed into, which matched the banner she was frantically waving above her blue-rinse hairdo. Alyssa had forgotten how much these people loved a cause.

Alyssa had specifically asked her parents not to be at this task, as she had to keep her work head on and didn't want people spotting them and making the connection. Perhaps she'd been naive bordering on stupid to hope memories wouldn't be jogged.

And how many of these people might remember her spilling her undying 'love' to that cretin on a stage, dressed as a damned turtle – only for him to waddle off without so much as a '*Thanks but get stuffed*?' Her soul was withering.

Her eyes shot back to Devan, who she now registered was wearing the same T-shirt under his open shirt and coat, only his was *definitely* too small. It was riding up his stomach in a way that said: '*I'm game for a laugh, and I'm a good-cause-supporting kind of guy. Oh, and look at my obliques.*'

How infuriating. She remembered now how the locals had always loved him, even when he displayed the morals of a street rat.

'Hello, Beryl dear. Long time no see!' said another voice.

Did they honestly recognise her, or had there been gossip even before she'd arrived? News spread here like Japanese knotweed.

Alyssa straightened herself and turned in the direction of the voices. 'I'm not Beryl. My name's Alyssa.' She'd practised saying it in the mirror and she didn't care if they believed it. If a person wanted to change their name to Sunny Flipping Moonbeams, others ought to respect that. She wasn't here to make friends or to get out her baby photo albums for a trip down hideous memory lane.

'A fibber?' The second woman scratched her head.

Alyssa summoned her last ounce of inner zen. It was a struggle. 'Alyssa,' she repeated semi-patiently, making sure the press heard her too. 'From Chelsea. I've never been here, though people often think they know me. Easy mistake to make.' She smiled as kindly as she could at the older residents, hoping any journalists might pass them off as a bit forgetful.

She'd chosen her new name not long after she'd fled Hartglove, feeling broken and desperate to reinvent herself. The name meant *logical*, and it went nicely with the new surname Heart, which she'd added once she'd got into love coaching. You could call yourself anything online, even if your passport still said Beryl.

'Alyssa Heart,' Devan repeated authoritatively, like he was trying to save things. She didn't need a hero in a too-small T-shirt. 'I did read that you were from London. Sorry for the confusion.' He extended his hand to shake, giving her an irritating conspiratorial look that told her he knew she was Beryl, but he wasn't going to harp on about it. Coming from the bloke who was named like the seaside, even though he lived in the Cotswolds. 'I'm Devan Shaw. I'm your Budding Ultimate Match.'

And suddenly, Alyssa felt unbearably hot.

The fan that had been blowing behind them had now been replaced by fire. Great, scalding flames licked the inside of the red air balloon, making it rise. It reared up behind Devan, taking shape with every agonising second that passed between them. The balloon formed itself into a gigantic red heart, pulsing and burning behind them. It had the words *We're 'Appy Together* emblazoned across the front – which couldn't have been further from the truth.

She'd managed many a year without feeling this wildly out of control – and that had been just the way she'd liked it. Right then, it felt like *all* of her worst nightmares were coming true. Worse still she'd unwittingly signed herself up to them, and there was nothing she could do but grit her teeth and play ball. How quickly could she get this farce over with?

## Chapter 12

Being stuck in a basket with an ex that she wanted to pulverise, trying to pretend her name hadn't been Beryl and that she'd never seen his manhood. This was not how Alyssa had imagined her day panning out. On the plus side, there was no way the app was going to make anyone fall in love like this. People were better off with a love coach.

As the hot air balloon ascended, Alyssa clung to the cable, trying to practise her deep *please don't let me die* breathing at the same time as smiling to the cameras below, acutely aware it was impossible to look good when people could see up your nostrils. At least she had a scarf to disguise the possibility of a second chin. Worst-case scenario, she could use it to strangle someone.

She didn't even have a spare hand to distract herself with something mindless on her phone. This was excruciating.

'Are you OK, B— ... Alyssa?'

It was Devan's voice, dangerously close to her ear. She tried to shuffle away, but there wasn't much shuffling room, and she bumped into Teijo who was on her other side with a camera around his neck, ready to record *'anything intriguing'* to release to the press and spread across social media. Behind her was their pilot, who was large enough to take up extra space and wore a pilot-style uniform with *Mr Hot* stitched across the jacket pocket. It did not suit him.

Alyssa couldn't help thinking about *rub-a-dub-dub, three men in a tub*. Falling out of a rotten potato would be just about her luck right then. Rufus had, of course, opted to keep his distance, though was probably now schmoozing. He'd be for the high jump later.

'Not really,' Alyssa hissed, in answer to Devan's question, as hot flames exploded above her and the safety of solid ground got further from her feet. 'I don't like heights, as your troublemaking love app knows.'

She wanted to add, '*And as YOU well know, you bloody dickweed.*' She was also bursting to ask if he'd called his stupid piece of software 'Appy Together, after *their* song – the one that had been playing when they'd had their first kiss – and then dragged her back to Hartglove to humiliate her with things she hated. Seven times over. And if so, *why*? What on earth had she done to deserve this? Wasn't he married now? Not that he was wearing a ring, she'd accidentally noticed. But saying any of that would involve admitting in front of Teijo that Devan had once dated her as gullible Beryl.

'I had no idea,' said Devan, blinking innocently behind the geek glasses that might have looked sexy on anyone else.

She tried to cling on to her smile until the camera lenses on the ground were out of sight. She was coming to wonder if holding on to the pretence she hadn't grown up here was unsustainable – with people already sussing her out. But her morning had been enough of an emotional whirlwind. Her online persona was a mask that protected her, and she wasn't ready to let that drop. Not by a long shot. For now, she had to style this out.

'So is there any truth in the suggestions that you two once knew each other?' Teijo asked, pulling a pencil from behind his ear and a small notebook from his trouser pocket.

Why was no one else gripping onto this basket like their life depended on it? Alyssa had never felt so dizzy.

'No,' she said quickly, before closing her mouth for fear she might vomit. She glared at Devan in case he dared to contradict her.

'Hmm,' Teijo replied, like he wasn't sure what to believe. 'Anyway, according to your answers in the initial 'Appy Together questionnaire, Miss Heart, "*Fears can be conquered. It's mind over matter.*" Wise words.'

Damn that stupid questionnaire, which had been as long as *War and Peace*, and twice as rambling. Goodness knew what else she'd written or what mess it might get her into.

'Mind over matter,' she said to the toes of her boots. 'Exactly.' She only wished she believed it.

Their barrel-shaped pilot, Mr Hot, moved to point something out and the basket wobbled. Alyssa stumbled, grabbing onto Teijo's strong arm. The soft navy wool of his double-breasted coat felt like a small comfort beneath her fingers. She did like a man in a nice coat. Maybe he would be a better distraction.

Devan cleared his throat. Teijo nodded towards him as though Alyssa should be holding on to her BUM. Well, that was never going to happen. She went back to clutching the side of the basket, her knuckles white.

'How do you think 'Appy Together is doing so far?' Devan asked her. 'Is it going up in your estimations?'

Teijo had his pencil at the ready, which was so old-school that it was cute. But this was no time to assess anyone's implements. If she sucked up her nerves and got this right, she could get one over on sneaky Devan's lechy love app.

'My estimations are plummeting, if that's even possible. I mean, how is this even a *love task*? Bobbing around in a basket is hardly going to make anyone fall in love – unless you're just going for the *falling* part? What will it dream up next? Wrestling with bobcats?'

She heard Devan's soft chuckle. He could stuff his attempts at being jolly.

'The app decides each task, based on our responses to the

previous one.'

'You can put this one down as ...' she stopped herself short of *utterly shit* '... not my first choice of the ultimate day out.'

'Mind over matter,' Devan replied, in a reassuring voice. He'd be saying *there, there* and stroking her head, if she didn't watch out. 'Don't you think 'Appy Together has chosen the perfect way for us to enjoy quality time, away from everything? Isn't that important for any relationship?'

Like he was so big on how relationships were meant to work. They absolutely weren't meant to involve impregnating your girlfriend's best mate. She hoped her eyeball glare said at least some of that.

'I don't see how the average matched couple would afford such a lavish first meeting,' she countered.

'Obviously, we have extra funding for our tasks, as this is part of a promotional campaign. The app's users can choose their budget, as they'd be paying for their own tasks.'

'Then how can this be a fair test, if you're throwing extra money at it? Not to mention your vested interest in making our match a success – so that your love app soars.'

'My question about quality time?'

Were his eyes actually twinkling?

'Quality time in a cramped wicker box, with Mr Hot the pilot trying to flame-grill my scalp, and a journalist as a note-taking chaperone?' Alyssa delivered her words with a smile, hoping she seemed witty, in control, professional ...

'Oh, you'd prefer it to be just you and me?' Devan asked.

'In your dreams.' *Oh God.* Why had she said the D word? Thoughts of *The Single Dream* flew into her mind. Bare skin. Tight boxers. *Nipples.* She did not need visions of his areolas.

Why was Teijo fanning her face?

'I'm fine.' She politely batted him away.

'What would a professional love coach have recommended for quality time?' Teijo asked, pencil poised.

'Something more grounded,' said Alyssa. 'The algorithm has got this all wrong. Two people need to feel comfortable, when they're first starting out. Not completely thrown off course.'

'Think we're going the wrong way,' said Mr Hot, scratching his head.

She could have kissed him for his timing.

'Interesting,' said Devan. 'But don't you think it's easy to get on when everything is plain sailing? Surely, how people react under stress shows you the true measure of them.'

Urgh. It was irksome when people came out with the sort of stuff a coach was meant to say, when that was clearly her job. So when Teijo was busy checking wind direction with the pilot, Alyssa delivered her discreet low blow.

'Maybe the true measure of you is how you behave when your wife's not looking.'

Devan swiftly put an arm around her shoulder and angled her away from the others. She would have elbowed him, if she wasn't quite so terrified of rocking the basket. 'I don't want Sylvie and Emmalina brought into this.'

So he wasn't denying anything? She waited for him to say they were separated or divorced or that Sylvie had run off with a fit rugby player with nice legs – but nothing. She could only assume his family were still in the picture. Well, perfect. Perhaps all of this was a publicity stunt for him too. He wanted to promote his app, and she wanted to reignite her career.

'If you don't mention the name Beryl, then I won't mention Sylvie,' she replied. She looked at him, his face maddeningly close, his breath warm against her cheeks. Could she smell a hint of amber on his skin? He should grow up and change his aftershave. She'd pull away in a second, when she'd given him enough of a mean stare. 'Anyway, don't you think it's weird that you've created a love app and then put your name down to be matched?'

'Why wouldn't I test-run my own product?'

She huffed. That was probably a thing. Although now she

came to think of it ...

'Hang on. If you're behind 'Appy Together, and by some *huge coincidence* you're my match – you're essentially paying me to date you? Aren't there laws against this?' she hissed.

But Devan was simply smiling, like she was taking it all far too seriously. 'So now we're dating?' He whistled. 'You move fast.'

'You're a prize fricking idiot. We will *never* be dating. This is all just business.'

She kept her voice low, although Teijo was now busy taking photos of them dangerously close. She shook Devan off, and he looked at her in a way she couldn't make out, other than it was sort of sad.

'Just business,' he repeated. 'One task nearly down, six to go.'

If they'd been keeping a scoreboard, she'd say she was up one nil – publicly, at least. She'd been shocked, ambushed and dragged headfirst into her worst fears, but she was still standing. And she'd never been further from falling in love, even at 3,000 feet. If anything, she and her BUM were Crappy Together – and she only had six more tormenting tasks to crawl through to prove her point that the whole thing was ludicrous.

Which she absolutely would.

## Chapter 13

'That couldn't have been more nightmarish if I'd been naked, falling from a cliff, and late for my high school exams.' Alyssa yanked the passenger seatbelt of Rufus's car around herself and thrust in the metal clip with a satisfying clunk. 'I cannot *believe* you actively lied about Devan's name not being anywhere near this deal, when he created the stupid damned app. Then you let me get paired with the two-timing arsehole, kick-starting the pantomime with a death-defying balloon flight for four. Is there anything else I should know right now?' She wished her glare could burn a hole in the side of his dumb head.

'You saw that beast of a contract. There wasn't time to talk through *everything*. Anyway, I didn't want you to cut off your hooter to spite your face. This is a great opportunity for you, and why should some poke from the past screw things up? I just want the best for you. Honestly. And I did think we'd get away without seeing him, with Teijo running things. Nobody could have known the two of you would be paired. That was in the hands of the algorithm. Weird, hey? I guess he was the most viable match.'

'Devan Shaw is *married*.'

Rufus shrugged and revved up the BMW, its wheels spitting up grass and mud as they turned.

'Anyway, algorithms don't have hands. Although the people who create them do.' Alyssa wouldn't have put it past Devan to have concocted this *match*, although she still didn't know why. He'd agreed it was all just *business*. Maybe he wanted his pathetic app to make him rich so he could afford some T-shirts that didn't show his belly button.

They drove through snaking country roads towards the converted barn accommodation that Alyssa had yet to see. She just prayed it wasn't dreadful. She clung to the shoebox containing her mouse friend, noticing all was quiet inside. From what she'd discerned, Pikachu mostly slept in the day. Perhaps she should set him free, but right then, his little box was warm against her lap, and it gave her comfort after such a horrendous day. Feeling inside her coat pocket she pulled out her other comfort – her phone. Some people liked to disappear inside the pages of a book. For her, it was her online world. A place where nothing was quite real, and that you could shove back into your pocket when you'd had enough.

'All good on the socials?' Rufus asked. 'Hope my bum doesn't look too big.'

'So vain,' she muttered, as she scrolled to check through.

She breathed a small sigh of relief that the photos posted about the first task so far weren't too unflattering, and the comments were mostly positive. There was some chat about whether she was the mysterious Beryl, but if it kept people talking, then their posts would stay current – and that much could be a good thing.

The video she'd posted of herself pretending to look brave before she'd got into the air balloon had lots of likes and shares. Aggravating @garypratt had said he hoped to see a close-up of her arse trying to get into the balloon's basket, though it had caused backlash from female fans, which simply boosted the post's popularity. And that was how an algorithm *should* work.

She'd even had two enquiries about her coaching, though they both looked a bit spammy, and she was too exhausted to think about fixing other people's catastrophes today.

'Let's hope for a juicy long task next time, 'cus we'll get paid more,' said Rufus, rubbing his hands together even though they should have been on the steering wheel.

'I'll be telling the app I like short ones,' she huffed. Maybe she would add that to the post-task questionnaire she still had to complete.

The narrow, winding roads did nothing for Alyssa's dizziness – but when they finally opened out again, she was surprised to remember how spacious this part of the country felt – even if the trees were looking a bit like skeletons and the grass was probably not greener. It was certainly different from the busy London streets and built-up suburbs she'd become used to. Though she'd always embraced the city hustle, because when you were busy, there wasn't much time for thinking.

The Cow Shed was on farmland on the outskirts of the town. Teijo had found it for her, as he was in charge of campaign logistics. She'd been sure to get photos of inside and out, after the grotty Hackney flat situation. At least he would presumably have picked somewhere reasonable, if they wanted her to stick out these tasks. Rufus had promised he'd checked things – for what that was worth – and he had the details they needed to get inside.

Hartglove would still be her closest place for food and essentials, but she'd hopefully be at a safe distance from any small-town gossip, and from her parents, whom she still hadn't seen and was in absolutely no rush to.

In fact, one of the last times she'd properly seen her mother had left her eyeballs and her thoughts about 'love' scarred for life. The image appeared again before she had chance to stop it, making the taste of bile rise up her throat. It had been the night she'd rushed home heartbroken, having just been publicly rejected by Devan. And Pearl Bagnor had been distinctly naked and bouncy – with a man who was not Alyssa's father. Yet despite that, and her father's various affairs, her parents were still together – presumably pretending that all was fine and dandy. She couldn't trust or respect either of them and it was no wonder she'd come to be sure love was a joke.

'We're here,' said Rufus, rousing her from her thoughts. *Thank God.*

She wiped the clammy moisture from her top lip, willing her heart to slow itself. She'd have to face the Bagnors at some point. Her dad would ramble on about her *appalling* pink hair and the fact she should get a *respectable job*. That much was comical. Her mum would probably be too busy eyeing up the milkman to care that her only daughter was back in town.

Rufus pulled into a muddy courtyard, with a decrepit-looking tractor in one corner and a huge pile of old tyres in another. There were no other vehicles or signs of life. Clutching Pikachu's shoebox, Alyssa climbed out of the car. The courtyard was flanked by ramshackle barns, most without doors or roofs. Only one looked habitable, and she hoped it was hers because it had been a *long* day, and she just wanted to eat, sleep and forget. Unless the barn still contained cows, it would do.

Alyssa paced to the door and read the sign. 'The *ow hed.*' It had lost a C and an S since the rental agent's photos had been taken, but it just about summed up how she was feeling. Though she wasn't going to cry over missing consonants.

Rufus darted back and forth behind her, unloading her things like he was terrified she'd change her mind. 'Key's behind the sign,' he told her. 'The owner's away, but I'm sure the place will have everything you need. It's a luxury conversion. High end. Bijou.'

Alyssa knew he was spouting random estate agent speak, and she doubted it was true. Though strangely, she didn't need his big talk. Something inside her already liked the place. It was quiet. There were no people around. And having been used to that horrible, stinky tower block, she was determined to make the best of whatever was inside, however fleeting her stay might be.

Rufus made a show of checking his watch. 'Anyway, gotta

go. Call me if you need me.' He waved his phone over his head, already getting back into his car.

She knew he'd be driving back to London, so wouldn't bother answering anyway. But that was fine. She was desperate for some peace. So she waved him off, took a deep breath and opened the door to her new little sanctuary.

'Oh,' she said, stepping inside. Far from being full of modern, stylish furniture, like in the photos, it was more or less empty. The front door opened straight into what she assumed was the lounge area, if people liked to lounge on hardwood floors. Well, she wasn't one for lolling about, so that was probably fine. She remembered there being an open-plan dining area on the pictures, but the table had clearly grown feet and walked off too.

'Reasons to be cheerful – I get to eat my beans on toast from a tray,' she said to the lid of Pikachu's box. 'Fewer surfaces to clean.'

A challenge was simply an opportunity dressed in crap clothes, as she told her coaching clients – when she had any. It was cheesy, but it helped. She put the shoebox down and dragged the rest of her things over the threshold.

As she looked around The 'ow 'hed, she could almost feel its potential. The walls were a plain but warm shade of cream nothing would clash with, and the exposed oak beams gave the place a cosy yet classy feel. If she was the sort of person who stuck around, she might have strung twinkly lights around them. And she wasn't sure why she was starting to imagine quirky art on the walls and plants dotted around, some dangling from macramé hangers. *Macramé*? She must have been spending too much time on Instagram. She was *not* here to make a house a home.

Getting back to logistics, she was relieved to see that the kitchen had the essentials, like a fridge, cooker and washing machine, and there was a double bed in the bedroom, even if it was crying out for new bedding. Another look at the letting agent's bumf, which was still stuffed inside her knock-off handbag, told her the barn was only meant to be partly furnished. Well, that was another lesson in reading the small print – much like the situation with the 'Appy Together deal.

'I needed to get food and supplies anyway,' she announced to herself in a pep-talk fashion. 'Let's see if I can get to the Hartglove shops and back in one unnoticed, undisturbed piece.'

## Chapter 14

Ten minutes later, Alyssa was marching towards the small town of Hartglove, the darkening night air fresh against her skin. Being unapologetically chilly, she felt like this time of year suited her. It was the season where you could huddle under extra layers, rather than being expected to strip things off. Because who wanted to feel exposed? She pulled up the hood of her parka, silently hoping it would help her to dodge being recognised as either Beryl or Alyssa – though she was beginning to realise the locals were as astute as ever. Or maybe it had been absurd to think a bit of hair dye and twelve years could change things?

She checked the time on her step-count watch, which she'd been gifted in return for social media praise, when she'd posted, 'Couples that exercise together, stay together.' She wasn't sure if that was true, but she found the watch judgemental and annoying – like a constant reminder she hadn't done enough, and she should get a bloody move on.

Hartglove had one main shopping street, which was called Apple Blossom Lane on account of the apple trees that lined it. In the spring their boughs almost drooped under the weight of apple blossom, which she seemed to remember filled the air with a sweet, floral smell. Then in autumn, the apples were ready, and the residents got busy making everything from toffee apple pies to flaky pastry turnovers, storing the rest to use over the year. Though right then, the trees would be dormant for winter, and no one would be bothering them. She could relate to that.

If her old town hadn't changed, there wouldn't be much open at this time, other than the convenience shop and The Rat and Raspberry pub. The latter was the hub of all gossip and was best avoided like smallpox.

Yes, she would be in and out quickly. She'd had quite enough blasts from the past for one day.

'Cooee, Beryl!'

Oh God. Did people even say *cooee* anymore? And who was that? It sounded a bit like Mrs Halfpenny, who she'd managed to avoid talking to in the field earlier – although she was not stopping to find out now.

Alyssa dipped her head and moved along the street, noticing that the apple trees were still there, though they'd grown since she'd last seen them. And either their branches were keen to prod her to say hello, or someone needed to prune the things. *Ouch.* She ducked further as she passed the pub's windows, ignoring the toasty glow from inside and the delicious smells of cooking. Her hand moved to her stomach as it rumbled. The shop would sell perfectly good microwave mash. And there it was, with the same old sign, its green paint flaking. She paused for a moment, feeling slightly dizzy as though she'd whizzed back in time. But that was silly.

'It's just a pile of bricks.' As she took a deep breath and stepped into the shop, the same old bell ringing to announce her arrival, she wondered who owned it now, because she wasn't in the mood for awkward conversations. At least it probably wasn't Mrs Halfpenny, if she'd just heard her in the street and she had possibly now retired. She grabbed a basket and pulled out her list, aiming to gather what she needed and get out of there.

If only it wasn't such a confusing maze of stuff, with no obvious order.

She noticed with a slight pang that the sweet counter was no longer there. An image of herself and Sylvie slipped into her mind. About eight years old and wearing summer dresses. Heads together, whispering something about fizzy cola bottles and gummy bears. Alyssa shook her head. It was good that the enticing array of sugar had gone. Sweets rotted your teeth, much like friendships gone bad ruined your soul. It would be best if she stopped thinking about them. She just prayed she didn't bump into her cheating ex-best-friend anytime soon.

'You OK?' A woman's head popped around the end of the aisle, making her jump. She was a bit younger than Alyssa and wore a green apron with *Halfpenny's* embroidered across the top. 'Let me know if there's anything you can't find. It can be a bit puzzling.' Her forehead crinkled. 'Do I know you?'

Alyssa shook her head.

'Oh, you have a list. Let me save you the headache.'

Before Alyssa could stop her, the woman was commandeering her piece of paper, introducing herself as Jess Halfpenny, and escorting her around the shelves. In London, Alyssa would have bristled at that level of interference – not that anyone in London would get so involved in her shopping. But it had been a long day, and it was surprisingly nice to have someone lend a hand. Warm joy at being useful seemed to exude from the small woman, who wore her dark hair in plaited pigtails tied with green ribbons. It was impossible not to defrost a little.

'This is quite a quirky list. Pillow. Mouse cage. Ready meals for one. Where are you staying?' Jess cocked her head.

'Erm.' Alyssa didn't like sharing too much, but Jess didn't seem like a psychopath, and who would know where one random barn was? 'The Cow Shed.'

'Up at the old farm?' Jess pointed in its general direction. 'Then you must be the Alyssa Heart everyone's talking about. Though didn't your name used to be …' Her voice trailed off as she seemed to realise she was butting in. 'Sorry. I've only been in Hartglove for six months, and I'm already becoming a gossip. Small-town life, hey?'

Didn't Alyssa know it. She smiled politely.

'Anyway, you sure The Cow Shed even has a microwave? The last people who stayed there mostly ate at The Rat and Raspberry, because even the oven's temperamental. And isn't there pretty much no furniture, apart from white goods and a bed?'

Wow. Alyssa felt her eyes widen. There really were no secrets around here. The woman would be telling her the colour of her cloths and curtains next. Judging by Jess trying to wedge a bundle of hand towels into the basket, perhaps there weren't any.

'Don't worry, the prices are cheaper than what you'll be used to, or you can start a tab?' Jess offered, moving towards the till.

'I'm fine without a tab,' said Alyssa. 'Not sure how long I'm staying.' Her lease might be for six months, but she wasn't convinced she could stick six days, if Devan was going to be in too many of them. And she hated to feel indebted.

Her eyes landed on the counter, where Jess had apparently been crafting with various balls of cord. *Macramé.* There were piles of multi-coloured hearts.

Jess's face lifted as she saw Alyssa taking them in. 'I'm making bunting. More Love in Hartglove, as my nan keeps saying. I could make some for you? I also do lampshades, coasters. Ooh, and some very nifty plant hangers.'

Macramé plant hangers? What were the chances?

'No! Thank you.' None of this was a sign she should fill her perfectly reasonable accommodation with homely bits and bobs made of string. She was here for business. Talking of which … 'Are you finding the relationship situation a struggle in this town?'

'Is that a pickup line?' Jess joked, giving Alyssa a playful nudge.

She wasn't used to friendly nudging and tried to hide her shock. 'I just meant, I should probably leave some business cards, in case people need me.' Alyssa pointed to her handbag, reluctant to pull any out, in case Jess wanted to become her client and started trying to foist friendship and macramé décor onto her. She was just about dealing with having a mouse to care about.

'Absolutely,' said Jess, holding out her hand for the cards. 'There hasn't been much love for me around here. Most residents are old enough to be my granddad.'

Well, she couldn't back out now. She passed a few cards over, being sure to keep most of them safely on her person. She was used to having online clients, not people she might have to console with tissues and tea.

'You know, my nan was sure she knew you,' said Jess, as she rung Alyssa's items through the till. 'But I get how stifling it feels when everyone knows your family tree and your mum's knicker size. Takes some getting used to.'

Alyssa nodded. It was strangely pleasant to be understood by someone who wasn't just a name from your social media followers list. Not that she'd be making friends here, because she wasn't staying long enough for it to be worth it. Not that it was ever worth it – real-life friends just let you down. Her stomach growled as she saw Jess ringing through pastries and blackcurrant jam, presumably for tomorrow's breakfast. *Handy.*

'If you need more furniture …' Jess began tentatively. 'I could ask around?'

'I'm fine!' Alyssa felt her hackles rising. That was why it was better to keep yourself to yourself. She didn't want half of the town knowing her business or showing up with their goodwill and potted plants.

'And you sound hungry.' Jess nodded at Alyssa's stomach.

For the love of actual … Were a person's bodily functions not even private around here? London had been *so* much easier.

'The steak pie is amazing at The Rat and Raspberry.' Jess looked at the clock. 'It will still be dead at this time. Get a booth and no one will bother you.'

Peace, privacy and a juicy pie. It sounded bloody perfect.

'Did Beryl just come in here?' yelled a distant voice from

beyond the counter in the storerooms, as another door closed. 'I have a very fetching "*Save Hartglove*" T-shirt for her, with extra hearts. I do hope she's sticking around.'

'I'll be off,' said Alyssa quickly. It sounded like the older Mrs Halfpenny, and she had no intention of being Beryl or dressing in soppy slogans.

## Chapter 15

And that was how Alyssa came to be at The Rat and Raspberry on a Saturday night, ordering a quick pie and chips on her way home, praying no one would disturb her. It was as good a place as any to lick her wounds after an awful day. She didn't often have as much as her one drink limit these days, but her nerves needed the cold comfort of a rhubarb gin – and with the added foliage, it would probably count as one of her five a day.

One speedy drink and a bite to eat and she'd be on her way. If she pulled on her hat and emanated *leave me alone* vibes, surely no one would butt in.

A long sigh escaped her as she settled into a booth, relieved at how quiet it was. She could hear the barman around the other side of the bar chatting to someone, and the occasional glass clinking. An open fire crackled in the nearby hearth, dispensing tiny red sparks and woody smoke that would have been frowned upon in busier places. As much as she hadn't come here to start liking things, she couldn't deny it felt cosy. And she didn't have much choice but to peel off her coat and settle herself, unless she wanted to pass out from heat exhaustion.

Her fingers traced the round imprints and scratches on the old wooden table, her mind remembering how she'd come here a lot in her college years. They all had. Some of the décor felt time-warpishly familiar. *Urgh*. She shook her head. She'd come for puff pastry, not a trip down memory lane.

Pulling out her phone felt like as good a distraction as any, so she let herself get absorbed in it for a while. Catching up with people she'd never met on social media was much safer than getting sucked into too much *real life* – even if checking she was still 'liked' online could become addictive. At least getting involved with these inane love tasks seemed to have quietened the recent clamour of Alyssa Heart doubters, after the post by Princess Trudy the bored London waitress.

The odd shadow passed her table, but she didn't look up until a young person brought over her steaming pie and chips. *Heaven on a plate*. She might even have groaned when she took her first mouthful. It was the closest thing she'd tasted to home-cooked food in a while, and it beat the hell out of packet snacks and toast.

After a few bites, she went back to her phone, clicking onto the 'Appy Together app. She needed to answer its questions after the day's first love task, and there was something about the warmth of the fire and the background noise that made it feel less overwhelming.

She couldn't help a sarcastic laugh at the first question. '*How was your first love task, Alyssa?*' she repeated back at her screen, with her best impression of a robot voice. Maybe the rhubarb gin had gone to her head.

She thought for a moment, her memory scanning back over the hilly views that had stretched out beneath them, in wintry shades of brown and green. Devan had tried to point out landmarks and pretend he wasn't a twat, whilst she'd clung to the side of the hot air balloon basket, hoping not to die. Objectively, it ought to have been beautiful up there. The cool air against her skin. The feeling of possibility and floating and being free from it all. But she'd been stuck in – no, outrageously tricked into – a confined space with a certain person she'd hoped never to see again. Teijo had asked a lot of bothersome questions and had forgotten the Champagne, and Mr Hot the pilot had smelt like a sweat factory. And she *hated* heights. She wouldn't have been surprised if Devan had told his idiotic app as much, just to throw her off-balance or to make for more interesting promo. Why had he lured her here and why was he doing this to her?

'Dreadful,' she concluded, typing that into her phone. Then in a stream of frustrated consciousness, she let her fingers tap out everything that had narked her about it. Better out than in, and she wasn't in the mood for being polite to the thing, after the day it had so-said picked for her.

After a few seconds of the app seeming to digest her words, it summarised them on her screen.

'*Is it fair to say you would prefer to be on the ground, Alyssa?*' she mimicked again as she read the app's words. 'You don't say.'

'And what do I think of my BUM?' She spluttered out her mouthful of G&T at that. '*Ridiculous.*'

'Erm?' A head appeared around the side of her booth, making her jump. The head cleared its throat. 'This is probably a good time to mention I can hear you. I'm in the next booth.'

Alyssa inhaled sharply and then pursed her lips, determined to stop the string of swear words that were bursting to come out. Devan Shaw. *Of bloody course.* There was no such thing as peace in this place.

She snatched up her phone and held it against her chest.

He was waving his lamely. 'I was just about to put that I quite liked my BUM.'

'Devan,' she said, through gritted teeth. How many more times was he going to pop his unbidden head into her life today?

She slid her plate away and made to stand up, suddenly not feeling hungry.

'Don't leave on my account.' His eyes seemed earnest – though she'd fallen for that look enough.

'I was just going anyway,' she lied, her plate still three-quarters full of what had once looked like delicious food. The gravy was quickly congealing.

His eyes flicked to her plate. 'But you love pie and chips.'

Her skin bristled at the over-familiarity. He did not know everything. As Alyssa Heart, she made a show of eating quinoa, even if it did taste like dust. Because *'Healthy lives make for healthy love lives'* as she liked to spout.

'I used to,' she answered, trying to keep her voice low and even, in case anyone was watching. 'What people love changes. Doesn't it?' She hoped that last part might prick at his conscience. If he had one.

She finally stood, pulling on her coat and gathering her bags from the floor.

'No honestly. Stay. We didn't have time to talk properly earlier, without media people and cameras. There's so much to catch up on. Stuff I want to tell you.' He moved himself to standing too, clearly keen to get his annoying, pleading eyes at her level.

What a trickster.

'Whatever it is, I don't need to hear it. This is all just business.' She smiled at him as politely as she could, hoping it would fool him. 'Anyway, I have a busy evening.'

Alyssa bent to pick up the final bag, a sad ready-meal for one and a packet of mouse food spilling out. Her heart sank.

'It looks like it,' Devan replied, trying to sound jovial.

She didn't need his jokes. He would probably be going home soon to his wife and child, in some comfortable house, with a roaring log fire and a pet cockapoo to fetch his slippers. It wasn't nice to mock people because they only had a rodent for company.

'I need to get back,' she said hastily, grabbing her dropped items before he could.

'Has anyone seen Beryl?' That voice in the distance again. The one that belonged to Mrs Halfpenny. 'I've got this *lovely* T-shirt for her.'

*For the love of all things good and holy.* Small-town life made

*Nightmare on Elm Street* look like a fun place to hang out.

She should have stuck to her plan to get in and out of this place quickly, because *no* good could come of getting cosy.

# Chapter 16

A barren old patch of mud. Was this *love* app having another laugh at her expense?

Alyssa trained her face into a smile she wasn't feeling as she paced forwards, noting there were local news cameras at the ready. She was heading towards what looked like some sort of veggie patch allotment area beyond a cluster of apple trees at the end of Apple Blossom Lane, which if she remembered rightly, used to be a parking spot. With it being winter, the trees still had no leaves, which made them look a bit like they were pointing their gnarly fingers accusatorily at her. Or maybe this place was messing with her head.

Anyway, weren't allotments usually somewhere more secluded, so old men could hide in their sheds smoking pipes? She had no clue what Love Task Two was about, as Teijo prearranged logistics for the app's chosen task with an air of mystery, and Rufus kept pretending he was busier than an elf at Christmas.

But whatever this was, she was going to style it out. No looking flustered, flappy or like a prize buffoon. She would sail through quickly, plant a few turnips for the cameras, and then disappear somewhere for a big, greasy brunch. As she arrived at the edge of the land, she noticed a wooden sign saying Hartglove

Love Garden, and the entrance had been decorated with white picket fences, strung with what looked like Jess from the shop's macramé heart bunting. Well, it was *Instagrammy*. Though she'd preferred the view from the angle where she could just see the barren trees and mud.

Somewhere in the distance the usual locals were whispering about something, some clutching their More Love in Hartglove banners. Then her eyes widened. Her parents. Holding hands like an unlikely pair of lovebirds and looking surprisingly muddy. *Urgh.* Her stomach twitched. Well, they'd better stick to the memo that she wasn't their loser of a daughter, Beryl, or she might be tempted to drop a few digs about one particular scorching memory she had of her mother. That dreadful night when she'd walked in on her doing the reverse cowgirl on top of a man called Dominic, right there on the family sofa. At least it had been wipe-down pleather.

*That* had been the scene she'd walked in on after rushing home, the night of the Devan and Sylvie bombshell. '*I thought you'd be at the dance*,' her mother had exclaimed. Followed by '*Family life gets so boring*,' which teenage Beryl had interpreted as '*Beryl Bagnor is so exceedingly dull that her boyfriend shags her best mate, and her mum would rather forge a whole new secret life.*'

What had made the slapstick scenario even worse was her dad walking in looking for his car keys, on his way to see his girlfriend from the bank. He'd simply waved at a naked Dominic like it was a standard Saturday night, and said he'd see him at the golf club on Tuesday. Her parents had gone on to admit they liked to play around. But even at nineteen, Beryl hadn't been able to stomach it. And she hadn't stuck around to spend any more time on the family pleather sofa, because London had seemed more inviting.

She rolled back her shoulders and lifted her chin. If she was lucky, she could spend the morning dodging her parents, like she had for the last two or three weeks – and in fact, since she'd first left Hartglove, more or less. The delay between tasks had been frustrating, and a suspicious part of her wondered if it had been orchestrated in the vain hope that Hartglove might get under her skin. But she wasn't that penetrable. When she'd complained to Rufus, he'd wittered on about trusting the process and the possibility he might bug them for more money.

And where was Devan? Not that she *actually* wanted to see him, but the sooner he arrived, the sooner they could get this love-themed pantomime over with. At least his imminent arrival would mean Sylvie wouldn't be showing her face. It surely wasn't a good look to bring your wife.

'Are you ready for whatever they throw at you, Miss Heart?' asked a reporter, jumping in front of her.

Alyssa tried to keep her composure. 'Yes, of course.'

She beamed for a few photos, determined to mask the odd jumble of nerves she'd been feeling all morning, and to ignore the members of the press pack who were still barking questions about Beryl.

'Is the app making you fall in love?' another journalist yelled.

Alyssa laughed, and this time it was genuine. '*No*. I'm all about giving this a go – in the interests of science.' *Or more likely, the getting paid bit.* 'But could an algorithm make *you* fall in love?' She smiled sweetly and handed him a business card.

There. That was slightly more *badass love coach* than the last time.

Teijo from the app's media agency appeared at her side. Thank goodness. He gave her a warm smile with those great teeth of his, and offered her his hand, which was warm and inviting. Hmm, chivalrous. Maybe she *would* ask him out for a drink when all of this was over.

With one swift move, Teijo handed her unsuspecting digits right into the open palm of Devan Shaw's hand. And unless they came gift-wrapped with a really nice bow, she did not like surprises.

Well, she was retracting that imaginary drinks offer. And where had Devan popped up from? He squeezed her hand lightly and she yanked it back.

'Ow! You just gave me an electric shock.'

Wasn't that something to do with a person's footwear? She eyed him suspiciously, silently pleased he wasn't dressed for gardening either. He looked annoyingly smart-casual in well-fitting jeans and a shirt, with a tight jumper on top. What was with him and the too-small clothes? Well, she hoped he was about to get filthy. She blinked a few times, heat rising to her face. Because she definitely hadn't meant it in *that* way.

Devan smiled and shrugged. 'Your body must be having a chemical reaction at the sheer sight of me.'

Teijo was busy scribbling.

'My body is perfectly under control,' Alyssa replied, signalling for Teijo to write that down too. 'Now, can we get on with this?'

It didn't take Teijo long to explain the app had taken on board Alyssa's dislike of heights in task one and given them a project on the ground. They would be cultivating one of the allotment plots in the town's new communal garden.

'Bringing more love to Hartglove,' said Teijo brightly. 'Devan's business has funded this new love garden to help bring the community together.'

Did Devan look embarrassed? 'It's a cause that's close to my heart.'

*Cheesy-tastic.*

'So, you're pretty much a gardening pro,' Teijo continued, checking his notes and looking at Alyssa. 'You listed horticulture and *taking care of the planet* as pastimes in the app's initial questionnaire.'

Had she? She'd got bored by the end and had quite possibly ticked space travel and competitive duck herding, for all she could remember. There had been *a lot* of pointless questions.

Devan muffled a laugh.

Alyssa felt herself bristle. 'Well yes, of course I like tending to gardens, and things. Obviously,' she bluffed. Devan probably remembered she hated getting muddy, but what did he know about her life these days?

'And you're always posting photos of delicious-looking beetroot juice on Instagram,' said her mother, Pearl, busy-bodying over. She gave Alyssa an exaggerated conspiratorial wink. 'As Miss Heart, of course.'

She could keep her sodding winking to herself. Alyssa grimaced. What was Pearl even doing here? She'd never paid Alyssa much attention when she'd been Beryl – probably because she'd been too busy practising her *hole in one* with Dominic from the golf club. And since then, they'd only kept in touch over the phone every month or three, plus the odd quick hello in London. Stilted conversations about superficial things. Why did Pearl have to come flitting around her now?

'Oh, I do enjoy Miss Heart's Instagram photos,' said Devan, putting his arm around her mum like they were besties. *So annoying.* 'They never fail to surprise me.'

Beetroot juice tasted like the contents of an earthworm's intestines – but as an inspiring role model, she couldn't go posting photos of her downing Vimto like it was going out of fashion. At least her white lies were about positive, well-meaning things.

Alyssa barely recognised Pearl, dressed in gardening gear and radiating joy as though digging up worms was the best fun ever. Her mother had never even boiled a vegetable since Marks & Spencer had started selling pre-cooked red cabbage, let alone grown one. And as for the flower borders, her mum had always had a man in to do that. And that's probably not all the poor man had ended up tending.

'Isn't it wonderful that the town will have these new gardens, as a space to bloom and grow? We residents have always taken pride in our apple trees, of course. And just you wait until you see our glorious spring blossom,' Pearl said to Teijo. 'It's simply spectacular. Move over, Japan!'

It wasn't *that* good. Was it? And since when had her mother given a fig about foliage?

'Did you know blossom is symbolic of beauty, love, hope?' Pearl continued to babble, pointing to Teijo's pad, as though he should write that down.

Lessons in love from Pearl Bagnor?

'Once we start filling this allotment with new life, and more couples come here to enjoy it, they'll soon stop calling us *loveless*. Well done, Devan, for funding it,' Pearl concluded. 'What a fantastic idea.'

Alyssa gave a small clap, which wasn't *at all* sarcastic. She was pleased to note Devan looked a little awkward.

Teijo nodded, made a few notes, and then went off to gather kit.

'This 'Appy Together app is brilliant.' Her dad arrived next to Devan and clapped him jovially on the back. Percy Bagnor, manager of the local bank and a man who never used to take his suit off, other than for getting naked with his bank staff in the stationery cupboard. Sickening. And here he was, wearing moth-eaten *corduroy*? 'We're so enjoying working through our tasks together.'

What was this, an impromptu meeting of the Devan Shaw fan club? And were these two using the damned app too? She vaguely remembered it claimed it could help both singles and couples in need.

Though her dad had always praised everything Devan did when they were growing up, even if *her* achievements only ever disappointed him.

'I'm feeling *so* romantic with it all. We might even treat ourselves to a second honeymoon,' Pearl enthused. 'Devan's parents are always off doing something lovely. I do envy their extended trip to the Maldives right now. Maybe I should dust off my bikini!'

'Always a treat.' Percy gave his wife a wink.

Alyssa's stomach turned.

'Anyway, look. Our plot is right next to yours.' Percy gave a smile that could light up nearby planets as he put an arm around her mother and planted a soft kiss on her dirt-speckled forehead.

Yuk. Were these two getting paid? How much could she pay them to just naff off?

And if this app wasn't powered by evil for *randomly* throwing her next to the Bagnors ... 'What a delightful year we're all going to have, working side by side,' said her mother, looking positively gleeful. 'Not that we've met you before.' Another exaggerated wink.

All. *Year*?

'Wait, what?' Alyssa snapped at Devan, as her parents wandered off. 'I thought we'd be done before lunch?'

'Creating an allotment takes time,' Devan explained, as though she was five. 'The app is encouraging us to have shared responsibilities. Mutual interests. Commitment. All important ingredients, wouldn't a love coach also say?'

'Committed to growing broad beans?' said Alyssa, through slightly gritted teeth. *Blooming marvellous.*

'More time for budding relationships to blossom and grow.' Devan gave her a winning grin. 'Talking of which, when are you going to stop denying those nice people are your parents, and that you're from here?'

'At around the time you admit you were a two-timing sleaze.'

Devan opened his mouth to say something, but was interrupted by a reporter wanting to talk about his bloody brilliant love app.

Alyssa had been relieved Devan wasn't wearing a too-small, stomach-flashing Save Hartglove T-shirt that morning – but perhaps she shouldn't have been. Because it looked like things were about to get worse.

'Dev, do you need overalls?' said a young guy, who'd been working on one of the allotments. 'Can't get your good stuff dirty.'

Teijo had disappeared somewhere with his list, looking flustered. Alyssa wouldn't mind betting he'd forgotten some supplies.

'Cheers, Cole,' said Devan, giving the guy a blokey arm clap as he handed him a pair of overalls.

Alyssa didn't recognise Cole, although most of the people they'd grown up with had moved away for work or uni and had never come back. Maybe that was why the town wasn't winning any awards for its love statistics. The youngsters had all got fed up and buggered off.

Devan was still smiling and chatting to anyone who passed, with an ease that was almost vexing when you weren't so good at it.

Though what was he doing now? Alyssa willed her jaw not to drop. The man was peeling off his clothes as though he was in some sort of gym changing room. In front of half of the town, and a bunch of people with cameras. Really? Didn't he get that overalls literally went *over all*? That was the actual point of them. You didn't need to do a striptease.

God, he was probably one of those guys who posed around communal changing rooms and dried his pubes with a hairdryer.

Alyssa wanted to feel more irritated at his bravado – but as the situation unfolded, she was struggling not to giggle. He was naked from the waist up now, which was clearly unnecessary, but the cameras were loving it. She cocked her head. Talking of gyms, was he working out more these days? He didn't used to have pecs that were quite so well-sculpted, nor abs that her gran could have scrubbed undies on. How did people get those, anyway? She'd once done sit-ups every morning for a whole week, and had got *nothing*, other than a strange twinging in her side.

'Everything OK, Alyssa?' Devan winked at her.

Damn, had she been staring? Well, it was his fault for parading around like a prize poodle. She willed her brain back to the pube drying image, which was safer all round.

'Just thinking about …' She searched for excuses. Pubes? Washboard stomachs? 'Outfits! Such a shame I didn't bring my garden wear.' Was that what people called it? Who knew. She did her best to hold eye contact, because it was rude to look at people's nipples.

'I've got spare overalls at the shop,' said a woman, from amid the throng. It was Jess, who'd served her in the convenience shop on Apple Blossom Lane a few times since she'd arrived here. 'You don't want to get your designer things ruined.'

Alyssa wasn't about to say her designer clothes were vintage, if vintage meant cheap and pre-loved.

'I'm fine, honestly,' said Alyssa. It was easier not to ask for favours nor get too friendly.

'Or I could pop home and get you something of mine?' Pearl offered.

Alyssa tried not to visibly baulk.

'I'll go straight away,' Jess replied, giving Alyssa a look that said *nobody wants to dress like a lady who may or may not be your mother.*

Alyssa's relief was palpable. Now and again, the universe threw her a bone, amongst the shit bombs. Perhaps it was OK to accept this one.

'That's a shame,' said Devan, who'd drawn close enough to whisper into Alyssa's ear, his breath making her skin prickle. At least he had his overalls done up now, even if he shouldn't be invading her space with his bothersome lips. 'I would have loved to have seen you in one of Pearl's floral trouser suits. Maybe that's a task for later.'

'You wish,' she hissed back, still smiling for the cameras.

These tasks might be hideous, but she could at least enjoy a touch of ribbing. Let the garden games begin.

# Chapter 17

'So I'm meant to dig over this entire patch of land with a hand trowel?' Alyssa asked Teijo, after ten minutes of trying and failing. She didn't know much about allotments, but following a few hot gardeners on Instagram had told her there had to be better kit. 'Haven't we got a proper fork?'

Teijo scratched his head and consulted his notes. He did that a lot.

'Here, borrow this.' Devan arrived back at their patch after having skived for half of the morning, under the guise of '*getting inspiration from other plots*'. Alyssa had blatantly seen him lolling about under the apple trees, chatting and drinking tea.

He was carrying an armful of gardening tools and looking particularly pleased with himself.

'I'm fine, thank you.' She was far from fine, on her hands and knees in a pair of borrowed overalls, pretending she knew about horticulture. She wasn't even sure what the word meant. But she wasn't about to accept help from Devan cocky Shaw.

'As someone who's big on "*tending to gardens, and things*" you'll know we need to dig this over and prepare the beds for sowing seeds in a month or two?' Devan swept his arm across the whole patch of land, which was the length of a good-sized garden. 'And that you'll need more than a tiny hand tool?'

'Yes, of course I know that.' He was the only *tiny tool* around here. She stood and brushed herself down. At least the overalls Jess had lent her were a nice shade of green and a reasonably flattering fit. She could not have faced this in ankle swingers. 'I'm just completing some ... ground testing. It's intricate work. Not everybody knows about it.' She wiped an arm across her forehead in a way that looked like she'd been toiling hard. She was blagging, of course. But it was better than being a tea-swigging shirker.

'And what do your ground tests conclude?' Devan asked, sagely.

'That it's about time you pulled your weight.' She snatched the only garden fork from him and swapped it for her hand trowel. There. That wasn't accepting help. It was simple fair trading.

When Alyssa got into the swing of digging over, she was surprised at how time flew. She'd only meant to stick around to pose for photos and pretend she'd given gardening a go. In fact, she'd only checked her phone a few times, having given up when her hands got muddy. Devan had borrowed another fork and was digging from the other end of the plot. Although at some point, they'd surely have to meet in the middle – and she wasn't sure how she'd navigate that part.

'You'll need to cover that with a thick layer of compost,' said Horace from the plot next door. 'Have you got some?'

Alyssa looked to Teijo, who was sitting on a deckchair, scribbling notes. He checked another list. 'We have *some*.'

'We've got spare, if you run out,' her mother called over. She was the ultimate nosy neighbour. Alyssa wasn't even sure what she'd been doing all morning, other than smooching Alyssa's father, posing for Teijo's social media promo photos and eating cake.

'We'll be fine,' Alyssa replied firmly. She knew she would have to woman up and face this predicament with her parents at some point, but she had quite enough on right then.

'Do you have wheelbarrows?'

Teijo jumped up from his lounging spot. 'Erm, I did order

one. Though I think there's something wrong with the wheel.'

Devan offered to take a look, but Alyssa scowled him down.

She marched to the shed and began shovelling compost into the wheelbarrow, unsure what she was doing but determined to style it out. The effort was making her out of breath, but somehow, the mud-slinging was satisfying.

From the corner of her eye, she could spy Devan leaning on his fork, watching her. He was probably waiting for her to cock something up so he could rush in and save the day. Well, he could bugger off. When the wheelbarrow looked full, she moved to lift it, bending sensibly at the knees like any good gardener would probably do, and took a deep breath. She *had* to get this right, because she could not go looking weedy-armed in front of Devan and his monster pecs.

'Heave,' she whispered to herself. 'Huh … *ohhhh!*'

Who knew she had such a strong right arm? The barrow tipped to one side, spilling half of her load and sending her cheeks a hot shade of mortified.

'Yes, well that was what I meant to do,' she said through a fixed smile, grabbing at the mess with her thankfully gloved hands and scooping it back into the barrow. 'Aeration. You know. Getting air into the soil.' That was a thing, wasn't it?

Teijo hadn't been joking about the dodgy wheel. When she got herself going again, it squealed and wobbled, coming to another juddering halt and spilling yet more compost.

'She's just aerating,' she heard Devan shout to her mother, using actual air quotes as he said it.

*Earthworm.*

'Here, duck. I've got a spare wheelbarrow,' said Horace.

He'd kindly offered them tea earlier and seemed like exactly the sort of man you'd want to adopt as a granddad. Not that she was one for getting too attached to people.

'No, it's fine, I …'

'It's OK to accept a bit of help,' Horace said, discreetly. 'I can tell you're one of those independent sorts, like Beyoncé sings about. But life's hard enough. When someone offers you a hand, grab on to it and don't sink.'

And though she had no idea who he was, beyond an old guy in a floral print twill jacket and bumblebee wellies, his words touched her. Then somehow, she was welling up. She blinked a few times. No. It had been a long morning – that was all. Trying to prove she was a brave-arsed coach who could deal with this love app's horseplay felt like *a lot*. Especially with half of social media gawping. Horace winked at her, the skin around his eyes crinkling, and she decided to follow him. She wasn't going to make a habit of accepting favours, but perhaps this town wasn't as bad as she'd remembered. Jess had said people meant well. Perhaps that was a thing.

'Do you think 'Appy Together is bringing more love to Hartglove?' Teijo asked her, during a quiet moment.

'It's bringing more heart-shaped bunting,' she replied with a wry smile, pointing at the white picket fences.

And when he asked her if she was falling for her BUM, she simply laughed.

The next couple of hours floated by, with Alyssa wheeling backwards and forwards with compost, and taking out her troubles with a rusty old fork. In fact, as long as she stayed at least five metres away from Devan or her parents, she might even describe allotment life as relaxing, and a surprisingly nice change from fiddling with her phone. Perhaps Devan's app should focus on matchmaking people with new hobbies and leave the relationship fixing to her.

Alyssa was curious about a nearby plot of scruffy land, complete with a shed that had been painted with the words *Tea and Sympathy*. Outside it were two large purple wingback chairs that looked suspiciously like something from the *Big Brother* diary room. She hadn't yet worked out who presided over it, other than there were rumours of upside-down apple cake on a good day – because apparently this town could still grow and store enough apples to bowl Aphrodite over, even if they couldn't harvest a decent love story. As for the chairs, she'd decided to keep a safe distance. Nobody had bugged her too much about whether she'd once been Beryl today, and that was the way she liked it.

'I'm just going to collect lunch,' said Teijo, interrupting her thoughts. Now she stopped to notice, her stomach was rumbling again. 'I've ordered greasy, doorstop bacon sandwiches. I'll bring plenty of ketchup, hot coffee …'

*Heaven.* She could taste the salty sweetness already.

'Not for you, of course,' Teijo clarified. 'What with you being extremely nutrition-conscious. I've ordered your favourite. Quinoa with mung beans, and a pea and pineapple smoothie.' He beamed at her.

Pea and *pineapple*? Did that even go, unless gammon was involved? The thought of it made her belly clench. Though she'd definitely posted about quinoa salads at least five times on Instagram.

She held in her sigh and smiled her thanks, briefly considering the thought of posting the odd photo of food she *actually* liked, before swiftly dismissing it.

'You're so healthy and inspiring. I'm proud of you,' her mother whispered, having barged over at the mention of food.

Alyssa blinked and looked away, because there it was. Her mother had only ever been proud of the version of her that didn't exist. Neither of her parents had ever thought Beryl was worth spending time with – well, not as much as their extramarital shag partners. At least as Alyssa she was vaguely respected, even if she didn't always believe in the good vibes she advocated.

'Swap you,' said Devan, coming to sit next to her on a bench, when the food had arrived.

His bacon sandwich was still wrapped in its paper bag and the smell that wafted from it was divine. She could feel the heat from it, and from him too, as he adjusted himself like his gym thighs needed more room.

Teijo had disappeared somewhere and most of the locals had little interest in what she ate. And she could almost taste that sandwich in her mouth. The softness of the bread, the ooze of the tomato sauce ...

She bum-shuffled away. 'No thank you. This quinoa is ...'

'Dreadful?' Devan leaned over to eye it. 'As dry as a bag of old toenail clippings?'

'Ew.' Now he'd really put her off. She would definitely have got into it if it wasn't for that. Well, probably.

'Your Instagram food pics are just for show, right? Nobody actually enjoys eating cucumber couscous sprinkled with galangal root.'

*Galangal* ...? She narrowed her eyes. Well, that was ridiculously specific. Had he been *memorising* her Instagram posts?

She was sure she could see his cheeks reddening. He *had* been paying extra attention to her words. Ha! And as for making his perfectly chiselled cheeks turn crimson. Alyssa squeezed her eyes shut and took a big spoonful of her quinoa, making an *mmm* sound that could have won her a BAFTA.

'All right, Meg Ryan.' He gave her a curious look and shifted away a little.

Then he opened his bag, took out one half of the sandwich and wrapped the other half up again. 'I'm just going to leave this here,' he said quietly, standing and placing the bag next to her. 'If you feel like indulging, be my guest. I'll never know.' He winked at her. 'And if you want to fling it in the bin.' He gave a nonchalant shrug. 'Your business.'

What was his game? Was he about to hide behind a gooseberry bush and take photos of her pigging out on a pig sarnie, with grease dripping down her chin?

He held up his hands as though he could sense her train of thought. 'No tricks – I can just hear your stomach rumbling. They don't call me *Good Old Devan* for nothing.'

Did she sense a tinge of resentment when he said the last bit? If she did, it was quickly replaced with his trademark grin.

He turned and began to walk away.

'Thank you,' she heard herself mumble, before she could think better of it. 'Not that I'll need it, or anything. I'll just ... feed the birds a few crumbs.'

'Of course.'

'And Devan?'

He stopped and turned to look at her, his eyes strangely hopeful.

'I hope you're not keeping your old toenail clippings in bags. That's kind of gross. Surely your wife has taught you better?'

His forehead creased, but he didn't have time to answer. Cole came over to let him know there was no rush to return the overalls, leaving Alyssa to ponder the sandwich situation and to feel *not at all* disappointed that Devan wouldn't have another excuse to strip.

With a quick sweep, she scooped the brown bag into her handbag, because it wasn't good to be wasteful or to litter public benches. She wasn't going to openly accept favours from Devan. But if she did find herself feeling absolutely starving ...

'You coming to The Rat and Raspberry, love?' her dad asked, when she'd finished stashing her swag.

'We still need to catch up properly,' her mum whispered, putting her arm around her husband's waist and pinching him on the bottom.

*Urgh.* Alyssa tried not to pull a face.

'No thanks.'

If she was honest, a small part of her had enjoyed having people around and remembering how it felt when the town pulled together – but she wasn't ready to embrace *everything*. These two were a step too far.

'You sure?' asked Devan. 'I didn't get much chance to catch up with you either.'

Oh, she was sure. She'd seen *far* too much of him today.

'We could talk about that exclusive for the media?' Teijo suggested, as he joined the circle. 'I keep hearing the odd whisper from residents that you have history around here. Is it true? And why did you leave?'

'Busy night!' said Alyssa, pulling out her trusty phone and waving it. 'Social media jobs, plus a whole list of online house shopping.'

The Cow Shed was still quite empty, even though Jess from the shop kept trying to offer her everything from beaded fly curtains to front garden gnomes.

'We can lend you …'

Alyssa cut her dad off. 'I'm all good!'

And that was exactly why she should get herself back to the barn. She could do without other people's interfering or her parents' cast-offs.

She had half a cold bacon butty with her name on it, and plenty of Instagram friends to catch up with. She would be just fine.

**Private message from @agent_rufusdiamond to @alyssa-heart_thelove coach:**

**@agent_rufusdiamond** – *Sorry I couldn't make it to your latest love task. Was getting my eyebrows done. I can highly recommend 'barbed wire' as a facial hair look.*

# Chapter 18

Peace and quiet. Yes, what a glorious thing that was. Well, it always sounded like a lovely idea, until you'd checked your phone for the gazillionth time, got fed up of the sound of your own thoughts and then realised you were excruciatingly bored. Even Pikachu was fast asleep, which was pretty much all her new mouse pet did all day. It was only at night that he decided to come alive like a mini vampire and keep her awake, incessantly running on his tiny wheel. Didn't he realise going around in circles got you nowhere?

Alyssa sighed. Because now, the most interesting thing she had to think about was her rodent's life problems.

She stretched out on her bed, wondering if she should paint her toenails again, for a bit of sport. Hanging around by yourself wasn't *that* tiresome. This was soul time. Space to be zen, away from life's noise. People paid good money for this sort of tranquil retreat. Ooh, maybe she could put on those snazzy yoga pants she'd bought to look wholesome and bendy on social media and try a bit of one-legged king pigeon. She considered it for a moment and then shuddered. No need to be extreme.

She rolled off the duvet and went to grab her phone again.

'Reasons to be cheerful,' she sing-songed in the direction of the clump of hay where Pikachu was snoozing. 'I still have my latest

'Appy Together post-task questionnaire to complete.'

If she said it in an upbeat enough way, she might even convince herself she wasn't dreading it. She had a feeling that awful algorithm was out to get her.

Or another thought. Maybe she was bringing some of this onto herself?

*Hmm.* If she hadn't told the app she was into horticulture, maybe it wouldn't have thrust them into a task where she had to pretend she was Alan bloody Titchmarsh. A task that could drag on for *months*, because they had yet to sow a seed. And she couldn't deny that feigning a love for quinoa and mung beans had lost her the chance of her own bacon sandwich.

In fairness, the allotment task hadn't been nearly as bad as she'd expected, and from the social media coverage, she hadn't come across as a *complete* buffoon. It might even open up a whole new pool of potential love coach clients if lonely men in sheds started following her on Instagram. Some parts of it she'd even enjoyed. The sense of achievement, the time outdoors, the people. She shook her head. Well, not *all* the people, because nobody needed too much of striptease Devan or her snogging parents, and it still felt awkward dodging folk who might say, 'Ooh, Beryl. *I remember when Devan dumped you like a numpty and ran off with your pretty friend.*'

Thank goodness she hadn't yet bumped into Sylvie, even if now and again she caught herself absently wondering about her. Her once best friend's betrayal had hurt, and Alyssa had made damned sure back then that Sylvie couldn't get hold of her to talk about it – because she did *not* want to compare notes on the size of Devan's schlong. She'd moved to London, changed her number and instructed her parents not to pass it on. At least they'd done her that courtesy.

But she hadn't come back here to moon over relationships lost.

Alyssa clicked onto the app's questionnaire. This time, should she blag a bit less? Not that she'd go admitting *all* her secrets, or anything wild. She had her reputation to keep, and people liked the version of her who ate mung beans. But would it hurt if she was a touch more honest, in the hope the algorithm would be kinder to her?

And if she wasn't going to fall for Devan, come hell or high water, what was there to fear?

She paced to the kitchen and sat up on the worktop, because it was the only place to rest her bum other than her bed or the floor. She really must think about more furniture. When she'd searched online the previous evening, she'd wavered at spending that much money on stuff she'd get rid of when she went back to London. And who wanted to spend their earnings on something as dull as temporary furniture?

Her fingers danced across her screen as she answered the app's questions with a touch less embellishment. She admitted she'd enjoyed being outdoors, though next time, maybe she didn't need the whole town there, waving banners and appraising her wheelbarrow skills. She held off on adding *and don't invite my slutty parents*.

It was still hard to believe Percy and Pearl were going through 'Appy Together's seven-step shenanigans too. Were they actually into each other, or still on the partner swap merry-go-round? And how on earth had the app managed to throw them into the same task, on the plot of land next door? Surely there was something – or someone – else at play? Although she wasn't going to spend her morning contemplating Devan Shaw. Or Pearl Bagnor.

'Hellooooo there.'

Alyssa froze. Had her mind just conjured up that voice as she'd been thinking about her mother? Because it sounded freakishly like her.

'Are you in? We've brought supplies!'

*We?* Was it really her mum? And who had she brought?

'Cooee! I've got a lovely T-shirt for you.'

Alyssa winced. Well, that one sounded like Mrs Halfpenny.

She guessed she couldn't dodge her past forever.

The voices were accompanied by a round of resolute banging on the barn's front door. It was not going away.

'The cow 'hed?' her mum seemed to be saying.

Ow indeed. Alyssa jumped down from the worktop, grateful at least that she'd showered and got out of her pyjamas.

She opened the door and was immediately surprised by the clamour. Had the whole of Hartglove descended on her doorstep, laden with packages and awkward-to-carry items? But it was February – not Christmas. What was going on?

'Someone need a kitchen table?' said Mrs Halfpenny, rocking a T-shirt that said, '*Aorta Tell You Hartglove's Got Love*'. She was holding one end of a rustic wooden table, with her granddaughter Jess clutching the other.

'And chairs,' said another woman, who was carrying one, with three children behind her sitting on the rest of the set like a row of tired ducks.

'You mentioned you didn't have a freezer when I tried to foist my batch-cooked casseroles onto you,' said an older man, who she instantly recognised as her wheelbarrow friend, Horace. He was pointing to the open back door of a van, which held a freezer, amongst other things.

'Which means you'll need ice cream!' said Jess, flicking her head towards the freezer bag on her shoulder.

'And kitchen items,' added Alyssa's mother, pointing to a large box at her feet. 'Because how can you make your lovely pea smoothies without a blender?'

'And quinoa!' said Sausage Sandra, who ran the local breakfast café. 'Not our usual order, but I'm sure you'll inspire us with your new fandangled ways.' She held up a box of what looked like Alyssa's least favourite pseudograins.

Jess was eyeing her freezer bag and mouthing 'potato waffles' and 'triple-cheese pizza'.

Alyssa put a hand to her head. All these *people*. She was used to conducting her '*friendships*' online. With followers she never had to meet and who couldn't lovingly share their Furby toys and then smash your heart to smithereens, like a certain ex-best-friend.

'Are you inviting us in?' asked her mother.

'Or we could leave the stuff outside?' Jess offered, looking almost apologetic. She must have been picking up on Alyssa's overwhelm and confusion.

'We just wanted to be helpful,' Horace added, looking charming in his flowery jacket and funky wellies. 'You're a good sort and we like you. But we don't want to be a bother.'

Mrs Halfpenny plonked down her end of the table and Jess followed suit.

'I know you've been avoiding me like an attack of pubic lice,' said Mrs Halfpenny, sounding nothing like the sweet old dear who used to serve her Sherbert Dips in the corner shop. 'So I won't beat around the lady bush. Folk who've lived here long enough know you're Beryl Bagnor and you weren't born with bubble-gum hair and an online fan club. But just like Shania Twain is really called Eileen, if you want to be known as Alyssa, we won't tell tales. Team Hartglove looks after their own – even if we're pretending we don't know you from Adam. Though I *do* think you'd look smashing in this Save Hartglove T-shirt,' she said, waggling one at her. 'Just saying.'

Alyssa looked at the sea of faces, her hand strangely drifting to her heart. They'd really brought all this stuff for her, and they weren't going to blow her cover? How could she possibly turn them away? As much as she'd been planning a serene morning it would be rude not to stick the kettle on. She'd lived away from small-town life for years, but you never forgot the etiquette of offering tea. And she *had* been feeling a bit on the bored side.

'Wow, well, thank you. Can I interest anyone in a cuppa?' Alyssa slowly backed away from her position of blocking the doorway, because she couldn't leave everyone out in the drizzle.

'Thought you'd never ask,' said Sausage Sandra, bustling her way in. 'I brought milk and teabags. And apple pie cookies – though I don't suppose you ruin your arteries with those.'

Alyssa gulped. She'd have to keep them away from her fridge, if she didn't want them spotting the junk food. Or could she trust them with that too? As people filed into her once-empty space, she couldn't help giving a cursory glance for Devan. *Not* that she wanted him anywhere near her home.

'Don't worry, *Signorina Cuore*,' whispered Anna Farina, who Alyssa had learned ran the local Italian dessert shop, Dolce & Anna, which was also on Apple Blossom Lane. 'I brought caramel apple tiramisu. I won't let you starve on this bean food.' She patted her own rounded belly. 'Apples are symbolic of love, you know.'

Alyssa raised her eyebrows. She'd have to be sure not to eat too many – not that she believed in love *nor* fruit with superpowers. Was everything made with a hint of apple in this town? She did remember people used to store or cook and freeze them, to use all year round.

Anna gave Alyssa a wink, pinched her cheek as though Alyssa was an adorable toddler, and bustled into The Cow Shed, like a short, sweet woman on a mission. Alyssa didn't know Anna from her previous years in Hartglove but could already tell she was going to like her.

And before Alyssa knew it, what seemed like half of the town and their friends, aunties and second cousins twice removed were piling into her small, converted barn, with armfuls of things she didn't know she needed.

'Where shall I put this air fryer?' she heard her mother ask. 'Everybody's doing it, you know. You're not alive until you've baked your cheese scones in a Ninja.'

'My mum does her whole roast dinner in hers,' said Jess. 'Gravy and everything.'

Sausage Sandra pulled a face.

'I brought you a heated clothes dryer,' said the woman who'd been carrying a chair earlier. 'I'm Mel from Splash 'n' Dash launderette. No idea why my husband bought me this for our anniversary, when I have thirteen industrial tumble dryers and a perfectly good washing line.' She lowered her voice. 'Romantic, hey? And they wonder why there's not enough love in Hartglove. You'd better give me one of your business cards.' She winked and moved away, her three children following her and copying her hip-swishing action.

Splash 'n' Dash. Well, it was an improvement on the days of Hackney's All Washed Up.

'Hartglove is perfectly nice,' Horace added, when Mel and her brood had disappeared towards the kitchen. 'It's just that youngsters move away in search of more excitement, and many of us have come here to retire, sometimes widowed.'

He fiddled with a button on his flowery jacket and Alyssa noticed for the first time that perhaps it was more of a woman's cut, as coats went.

Anna came past and squeezed his arm. 'Me too, *tesoro*.' Were her eyes welling up?

Before Alyssa could be sure, she'd sniffed loudly and was ambling off.

'It means treasure, you know. Or maybe even *darling*,' Horace said, absently. 'It's amazing what you can search for on this internet, isn't it? My mobile phone tells me everything. Have you heard about apps?' He smiled up at her, his eyes a touch teary too.

'I have heard about apps,' said Alyssa, her heart warming a little further, despite her best intentions. 'Though you need to be careful with some of them. Shall we get you that cup of tea?'

As they arrived in the kitchen, the kettle was already on. Her mother was setting up all manner of gizmos and gadgets. Jess was sitting on the worktop eating raspberry ripple ice cream with stewed apples, and saying how she loved it when it rained, because you got to huddle in. Alyssa hadn't noticed until that point that it was hammering it down.

Somebody had plugged in an old radio and Anna was dancing

solo to something that sounded Italian and operatic.

And were Mel and her children *actually* hanging the contents of her washing machine onto the heated clothes horse? Were those her favourite knickers?

Horace chuckled. 'No secrets in this town, hey, duck?'

'Or much in the way of peace,' Alyssa replied.

She blinked a few times, not sure how to take it all in. She ought to be outraged that a small person was now spinning around her kitchen floor with a pair of her tights, singing to Pavarotti. Or that her peaceful morning was now completely shattered. But there was laughter and warmth and a sneaky chance of tiramisu. And everybody meant well. So just for once, Alyssa decided to go with it. It wouldn't be forever. She'd be back to her old, less overwhelming and more discreet London life soon enough. The one where she kept real people at bay, because if you weren't careful, they had a funny habit of muscling in.

But it wouldn't hurt to loosen the rules and accept a bit of kindness, just this once. Would it?

# Chapter 19

Alyssa breathed a sigh of relief as the last of her surprise guests began to leave. It had been an unexpectedly uplifting morning, other than the general chaos and having to field interference in everything from her fridge contents to her clean undies. But now, she needed to hide in a cupboard and eat leftover cookies. She deserved it.

'We should go to the quinoa bar!' her mother piped up as Alyssa was handing over her Burberry trench coat. She'd apparently splurged on it after seeing Alyssa wearing one on Instagram. Alyssa didn't like to say she'd grabbed hers for twenty quid on Vinted.

'Hmm,' said Alyssa noncommittally, her stomach clenching at the thought of hanging out with Pearl, consuming quinoa. And at a bar? What were they doing, turning it into mojitos? 'We'll do that soon.' *Or not.*

'Let's go now.' Her mum gripped her arm, her eyes wide with something that looked like hope. 'We still haven't caught up properly, just you and me.'

'Erm.' It didn't feel good to worm her way out of it, and maybe they should make peace. She couldn't unsee the image of her mum getting jiggy with Dominic, or unhear the lies that came before it to cover up her parents' affairs. And *quinoa*? 'I'm tired. Maybe another time.'

'Tired? Nonsense! You're always up to energetic things on social media. It's so impressive.'

Pearl was squeezing her arm now, like she was proud of her. Her mum had always been too busy to care when she'd been boring Beryl.

'I'll tell you all about what that dishy Devan has been up to, since you left. Not that I'm one to gossip.'

Dishy. Alyssa rolled her eyes. Though maybe she should get the lowdown, in the interests of not being duped.

'And we *must* talk about Teijo. He keeps asking me and your father about whether we have a connection to you, and some sort of exclusive?' Pearl giggled. 'You'll have to give me media training on what I'm allowed to say!'

Damage limitation. Alyssa sighed and grabbed her umbrella and coat.

'They do this wonderfully cleansing matcha and lychee tea,' said Pearl, as she hustled Alyssa along the rain-damp main street of Taybury – their nearest big town. There was no way you could get matcha anything in Hartglove. Thank God. Maybe there was something to be said for the simple quaintness of Apple Blossom Lane. Though at least Taybury's central shopping street wasn't full of trees that tried to poke you.

'I'm not really into …'

'I saw you raving about the wonders of matcha on Instagram. Who knew it had so many protective polyphenols?'

Who knew indeed. Alyssa tried not to feel guilty that she never drank the stuff, because it tasted like something a cow would spit out. Though at least her healthy living images were doing other people a service.

Her soul drooped as her mum pulled her past the inviting smells of pizza places she'd much rather indulge in. All that delicious, melty cheese. The pure joy of a carb fest. Would it be so bad to steer her mum towards Pepperoni Franco's? But that wasn't the version of herself that impressed her mother. Or anyone.

It didn't take long to shake off their umbrellas and settle themselves into The Keen on Quinoa Bar, where disappointingly, cocktails were not a thing – because right then, she could do with one. It was no more than a fancy café.

'I ordered us chocolate quinoa cake,' said Pearl, looking pleased with herself.

The teenager inside Alyssa was daring her to say '*urgh, gross*' and '*are you still shagging that bloke from the golf club?*' But she opted to wear her adult pants and stay open-minded. So many things had not been as she'd expected since she'd returned. Perhaps a miracle would happen, and her mother would turn out to be one of them.

While they sipped their smoothies and waited for the dubious cake, Alyssa instructed her mum not to tell Teijo or anyone else who she was or anything about her past in Hartglove. Their early press release had kept journalists off the scent, but Teijo was closer to the action and a touch too curious.

'What are you ashamed of?' Pearl asked, looking a little sad.

It was possible that something inside Alyssa panged slightly. Or it might have been smoothie brain freeze.

'My past is not for sale, that's all. It's just … *embarrassing*.'

Her mother had the good grace to blush. Maybe Devan had caused the first wound, but like any dumped teenager, she could have festered at home and got over it, even if she would have needed a new circle of friends. But rushing home to find out her parents' marriage and their entire 'happy homelife' was a sham had been too much to bear. Not to mention her ruined memories of the family sofa.

'We're so sorry about our extramarital thingamajigs, love,' her mother said quietly. 'And that *very* discombobulating scene in the front room. You were never meant to see that. Goodness knows,

I'd have been mortified if I'd ever caught your gran doing the naked mambo.'

'*Wow.*' Alyssa baulked. 'Thank you for adding *that* mental image to my back catalogue.'

'It all feels like a lifetime ago now. Your dad and I both used to enjoy a bit of *shopping around*. But as we got older, we realised the plums are always juiciest at home. And now look at us, doing this love app challenge, just like you! Perhaps we'll all fall in love again, together.'

*Juicy plums?* Alyssa pushed her drink away, suddenly queasy. She would not be *falling in love* with anyone. Love was a fantasy. A whimsical idea milked by film-makers and jewellery shops. And, in fact, by herself as a love coach – when she had any actual clients. *Love* was a fruitful business. But like Santa Claus and the tooth fairy, there was no tangible evidence it existed.

And she had plenty of evidence that her parents were massive liars – so who could tell what the truth was with them?

Pearl reached over and touched Alyssa's hand. 'Are you OK? You look a bit pale.'

'I'm fine. Thank you.'

It was her staple answer to most things. The words you said to be polite, because the truth was inconvenient. If she started unpacking it here, it would probably put Pearl off her quinoa cake. And nobody wanted that.

'I know I haven't had chance to say it in a non-whispery way, but I *am* proud of you,' said Pearl, squeezing her daughter's hand. 'You're doing so well for yourself as Alyssa Heart.'

*Compared to Beryl, who clearly nobody had chosen first.* Or was Pearl lying now too?

'Your dad's proud of you as well, you know. He's just a bit rusty on how to show it. And he doesn't understand what being a love coach is all about. He'd always wanted you to get a job in banking. He's learning.'

Alyssa tried not to scoff. Percival Bagnor had probably done more *bonking* than banking, and why was it he could appreciate Devan's love app, but not her work?

'And before you ask, he takes his role seriously these days. Absolutely no staffroom hanky-panky.'

'Right,' said Alyssa.

'Perhaps you could have a lovely heart-to-heart with him too? Go for a nice pie in The Rat and Raspberry. Heal some old wounds?'

Alyssa had had even less contact with her dad than her mum since she'd left Hartglove. He wasn't much of a phone chatter and had never bothered her to do *awkward brunch* in London like her mum sometimes had.

'I'm not into pie,' Alyssa lied.

'No, of course.' Pearl flapped a hand. 'But they do a good side salad.'

*Side salad*. She had more or less *been* her dad's dull side salad, while he went off in search of tasty meat. He'd always been too busy 'working' to spend much quality time with her when she'd been growing up. She now knew his version of work wasn't quite so wholesome as hers.

'I'm busy,' Alyssa replied more firmly, enjoying the sense of satisfaction it gave her.

Her mum pursed her lips but seemed to take the hint.

After a halt in conversation, their chocolate quinoa cake arrived. With a bit of prodding and a wary taste test, Alyssa was amazed to find she didn't dislike it.

'So, you must be wondering about Devan. You, him and Sylvie used to be such good friends when you were younger. Why do you never ask about them?'

Well, that was enough to put anyone off their cake.

'It's not my concern.' Alyssa didn't like the fact Devan was presumably still married, though with all the media coverage, Sylvie must be in the know. The love task stunts were just promo for his app and a boost for the town. Just business, as they'd both called it. And yet ...

'He's not married anymore, of course. He and Sylvie split up years ago.'

Did they? Alyssa couldn't stop her ears from twitching. She wanted to know more, yet she felt compelled to keep a poker face. How embarrassing that she even cared what had happened between them. It was years ago. She was the bigger, completely un-nosy person. She made a show of inspecting her sparkly nails as though they were far more intriguing.

'They still lived in the same big house, until recent months,' her mother went on. 'Though they were being *platonic*.' She said the word as though it was something that had been invented by three-headed Martians. 'There have always been *lots* of rumours about what went on behind closed doors, but he always does the right thing, does Devan. He stayed in the family home until Emmalina was settled at senior school. Very respectable.'

*Rumours. Respectable?* Alyssa nearly choked on her super berry smoothie. 'Always does the right thing?' she heard herself saying. Like shagging the tits off Sylvie, when he'd meant to be dating her? Though she wasn't going to say that out loud.

'Oh yes, he's known for it,' Pearl ploughed on, seemingly unaware her daughter was quietly seething. 'Good Old Devan, they always call him. I think it suits him.'

Alyssa narrowed her eyes. She did remember him mentioning that, although he hadn't looked particularly pleased about it. Though he probably was pleased Good Old Devan could be abbreviated to GOD. It was an upgrade from being a BUM.

'He's been doing a lot to try and regenerate Hartglove too, although he's a bit bashful about it. The town is proud of him.'

*Not like a certain daughter, who completely denies all ties to it.*

'I was never convinced by those two,' said Pearl. 'Devan and Sylvie. They were always perfectly nice to each other, but I never once saw them being *lovey*. Not even when they were newly married. It was as though the spark was missing. No one was surprised when they got divorced. She wanted to explore *other avenues*, although I never hear about Devan dating. Well, not until now ...' Pearl seemed to ponder it for a moment, then beamed as though she'd solved the world's problems. 'Maybe he's been waiting for his perfect match. Wasn't he sweet on you, when you were both younger?'

Alyssa blinked. Her young infatuation had been all-consuming. Did her mother honestly not remember? If she hadn't, perhaps the rest of the town had forgotten too. And yet she'd been too humiliated to come back to Hartglove for twelve whole years because of it. Had she built up that one excruciating night of being publicly dumped to be more than it was? Everything that had followed in her life had been coloured by it.

Alyssa composed herself and waved a hand. 'It was nothing. We weren't compatible.' She tried not to think about the nights they'd lain on his bed, listening to Coldplay, singing out of tune and giggling when they'd got the words wrong. Watching their favourite romcoms, because they'd both *loved* a love story. A grand gesture. A happy ever after. They *had* had so much in common. She'd never met anyone who she'd felt more connected to, other than her former best friend. And all along, he must have been sleeping with Sylvie, when he wasn't even sleeping with her. Because Good Old Devan had the good grace to only stick his penis in one girlfriend at a time. Well, she wasn't a hopeless romantic anymore.

'This love app of his must think you have plenty in common now,' said Pearl. 'It's matched you together, of all the people in the world. Can you imagine? Onlookers say you have chemistry.'

'Dynamite,' said Alyssa, sarcastically, thinking about all the ways she'd like to see him spontaneously combust. 'Anyway, there can only be half a dozen people on the app, if it's thrown us together. Or Devan the app master engineered it.' Her parents had chosen to be matched to each other, and she knew it was possible. Though presumably both parties would need to consent to that.

'Or maybe it's fate.' Alyssa's mum tapped her finger on her nose. 'Because "*fate isn't written in the stars. It's written in our hearts.*"'

Alyssa tried not to groan. She recognised it as something she'd once said on Instagram, quite possibly tweaked from Shakespeare, because he'd been good at these things. The post had got a lot of hearts but so had pictures of her breakfast.

They left the quinoa bar soon after that, Alyssa feeling hungry for some proper tea.

As they walked down the high street, the sun now glinting through the clouds, another shopfront caught Alyssa's eye. It looked more modern than when she'd last seen it, but its name was the same. I Scream for Ice Cream. She, Devan and Sylvie had all loved going there, sometimes as a trio, but often just her and Devan. They'd been suckers for The Peanut Butter Triple Beast, with extra whipped cream. It had tasted like bliss, and so had Devan, every time she kissed him after they'd shared one.

Then, as though fate was an actual thing, there he was. Walking out of the ice-cream shop like the last twelve years hadn't happened. Only he was broader now, and his hair a little untidier. His eyes crinkled at the sides when he smiled, and sometimes he wore glasses. He was wearing them right then, and the winter sun seemed to be dazzling him. As he stopped to adjust them, he spotted her. Had she been staring? She straightened herself and closed her surprised mouth. Thank goodness her mother hadn't spied him.

He held his ice-cream milkshake towards her in offering, a single straw sticking out. They'd always gone for two straws when they'd shared a drink, though they'd never cared whose was whose. Alyssa shook her head. Was he really standing there, and what were the chances? Maybe he'd followed her. Or could he track her on the app? As if he'd want to. Even if he wasn't with Sylvie anymore, this was just work – for both of them.

She bowed her head and kept walking. Did she feel a little *different*, seeing him and knowing he wasn't married now? She wasn't sure. But she wasn't going to stick around to find out. They'd be thrown back into the thick of their love tasks soon enough. What could 'Appy Together possibly come up with next?

**From: teijo@luckysevenmedia.co.uk**
**To: alyssa@alyssaheart.co.uk**

*Greetings Miss Heart*

*Thank you for completing your latest questionnaire.*

*'Appy Together has now chosen Love Task Three. What a treat you and Devan have in store. ALONE TIME! ;-)*

*I'll keep you posted with dates, as it will depend on the weather. When the time comes, we'll set off bright and early. Devan too.*

*Road trip!*

*And you'll need to pack for the whole weekend, with plenty of warm spare clothes. (I'll try not to forget the essentials. Again.)*

*Kindest regards*

*Teijo*

*P.S. Excited to see from Instagram that you've discovered a quinoa bar. I'll be sure to pack some more nutritious quinoa meals for you. Have you tried it with spinach and figs?*

*P.P.S. You must tell me whether you used to be called Beryl. What's the mystery about your Hartglove history? Ooh, that's a great name for a newspaper exclusive!*

# Chapter 20

Alyssa huddled inside her parka, wriggling her toes inside her boots to try and keep them warm. Spring might just about have arrived, but at this time of the morning the sun was still half asleep. And so was she. At least Teijo had heated seats in his car, so her rear end was toasty. They were on their way to Love Task Three, and for some reason, Alyssa couldn't help stealing glances at Devan, who was sitting in the front.

It wasn't that she *liked* looking at him. Of course she didn't. But she couldn't escape the weird thought that he seemed sort of different, since her mother told her he'd been separated from Sylvie for ages. And what was that thing she'd said about those two never having had a spark? Alyssa shook her head and looked away. She'd insisted on sitting in the back of the car, away from him. What on earth was she hoping to deduce from scrutinising the side of his head? As if anybody's ear ever gave away trade secrets. Anyway, he surely looked the same as he always did. Irritatingly laid-back, and nice to the point of smarmy. Only this time, a little rumble of something like guilt stirred in her belly as she thought that.

From what little Teijo had mentioned in his email, she might have *all weekend* to stop judging Devan on past crimes and confront him. The thought was mildly terrifying. On second thought, maybe a liar never changed their spots – or whatever that saying was.

'Can you divulge where we're going yet?' Alyssa asked, her gaze fixed on the trees and fields beyond her window. Somewhere in the middle of nowhere, as far as she could make out. This had better be swanky, because she'd entrusted Pikachu to Jess from the shop for the whole weekend. Who knew what the going rate might be for mouse-sitting.

Devan hadn't asked Teijo any nagging questions, though maybe he'd plotted this himself, complete with big hairy spiders and buckets full of quinoa. Or was she being a bit unfair on him? He'd arrived at the car with a cinnamon apple latte, an Americano and a green tea, and had given her first choice. At six a.m. on a weekend, she hadn't even pretended she was going for green tea, and he hadn't smirked when she'd grabbed the latte. But it would take a hell of a lot more than a nice drink from Apple Blossom Lane to fix his list of misdemeanours.

'You'll see,' Teijo replied. 'But I can tell you're going to love it. 'Appy Together is just brilliant at creating the perfect tasks.'

'Bit of a shame it's so far away from Hartglove,' Devan said absently. 'I ran a poll to see if the locals were feeling more love lately, so we can shake off that dreaded "*loveless*" stigma and make our town a more attractive place to live, though our efforts don't seem to have changed much. Maybe we need something more.'

More than flying over the town in a heart-shaped hot air balloon and breaking your back digging over a damned *love garden*?

'I must hand out more of my love coaching business cards,' Alyssa said fake-pleasantly.

The car arrived at a clearing in a wooded area next to a lake, Teijo jumping out like an excited puppy and pulling out supplies from the boot. Alyssa and Devan joined him.

Alyssa did her best to stop her heart from sinking as she took stock of Teijo's goods. She knew she often gave off outdoorsy vibes on social media, because photos of nature and lovely walks were far more uplifting than snaps of her watching *Bake Off* and eating a meat feast pizza. But Teijo's equipment looked a hell of a lot like there would be camping involved. Had she really signed up for *this*?

'Camping?' Alyssa asked casually. 'Just for the photos though, right?' If she could go home to her own warm bed after a little photoshoot, she'd do the best smiles ever.

'The seven love tasks are a genuine experiment, Alyssa,' said Teijo, as though she'd mortally wounded him. 'Real life isn't just a thing we do for the pics.'

Said the guy whose middle name ought to be '*When am I getting my exclusive?*'

'What will we be doing?' asked Devan, helping Teijo to organise the kit.

'Great question,' said Teijo. 'We have Alyssa to thank for this one. She asked the app for something involving fewer people, after the allotment task. And we know from her initial questionnaire that she aces everything from white-water rafting to campfire cuisine.'

Alyssa grimaced. She must get a touch more honest and update that bloody thing.

'And Devan is clearly fit and adventurous,' Teijo added, sweeping an arm at him.

Adventurous in his choice of clothing, Alyssa noted, eyeing his latest Save Hartglove T-shirt, emblazoned with '*Don't Play Hart to Get*', which he'd insisted was Mrs Halfpenny's brainchild. *Likely story*. At least it vaguely fitted this time, and he was wearing it with suitable layers.

Devan shrugged. 'I have most of my adventures behind a computer screen, but I'll try.'

'Teamwork and trust,' said Teijo. 'The app thinks you could both benefit from less time paddling your own canoes.'

Devan raised his eyebrows.

Teijo explained they'd be building a raft from logs, to get them across the lake to their wild camping spot. He was churning out other words, but Alyssa's thoughts were too busy spiralling.

She'd be sleeping in a tent. With Devan. In *March*? Who even did that?

'Hang on, won't it be freezing?' asked Alyssa. 'What if we need anything? Are there shops? And places to eat?'

'I've packed everything you need,' Teijo insisted. 'And written instructions, because phone reception will probably be non-existent.'

Alyssa gulped. She knew about Teijo's haphazard organising from the one wonky wheelbarrow situation – and that was before she got started on the quinoa. And no phone reception?

'You'll be staying with us, for backup though?' Hell, she'd even consider giving him his stupid exclusive, if he'd give her a lift home when it got chilly.

'I'll be leaving you two to take the photos, which you can send to me later. The app thinks you need some *alone time*. Wouldn't a reputable love coach like you agree?'

Her chest tightened.

'But we don't need to build a raft,' she blurted. 'No love coach would advise putting unnecessary strain on an already fragile situation. We could just walk around the lake. A few pics with a tent, and then …'

'I've packed waders,' Teijo replied. 'Because life is about enjoying the journey, Miss Heart – as your Instagram quotes are always reminding us. Embrace the ride.'

She'd quite happily shove the ride up someone's ridiculous T-shirt.

But as Teijo threw a pair of rubbery-looking trousers at her and pointed to the lake, she knew she'd better suck it up and start smiling, if she didn't want to breach her contract or look like a quitter. No wonder her agent had opted to stay at home again. Rufus had all but promised her the tasks would be quick and painless. And he had *not* mentioned when questioned the very real danger of being faced with Devan Shaw. Or indeed the possibility she might be sleeping face to face with him in what was bound to be a particularly small tent. Awkward to the power of a million.

It wasn't long before she and Devan were listening to the quiet purr of Teijo's engine, as he disappeared for two whole days – and something inside Alyssa was silently screaming. The purr had barely disappeared before she was eyeing up routes around the lake to avoid going over it and wondering how long she'd have to hike to a road to hitch a ride.

'You know he wants photos of the finished raft with us on it?' said Devan, clearly guessing she was considering escape routes. 'Shall I get some logs?'

She supposed she ought to at least complete some of the task, before trying to leg it. 'I'm perfectly capable, thanks.'

'I don't doubt it,' he replied. 'You're determined enough to make fourteen rafts and a shed to put them in. You just don't look like you fancy doing this.'

She paused for a moment. Did he think that about her? That she was determined? It was always strange to hear other people's take on you, especially when they'd known you well. Though they were both different now.

'It's just not my idea of a fun weekend, that's all,' she heard herself admitting. At least Teijo and his notepad had gone.

'I wondered.' He sat on a log and grabbed Teijo's instructions on how to make a raft. 'So why do you tell the app and your followers that you're into this sort of thing, if you're not?'

He kept his gaze trained on the paper in his hand.

'Are you saying I make stuff up?' she asked.

'I don't know. *Do* you?'

His words hung in the air, which still had a chill, even though the late winter sun was rising. A bird squawked somewhere in the distance.

Alyssa opened her mouth to reply. There were so many things

she wanted to say. This fresh, clear air was almost inviting it. A small part of her felt like telling him she'd built this whole persona to feel accepted and liked, and that it was all becoming a bit ridiculous. She imagined the great weight of it lifting as they chuckled at the unlikeliness of her eating mung beans on a white-water raft, wearing painful yoga pants ...

The distant bird screeched again, bringing her instantly back to her senses. What on earth was she thinking? Of course she wasn't going to start spilling all *that*, to Devan Shaw, of all people. She'd only been alone with him for approximately three minutes, and already she was getting extremely strange ideas. This was going to be a long weekend.

'I'll find some wood. We'll go separate ways.'

'You know, it will be easier if we work together,' Devan said cautiously. 'I've never made a raft before, have you? And let's face it, Teijo's instructions are likely to be shit,' he joked.

That was something they could agree on.

'So I guess it's teamwork or drown?'

Alyssa couldn't help the laugh that burst out of her. 'Now there's a saying for Instagram.' Though for once, she didn't want to share it. 'You know, that's probably the only reason I'd agree to teamwork with you,' she said lightly. 'Survival.'

'Oh yeah. The only reason?' He ran a hand through his wayward brown hair, the natural streaks of auburn flashing in the low sun.

Alyssa tried not to notice how the misty air had turned a few strands adorably wavy. She'd probably think the same about a spaniel.

Devan quirked his eyebrows, showing off his deep blue eyes. He wasn't wearing his geek chic glasses today. Not that his eyeballs were any of her business. One corner of his mouth was twitching into a smile, as though he knew his jokey efforts to look seductive were too much. Then, inexplicably, one hand moved slowly up his thigh towards his groin. Alyssa's mouth dropped. What on earth was he ...?

She shook her gaze away and glared at him.

'Not even for my massive ... bar of chocolate?'

Alyssa let out a relieved breath, mixed with a snort of laughter.

'Chocolate is survival,' she said, letting her eyes dance across the chunky Yorkie bar he was pulling out.

'And here was me thinking I could only impress you with a smile like Teijo's and a packet of goji berries.'

'Teamwork or drown,' said Alyssa, holding out her hand for her share of the chocolate bar Devan was already breaking in half.

'Is that a deal?' he asked, his eyes twinkling.

## Chapter 21

'Oh my God, that was incredible!'

Alyssa jumped off the raft and hopped towards Devan, who was already at the side of the lake, looking for somewhere to tie the raft's rope. Before her sensible head could catch up with her endorphins, she flung her arms around his neck and gave him a brief squeeze. He smelt of amber and something woody, invoking memories of being close to him all those years ago. She closed her eyes momentarily, before shaking her head and quickly disentangling herself. He might not be with Sylvie now, but he had been. And she'd been fooled by his charms before.

'That's what all the ladies say,' he joked, giving a small bow.

'Don't be a twat.' She gave him a light swipe. Hell, what was she, eleven years old? 'I just meant maybe there's something in this *enjoy the journey* stuff.'

Her heart was still racing from their wobbly ride across the water on the crappy contraption they'd hashed together using logs, a saw and a whole lot of rope. Teijo's instructions had been as useful as a bag of sand in the desert, but somehow the 'teamwork or drown' motto had got them across the lake without sinking. Alyssa had to admit, she felt more alive than she had in ages. The unexpected rush of adrenaline could be the only explanation for her having just flung her limbs around Devan like a total goon.

'Sorry,' said Devan, clearing his throat and going back to his task with the rope. 'For the stupid comment. I'm not always a twat. I just ... don't always know what to say around you. I come out with all this nervous bravado, and that's not really me.'

'Like the time you stripped in the love garden, when you could have just put the overalls *over* your clothes?'

'Yeah.' He winced. 'I wouldn't normally get semi-naked in front of your parents. When you're around I sometimes do odd stuff.'

Were his cheeks going red? A tiny part of her almost liked the way they could poke fun at each other, and how their jesting was becoming a touch less barbed.

'Just be yourself, Devan.' She sat down on the bank of the lake, pulling out the last square of Yorkie she'd saved in her pocket. She wanted to add *because everyone else is taken*, like she might have said on Instagram. The quote attributed to Oscar Wilde was a good one. Though as she saw his eyebrows gently raised in question, she knew this wasn't the time to throw out advice she wasn't sticking to.

'*Alyssa Heart* is a role I've come to play,' she heard herself mumble, through a mouthful of chocolate. 'We all have our reasons,' she added, more firmly.

'I get that.'

Did he? She didn't answer because she'd said more than enough.

And she *had* been meaning to somehow escape this task as soon as the raft thing was done. But Teijo would be expecting photos of them next to a pitched tent, so she supposed she ought to stay for that bit. Contractually speaking.

By the time it came to pitching their tent, Alyssa had learned it would be faster to work with Devan than to obstinately do her own thing. It was curious how quickly they fell into step as they worked, like some strange, historic muscle memory was taking over. They'd built dens together as kids and had worked on school projects. They'd both been in Scouts, and he'd even joined country dancing, until they'd tried to get him to wear a flowery hat and braces. Their bodies and minds knew how to work together, even if Alyssa had tried to resist it. If nothing else, it was useful for getting things done.

When the tent looked like it probably wouldn't collapse, they set up a campfire. Perhaps she ought to stay until they lit it later, because that would make for good photos too. She absently wondered if Teijo had managed to pack enough blankets and thermals, because it would surely get chilly. For Devan, that was. She'd have worked out how to get signal and order an Uber or something by then.

'Lunch,' Devan announced, when the afternoon was getting on.

It was quite possibly the best word she'd ever heard him say, and there was no way she was missing that bit. They'd had an active day, and her stomach was all but yelling.

'Is the quinoa salad yours or mine?'

Alyssa looked up to see the familiar twinkle in his eyes as he said it. He'd bailed her out before and she didn't need him to. She should just be honest with Teijo and let him know she only liked quinoa when it was disguised as chocolate cake. But her failure to do that was her problem, not Devan's.

'Salad's probably mine,' she said with a smile that didn't reach her eyes. Nobody's eyes could smile about pseudograins – especially if they'd probably been cooked to gritty imperfection by Sausage Sandra, as lovely as she was.

'Whatever he's sent, we'll share. Team *Delyssa*,' he said, combining their names and holding his hand up for a high five.

'Yep, you're doing that awkward bravado thing again.'

'What? That was better than Team *Alyvan*, right?'

'Still not a team.' She laughed and rolled her eyes.

They were back on the bank of the lake by the time they got around to sharing Teijo's thrown-together picnic. His notes said they'd have to catch fish to cook and eat for tea, and in the interests of getting photographic evidence she'd done her best with this task, they made a start. Teijo had sent a list of which fish they were allowed to eat, even if the rest of his instructions were dire and she did *not* plan on sticking around to gut a trout.

It was surprisingly peaceful sitting by the water like a pair of gnomes, each perched on a rucksack and dangling a fishing rod, their lunch spread out between them. Alyssa noticed how the quinoa salad was more or less bearable when you only had to eat half of it, and it helped that she had half of Devan's ham and pickle baguette to sweeten things.

'How did the Alyssa Heart thing come about?' Devan asked, after an almost amiable silence she'd been quite enjoying. She wasn't sure how much of her private life she wanted to share with him, after the last time she'd foolishly trusted him. But most of her love coach story was on her social media, and they may as well talk about something as they pondered the surface of the water.

'After I ... left,' said Alyssa, the last word feeling uncomfortable, 'I went to London and juggled various crap jobs. Then this life coaching course came up and I had no better plans, so I went along. I had no idea what to specialise in until one of mum's old friends, Dina, turned up drunk at my bar job. She was on the verge of divorce, and I started giving her informal coaching. My words helped to save her marriage. Dina suggested I could be a love coach.' She gave a small laugh. 'After everything that had happened in Hartglove, I can't say I thought much of the *big romantic dream*.' An image of a stage and an embarrassing costume invaded her mind, and she shook her head. 'But I'd found a strategy that helped people. Then when I set up my business, I was ready for a complete new name. A fresh start.'

'You seem good at what you do,' he said a little awkwardly. 'Do you enjoy it?'

Alyssa let out a long sigh. 'I used to.'

'And now?'

She stole a glance at the side of his head, as though sizing him up. What the hell. If he blabbed, she could always deny it. He had a history of lying.

'Like all careers, it has its moments.' She wasn't about to admit business had been rubbish for a while, or that she'd received a few reasonable enquiries since the love tasks began, but somehow, she was still holding back from them. It didn't yet make sense to her either.

'And the persona?' he asked gently.

She watched the lake ripple. Was that a fish?

'Not always me,' she conceded, when the water stilled.

'Why did you drop Beryl?' he asked, his voice still soft. He was probably trying not to scare off his tea.

'People weren't that into her.'

'I was into her,' he said, with a sudden firmness. 'I liked her just how she was. She didn't need to pretend to be ...'

Her head swung around to face him and his followed. Her eyes dared him to continue but he halted.

'You clearly didn't like her enough,' she challenged.

His gaze held hers for as long as she would let it, hurt seeming to flash across his face. *He* was hurt? Tears stung her eyes and she turned back towards the water, a stir of old emotions broiling. As he started to speak, she shushed him.

'We have a fish to catch. Then I'm getting out of here.'

Nearly an hour passed, with nothing pulling at their rods or swishing the water. Even the trout didn't want to breathe their uneasy air. Alyssa could feel the tension building inside her. Should she have seized that moment to scream out her hurts or address the stampede of unspoken elephants? Could she honestly continue like this? But blurting out her feelings would be like saying '*Here's the ugly scab you made; come and pick it.*' Like showing her weakness. Letting go of her power. She wasn't down for that.

So she quietly seethed.

'Maybe we should give up and order you a takeaway, if you're staying. And me a taxi,' she finally said, when her backside was numb and her patience had reached its limit. She had no idea if they were close to food or phone reception, but anything was better than this passive-aggressive waiting game. In fact, if they could get a car to bring takeaway, she'd get a lift home.

'Alyssa Heart.' Devan put his hand on hers, clearly trying to bring back the easy humour from earlier. 'You would cheat?'

She. Would. *Cheat*. That was the wrong choice of joke. She stood up quickly, her fishing rod catapulting into the water. She glared at him, his last word still echoing across the lake. How did he have the audacity to look confused?

'What did I say? I know you're not really a—'

'No, I'm not,' she said pointedly. 'Shame about *you*.'

His forehead creased, as though his brain was on rewind. 'Oh right.' He rubbed the back of his neck, as people often did before they told a massive lie. *Again*. Alyssa wasn't stupid. 'I know it looked bad back then, but it was complicated, and—'

'It looked bad? When my best friend ended up pregnant by my boyfriend. The boyfriend who hadn't yet slept with me, because he wanted the moment to be "*right*".'

Devan put down his fishing rod carefully, slowly standing, his hands raised as though he was fully expecting missiles.

Alyssa wasn't finished. 'And before I'd realised all of that I made an absolute idiot of myself, announcing my "*love*" for you on a stupid stage, with everybody gawping. You legged it from the room, leaving me alone up there. Then, to make it even worse, Sylvie's dad started yelling that you were marrying her because you'd got her up the duff. And that's the last time I'm drinking cheap-shit wine.'

'Did you?' He shook his head, as though it was helping the thought to settle. 'Why did nobody tell me that? I must have left the room before you said that, though I heard the gossip about what Sylvie's dick of a dad had shouted.'

'Like it would have made a difference.' She thrust her hands on her hips, so she didn't whack anyone with them. 'You'd made your choice, and it wasn't me.'

'No, Alyssa. It wasn't like that. I tried to speak to you. I wanted to explain. I called you, I knocked on your door, I threw stones at your bedroom window. Hell, I even tried to climb a tree and get in. You wouldn't let me near you. And then you left so quickly. You changed your number. I didn't know your address and your parents said they were under strict instructions not to pass your contact details to anyone. They had their own stuff going on and they got sick of me and Sylvie bugging them. We had to back off, but we *wanted* to explain. I know it must have seemed terrible to you. The worst. But the truth of it was such a mess. Sylvie was gutted too. She missed you. But she was so ill through her pregnancy and then Emmalina arrived.' He couldn't hide the small smile at the mention of his daughter's name. 'Please believe me, Alyssa. There was so much more to that story. Things I couldn't share and still can't, because it's not just my story to tell. But I promise you this: I thought the world of you, and I *never* meant to hurt you.'

He took a slight step towards her, but she backed away. Her head was spinning. She'd known Devan all of her life. From everything she could see on his face and through his body language, he looked honest and sorry to the point of desperation. But she knew how getting pregnant worked, and he'd married Sylvie. His actions *had* hurt her – beyond measure.

She screwed her eyes shut and exhaled. 'Whatever. It was a mess back then, but none of it's my problem. We're just two people, trying to get through seven tasks without killing each other. I need to get paid. You need to promote your app. Nobody needs any pointless heart-to-hearts.'

'Alyssa … The rod. I think we've caught something.'

## Chapter 22

They hadn't managed to kill the fish. At least that was another small thing they could agree on.

Teijo's instructions had said something about bashing the poor thing on the ground before gutting and flame-grilling it. They'd looked the fish in the eyes before eyeballing each other, taking the requisite photo, and then unhooking it and placing it gently back into the water.

Night had fallen quickly after that, and suddenly it seemed too late to try and hike her way out of there. As much as sharing a tent with Devan would be as irritating as a bad case of ringworm, it was mildly preferable to getting murdered in the deep dark woods. There was still no phone reception, and she was rubbish without Google Maps. Though now they were huddled around the campfire getting hungry, having released their last chance of dinner back into the lake. Raiding the remnants of their backpacks had only unearthed a packet of stale wine gums and some dry old crackers.

'If you promise to call a truce until Teijo picks us up tomorrow, I'll see if I can work out where the coffee and cake hut is, for breakfast,' Devan offered, as she crunched through her third cracker, doing her best not to think about cheese.

'Wait. You think there's a café nearby, and you only just thought to mention it?' He knew how to make her blood boil.

He shrugged. 'We're meant to be sticking to the rules and working together with what we have – in the interests of proving whether 'Appy Together's tasks work.'

And as much as she wanted to scream '*cheat*' at him, she'd done enough sniping for one day, and maybe her thoughts would never stop spinning, trying to work out his odd suggestion that there was more to the story with him and Sylvie. Why couldn't he explain? Or was it all more smoke and mirrors to try and make it look as though he wasn't a heartless, deceitful dickwad? Maybe she would never know, and none of it really mattered. When she'd seen out her duties, she'd take her earnings and get back to London, with far more opportunities lining up for her.

Now there was a faint hope of coffee and sweet treats, she could just about crawl through one night out here. Even if their tent felt dangerously small now they'd crammed all their stuff into it. At least she could use their bags as bolsters, so she didn't have to touch limbs.

'We scoffed tomorrow's breakfast when we were fishing,' he continued. 'And neither of us could stomach being hunter gatherers. So …?'

'*Temporary* truce,' she agreed, with the emphasis on temporary. But mainly because of the cake. And by truce she meant she promised not to kill him in his sleep. 'I'm going to investigate the bag of bedding. It's not getting any warmer and I'd gladly hide in my sleeping bag until coffee time.'

'That's assuming our disorganised organiser has packed sleeping bags.'

'Don't even go there,' she warned.

Though as she finished unpacking the last bag Teijo had left them with, her heart sank. 'What's worse than having no sleeping bags?' she asked quietly, her brain trying to work out how they'd get around this. Her body was already starting to shiver, but she wasn't going to play the *I'm a woman* card.

'Two adult-sized shark onesies made from particularly flammable flannel?'

She snorted a laugh, even though none of this situation was funny. She hadn't snort-laughed for years, before she'd come back here.

'I love it when you do that,' he said earnestly.

'You mean you love that you think you're hilarious.'

'That too. Was I right about the shark onesies? No wait. I hope I got one of those mermaid blankets, because I think I could rock a fish tail. Though not practical if we need to get up in the night and leg it from wild Cotswold beasts.'

'Devan!' She grabbed a tissue for her snorty nose. 'Will you take this seriously?' The look on his face was doubtful. 'What's worse than no sleeping bags is one sleeping bag. Because then we have to decide who freezes in the night.'

He looked confused. 'You get the sleeping bag. No question.'

'I don't need your chivalry.'

'It's not chivalry. It's the basic law of Finders Keepers. You found it. Anyway, I have my layers of hunky muscle to keep me warm.' He gave her a wink.

Her mind whizzed back to him stripping off at the allotments and she tried not to blush.

'I'll be fine, Alyssa. Seriously. Your concern for me is sweet, but I'm a big boy.'

She stood up quickly and busied herself taking the bedding to the tent, in case he was throwing out more of his nervous innuendos. It was safer to conjure up the imaginary vision of him hair-drying his pubes in a gym changing room.

Alyssa went to bed quickly after that. Being around the campfire was making her sleepy and she had a lot to process after the days' events. At least if she curled up in the single sleeping bag she could drift off before Devan got his head down. There was nothing more awkward than trying to get to sleep in a confined space with someone you didn't want to be close to. Listening to each other's breathing and being uber conscious of every movement was not her idea of fun.

Once she was tucked into the one sleeping bag like a glow worm, the only hot water bottle toastily inside with her, she pulled a line of bags across the tent to form a central barricade. Surely this night would be over swiftly, and then there would be cake. Only, the more she thought about the inviting prospect of sleep, the more it evaded her. Minutes passed. And then tens of minutes. It had probably been at least an hour before Devan came into the tent, burrowing himself under a pile of clothes on the other side of her great divide.

His breathing was calm at first, his body seemingly still warm from the campfire. Though as the tens of minutes continued to pass, his breaths sounded more jittery. His limbs kept moving, as though he was trying to create heat. Or maybe he was just restless. It wasn't easy sleeping under a sheet of flappy nylon.

If anything, Alyssa still felt a bit too warm. She had thermals, thick pyjamas and a hat. The hot water bottle, which Devan had helped her to fill with campfire water, was almost burning her leg. In theory, she *could* invite Devan to her side of the barrier she'd carefully constructed. It wasn't that she was stingy about sharing her heat, as such. It was just that if she agreed to let him into her personal space, what would that mean? And where might it lead? She could absolutely keep her hands to herself. *Probably.* But that sort of closeness with the man who literally showed up naked in her dreams might nudge her soul in ways nobody had any business poking. To add to the weirdness, he was paying her to be a part of these tasks. So if anything *accidentally* happened between them ... *eww*. She was not here to get paid for that.

Hang on. Was that the sound of his teeth chattering?

'Devan, are you OK?' She held her breath, using her senses to tune in to him.

'I'm f-i-ine.'

He did not sound fine. 'Here, let me give you this hot water bottle.'

'No! I w-want you to have that.'

'Why on earth?' She was already shifting to pull it out for him. She was not having his death on her conscience. What if she went to jail for withholding a vital heat source?

'If you pass the heat to me, t-then you get c-cold. How does that help us?'

He was probably right, but that didn't mean she was going to let him turn into an ice sculpture. Who would show her where the coffee hut was?

She let out a long breath, barely believing she was about to say this. 'Then come here. We'll share the warmth. Strictly for survival purposes. That is all.'

'I'm f-f-fiiiiine,' he said again.

Did he sound a bit sleepier this time? Wait. What was it about not letting people fall asleep in extreme conditions when they were feeling cold? Not that they were in the North Pole, or anything. But that didn't sound good.

'Stop being Good Old Devan, you idiot, or you're going to end up snuffing it.'

She wasn't sure how true that was, but she wasn't waiting around until the morning to find out. With one gigantic heave, she pulled herself onto the top of the bag barricade and rolled herself over it, like a giant, slightly too hot caterpillar. As she crash-landed next to Devan, she was relieved to hear his chuckle.

'You never did treat me like G-good Old Devan, d-did you?'

'Rest assured. You'll never be G-O-D to me.'

'It's just a persona, you know. Like yours. Sometimes I wish I could drop it.'

'I'm loving your honesty, but let's just keep you alive.'

The humour helped as she began to do what might otherwise have felt overly familiar and painfully embarrassing. Snuggling herself into Devan under his small heap of spare clothes, she unzipped the snug protection of her sleeping bag and wrapped half of it around him, allowing half of her heat to seep into him. Feeling his chill, she instinctively pulled herself to him, the fronts of their bodies firm against each other, the hot water bottle at his back.

'Ohhhhhh.' He shivered against her as his body adjusted to her heat. 'This is s-soooo good.' His voice was deep and guttural, his cold lips softening against her neck. 'I mean, for s-survival. N-nothing weird.'

'Nothing weird,' she repeated, quickly taking his cold hands and pushing them up under her clothes so they were touching her bare skin, worried he might get frostbite. Did people's fingers fall off if they got cold? She did not want to be held responsible for a stumpy Devan.

And all of this *should* have felt peculiar. Getting so absurdly close and almost intimate with her cheating ex-boyfriend – even if he was single now and he seemed adamant he hadn't meant to hurt her. She did not want to let go of her heart for anyone, because unguarded hearts got besieged. Yet none of this felt strange. Just like earlier, when muscle memory had kicked in and they'd worked together in tandem, their bodies seemed to know what to do.

Except she was *not* going to let her body do a fraction of what it was traitorously whimpering for. As he warmed against her, his shivers calming to contented sighs, his fingers curling into her back and tangling with her nightclothes, there was a heat building between her legs that could have kept them both sizzling all night. Her nipples were hardening against him, even though she definitely wasn't cold. Her body was reacting to his. Longing for more of him. Though if she dared to be honest, perhaps it wasn't just her body that was falling.

But that was ridiculous. They were both tired, and probably a touch delirious from being out in the elements. They were two semi-lost people, clinging to each other for survival. Just for one night. She was not going to go taking advantage of Good Old Devan, just because the poor guy was freezing his knackers off.

'You're so warm,' he whispered into her skin.

OK, so maybe he wasn't at death's door anymore. That didn't mean she was going to get wild.

'Just call me Good Old Alyssa,' she whispered back.

'You are good, you know,' he said, after a pause. 'In here.'

With a slowness that was almost agonising, he moved one of his hands from the naked flesh of her back, trailing it over her hip in a way that made her shiver, and up past her belly button until it landed on her ribs. Just under her breasts. Polite, but utterly sensual. How much she wanted to grab that hand and push it upwards, until it touched the nipples that were throbbing for him. She was on fire – and he hadn't even kissed her. There was no way she could let him, or there would be absolutely no end to this. She would be his. And she'd spent so many years making sure she would never be anybody's again.

'In here,' he repeated, his hand dangerously close to her beating heart. 'You're so good. I wish you knew that. I wish you knew you've always been perfect, just as you are.'

Now he was definitely feverish, if that was a thing. Exhausted and rambling. Wasn't he? Either way, he would forget all of this by the morning. Thank goodness.

'I can't explain exactly what happened back then, without betraying other people's secrets. They're not just my truths to tell. And I don't expect you to trust anybody who can't tell you the truth.'

His voice was low, his breath warm against her neck. Every inch of the flesh he was touching was rising up to him in goosebumps, aching to be caressed.

'Though I do want you to know that it was always you. I never dropped my torch for you. Never will.'

She could feel her eyes welling up.

'I can't go on being Good Old convenient Devan forever. We

all deserve our own true love story. Don't we?'

Each word was getting quieter, as though he was falling asleep against her. She guessed it was safe for him to drift off now his body was warm. In fact, it was safer all round if he did. Who knew what might happen between them if he stayed awake. If he kept talking, even if it was surely nonsense. If they kept holding each other so tightly.

Because something was shifting inside her, inside and out. And if things were allowed to move too far in unexpected directions, they might never be the same again.

# Chapter 23

Alyssa woke up feeling snuggly and heaven-like, with something breathy and warm against her, and the promise of sunlight dancing across her closed eyelids. The usual feeling of first-light emptiness seemed to have disappeared somewhere, and ...

*Oh God.* Her memory caught up with her and she flinched, remembering she was in a tent, sharing a sleeping bag for one – with Devan. What had felt necessary and strangely instinctive under the cloak of darkness suddenly seemed glaringly awkward.

She wriggled her way free from him, trying to ignore his gentle whimpers of protestation. He was still asleep, otherwise he'd surely be equally mortified. He'd said some odd things as he'd been drifting into slumber the night before, his thoughts doubtlessly jumbled. Something about never having dropped his torch for her. She'd do him a favour and not mention it. He might already have been dreaming, and she, as much as anyone, knew dreams could be unruly. If nothing else, it would be easier on her own confused feelings if they drew a line under last night. It had simply been about survival. *Hadn't it?*

And anyway, admitting a tiny part of her heart might be warming to him would be like conceding that a love app and its crazy tasks were having an effect on her. Which couldn't be the case.

Alyssa grabbed a coat and unzipped the tent as quietly as she could, climbing out onto the bejewelled morning grass. There was sunshine again. Was it bizarre that all of their love tasks had been unseasonably sunny? But the incumbent weather conditions couldn't possibly revolve around her, Devan and a stupid phone app.

Her hand reached instinctively to her coat pocket. She would usually start her day scrolling through social media, seeing what was 'happening in the world', chatting to relative strangers and checking how many people had liked her posts. Somehow, she didn't feel the pull of it today – not that there was any reception here, anyway. For once, she was almost looking forward to real-life things, like finding coffee and cake. And maybe she was curious to talk to Devan a bit more, seeing as they were on a temporary truce – at least until Teijo arrived later on. She found herself wondering what else he might share about his life since she'd last known him. But she knew parts of it might hurt, like the stuff about Sylvie.

Alyssa sat on a rock and listened to the birdsong as she pondered her old best friend. She still missed Sylvie, as much as she didn't want to – and being back in Hartglove made her think of her more. They'd grown up together, shared so many memories there, made so many plans together. Their roots were still entwined, even if many of their branches had snapped off or grown apart. If this tricky camping task had taught her anything it was to embrace the journey, and that it wasn't always bad to talk. Should she seek Sylvie out? Because, really, Alyssa's loneliness had begun when she'd left Hartglove – so perhaps hitting the rewind button might help her to untangle her knot of feelings. Or she could keep her head down, hope not to bump into her former friend, avoid the pain and upset that conversation would stir up and get out of town as soon as these tasks were over.

*Weigh up the pros and cons and then follow your gut.* That's what she would tell one of her coaching clients.

Devan stuck his head out of the tent, pulling her out of her thoughts. 'Did someone say cake?'

Talking of following your gut. She smiled to herself.

His hair was all over the place and his face had sleeping-bag creases and the imprint of what looked like a coat button on one side.

If Alyssa's heart was open, she might have thought that was cute. 'No.' She laughed.

She hadn't mentioned cake, but she'd thought about it. And if he could hear what else had been going on in her mind recently, she might be in trouble.

They eventually found the coffee hut that Devan had remembered, even though it had taken the best part of an hour and a lot of getting lost. But as they stepped into the small, warm wooden construction, which smelt gloriously of rich coffee beans and baking, Alyssa knew it had been worth the trek.

'Mmm.' she said, inhaling the air. 'If cake for breakfast is wrong, then I don't want to be right.'

It wasn't long before the dark-haired café owner, Meena, was bustling over in her peacock-patterned apron, holding a tray with two artfully topped lattes and the most gloriously fruit-laden flapjacks Alyssa had ever seen.

'Delicious treats for you and your ... girlfriend?' Meena asked Devan, before beaming at Alyssa.

'No, we're not ...' Devan started.

'We're just ...' Alyssa flapped her hands between them, like her frantic movements would explain everything.

'She's my BUM.'

Meena's big brown eyes widened.

Devan didn't usually get so flustered. Perhaps he needed coffee.

Alyssa tried to stifle her laugh. 'We're just friends,' she explained quickly. 'And thank you. This looks delicious.'

'You're welcome. Enjoy your alone time while it lasts,' said

Meena, waving a hand around the empty café. 'Whatever it is you're up to.'

Then she winked and left them to it.

Meena had made heart patterns with the milk froth on the tops of their coffees. Alyssa blew on hers, watching it wobble.

'So we're friends now?' Devan asked her, once Alyssa had won the fight over the slightly larger piece of flapjack.

Alyssa shrugged. 'It was just easier than explaining the stupid BUM thing. Did you make up that acronym?'

'Yep. Us computer nerds have to entertain ourselves somehow.'

He was wearing his thick-rimmed glasses again, and he pushed them up his nose a touch, as though to make his tech geek point. She noticed now that they were tortoiseshell, the chestnutty tones complementing his still-mussy hair. The glasses sat perfectly on his cheekbones, and if this was what a nerd looked like, Alyssa liked them a little more.

She shook her head. As a *friend*. She busied her hands and thoughts by slicing up her flapjack.

'How are things going with the app?' Work stuff was safer territory than gawping at the shades of his hair.

If she'd thought asking about his app would make the conversation dull enough for her to focus on her breakfast rather than his cheekbones, she'd been wrong. A different part of him seemed to come alive as he spoke about his love app creation. She couldn't pretend to understand what he was talking about, with all that coding, programming and algorithm lingo. It ought to have been as dry as a bag of old bones, and about as appealing. But the way his deep blue eyes twinkled, and his strong hands drew shapes on the table had her completely transfixed. She found herself asking more questions, as though each one was allowing her one step closer to the fire that burned inside him. She wanted to know all of it, to hear him talk and talk.

Which was weird.

Because she was meant to be rallying against this app and

trying to prove it couldn't work. But if these tasks were strangely softening her and changing her feelings towards Devan ... well, who knew what that could mean? Tread carefully was what it meant, she quickly reminded herself.

Meena fluttered around them, tidying tables for non-existent customers and doing who knew what – but Alyssa was barely aware of her. Against her better judgement, she was hanging on to Devan's every word. Was her mouth actually open? Perhaps 'Appy Together wasn't the soulless, dreadful piece of tech she'd built it up to be. From Devan's words, he'd created it from a place of passion. Not just for the challenge of getting the coding to work, but the intriguing idea that his algorithms could bring people together. And he certainly had more desire for his work than she did, these days.

'So your app's taking off,' she conceded. He'd explained that although the app was free for users, it did well through sponsorships and advertising. 'Though you mentioned in the car yesterday that the polls aren't showing Hartglove to have any more *love* since our 'Appy Together promo started. Why do you care so much?'

She remembered her mum saying his business had invested money into the town too, to help regenerate it. And he'd probably funded those terrible T-shirts.

'I'm just proud of where I'm from. Not that I'm saying you're not,' he added quickly. 'I mean, I loved growing up there, and it's been great to see Emmalina enjoy the town too. But it's not what it used to be, and young people are leaving. I'd hate to think she might have no choice but to move away because there aren't enough youngsters or jobs. If she wants to spread her wings, that's incredible. But it would be sad if leaving was her only sensible option.'

For a second, Alyssa wanted to say that fleeing wasn't all it was cracked up to be. But the thought surprised her, so she kept it to herself and simply nodded. She did feel a pang of something in her chest for his so far unsuccessful plight. He seemed to genuinely care about Hartglove and his work. Part of her wanted to do something – but what did she know? She still had her own life and career to sort out.

'Is it true the app chooses the love tasks?' she asked, with a wry smile. 'Or do you hide behind the curtain like the Wizard of Oz, trying to orchestrate things?' She was more than curious about whether he'd fixed their weekend of camping alone-time, or indeed, all of this. 'And did you match us on purpose?' Was this part of his still holding a torch for her? Would it be sweet if he had, or just plain creepy?

Devan blinked a few times and repositioned his glasses. 'Of course I don't orchestrate things. And I definitely didn't match us. I want to know if the app actually works, without me poking my nose in.'

'But you *did* tag me in that Instagram post on New Year's Day?' she asked, cheekily.

He seemed to contemplate the question for a moment, one corner of his mouth trying to twitch into a smile. 'I don't make my part-time social media person work on public holidays. I do my best to help out.'

They held each other's gaze for a moment, their eyes twinkling. 'Anyway, how about you?'

His question broke the spell and brought her back to reality with a bump. She didn't want to talk about herself. Listening to Devan had been absorbing, even if her mind still carefully questioned everything he said.

Alyssa leaned back in her chair, absently rubbing her chest as though something had actually been hooking her. Maybe flapjack gave you heartburn. She took a swig of water.

'How are things with your love coaching?' he asked, when she'd forgotten it was her turn to speak. 'Is trying to prove my love app is utter nonsense helping you rake in those *love-stuck* clients?' His tone was friendly rather than treating her like an arch rival.

'Oh, that.' She was still making a hash of getting things off the ground again, but she didn't want to spoil this perfectly nice coffee by digging into whatever it was that was oddly holding her back from signing up some clients. So she settled on: 'It's all fine.'

He raised his eyebrows.

She guessed he wasn't stupid. Fine never meant marvellous or the best thing since sliced flapjack. It generally meant *a little bit pants, but I don't want to talk about it.* He seemed to take the hint.

'Have I seen fewer posts from you on social media lately?'

She waved a dismissive hand. Though was he right? Maybe she'd been a bit busier with actual life. Or maybe something inside her was slowly changing, and she wasn't sure who she was or what she wanted to say. She let the thought settle for a moment. Much like finding your way to some random café in the woods without a map on your phone, it was disorientating.

She grabbed her coffee. 'We should drink up and go. We're taking up all the space.' She made light of it, because it was early and they were still Meena's only two customers.

As much as she hadn't hated this angst-free time with Devan, she needed fresh air and thinking space. Because that was the thing about real-life friends, she was suddenly remembering. They were intuitive. They got under your skin. And they asked inquisitive things that you didn't always want to address.

She was used to being the coach. The one who asked questions. The one who stayed in control of conversations and fixed other people's woes. Was she willing to go back to a life where she let people in? This weekend had shown her it might not be *so* awful to rally less against Devan, even if there was no way it could progress. There were still so many questions left unanswered, and he'd made clear he wasn't going to answer them. And she wasn't the type to go digging – outside of allotments. Was she?

*Private message from @agent_rufusdiamond to @alyssa-heart_thelovecoach:*

**@agent_rufusdiamond** – *Sorry I couldn't make it to your latest love task. I had to take my neighbour's Jack Russell to get his nails painted. Great news – we went with 'Iridescent Peacock'. He's looking quite dapper.*

# Chapter 24

'Wow, hello, Apple Blossom Lane,' Alyssa found herself saying as she rounded the corner into Hartglove's main street.

She'd only got back from the weekend's camping task the evening before, and perhaps it had been a short while since she'd wandered into town. But she hadn't been expecting *this*. Her hand moved to her chest as she stopped to take it all in. The apple trees that lined the street had blossomed and the abundance of pinky-white petals made the whole place look transformed.

And the fragrance. Honeyed and almost fruity, like the tease of apple crumble. Since when had she become the sort of person who sniffed the air and had floaty thoughts about apple blossom?

She laughed to herself and started walking.

Of course, she guessed the blossom had been budding for a while – though she hadn't properly noticed it. And she remembered many such apple blossom springs from her childhood, when some residents used to say that the trees' tendency to blossom early was magical – though more sensible folk said they were simply unusual Hartglove hybrids. Either way, she was absolutely ignoring her weird impulse to start shaking boughs to make it fall like confetti, like her gawky younger self would have done.

Alyssa paced along the lane, wondering if she had more of a

bounce in her step than usual. The sky was bright and perfectly spring-like, and was it just the surprise of the blossom that was encouraging her to fully see her old town for the first time since she'd returned? Why was she suddenly noticing how beautiful the honey-coloured shops were, with their pastel-painted signs, pretty bow windows and inviting displays? Wisteria vines trailed along the fronts of them, and she recalled that by summer, they'd be heavy with honey-scented purple flowers that would take over from the apple blossom and complement the street's colourful bunting.

Did it feel like there was something different in the air today – beyond the flora? Maybe it was just the tempting coffee and cream fragrances wafting out from Anna's gorgeous Italian dessert shop, which had bistro tables outside, now the weather was brighter. And had some of the shops had their paintwork touched up?

It was Monday morning, and Alyssa was stepping into town to run a few errands. She hadn't been gone long, but something inside her felt good to be back. Had she missed the place? Her forehead creased. How could that be, when she'd managed not to pine over it for years? She would have to be careful about that, because after these tasks were done, she wasn't sticking around, however nice the flowers were. She preferred a place with more prospects and fewer ghosts.

The old community hall snagged her attention as she walked by, even though she usually kept her head down when she passed it. It held sweat-inducing memories of *that night*. Her humiliating grand gesture, which did *not* turn out like a happy romcom. It was boarded up now, and she was surprised to feel a pang of sadness for it. Growing up, there had been all sorts of local events there – from spring balls to bake-offs and barbecues, and Morris dancing with funny sticks. Not all the memories had been bad ones. Hartglove Hall had been like the heart of everything. She remembered what Devan had said about missing the way things used to be. The sense of community that made people want to stay. His words had briefly resonated, before she'd pushed them away. As someone who wasn't planning to stay, that wasn't her problem. She shook her head.

'Good morning, Miss Heart. Nice weekend?'

Horace from the allotments was waving at her from across the road. He was wearing his usual bumblebee wellies, but was that a new jacket? And he seemed even chirpier than usual, if that was possible.

'Yes, Horace. I did have a good weekend.' As she said the words, she realised she meant them. *Wow.* 'And you?'

'Oh, exemplary.' There was a twinkle in his eyes that Alyssa couldn't miss even from twelve paces. 'And doesn't Hartglove look glorious in bloom?' He raised his arms up, as though she might not have noticed the eleventy-billion tiny buds that had sprouted.

'Erm. Well, yes.' She couldn't lie about that.

'Blossom is a sign of new beginnings. I think we're just about ready for them.'

He bustled off, still beaming, before she could argue or ask more about his *exemplary* weekend.

With the sun on her face and the scent of tiramisu on the breeze, she sat on a painted bench, feeling drawn to update a few more of her personal details inside the 'Appy Together love app. Against the odds, she'd sort of enjoyed her weekend with Devan, even though the app was not getting her to *fall for* anyone. Their candid moments had been a good thing, even if she was still treading with extreme caution. Maybe it was time to sprinkle in a few truths of her own.

Smiling to herself, she typed '*we're on a break*' next to where she'd once raved about quinoa. And white-water rafting was promptly deleted, even if the much tamer wobbling around on a raft with Devan had turned out to be surprisingly uplifting. '*Horticulture and taking care of the planet.*' She rolled her eyes, because buying the odd basil plant from Waitrose did not count. What were her hobbies, now she wasn't pretending to enjoy unlikely sports and bendy yoga, and wasn't quite so addicted to her phone? She typed '*Open to ideas and still learning.*' There. That was better than ruining her reputation by admitting she'd stretched the truth further than an elephant on a bungee cord.

As she looked up, the flapping macramé hearts of the love garden allotments caught her eye in the distance. The trees that huddled close to the entrance of the gardens had blossomed too, making it look undeniably more inviting. Perhaps she should get on with the next stage of planning and planting on their patch. She'd lied that as the 'expert' she would get on with it herself, having been desperate to avoid further muddy dates with Devan. Though after their camping weekend, she was coming to wonder if team *Alyvan* wasn't the worst thing in the world – in the interests of getting through these tasks in one piece. Though it did need a better name.

'You'll never guess what,' said Jess, as Alyssa pushed her way into Halfpenny's shop, a few minutes later.

She pulled Pikachu's cage out from under the counter and popped it on top.

'You've been arrested by the Cotswold constabulary for harbouring mice in a food shop?' Alyssa joked. It still felt new that she could have fun without the urge to stay professional – but she was coming to like it, in small doses.

At least Jess was giggling back. 'No! And he's been staying at mine. But look.' Jess moved the bedding around. 'Meet Minnie. Pikachu's got himself a girlfriend.'

Jess explained the stray mouse had been sniffing around, and when she'd opened the door to see if Pikachu wanted to play, his new mouse friend had jumped in and nose-kissed him.

'And now I have two pet mice to contend with?' Alyssa mock-huffed.

'They breed quickly, signorina,' said Anna, who appeared from the baking and other random objects aisle with a basket of supplies. 'Just like the blossom swiftly blooms. You'll soon have more than two.' She clutched her ample bosom and pulled a swoony face.

What was going on in Hartglove today? Was whatever was in the air out there seeping inside too? It had been easier when all she'd needed to dodge was awkward encounters and badly cooked quinoa.

'Anna's dating!' Jess blurted out. 'Hasn't it given her a whole new glow?'

Anna put her basket on the counter, her cheeks flushing. Her tiny cake earrings jangled as she fanned her face. 'No, *bella*. We have only completed one love task. It is early days.'

'She's been matched with Horace. They're road-testing the app too, beginning with their wine-tasting and pizza-making task,' said Jess, clearly on a roll as the town's unofficial news station. 'Their promo photos look incredible. More love in Hartglove!'

'So that's why Horace was looking so chipper.' And perhaps why he had a flash new coat. Hadn't he said his old one belonged to his late wife? As much as he'd looked sweet in it, perhaps he was ready to lay some of the past to rest.

Alyssa blinked a few times, wondering if there was a lesson in there somewhere.

'Horace is my BUM,' Anna confirmed. 'Everything that's been going on in the town, and with you and Devan, finally inspired us.'

'I've signed up too,' said Jess, fanning her own face as though the lovey-dovey air was getting far too hot.

She had a point. Alyssa was starting to feel stifled. 'Right, well, I'll probably take my mouse and go.'

It wasn't that she didn't feel happy for them, but what if it was *catching*? Or like when you'd eaten far too much caramel apple tiramisu, a tad too sickly-sweet.

'Mice,' Jess corrected her, nodding at the cage, which was now making squeaking noises, the bedding vibrating. 'Did you know they can have fifty pups a year?'

*Fifty?*

The three women stared.

'Everyone's at it,' Alyssa said quietly. She wouldn't even be able to escape it in her own home, if these two critters carried on.

'Even your parents,' Jess added, before clapping a hand over her mouth. 'Oh sorry. Eww! I mean, they've just gone away on a second honeymoon. *So romantic.*'

'*Right.*' Well, that saved her having that awkward heart-to-heart with her dad, which her mum had been so keen on, anytime soon. She might have thawed to Pearl a touch since their quinoa cake date, but she didn't feel ready to let Percy off a lifetime of lying about his secret office bunk-ups. Especially when he'd often made *her* feel like the one who should get a more respectable job.

'And Devan's parents will be back from their long, romantic Maldives trip any day,' Jess continued. 'All this extra love in Hartglove. We'll have to get you wearing that Save Hartglove T-shirt!'

Alyssa smiled politely. As well-meant as Mrs Halfpenny's offering had been, she still hadn't worn it. She had enough of her own things to save.

Then her thoughts were pulled to Devan's parents, who she hadn't seen since she'd left Hartglove all those years ago. Alyssa had adored Devan's mum, Dawn, and had got on with her far better than her own. Dawn had always been the one with tissues and hugs, when she'd needed them. And now she allowed herself to think of it, Devan's mum and dad had always been the epitome of the perfect couple. *In love* – if Alyssa had once believed in such a thing. They'd been gorgeous together. Hadn't she often daydreamed of having a relationship like theirs one day? *With Devan.* But young dreams were wild like that.

'Earth to Alyssa.' Jess gave her a nudge. 'Are you OK?'

'Yes, of course.' Was she welling up? What a strange morning. She'd only come out to do a few jobs, and now she was nearly sobbing in the convenience shop, whilst her mouse shagged his new girlfriend, and everyone mooned over their BUMs.

Seeing everyone else getting themselves together reminded Alyssa that her own life was becoming *more* confusing, especially after that weekend. If she dared to be honest, she sensed there were feelings stirring inside her. Old feelings mixed with new ones. For *him*. And she had absolutely nowhere to put them.

'How did your love task go?' Jess asked, putting a gentle hand on Alyssa's arm.

Anna was happily humming 'Love Is in the Air' as she emptied the contents of her basket onto the counter. The bell above the door rang and a young couple barrelled in, chattering and nibbling each other like a pair of actual lovebirds.

And suddenly, Alyssa needed to be somewhere else.

'I'm going to get some air.'

She said her thank yous and backed out of the shop, clutching a few essentials Jess had thrust at her, the mouse cage under her arm.

She took a gasp of fresh air and looked around, her eyes landing on the allotments. Yes, that was exactly the place for quiet thinking time. She could hide and make plans about runner beans, with nobody to disturb her.

## Chapter 25

'Cup of tea?'

Alyssa looked up to see Jess's grandmother, Mrs Halfpenny, sitting outside an allotment shed on one of the two purple wingback chairs Alyssa had previously spied there. So that's who was in charge of that quirky plot. She should have guessed. The older lady was wearing a top that said *'Hartglove – Love Is a Bug'* under her thick coat, with a ladybird bobble hat pulled over her blue rinse. A chintzy teapot and two mismatched cups balanced on a rickety table in front of her – because who didn't conduct solo Mad Hatter's tea parties next to a barren vegetable plot? The second chair was glaringly empty.

Alyssa winced at the roughly painted words *'Tea and Sympathy'* on Mrs Halfpenny's shed, because she hadn't come here to chat. But Mrs H was beckoning her over and it would be rude not to step closer. Now the sun had disappeared behind a cloud there was a chill in the air. Perhaps they both needed to warm their hands around a cuppa.

Mrs Halfpenny ordered her to put her mouse cage in the shed and grab two blankets. Was she honestly shivering or putting it on? Alyssa could feel her resolve to find some peace and quiet waning. She did as she was told and then moved cautiously to the empty chair.

'Though I don't need any ...' Alyssa waved towards the sign's S-word.

'Nonsense. It's not a sympathy chair. Now, sit your skinny bum down.'

Alyssa laughed and sank into the empty chair, pulling one of the blankets over her legs.

'It's a truth chair,' Mrs Halfpenny clarified, with a cheeky smile. 'And I only invite people who need it. Now pour the tea.'

Alyssa gulped and started pouring. Not that a chair could make a person say anything they didn't want to, surely? It wasn't like Mrs H was about to strap her down and spike her in the backside.

'I like what you've done with the place.' Alyssa nodded at the allotment.

Mrs Halfpenny spluttered out her tea. 'Now I know you're telling porkies.' In fairness, it was pretty bare – other than the odd weed. 'I come here for tea and company. Sometimes people bring cake.' She raised her eyebrows towards the Halfpenny's bag Jess had thrust at her.

Alyssa pulled out a pack of fruit cake slices that Jess must have packed.

Mrs Halfpenny's eyes lit up. 'Those will do nicely.' She commandeered the packet and dished two out.

This wasn't exactly the solitude Alyssa had been expecting, but it was peaceful, in its own way. The still air and the gentle chink of crockery. The backdrop of blossoming apple trees. Mrs H's almost inaudible hum of happiness as she ate. Alyssa had never had a close relationship with any of her grandparents, but she remembered different generations coming together in the days when Hartglove Hall had been vibrant. She used to ice cupcakes for the fetes with Devan's gran, listening to her stories and then stirring the bubbles for her washing up. Being around people who were no longer rushing through life held a certain kind of magic. Like calm for your soul when everything else was cartwheeling.

Alyssa shook her head. What on earth had Mrs H put in this tea?

'Life can be lonely, when you don't let people in,' said Mrs Halfpenny, her hands around her cup, her eyes looking out over her scruffy patch of land. 'Can't it?'

Alyssa wasn't sure where this was coming from, but it felt rude to interrupt.

'I didn't do much after Mr Halfpenny died. I shut up the shop and stayed indoors. Didn't want to speak to people. It was easier that way. Keeping folk at bay, so that if anyone else let me down by snuffing it, it wouldn't hurt as much. Because it *does* hurt when people let you down. Even when they don't mean to.'

The sentiment hung in the air, Alyssa unsure whether her companion was still talking about her departed husband or if she was trying to hint at Alyssa's past.

'I'm so sorry to hear about Mr Halfpenny,' Alyssa said gently, reaching over to put her hand on Mrs Halfpenny's. 'I do remember him. You two were lovely together.'

'Childhood sweethearts.'

If any more poignant words were allowed to rest in the air, Alyssa might let out a sob.

'It took me a while to start healing after he broke my heart by popping off, God rest him. Not that it was his fault. But let me tell you. The day I decided to let people in and start trusting again.' She shrugged. 'Well, that was a good day.'

They squeezed each other's hands.

'And I know you're meant to be Alyssa now,' the woman said more quietly. 'But I remember when you were young Beryl. You and Sylvie, always thick as two thieves in a pot of marmalade. You'd come into the shop with your pocket money, sharing a packet of Cherry Drops or hankering over the latest copy of *Mizz*.'

'We did love that magazine,' said Alyssa, the memory of poring over the latest pop stars with Sylvie bringing an unexpected smile to her face.

'And don't get me started on that summer when I let you share the paper round.'

Alyssa clapped a hand over her mouth. Sylvie had ridden the bike, with Alyssa on the back, trying to keep hold of the huge bag of newspapers. They'd had so many complaints about lost papers and shredded front pages that Mrs H gave the round to the more reliable Devan.

'I'm sorry,' Alyssa said. 'We weren't the best at that paper round.'

'But you were the best of friends.'

Alyssa's heart felt strange for a moment. She rubbed it, though that didn't seem to do the trick.

'You'll find her at Clucky Ducks Retirement Home, if you're brave enough. She volunteers there with the oldies, on a Monday.'

'No, I . .' Alyssa felt herself squirming in the truth chair. It really wasn't as comfortable as it looked, if you stayed for too long.

A surprisingly strong hand shot out and clamped itself onto Alyssa's knee. *Ouch.*

'Don't shut people out, like I once did. Don't think I haven't spotted you doing the same with Devan. You and that boy had a special thing. Sparks used to fly off the two of you, like you'd been electrocuted by a wet toaster. And I'm sure it must have stung when he ended up with Sylvie.'

*Thanks for the reminder.*

'But that's the thing about pain,' Mrs Halfpenny continued, whether Alyssa wanted to hear it or not. 'If you keep circling around it like a lost idiot on a roundabout, you'll never get anywhere. You've got to face it, head on. You've got to go *through* it.'

'Like a collision?'

'Like the brave person you've always been, under all that pink hair and fancy mascara. Real life hurts, Miss Heart. But not as much as being a lonely, stubborn goat living in a cow shed for one with a mouse for a best friend.'

'Two mice,' Alyssa protested, a little meekly. 'And I am starting to make more friends, since I arrived here.' She pointed towards the shop, where she'd just been chatting with Jess and Anna Farina, even if their *lovey* chat had got a bit too much. 'I'm even getting on better with Devan. I don't actively want to cause him grievous bodily harm. In fact, there are certain times when I look at him, and …' Her voice trailed off and she could feel her cheeks reddening. Damn that truth chair.

'So the story ends there? She loved, she lost, she gave up, the end? Is that what you'd tell one of these people who come to you to have their love life fixed?'

In truth, she barely knew what she might tell a love coach client anymore. Maybe that's why she was strangely avoiding having any. And perhaps if she stopped ignoring the keys to whatever had been keeping her heart locked, things would become clearer.

Her mum had mentioned there being a lot of rumours surrounding Sylvie and Devan. Devan had said what had happened between them wasn't his story to tell. Was it Sylvie's?

'Going round and round that roundabout is making you dizzy,' said Mrs Halfpenny, clearly noticing Alyssa's confused face. 'Follow the signposts.'

She nodded to a nearby wooden finger post. One of the places it pointed to was Clucky Ducks Retirement.

'Or you can keep on spinning. It's not for me to interfere. Obviously.'

## Chapter 26

Alyssa wasn't quite sure why she was walking in the direction of Clucky Ducks Retirement Home, because she was absolutely not going there. Was she?

And yet somehow, her feet were taking over while her brain was still processing. Of course, it wasn't too late to keep on marching and go straight home, where there would be precisely no revelations or heartbreak, and a whole lot less jolly apple blossom. Though did Mrs Halfpenny have a point about going *through* things, rather than skating around them?

Because try as she might, the more time she spent here with Devan, the more she couldn't stop thinking about the past – and the pieces of the puzzle that still didn't fit. And it was simply annoying to have a puzzle with chunks of the picture missing.

Alyssa halted, propping herself against a lamppost, her head swarming with thoughts. Her arms were full with a mouse cage and shopping. The wind was picking up pace. There was a version of her who would have gone back to her cow shed for a nice hot chocolate and an aimless scroll through social media.

Though there was a brand-new part of her that seemed desperate to emerge. A part who wanted to know more. And *feel* more? Because she couldn't deny she was feeling a lot more for Devan, even if that was terrifying. He'd been so vague about the past and her pain at being cheated on was still real. Mrs Halfpenny's weird purple truth chair had made her realise how much she'd missed Sylvie too, despite everything.

So she took a deep breath, pushed herself off the lamppost, and allowed her feet to carry her straight into the building where Sylvie would be – and where she could get some answers.

The place was noisy with the sound of older people chatting loudly, knitting needles click-clacking and the odd pair bickering over newspapers or the last Bourbon biscuit. Alyssa's first instinct was to back out. But it was too late for that.

And then she saw her. Her once best friend. Alyssa's breath caught for a moment as she watched Sylvie, fussing over the residents, smiling, paying compliments. More than a decade had passed, and though Alyssa's bitter memories of Sylvie may have hardened her edges, the real-life version of her looked as soft as Alyssa had known her to be. *Before the revelations.*

Sylvie seemed to sense someone watching her and looked up, a small gasp escaping her as she locked eyes with Alyssa. She quickly took off her tea-stained apron and stepped over.

'I'd been hoping you'd come,' Sylvie said softly. 'Can I?' She opened her arms sheepishly, asking for permission to hug.

Alyssa felt her body tense. She wasn't accustomed to friendly hugging these days, and she wasn't sure she was ready for … *Oh.*

Sylvie was going in anyway.

The uncomfortable mouse cage was squashed between them, but Alyssa got a waft of the familiar scent of Sylvie's light brown hair, which had always been long enough for her to sit on, but messy, in a kind of cute way. Peaches and vanilla, now with a faint tinge of tinned biscuits. But she shouldn't be swayed by shampoo and nostalgia. Life wasn't that easy.

Alyssa cleared her throat and pulled away. 'We should talk.'

Sylvie nodded. 'Ladies' toilets.'

Well, it was the undisputed champion venue for private girl chats.

Sylvie unburdened her of Pikachu's cage and beckoned her into the loos. Then her old friend checked the cubicles were empty, gave the sinks a customary wipe with a green paper hand towel, and hopped up to sit on the sink unit, like they'd done as teenagers. Alyssa sighed, double-checked Sylvie hadn't left her a wet patch, and followed suit.

'You don't trust me?' Sylvie said quietly, noticing her actions.

'You guys hurt me,' Alyssa replied, trying to keep her calm. 'Wait, no. That's the understatement of the century. You pretty much broke me.' That and Pearl Bagnor's reverse cowgirl. But she wasn't here to talk about her parents' joke of a marriage.

'Oh God, I'm so sorry about everything,' Sylvie said suddenly, putting her hands over her face and letting her head fall. 'I don't know where to start.'

Alyssa took a deep breath and blew it out slowly, trying to centre herself as best she could with a cold tap jutting against her bum cheek. 'Begin at the beginning.' It was something she'd said hundreds of times to her love coaching clients, and it was all she could come up with right then.

So Sylvie began to fill the room with her story, Alyssa reminding herself to listen with an open mind and not jump in.

'Devan and I never had an affair. We've never even slept together. Not once.'

They hadn't? But how …

'Emmalina isn't biologically his. *Obviously*, he knows that.' Sylvie flapped a nervous hand. 'Emmalina does too, now she's a bit older and Devan isn't living with us – though she isn't ready to tell people he's not her real dad. Emmalina is too young to know this next part, but I … I became accidentally pregnant after a one-night stand with that bloke who'd visited town on a stag do. Do you remember me mentioning him? I thought I was *so* grown up, losing my virginity to an older guy who wasn't local.'

Alyssa nodded slowly, letting the other information sink in. She did vaguely remember Sylvie's story about stag-do guy, though she couldn't remember his name and hadn't met him.

'Well, he turned out to be married – and not at all interested in the status of my womb. The total nobwomble.'

Alyssa, who was still processing, couldn't argue with that assessment. *If* Sylvie's story was true.

'And you know what a violent drunk my dad could be,' Sylvie said meekly.

'I do.' Alyssa could feel her eyelids heavying with the threat of tears at the thought. She'd often seen Sylvie's mum with unexplained bruises, and both Sylvie and Alyssa had been known to throw themselves between Sylvie's parents when her dad had kicked off. Some parts of Sylvie's upbringing had been frightening. At least Alyssa's parents hadn't put her through *that*.

'He had *such* strident views about sex before marriage and having babies out of wedlock. I was honestly terrified for myself and my unborn child.' Her hand floated to her stomach as though Emmalina was still in there. 'When he'd seen Devan consoling me, he latched on to some ludicrous notion that Devan "*should make an honest woman of me*". Talk about archaic bullshit. Then he was spreading his "*news*" before I could stop him. And you heard Dad's drunken rants, then before I could explain it you were gone, and then …' Sylvie let out a long, strangled sound, her eyes filling up. 'When we couldn't get hold of you, Devan and I ended up feeling pushed to go along with Dad's story in the short term – to keep the peace. It was only ever meant to be a temporary fix.'

Alyssa grabbed a fresh toilet roll and passed it to Sylvie, accepting a few pieces for herself. Coming from anybody else, Alyssa might have thought some of Sylvie's story was outrageously unlikely. Though as much as it pained her to admit it, Sylvie had never been good at lying. Her neck would flush, and she'd get all twitchy. Alyssa knew her tells, even though Sylvie had only really fibbed to avoid her evil dad's wrath when they were growing up. Alyssa hadn't spotted any obvious signs Sylvie was making things up. Though after years of mistrusting people, Alyssa was far from ready to merrily accept everything she was told without time to think things through.

She tried to slot the pieces of new information into her mind, replacing the old beliefs that had never quite fit with the versions of Sylvie and Devan she'd always known. Unless Sylvie was lying, she'd just entrusted her with the truths Devan hadn't been able to share, because they weren't just his. And they didn't seem like the sorts of things anyone would lie about, because they involved Sylvie's most precious thing – her daughter.

'Can you forgive me?' Sylvie asked, her face contorted with hope, her eyes teary.

'And please believe me that Devan did do his best to get hold of you,' Sylvie continued, when Alyssa didn't immediately answer. 'I continued to suffer with sickness through my pregnancy, but Devan and I were both *frantic* with worry. We desperately wanted to explain things to you and maybe come up with a way to tackle it together. But it seems you were equally desperate not to be found. We didn't manage, and things eventually moved on – even if I know that Devan's feelings for you never lessened. He was *heartbroken*. We both were.'

Alyssa's chest felt tight. She'd done everything in her power to stay under the radar for the first couple of years she was in London. New contact details. Even a new name. What if she'd stuck around and listened? Would she have believed them? Would she have stayed with Devan and been there for Sylvie and Emmalina? She didn't know, and she couldn't change history. But that wouldn't stop her wondering. Sometimes the truth *did* hurt.

'You didn't tell me you were pregnant,' Alyssa said quietly, the pain evident in her voice. 'Why did Devan know before me? We were meant to be best friends.'

'We were best friends. You're the best friend I've ever had, and I still haven't replaced you. There is *nobody* I would rather share my Sugababes posters with.' She gave a shy grin. 'But truthfully,

I'd only just found out myself. I'd been ill a lot, and my parents took me to the doctors. I peed in a cardboard cup and then wham. The biggest surprise of my life. A positive pregnancy test. My dad hit the damned roof. I'd been trying to call you that same night – the night of the Hartglove ball, but you didn't answer.'

'I left my mobile at home,' Alyssa remembered, her brow creasing. 'Couldn't work out what to do with it, wearing that stupid fancy dress costume. I saw your missed calls later that night, but I was hating you by then.'

'Fair,' said Sylvie, simply, still blubbing a little. 'But I started feeling rough again, and my parents were out at the dance. The only person I could get hold of was Devan. I called him and he said he'd be straight round.'

Reliable Devan. Alyssa nodded slowly, taking it all in.

'That's why he arrived at the ball and promptly left again. He was just answering my call. I *did* ring you first.'

'And when had your dad decided you and him should be a thing?'

'Devan had dropped around to mine earlier that evening to lend my brother a textbook and I'd ended up blubbing on him. Stupid pregnancy hormones. I think that's when Dad got the seed of his outlandish idea, though neither of us knew that until we heard what rubbish he'd been spouting at the dance.'

It was *a lot* to take in. And was she willing to accept it, after more than a decade of believing something different?

'I guess you'll need to think,' said Sylvie, seeming to read Alyssa's hesitation. 'But I hope you'll find it in your heart to forgive me. Devan too. He was just being *Good Old Devan*, doing the right thing. He loves you, you know. He always did.'

'But you guys got married. Brought up a child together. And you're saying you never even slept together? He might be good, but he's not a saint.'

'We didn't get married,' Sylvie confessed. 'I just started wearing a ring and we pretended we'd had a quick registry office thing.

People gossiped, of course. We lived together, in separate bedrooms. Devan was so great with Emmalina. They're adorable. But no, I haven't slept with any man, other than that once with Emmalina's sperm dad. I realised guys weren't my preference after that idiot – or perhaps even before.' She shrugged. 'Anyway, Devan always felt more like a brother. Seeing his todger would just have been wrong.' Sylvie pulled a *gross* face and shuddered. 'No offence. I'm sure it's perfectly nice, if you like that sort of thing.'

Alyssa spurted out a laugh. 'None taken.'

'After Dad died, it seemed ridiculous to carry on with the pretence. I'm not sure why we did for so long. Though as much as I often hated my dad, I couldn't stand the thought of being a disappointment to him, you know? Or of him treating Emmalina differently or ranting about us or causing trouble. Because he would have.'

'He was a dick,' Alyssa said firmly. 'In my professional opinion.'

'He was,' Sylvie agreed, snottily. 'And now, it's time for Devan and me to look for our own love stories. Even Mum has found hers – though she moved to the other side of the country to find it.'

Did Alyssa bristle at the L-word a little less than usual? She was happy to hear about Sylvie's mum too.

'Devan's always kept that torch burning for you, you know.'

'Hmm.' He'd said the same himself, but Alyssa's thoughts were still reeling. It was as though she'd spent the last twelve years believing the sky was green and now she had to squint hard and try to see blue.

'Maybe you could meet Emmalina one day?' Sylvie asked cautiously. 'She's into girl bands, sweets and pre-teen magazines – just like we were. Though she's way more grown up than I'll ever be. I think you'd like her.' Sylvie's face brimmed with pride as she spoke about her daughter.

Alyssa paused for a moment. 'Emmalina sounds great,' she said earnestly. Though she wasn't sure if she'd ever be ready to play happy families, when she barely remembered what that looked like. She stood up from her perch on the sink and shook herself down, all parts of her numb. 'But I need time to process. I'm honestly not sure how I feel about anything right now.'

Sylvie nodded and stood up too. 'I get that. I'm here for you, if and when you're ready. Let me give you my number.'

## Chapter 27

Since her conversation with Sylvie in the Clucky Ducks ladies' loos, it was as though something inside Alyssa was starting to unlock. She'd spent days going through all the emotions, from frustration with herself for running from her hometown without letting Sylvie and Devan explain, to deep regret for what could have been. She'd moved the jigsaw pieces around in her head, wondering if her parents could have been less self-centred and have tried to reconnect them, or whether Sylvie's dad could have been less of a drunken shit.

But her conclusion was always the same. Life was life. It dished out its lessons and you just had to learn from them. She was sad for the things she'd missed – but like Mrs Halfpenny's lost idiot on the roundabout, she couldn't go backwards. There was only ever onwards. It wasn't always easy to list her reasons to be cheerful, but with a lot of deliberation, a bit of allotment *Tea and Sympathy*, and a treat or two of tiramisu, she was getting there. It was gutting that she hadn't been around for Sylvie, but at least Devan had been. He'd done a selfless thing, and being a doting parent to Emmalina was a much worthier cause than their teenage crush.

And another thing had occurred to her, since Sylvie's words.

Perhaps the nineteen-year-old Beryl hadn't been rejected or unloved in the way she'd always thought – at least not by her friends. If that was so, maybe she'd constructed her new persona for all the wrong reasons. Was she ready to let down a few walls and dare to be herself? And would the right people accept her?

These novel thoughts could be the only reason Alyssa was now bouncing along the road, wearing *'clothes you wouldn't mind getting bodily fluids spilt on'* as the app had bizarrely suggested, on her way to Love Task Four.

Wait, she was bouncing? It had been a long time since her trusty flowered army boots had seen her being *that* energetic. If she was honest, this was the first time she'd been actively looking forward to seeing Devan for one of their tasks, even if that felt confusing. Since Sylvie had revealed her relationship with Devan had been a front and he hadn't made her pregnant, each time Alyssa played things over in her mind, Devan emerged as a good guy, rather than the liar and cheat she'd spent years wrongly casting him as.

And, as unnerving as it was after all this dormant time, she could almost sense her feelings for Devan growing, like a strange, untamed thing. Part of her wanted to run for the hills or deny it. And she was a *long* way off believing in a thing called 'love' – or perhaps even trust.

But was her heart slowly coming back to life? God, she'd better warn her ribcage.

She took in her surroundings as she walked, which she found herself doing more and more lately, rather than ignoring the loveliness in case it had a chance to seep in. It was one of those postcard-perfect streets with Cotswold stone cottages, some with thatched roofs and pretty rose bushes. Birds sang from hedgerows, and she could hear the distant trickle of the stream they used to dip their toes in, as children. A place that invited you to relax. *To stay.*

Alyssa shook her head. If she was going to let these unusual feelings keep growing like the roots of an apple tree, she would have to talk to Devan about what Sylvie had said. Could she do that today? And what kind of dangerous new world might that lead to? Life had been much safer before she'd started bouncing along, appraising people's perennial bushes. But she couldn't forget what Mrs Halfpenny had warned about shutting people out and staying lonely.

'Oh!' Devan stepped out onto the pavement in front of her, making her jump. 'I wasn't expecting to see you yet.'

He'd just emerged from the front garden of a quaint-looking cottage. Did he live there?

'I wasn't expecting to catch you checking out my foliage.'

He winked at her and moved in for a swift kiss on the cheek. For once, she was angling her face towards him, with zero impulse to throttle him.

'Ohhhh,' she heard herself say again, kind of stupidly. It was just a peck. His lips had touched her for one single second. That strange spark couldn't actually have happened, unless he'd spent the morning rubbing a balloon against his hair to make himself electric. She cleared her throat. 'I mean, hi! I was on my way to the task. You know. In my best outfit for getting splashed in bodily fluids.'

She winced. That really did sound awful. And why was she acting like some sort of weird, love-drunk puppy? She was *not* going to start conceding to herself that the *L word* was a thing.

To her relief, Devan just laughed, linked his arm through hers, and continued to walk with her along the road. Wow, they were arm-linking now? Though as her latest spicy dreams kept reminding her, they had spent a whole night temptingly close together on the camping task, even if it had mainly been about survival.

'Any clues on what the bodily fluids thing is about?' He gave her a gentle nudge. 'Shooting a dodgy porn movie? Clearing up geriatric wee?'

Well, that last option would certainly dampen the flames.

Maybe she'd better hope for that one.

'Just to be clear, I'm not available for low-quality porn. Or any quality porn,' she added quickly. 'No porn happening today. Or any day! I don't even own nipple tassels.'

God, she was rambling nonsense. The sooner they got to their hopefully un-kinky destination, the better.

'Any idea what this task is about?' She gave him a gentle nudge back, enjoying the feel of her shoulder against his and the way it brought them closer. 'Handy that it's apparently on your doorstep, so you could pretty much roll out of bed.' *And back into it*, her wayward brain added, trying not to dwell on how their last task ended in a *just one sleeping bag* situation.

If she couldn't keep her mind and body in check, it was going to be a long day.

'No clue. But we seem to be here.' He stopped outside the address they'd been given, and they both looked up. 'Hartglove Animal Rescue Centre,' he read. 'Where no stray is turned away.'

'They obviously haven't met us yet,' Alyssa replied, praying they *did* turn away big snakes and hairy tarantulas, because they were fears she was absolutely not ready to face. Being around Devan with a confused heart and diminishing reasons to be mad at him was challenging enough.

'How are you around mammals giving birth?' The spiky-haired young woman behind the desk of the animal rescue centre, whose name badge said '*Hedgehog – She/Her*', seemed flustered.

'I don't have any experience of it,' said Alyssa, hoping it was just a random question and that she'd soon be petting bunny rabbits or feeding cute kittens.

'I ... erm ... prefer to steer clear of the business end,' said Devan, running a hand through his hair, his cheeks pinkening. 'When it's not strictly my business.'

'Today, everything's your business,' said Hedgehog, throwing them both '*Save Hartglove – I'm* Sow *into You*' T-shirts and rummaging under the desk for further supplies. 'It's all hands on deck, because there's only us three. and all of *this*.' She pointed to a long, complicated-looking spreadsheet. 'Vet's on her way from Taybury to check on our mini pig, Nicole Pigman – the *Sow*. She looks like she's ready to give birth, but she's making a fuss about it. Much more of a diva than her celebrity namesake, and not nearly as good at singing.' A look of love spread over her face. 'She's a beauty though. She'll steal your heart, if you let her.'

'I know the feeling,' said Devan, almost to himself.

Alyssa dared a swift glance at him. He looked adorably flustered.

'I mean, being no good at singing,' he added quickly. 'Bet the pig's better than me.'

'Riiiiiiight,' said Hedgehog, glancing between them, sensing who knew what, and grinning. 'This is your fourth love task, isn't it?' She checked her notes. 'Teijo's running late, but he says the app has chosen this task to help you work on trust, communication and your spirit of commitment. And if you end up helping N-Pig to spurt out the world's cutest pig babies, you can throw vulnerability, emotional support and a whole lot of heart-eye emojis onto the list. Prepare to fall head over heels.'

'I'm in full control of my heart-eye emojis,' Alyssa confirmed. Though she wasn't sure how true that was today.

'Miss Heart, Teijo wanted your thoughts on the app's choice of task and the importance of the relationship ingredients it aims to help you with.'

Alyssa didn't feel her usual compulsion to rally against 'Appy Together nor to reel off her usual derogatory jibes. In fact, she might even wear the horrific-looking T-shirt. She settled on: 'I'm open to seeing how it goes.'

'It's a miracle,' Devan breathed.

'Teamwork, guys,' Hedgehog reminded them. 'Your mission today is bigger than yourselves. Can I trust you to work together?'

'Team Alyvan,' Alyssa joked, snapping a few selfies with Devan for social media, even though she usually made sure he was nowhere near her pics. 'You and the animals can count on us.'

Their first job was to check on Nicole Pigman.

'Wow, Hedgehog wasn't exaggerating about feeling heart-eyes towards this beauty,' said Alyssa, surprised to find the small pig so endearing.

Nicole had the cutest baby-pink skin with a smattering of black spots, and a downy layer of cinnamon-coloured hair that had perhaps inspired her near-celebrity name. She'd made herself a nest of hay in her indoor pen, and was lying on it, looking entirely worn out.

Alyssa knelt next to Nicole, instinctively rubbing the pig's belly. It was balloon-shaped and must have been uncomfortable, housing a team of wriggling piglets. The pig made panty, snuffling noises and nuzzled her wet nose into the side of Alyssa's leg. 'You poor thing. We'll be here for you.'

'It'll probably be the middle of the night, so you may not want to promise that,' said Hedgehog. She was standing in the doorway next to Devan, who still seemed a bit awkward about coming in, even though he'd presumably seen one more birth than Alyssa. 'And sometimes there are complications. It can be stressful, and it's not for everyone. Hopefully a colleague or the vet will cover it. Or she'll manage.'

Something inside Alyssa sank at the thought of leaving the creature to navigate birth and the start of motherhood alone. She looked up at Devan, who seemed to have similar thoughts etched across his forehead.

'Animals know what to do,' said Hedgehog, matter-of-factly. Maybe it was wise to keep some level of distance with animals coming, going, and surely not always living. 'I need to cover the desk. You two can come back later, after you've sorted the cats, dogs, rabbits and various goats. Not to mention Terrance the turkey and that new family of chinchillas.'

The morning whizzed by, with a montage of scenes that were

worthy of Teijo's camera, when he finally arrived. Everything from chasing an escaped, gobbling Terrance to mastering the goat poop scoop was certainly testing their teamwork skills.

And Alyssa being close to Devan while resisting her odd new impulse to touch him was a test for her too.

Her T-shirt must have been going to her head, because as she and Devan worked, they began batting around ideas for how they could bring more love to Hartglove through the animal rescue centre. They came up with thoughts of open days, volunteering opportunities for young people, and even sponsoring animals. Devan agreed to run the ideas past the centre's manager, and to see what funding he could arrange. It was becoming impossible not to *really* like him. Not just because he cared about things, but also, they *did* make a great team.

'If I had to choose anyone to mop up cat sick with on a Saturday morning, it would be you,' Devan said with mock seriousness, taking Alyssa's blue plastic-gloved hand in his and holding it to his chest.

A laugh burst out from her, and she tried to ignore the fizz of whatever it was as his warmth enveloped her fingers, her heart pulsing. The more time she'd spent with him that morning, the more her desire to talk to him about what Sylvie had said was growing. She wanted to hear the story from his point of view, to understand more about his decisions and how his life had panned out. And perhaps to probe a little about how he felt about her, or was that too weird? But if they cleared the air, what would be left to stop her heart from falling for his? Falling, was a frightening, uncontrollable thing.

So it was just as well there hadn't been a good time to start selfishly asking her questions, with all these schnoodles howling for their dog biscuits.

'Nice shot,' said Teijo, taking a snap of Alyssa gazing into Devan's twilight blue eyes like she was a love-sick spaniel.

God, how long had she been doing that? At least he'd been

gazing back at her, even if it was just for Teijo's photo.

'You're so photogenic together today. Has something changed?' Teijo asked, whizzing back through the images on his screen and smiling with an *aww that's so cute* face.

Alyssa pulled away from Devan and straightened herself.

'I'm covered in animal hair and puke, and I'm not sure if I'll ever get whatever this is out from under my nails. But apart from that, it's business as usual.' She looked towards Devan, expecting him to say something similarly noncommittal.

He looked at her for a long moment, as though Teijo, a whole lot of yelping animals and various wafts of pet stink weren't part of their current equation.

'I think every task has changed me,' Devan said finally, his voice almost uncertain. 'I created the app, so I guess I thought I knew how this journey would go. But it's been more challenging and rewarding than I'd given it credit for. I've learned that we can't control how things will be, because we make the path as we walk.'

'That's sooooo good for online,' said Teijo, grabbing his pencil and scribbling.

Devan shook his head, like it was the strangest thing he'd ever come out with. 'It is, isn't it?' His eyes searched Alyssa's. 'Did you say something like that on social media once?'

Alyssa shrugged. 'Probably.' If she did, it was more thought-provoking coming from Devan – because it was genuine and not inspired by a quick search on Google.

Were the two of them beginning to make their own, new path as the tasks progressed? Was this app actually working at bringing them back together? Or did she need to stop thinking peculiar thoughts and get back to mopping up cat sick?

# Chapter 28

The evening had grown dark by the time Hedgehog was getting ready to lock up the animal rescue centre. They could have left earlier, when Teijo had stopped taking promotional photos and they'd completed their list of animal-related jobs. But in truth, Alyssa had been enjoying herself. That sense of feeling useful and needed, not to mention the animal cuddles, and spending so much time with Devan. She couldn't help relishing their easy banter and the fact she felt so at home with him, as though the imprints of their souls still knew each other – or something kooky like that.

'Get going, you two,' Hedgehog insisted, all but shooing them towards the door. 'I'll check on this pig, and then I'm out of here. You've done more than enough.'

Alyssa's eyes met Devan's across the now-dimmed lighting of the reception area. Something unsaid passed between them.

'We'll come with you,' said Alyssa. The last time they'd looked in on Nicole Pigman she'd been restless, and still desperately rearranging her nest. Alyssa wouldn't sleep if she was worrying about her, and she sensed Devan felt the same.

They weren't wrong to check. Nicole was lying on her side, panting, and looking like she was trying to push. Alyssa didn't know much about giving birth, but it surely looked a lot like that.

Hedgehog sighed. 'I knew you were a diva, Miss Pigman. I'm due at an engagement party in Taybury in one hour.' She checked her watch. 'I literally can't miss it, because it's mine.'

With a lot of wows and congratulations, a call to the vet, and thrusting of various guidebooks and blankets, Hedgehog was rushing out of the door, looking apologetic.

'Go and enjoy your night,' said Alyssa, in her best *we've got this* voice. She hoped somebody did.

When Hedgehog had gone, Alyssa went to crouch next to Miss P. The indoor pen was dark, other than the orange glow of the heat lamps, and oh so warm. Alyssa began stroking the animal's side and making reassuring noises. Devan knelt next to her in the hay. They stayed that way for a while, not quite knowing what to do other than hope for the best. Their pig friend calmed again, as though she'd gone off the idea of popping out piglets.

They settled themselves down, Alyssa pulling a blanket over her knees, Devan reading through the guidebooks.

'Were you there when Emmalina was born?' The question was out before Alyssa had chance to decide whether to ask it. There was something about this warm, bosom-like darkness that made it easier to talk.

'Yes.' Devan's face lit up. 'It's such an experience. All of it.' He turned to her and grabbed her hands, squeezing them, as though he couldn't keep the joy of it to himself. 'I mean, I was still young, and I stayed firmly at the head end of the bed. Sylvie did an amazing job with all that pushing. But when I first got to hold Emmalina ...'

They held each other's gaze for a moment, Alyssa transfixed by how alive he looked. Then he remembered he was still grasping her hands, apologised quickly, and dropped them.

'It's OK.' She took a deep breath, sensing it was time to ask the question she'd been keeping in all day – even if the truth of it frightened her. Because once she knew, there might be one less barrier to hold her tumbling feelings back. 'Can I ask you something?'

He nodded.

'Sylvie said she was already pregnant when you agreed to marry her, and that the two of you were never really …'

He exhaled a long breath and took hold of her hands again. 'That's right. Emmalina will always be *mine*. I love every inch of her, and she's got my heart for life. But I'm not her biological dad, and she knows that now. She's been surprisingly cool about it.' He let out a soft chuckle. 'I think she sensed we were different to her friends' parents, with our separate bedrooms, and the way we were with each other. And yes, it's right that Sylvie and I have never been *together*. Her wedding ring was for show, and I never even wore one. Behind closed doors it was strictly friendship. A pretence, to protect them both from the wrath of Sylvie's dad, and to keep people away from the truth of things.'

Alyssa knew all about keeping up a pretence.

He explained the story from his point of view, which was much the same as Sylvie had told it, other than he used less polite words about Sylvie's now deceased father.

'Not that the truth was anything *at all* to be ashamed of. But it wasn't as easy back then, in such a small community. People's judgement can scar you. I know it would be different now. Maybe it was naive of me, still being in my teens and not knowing what the future held, other than I'd always dreamed it would involve *you*. It kills me that you found out like that, and I didn't get chance to explain.' His eyes were heavy with apology. 'But I'd do the Emmalina bit all over again in a heartbeat. Being there to raise her and help her grow has been an honour.'

Their hands were still entwined, connecting them, his warmth pouring into her. But now, there was something more. Like an invisible *something*, joining their hearts, pulling her closer to him, as though he was her north. Which could be the only reason their faces were drawing towards each other, her eyelids flickering shut. Her mouth was moving instinctively, edging towards him, as though the memory of what to do was taking over from any logic. And like she was in the sweetest dream, Devan's lips were on hers. Warm, soft. Sending a ripple of relief straight through her. She heard his intake of breath, felt the pressure between their lips increasing, his hand finding the base of her neck, her fingers grabbing his hair …

*Grug, grug, gruuuug.*

They pulled away from each other sharply.

It was Nicole Pigman. Well, she had immaculate timing. With a lift of her back legs and a few more jerks, a small, four-legged ball of slime popped out of the mini pig, attached by an umbilical cord which promptly broke free.

'Whoa! Oh my goodness.' Alyssa slipped on some rubber gloves, trying to keep her voice and movements calm, even if no part of her felt it. 'Her first piglet. What are we meant to do?'

Devan shakily put on gloves, then passed her a towel. 'The guidebook – thankfully *not* written by Teijo – says to wipe them. Mum pig is likely to stay where she is, getting ready to birth the next one. Piglet should snuffle around for a teat. Help them if they get lost.'

Alyssa gave the tiny new life a gentle rub with the towel, her own heart filling with affection as she watched it wriggle and squeak, its eyes closed, its body determined to move and find its way.

'It's alive,' Alyssa said unnecessarily, never having seen a creature enter the world before. She felt strangely protective of it, like she wanted to keep it safe, even though it wasn't strictly her job, and she should probably let go now. 'How many more could there be?'

Devan consulted the book. 'Hard to tell, but maybe up to a dozen or so? Hope the vet gets here soon.'

As he said it, Nicole Pigman lifted her back legs and treated them to another live piglet. Devan grabbed a towel and came to help.

Nearly two hours passed, with Nicole successfully popping

out seven tiny pink and black piglets, all as cute as buttons, and thankfully alive and well. The vet arrived, decided Nicole was healthy and had finished, and there was nothing for her to do. Alyssa and Devan decided to stay a while longer, feeling a pull not to leave the mum and her little ones – and perhaps not to leave each other.

'It's like we're in a bubble,' Alyssa whispered to Devan as she leaned against him, both sitting in the straw with a blanket over them, watching the tiny, snuffling brood. Alyssa's tired head rested on Devan's shoulder and his arm draped lazily around her. 'Like a strange, magical space of new life and fresh beginnings.'

Devan took a deep breath. 'Doesn't smell that fresh.' His soft laugh vibrated through her. 'But I know what you mean. Though I think we're more enamoured with the idea than Nicole there. She's snoring like a P-I-G.'

Alyssa chuckled too and then stifled a yawn. 'It's just so special, isn't it? Seeing a living thing come into the world and take its first breaths. To witness the strength of instinct to find belonging and to live.' She rubbed her chest, remembering what Hedgehog had warned about heart-eye emojis and falling head over heels. 'Not that it's the same, of course – because she's absolutely *not* a piglet. But I think I sense a fraction of how you must have felt with Emmalina.'

Alyssa looked up at him. His face lit up like she'd just mentioned his specialist subject. 'My heart was bursting for her from the moment I saw her tiny scrunched-up face and those grabby little fingers. Biology didn't come into it – I just wanted to protect her. Still do. Hey, you should meet her.'

'Sylvie said that too.' Not for the first time, she chewed the thought over. The more time she spent with Devan, the more she found herself wanting to explore his world. Toying with her growing feelings for him was one thing. But something else had been troubling her. 'What if I let her down?' The thought was out before she could stop it. 'All this time I've spent mistrusting people. What if it's me who can't be trusted? I make rubbish decisions. When the going gets tough, I run. Can I start letting myself back into your life, and into Sylvie's and Emmalina's, if I'm not sure I'll stick around?'

He gave her shoulder a gentle squeeze. 'You're being too hard on yourself,' he said softly, stroking back her hair and kissing her forehead. 'Your decisions aren't rubbish, by a long shot. We're all just doing the best we can with what we're dealt. Whatever you decide, I trust you.'

'Thank you.' She yawned. All this emotional stuff was exhausting.

'My mum's looking forward to seeing you when she and Dad are back from their Maldives trip too. But no pressure.'

'No pressure,' she repeated, sleepily. She had adored Dawn, though now wasn't the time to commit to too much.

She wasn't quite sure when she let the final part of her guard down and fell asleep on him, her head nestled into the crook of his neck, both of his arms now wrapped around her. She wasn't sure if she subconsciously felt his warm hands stroking her arms and smoothing her hair, or his breath tickling her face, or if that was part of a dream she was definitely enjoying.

When she woke, it was nearly four a.m., and Devan had drifted off too. Her stirring to life woke him.

'We should probably go soon.' She yawned again, looking over at the sleepy brood and their dozing mother. 'They all seem fine, and we'll give the morning staff a shock if we're still here, like shepherds in a manger.'

They stood, quietly gathering their things, Alyssa stopping for a moment to take it all in.

'This has been special,' she breathed, turning to Devan, who'd been standing behind her. 'Being here for this. With you.' Their faces were close now, as though something had drawn them back together. Noses nearly touching, eyes drinking each other in. Alyssa reached to touch his fingertips, their fingers entwining.

'I'd forgotten what a good person you are, Devan. I'm glad I got to come back here and start to remember.'

She'd thought they'd been about to kiss again. Every part of her had wanted to. Instead, a brief sadness flashed across his eyes, and he nodded, stepping back from her.

'I'll send Hedgehog an update and then we'll leave these guys in peace. I could call you a taxi? You can't walk down dark country lanes at this time, even though the murder rates aren't too abysmal.' He checked his watch and then winced. 'Actually, you won't get a taxi out here at this time. I could drive you? Or you're welcome to stay at mine. In a separate room, obviously. You don't want to relive the *only one sleeping bag* night.' He ran a hand through his hair, as though it was helping him to think through logistics.

Alyssa looked at him. His eyes were tired, and she didn't want to trouble him with driving when he looked like he might nod off. And a secret part of her *did* want to relive that intimate sleeping bag situation, albeit somewhere less chilly.

'Can I stay at yours? Just for a few hours.' It was nearly morning anyway. 'I won't get in your way.' Not that she really wanted to promise that last bit.

'Of course.' He nodded.

'Thank you. That's so …'

'Good of me. I know.'

When he tilted his mouth into a smile, Alyssa noticed that the hint of sadness she'd seen in his eyes had drifted down to it.

Had she said something wrong? Or maybe she'd had one of her sexy Devan dreams when she'd fallen asleep on him and had been accidentally rambling about his amber-scented skin or his washboard stomach. If she was about to stay at his, perhaps she *should* stay strictly in a separate room.

## Chapter 29

'Good Old Devan,' said Alyssa, realisation hitting. 'That's what I implied, wasn't it?' She clapped a hand over her forehead as they stepped through Devan's front door. It was a relatively new-build Cotswold stone house, and Alyssa could already tell from the neat, fresh-smelling hallway that Devan was still the tidy sort. 'I'm sorry. I mean, you are a great guy, but I wasn't implying that's all there is to you – like you're dependable, but a bit dull.'

They took off their shoes and moved to Devan's main living space, which was decorated mainly in neutral shades, with a dark green feature wall and tan leather furniture. There was a big-screen TV and various laptops and hints of technology dotted around, though it was surprisingly well ordered for what she guessed was now his bachelor pad, and she spotted at least three houseplants that looked reasonably well cared for. She should ask Jess to hook him up with some macramé plant hangers.

'Thank you,' he finally replied. 'I guess that's why I went a bit quiet back there. That, on top of our chat about you being what the police might call a flight risk,' he added wryly. 'You might lure me in and leave town again.'

'It's entirely possible.' She winked at him. 'But it's better to have loved and lost.' It was OK to use the *L-word*, as long as it was a cliché.

'Ouch.' He seemed to think for a moment. 'And as for the G-O-D thing. It's not that I don't want to be reliable. I actually do. But one day, maybe I'll get to be more than just *that dependable guy* to someone. You know?'

Oh – he wanted to be *the hot guy*. Perhaps she should scrap the macramé idea, or he might get a complex.

'I know,' she replied, resisting the urge to tell him he was definitely morphing into the *hot guy*. In fact, she was trying not to imagine him hotly stripping off that *'I'm Sow into You'* T-shirt in a welcome re-enactment of the shared garden task.

Wow, tiredness was doing dangerous things to her. Or maybe in a bizarre twist of technology, 'Appy Together had thrown them exactly the right task to help them open up. And now that they had …

'Erm. Coffee?' He pointed towards the open door of the kitchen.

'I am tempted by that incredible-looking coffee machine,' she said, making her way to the kitchen with him, curious to see more of his home. 'Though coffee would wake me up, and I could do with sleeping.' Her nose crinkled. 'And maybe having a wash?'

'You always smell good to me,' he said, flicking the kettle on. 'Though you're welcome to use the shower if you want to de-pig before you sleep. You can take my bed, because the sheets are clean. I'll make up Emmalina's or nap on the couch. And if I was being *Good Old Devan* – which I'm not – I'd wonder whether you fancied hot chocolate instead of coffee. And then I'd suggest pre-bed Penguin biscuits which are particularly good for dunking.'

Alyssa felt her stomach rumble. 'Please tell me they're orange flavoured?'

'You'll be happy to know I stock all flavours.' He gave a small bow, his easiness starting to seep back. 'I don't disappoint.'

She raised her eyebrows, stepping towards him. 'Oh, you *are* good. Though if you want to shake off your image and channel your inner *bad boy*, you'll have to be less accommodating.'

'What, like offering you crap biscuits and making you sleep on the couch?'

'Oh, that would be *bad*.' She laughed and gave him a peck on the cheek, sitting on one of his high breakfast bar chairs, before she got the urge to touch him again, or whisper where she'd really like to spend the night.

They sat drinking hot chocolate, dipping Penguin biscuits and debating the best way to eat them. They both enjoyed nibbling the top off first, although Devan admitted he only did that when Emmalina wasn't looking. Alyssa loved how he wasn't self-conscious about drinking hot chocolate with extra squirty cream and glittery pink sprinkles. They talked easily about the things Alyssa had thought would be difficult, like his life with a young child, and having to pretend he and Sylvie were a couple to onlookers, though neither of them had ever felt that way about each other. Then moving out and not seeing Emmalina every day was still tough for him too.

Alyssa could see more traces of his pre-teen girl in the kitchen, even though she mainly lived with Sylvie. Heart mugs, and the odd beaded bracelet and hair scrunchie. They were a nice contrast to his organised space.

By six a.m. they were both yawning again. And though the rest of the town would be getting ready to wake, they had hardly slept, and Alyssa really did want that hot shower.

'Can I?' she asked, pulling at her clothes like she wanted to get out of them. 'Get clean, I mean.'

'Yes, of course.'

After a quick tidy-away she grabbed her things, and Devan showed her upstairs to the bathroom, Alyssa only briefly imagining an *only one shower* situation, before telling her brain to behave.

'When you're ready to sleep, take my room.'

He pointed to an open door where Alyssa could see a double bedroom. A large bed with clean, inviting sheets sat in the middle of a room that was painted in grey shades with deep blue accents that she might have said matched his eyes, if she'd been there to appraise things. Though she was a little too sleepy for that.

Alyssa showered quickly, wrapping herself in Devan's deliciously soft white towels that smelled of fresh linen, and went to Devan's room to dry her hair. She sat on the bed as she ran the dryer over her messy pink waves, her body sinking into the comfort of the mattress. Devan had lit the fireplace, which was built into the wall and looked like real flames. It gave the room a cosy glow and a burst of much-needed warmth.

She could hear the shower running again and blinked away the thought of Devan naked inside it, water cascading down him. She wondered how that might look now, remembering *again* how he'd yanked off his top at the allotment and she'd noticed a whole lot of gym muscle he hadn't had at nineteen. She was willing to concede he probably wasn't the sort of poser who dried his pubes with the changing room hairdryer, after all.

As though the universe was answering her, she heard the bathroom door open, and Devan stepped out, a long bath towel around his lower half, his top half bare. Her eyes devoured what she saw, even though she knew it was rude to stare. In that moment, she couldn't help it. When they'd been gardening, she'd been too busy being annoyed by his bravado to notice the light smattering of brown hair, or the deep shade of his now-hard nipples. And she definitely hadn't had chance for an eyeful of the sweep of hair that led from his navel to his substantial bulge, which was quite frustratingly hidden by a layer of towelling.

'Oh, sorry.' Devan looked up to notice the bedroom door was open and her gaze was fixed on him.

Or more accurately, her eyes were sizing up his manhood, with her mouth slightly ajar. She clamped it shut and mumbled an apology back.

'It's your house,' she said meekly. 'You're welcome to ...' She waved an arm, trying to convey that he could wander around half naked on his own landing, if he wanted. The words had somehow escaped her.

'I was miles away,' he muttered back. 'A hot shower can transport you. Erm. Yeah. I'd better make up the other bed.'

She could see he was shivering, and not at all full of the semi-bare swagger she'd seen on the allotment task. He'd suggested that had just been nerves. Was he nervous now? Seeing him step out of the shower room had certainly given her butterflies.

He opened the only other door on the upper floor, and she heard him sigh. Craning to see, she spotted a pink-painted room with a single bed piled high with clean washing, boxes of board games, and other random items that looked like they needed putting away.

'So that's where you keep your mess.' She chuckled. 'I was beginning to think you were superhuman.'

'Everyone has their secret junk piles,' he answered, still shivering, his torso not properly dry. 'And pre-teens make a lot of mayhem.'

As much as she was enjoying his rear view, she couldn't leave him standing there.

'This is no time to be sorting out your ironing. Come and sleep in with me.' She could feel her own heart racing at the thought of it, even though it was surely just sensible logistics.

'No, it's fine. Honestly. I'll pull out the duvet and sleep on the couch downstairs. I can't invite you here and then pull an *only one bed* situation – especially after the incident when we only had one sleeping bag. I'm not *that* guy.'

He'd turned to look at her, his eyes honest. She knew he wasn't that guy. He was a good one. Though parts of her longed to encourage a bad streak.

'And for the avoidance of doubt, you're one hundred per cent off duty now. My love app business is not paying you to be in my bedroom.'

She had to smile at that.

Alyssa patted the bed next to her. 'I insist. It's your house, and we've slept together before. I mean, not actually *slept together*. But, you know.' She was waffling again too.

And he was still shaking. She jumped up and pulled him by his hands into the warm room, shutting the door behind him. She took a spare towel from the radiator and placed it around his shoulders, rubbing some heat into his upper arms.

'There. At least we don't have an *only one towel* situation.' She nodded to the one wrapped around his waist. 'If you remove that, my poor eyeballs won't know where to look.'

He smiled, gazing down at her, their faces getting closer with that inexplicable pull. 'Then I'll be sure not to remove it.'

There was a cheeky tease in his voice, and she couldn't resist returning it.

'That seems a shame,' she replied, hooking her fingers over the waist of his towel and pulling him in closer.

She heard his sharp intake of breath as the tips of her fingers touched his lower stomach, dancing dangerously close to what lay beneath. His sudden powerlessness to her touch gave her a thrill. She hadn't been planning this, as she'd been yawning and drying her hair, thinking absently about his muscly pecs. But now …

'Oh God, Alyssa. I'd honestly better sleep downstairs if you don't want this to go any further. I don't think I can be here with you, like this, and not want to …'

She put a finger to his lips. Because if he said *throw you on the bed and do hot things to you*, she might just explode.

He moved her finger away, his face coming down to hers. Their lips found each other, touching gently at first, as though neither of them could quite believe this was happening again. And this time, they wouldn't be interrupted by a hoofed hog called Nicole Pigman.

She felt his lips twitching into the biggest smile, before something like lust must have taken over him too. Then their mouths moved together, his groaning with a deep *at last* pleasure, hers falling into a trance that felt oh so familiar. She knew this kiss, she remembered every part of it. Maybe not this exact one, but the memory of how it felt to kiss him properly was flooding back. She'd dreamed about it more times than she cared to admit, but the reality of it felt so instinctive, she didn't even need to think.

It wasn't long before they fell into Devan's fresh, white bed, kissing deeply, arms wrapped around each other, like they had forever to remember the way. As much as she'd imagined him naked in the shower, now their bodies were entwined, soft towelling still between them, there seemed no rush for anything. It was as though they didn't need anything more, in that moment, but to hold each other and let their hearts and bodies reacquaint.

# Chapter 30

'I told you I was good.'

Devan walked into the bedroom with a breakfast tray, still wearing nothing but a bath towel wrapped around his lower half.

Alyssa sat up in bed, her own towel still loosely around her, her eyebrows raised in question. His cheeky tone and accompanying wink suggested he meant *good in the bedroom*. Though they'd done nothing more than luxuriate in slow, deep kisses and slip into an exhausted sleep in each other's arms. That much had been heaven enough.

'Good at ... making breakfast?' she asked, eyeing the tray of pastries, fruit, toast, various jars, and huge tubs of peanut butter and chocolate spread. And she'd be giving him extra marks for the cafetiere and range of mini coffee syrups.

'Good at not being bad.' He put his tray on the bed and climbed on. 'I just slept next to the hottest woman ever, who I have *uncontrollable* feelings for.' He rubbed his bare chest to signify feelings above the waist, though Alyssa hoped he had a heady mix of both. 'And your towel and modesty are still intact.'

She smiled as he kissed her on the nose, leaving a buttery smudge that told her he wasn't so good at resisting toast.

'You do know that was the best night of my life?' she heard

her mouth saying, before she had chance to stop it. She grabbed a pain au chocolat and bit down, before anything else tumbled out.

'Being knee-deep in a litter of squealing piglets, then falling asleep next to a man in a wet towel? You must have had some dull nights before you came back to Hartglove.'

She gave him a jokey nudge.

'You know what I mean. Just ... being with you, I guess.' She busied herself with pouring coffee, not used to allowing herself to have much in the way of feelings, let alone talk about them.

'I felt it too,' he said softly, layering peanut butter and jam onto a croissant. She knew she had good reason to like him.

'And you do know that once breakfast is done, I'm going to invite you to stop being *Good Old Devan*?'

He started coughing on his mouthful, and she thrust him some water. When he looked at her, his eyes were a mix of lustful imaginings and wateriness from nearly choking.

'Like, unleashing my inner bad boy?'

He was wearing his geek-chic glasses, which were doing *everything* for her inner bad girl.

'Yes please,' she replied simply, as though ordering a slice of toast.

He made to take his glasses off.

'Nuh-uh. I'm going to need you to keep those on.'

He nodded slowly. 'And the towel?'

'Oh, I'm going to enjoy taking that off you myself.'

And suddenly the tray was on the floor, and they were kneeling to face each other on the bed, towels still tantalisingly wrapped. Devan's hands reached out to cup her face and she shuffled into him, their lips pulling together in another deep kiss. All parts of her were flaming to life.

His hands moved to her hair, grasping as though desperate for her, wanting to get closer. All at once she felt adored, desired, lusted after – and she *loved* the sensation. She groaned, to let him know how much.

Her hands ached to tear his towel off right then. To get her eyes on *all* of him. To touch him, to feel him inside her, to move with him, over and over ... And yet, the slowness of last night's kissing and waiting and wanting had been divine. She longed to savour this. She'd wanted him for so long – she'd literally dreamed about it for years. Yes, she wanted him to be unrelentingly *bad* with her, that morning. But she wanted to bask in every ruthless moment.

'I'm waiting for your guidance,' he groaned into her mouth.

She let her fingers trail down his chest, stopping just below his belly button, before pulling away with a tease. 'Mr Shaw, you're being far too polite,' she breathed, moving one of his hands to the top of her towel and encouraging him to undo it. 'But seeing as you ask, I want you to devour me. *Slowly.* So I can enjoy every glorious moment.'

Alyssa wasn't quite sure where the words were coming from. She didn't usually indulge in kinky bedroom chat nor demand *bad* things. But there was something in the way they already knew each other and how he made her feel accepted just like she was, that carried her tongue to unexpected places. She was curious to find out where else it might travel.

'Let me savour this first too.' His eyes widened as he ran his hands gently over her towel, as though imagining her for one last time before she was his to unwrap.

She felt her breasts throb as his palms rested there, before his hands ran down her front, stopping to clench her waist and then slipping to her bum, to rock her gently into him.

She looked down, both seeing and feeling his desire, pulsing beneath his towel. The bulge she'd ogled yesterday was growing.

'Oh *God*, Alyssa. You do not know how many times I've dreamed about this. And so much more. Am I even awake?' He shook his head. 'I keep having this *really* hot dream, when we're right back in my teenage bedroom. Only in my version, I am *not* being as good as I was that night.'

She laughed softly. 'Can I tell you a secret?' she whispered into his neck, her mouth moving towards his ear. 'I've been having that dream for a *long* time. And I'm ready for the real one. Do you want to show me how your version goes?'

His hands moved back to the top of her towel, and at last he untucked it, letting it fall to the bed. She heard his sharp intake of breath, saw his eyes widen again as he took her in. She'd been his fantasy, as much as he'd been hers. But now, it felt like so much more. They could close their eyes and live out their fantasies with anyone. But she only wanted *him*. Smelling of fresh towels and buttery croissants, hair mussy, glasses on, off or quite honestly anywhere.

So she reached her hand to the top of his towel and finally undid that too.

## Chapter 31

Alyssa had seen him naked below the waist before, when they'd dated. She'd seen him excited, she'd touched him – even if she'd been shy and inexperienced then. But he was a full-blown, hot-blooded, *raging-with-desire* man now, and she was a woman who knew what to do. Though as his towel fell to the bed, exposing his fully erect manhood, the sight was even more impressive than her Devan dreams had prepared her for.

She reached out to touch his lower stomach, letting her fingers slip downwards, watching him twitch to be held by her. Her hand encircled his penis, moving up and down with a gentle but sure tease, his hips rocking towards her, his eyes closing in pleasure. Watching how much he wanted her, how desperate he looked for her touch, made her own pleasure swell.

He put a hand on top of hers, urging her to slow down.

'I want this to last,' he said, his voice hoarse, his eyes flickering open to drink her in again.

She shrugged. 'I have all day.'

His knees buckled and he fell backwards onto the bed, pulling him with her.

They laughed at the messy way they landed, kicking away the towels, making space on the bed to lie back and enjoy each other.

'What do you want from *Very Bad Devan*?' he asked, before blinking a few times, his eyes still lustfully gorgeous behind his thick-framed glasses. 'Sorry. Too pornstar-ish?'

She laughed again, loving that they could be hotly intimate and still make light-hearted fun. 'Not pornstar-ish enough.'

'Then show me where you want me.'

'Everywhere,' she concluded. 'One room at a time, and there should definitely be a shower involved, at some point.' She winked at him, enjoying the way his mouth opened slightly, as though imagining it and liking what sprung to mind. 'But before a hot shower, we ought to get dirty.' She reached over and grabbed the jar of chocolate spread, handing it to him, before lying back on the bed. 'Do your worst.'

'On my white sheets?' He eyed the jar and began slowly opening it, getting back up onto his knees and taking up a position between her legs. 'You *are* asking for bad. It's a good job I use a reputable brand of washing detergent.'

She put a finger over her lips to indicate an end to the clean talk.

Her nipples were on fire for him by the time he'd smeared them with a thin layer of chocolate, taking his sweet time and watching her squirm in anticipation. He lowered his head towards them, holding eye contact in the most erotic way, his lips parting. She heard herself gasp with joy as his tongue reached one, teasing the tip and tracing slow circles that made her mind spin. She grabbed his hair and pulled him down insistently, her body writhing as his mouth began to suck.

Was a nipple orgasm a thing? He was *making it* a thing.

'Dare I say, you taste better than a pain au choc,' he teased.

'You may dare,' she breathed back, encouraging his hand towards the soft spot between her legs that was now violently pulsing for him.

'I can do better than that.' He reached for the chocolate spread. 'If you like?'

'I like,' she heard herself squeak.

*Like* turned out to be an understatement, as he swept a sliver of chocolate between her legs and moved in swiftly to lick it off.

'More,' she managed to say, as he made to move his head away. '*So* much more of that.'

'This is reminding me of my Alyssa *hot* dreams.'

She was a big fan of his dreams already.

She rocked her pelvis into him, gasping through every moment of deep, delicious pleasure. His hands grasped her hips, pulling her into him, her groans becoming uncontrollable. Together, they moved faster, her hands in his hair, guiding him, clutching him, wanting his tongue to be firmer, deeper, *badder*. And soon the waves of sheer bliss were unstoppable. Rippling through her again and again, flooding her, washing over her, filling her up.

And then his fingers eased gently inside her, moving further than his tongue could reach. *Yes, there.* Oh God, she was his.

The world went white as she made her final thrust towards him, desperate to feel him against her and inside her in every way. The throb became an undulating thrill, and she was on top of every world as pleasure buzzed and the whiteness turned to a kaleidoscope. *Just like in her dreams.*

As her orgasm came to a shuddering end, Devan gently released her, coming to lie beside her, to hold her. Noticing her shiver as her body cooled down, he pulled up a stretch of duvet, even with the threat of more chocolate spread to wash off.

'Are we dirty enough for that shower?' he whispered into her ear as they lay together, his arm around her, smoothing her now-damp hair.

'Not even close,' she whispered back, leaning to pull her handbag from the floor and searching for the condoms she knew were inside.

'Cherry flavour,' he read, as she placed it next to him.

'You're not the only one who wants a taste sensation,' she chuckled. 'Or maybe I'll taste you before I put one on, if you're game?'

'Sounds like my kind of game,' he confirmed, as she moved down his body, tongue first, to return his gift.

Like her, it didn't take him long to come, as though they'd waited for each other for far too long already. Hearing him gasp her name and become devoured by desire for her, his body contorting, defenceless to her touch, made her own yearning rise again. She slid up next to him, wanting to luxuriate in the aftermath of his climax, to hear his ragged breath, to feel the pounding of his heart.

*His heart.* It didn't feel like long ago that she would have denied love was a thing. She would have insisted a heart was only there to keep you alive. But the more time she spent with Devan, the more she knew hers was beating for something way beyond survival. His might be pounding from physical exertion right then, but she sensed, like hers, that it was filling with something else too. All of her adult life, she'd had boyfriends – for convenience, or company, or for someone to be seen with. There had always been bedroom action. But she hadn't even had full sex with Devan yet, and already her heart was turning to ... mush? Her legs were wobbly, her soul was like jelly, her insides felt warm and wanted. And that was both exhilarating and terrifying.

Yet for once, she didn't want to run – at least not in that moment. She wanted to feel *all* of it. Right there. With him.

So she listened to her tumbling emotions and the thing that was beating for him in her ribcage and right through her body, and pulled open a condom wrapper. And with Devan's nod of approval, she teased him awake and slid it onto him. She wasn't ready to admit what she was starting to wonder about love, but if he could *make love* to her with his mouth like that, she was willing to evaluate what else he was capable of.

She straddled one leg over him and hovered for a moment, his firmness tantalisingly close. They took a few beats to look at each other, eyes locked, as though savouring this one last instant before everything changed. Then his eyes moved down her, taking in her small but firm breasts, the dip of her navel, the slight swell of her satiated belly. But there was at least one part of her that was ready for more. As his hands moved to her hips, she slipped herself down onto him, relishing each glorious second as he eased into place.

'Oh t*hiiiiissss*,' she yelped, as the last incredible inch pushed into her, more deeply than she'd ever felt a man before him. Her dreams had *not* done him justice. Had he been working out his penis muscles too? She mentally changed his name from *Devan* to *Heaven*.

As he thrust his hips so he was even further inside her – if that was humanly possible – she decided this was going to be one life-altering day. And they hadn't needed a love app to plan it.

**Instagram post by @alyssaheart_thelovecoach:**

*Feel like I haven't checked in for a while. Current status – WOW*

*#heavenisaplaceonearth*

*#reasonstobecheerful #chocolatespread*

*Email from: alyssa@alyssaheart.co.uk*

*To: sandiandandi@not-mail.com*

*Dear Sandi and Andi*

*Apologies for not getting back to you sooner in response to your love coaching enquiry. Let's set up a call! I'd be thrilled to help you.*

*Email from: alyssa@alyssaheart.co.uk*

*To: teijo@luckysevenmedia.co.uk*

*Let me check with Devan about the exclusive on my past in Hartglove, but YES – I think we can sort something.*

**Private message from @agent_rufusdiamond to @alyssa-heart_thelovecoach:**

**@agent_rufusdiamond** – Sorry I couldn't make it to your latest task. I had something stuck in my U-bend. All sorted now. Right mess, it was.

## Chapter 32

'Well, you've changed.'

Alyssa looked up from her spot in the allotment, where she was on her knees, sowing seeds. Beetroot, broad beans, Swiss chard – whatever that was. Yes, it felt like a time for new beginnings – at least for her vegetables. Even the spring air, laced as it was with the scent of sweet apple blossom from the nearby trees, held the promise of it. Or perhaps someone was harbouring another stash of that upside-down apple cake.

'Have I?' Alyssa replied, shielding her eyes to see Mrs Halfpenny, who was sitting in her purple wingback chair, drinking from a chipped china cup.

She could feel her cheeks colouring slightly, which was all the more obvious when you didn't bother with foundation. She'd opted for minimal make-up, keen to feel the spring sun on her face, and not even paranoid that people might gasp at her lack of under-eye Touch Éclat. She was getting used to the fact no one around here much cared whether or not she'd faffed with false lashes, or if she wore a hoodie that was only from Primark, or even if her pink hair looked dishevelled in a ponytail that her choppy waves kept breaking free from. And she kind of liked that – for now.

'Getting stuck in, even though that guy with the camera

isn't here.' Mrs Halfpenny's brow creased. 'And something else. You're smiling like a noodlehead. Have you been playing hide the sausage?'

Alyssa spluttered. Well, she hadn't been expecting that. 'No, you?' she replied, unable to disguise the wry smirk on her face.

'Not on your nellie. No one's getting near my baps. Anyway, we might be improving a bit in the polls, but Hartglove still holds that most loveless award. Though something's definitely cheering you up, and it's not those knobbly artichokes.'

Alyssa gave her allotment friend a wink and carried on with her seed sowing. She didn't exactly know what she was doing, other than a few tips she'd gleaned from Horace, when he wasn't busy with Anna Farina's tiramisu. But Mrs H's words rang a bell in her head that had been sounding more since that first morning in Devan's bed. Hartglove did deserve more *lovey-ness*. Alyssa had spent the last week feeling like she was dancing on the ceiling in sequin hotpants. She wasn't quite sure if she was ready to concede love was a thing – but whatever the hell kind of magic this was, surely everyone deserved a sprinkle.

And she may have come to Hartglove with no intentions other than getting paid. Though for the first time in a long while, she actually wanted to help people. To discover *their person* or to find their way back to them, if life had thrown obstacles in their path. And it wasn't just for the social media esteem. Dare she say it – she simply cared. Her hand fluttered to her chest.

'Got into your heart as well as your bloomers,' Mrs Halfpenny said knowingly. 'He is a good sort, that Devan Shaw.'

Alyssa blushed again, remembering plenty of good and unashamedly *bad* fun she'd been having with Devan. Although they'd spent a lot of time just chatting too, and watching romcoms like they used to, giving them a 'cheese rating' out of ten – even though she'd been sworn off love stories for years before she'd come back here. They'd even been getting into *quinoa cake*.

'I heard you spoke to Sylvie after our chat in the truth chair.

You made peace with your dad yet?'

Was Mrs Halfpenny nodding towards her chair again? Well, Alyssa didn't have time for that. And anyway, her parents were on their second honeymoon, which was a convenient reason not to have that heart-to-heart.

'No,' she said quietly.

She hadn't been in touch with Sylvie again either – although Devan had told her she'd put her name down to try and find a match through 'Appy Together, which sounded positive. A huge part of Alyssa wanted to fling her arms around her old best friend and get things back to the way they were. But like she'd admitted to Devan – she couldn't promise she was sticking around. She certainly hadn't planned to. As nice as this all felt in the short term, how long could she last here? Right now, it was a town with no prospects. It wasn't close to London, where the bigger opportunities were.

And more than that, she just wasn't accustomed to letting people into her business for any length of time. What if she felt claustrophobic and wanted to run? What if she was so unaccustomed to dealing with emotional stuff that she didn't know how? What if she was dreadful at being a good friend or a committed girlfriend or even a loving daughter? Not to mention that staying here long term with Devan may involve whole new stepmum-type role-model responsibilities. What if she simply wasn't *enough*?

She shook her head. Bloody hell, she should just get back to concentrating on the vegetables.

'Talk of the devil,' Mrs H declared.

Alyssa jumped and turned her head. Phew, it was Devan. She'd invited him to the Apple Blossom Lane gardens herself – and not just for the broad beans.

'Cup of tea, lad?' Mrs Halfpenny asked him. 'And have you brought biscuits?'

'Custard creams, at your service.' Devan winked at the older lady and edged the packet out of his pocket. 'Though I'm sure you have endless supplies of stored apples and cake in that shed of yours.'

Mrs Halfpenny tapped her nose like she wasn't giving away any secrets.

Alyssa smiled, happy Devan wasn't completely shaking off his good-boy side.

'Can I interest Miss Heart in anything?' he asked, stepping towards her.

She stood, giving his trouser pockets a discreet once-over, in case any more treats were about to emerge.

'I'll let you know,' said Alyssa, her voice sounding huskier than she'd expected as Devan got so close she could feel his warm breath against her cheeks. Did he smell faintly of chocolate spread this morning? Now she was definitely blushing.

They'd agreed to keep their budding relationship to themselves for now, not wanting to put pressure on things nor to be hounded by Teijo for more details. And Devan had Sylvie and Emmalina to think about, so they needed to deal with matters sensitively, and in the right order. Though Alyssa was already enjoying the thrill of their covert operations.

And if she was honest, she wasn't yet ready to publicly admit defeat on her mission to prove the love app couldn't make her fall for anyone. She'd spent more than a decade carefully constructing her persona and the fences around her heart. She wasn't about to let it all come crashing down because he served an exceptionally thorough breakfast. Not to mention that the last time she'd declared her feelings for him she'd been left looking like a *noodlehead* in turtle's clothing.

'You two aren't fooling me,' their friend in the purple chair chimed in. 'You know, Mr Halfpenny used to enjoy his conjugals in the great outdoors, so don't think I won't know if you try nipping off. Just watch out for gooseberry bushes. Those thorns wreak havoc on your backside.'

Alyssa spluttered out a laugh. 'She was not this cheeky in the days when she used to dish out fizzy sweets in the corner shop,' she whispered to Devan.

'We'll watch out for those gooseberries,' Devan called back, giving Alyssa's bum a quick squeeze and making her jump.

When they'd grabbed tea from Mrs H and found themselves a quiet spot to sit under the apple trees, Alyssa talked Devan through her allotment plans and he offered to help, even though it wasn't an official task day. Alyssa had once thought it was sneaky of the app to throw them into an ongoing project, but much like they'd both enjoyed going back to check on Nicole Pigman and had agreed to help out more at the animal rescue centre, Alyssa was coming to embrace most of the app's ideas. Which brought her to another reason she wanted to talk to Devan.

'Can we influence the love tasks 'Appy Together chooses for us?'

He ran a hand through his hair. 'No.'

Did he sound a little shifty?

She gave him a teasing nudge. 'Go on. You fixed it for us to get stuck in that tiny tent, didn't you?'

'I did not! I would have arranged something swishier than a piece of two-man polyester. Thanks for your faith in my taste in romantic dates, but nope. You can't beat the algorithm.'

'But did you try?'

'What do you take me for?' He nudged her back. 'I only use my powers for good.'

'Would it count as *good* if I wanted to use our next task to bring more love to Hartglove? I know it's a cause that's important to you, what with Emmalina and your general adoration for this kooky place. Not to mention that you and your T-shirt twin always like an excuse to get new tops printed.' She nodded to Mrs Halfpenny's current '*Save Hartglove – Lettuce Be Friends*' number.

'I do love an ill-fitting, badly sloganed T-shirt,' he admitted. 'So what are you thinking?'

It didn't take her long to reel off her idea, even if part of her was still petrified at the thought. It would mean facing something she'd barely been able to think about since she'd come back here. There would be a lot of cobwebs to dust off, both real and metaphorical. But like Hedgehog from the animal centre had said – sometimes your mission had to be bigger than your own crap. And now and again, your mission had to change its course – even if she wasn't going to make a song and dance about it.

'Miss Heart, are you starting to care about your little old hometown?' Devan asked quietly, when she was finished.

'Shh, we can't have people saying that,' she joked. 'It would be bad for my *high-flying, girl-about-London* image.'

'True,' he said. Although she wasn't sure his smile met his eyes.

Then he stood a little abruptly as though he was as spooked by the L-word 'London' as much as she was by 'love'.

Perhaps he was stuck with the thought that she'd once chosen it above staying here and being with him, and she could again.

He brushed himself down and began to stroll, so she followed.

'You're not missing your yoga retreats and the glamorous London parties?' he asked. 'I mean, I wouldn't blame you.'

She laughed, a touch sadly. 'Some of it was just for the pics. Yoga gives me a crick in the neck, and don't get me started on fake-smiling until your face cracks.'

'Damn it. I quite enjoyed your Instagram snaps in those extremely figure-hugging yoga pants.'

'How dare you!' She gave him a play slap.

'Though I prefer you in the flesh, wearing allotment-muddy joggers. Or anything.'

They'd reached a spot near some bushes, and he pulled her towards him by the waistband. She giggled, their faces coming close.

'Apologies for my weird, *jealous of London* moment. And I'm sorry I can't hack my own app to help with your idea. But I know you could make it happen without an algorithm fixing it. And I'm here for the donkey work. I know the community would be right behind you too, with their bunting and banners.'

'And probably a lot of apple-themed cake,' she added. Because thinking about sugary offerings detracted from the part of her brain that was screaming, *What fresh hell are you getting yourself into?*

'You had me at cake,' he whispered, his hands moving around her waist and settling gently on the small of her back, giving her happy shivers.

Their faces drew nearer, and she couldn't resist pressing her lips to his, even if she wasn't usually the sort for making out in the town centre's foliage.

Pastel pink blossom petals wisped around them in the light breeze, one landing softly on her cheek but not distracting her. Her hands slid up to his hair, her fingers running through the back of it, tugging him down so they could kiss more deeply.

'You are going to single-handedly ruin my good-guy image,' he groaned, as she let her hands move down his back to that firm bum of his.

'Who says I'll only use one hand?'

When they finally pulled away from each other, Alyssa trying not to think about bare bottoms and gooseberry bushes, she thought she heard movement close by. Did she just spot someone with a phone angled towards them hiding in the next row of shrubbery? But whoever it was ducked away quickly and disappeared.

Then Alyssa laughed. They'd probably just been waving their phone around to get a signal, because reception *was* pretty iffy. She wasn't living in a spy movie, and nobody around here much cared what Alyssa Heart got up to. And she was learning she liked it that way.

## Chapter 33

'I thought you were going to let *me* know any exclusive news first?'

It was Teijo's voice accosting Alyssa through her phone, which she had balanced on a pot of spiced apple jam as she made her toast. She was padding around her kitchen in The Cow Shed, wearing floral PJs with her hair in a towel, so at least it wasn't a video call.

She'd been adding a few bits to the old barn lately, to make the place more homely and for a better backdrop for Instagram pics. A few fake plants, so she didn't have to commit to watering. Some artfully positioned books to make the shelf less naked, though she still preferred a trashy magazine. Even a designer mouse habitat for Pikachu and his mouse girlfriend, who thankfully hadn't yet produced fifty rodent babies.

Luckily, she'd managed to dodge Jess's frequent offers of macramé heart bunting – though it was only a matter of time.

'I am,' she yawned, not really in the mood for a telling-off. She had half promised Teijo something exclusive about her past in Hartglove, but she hadn't quite got around to it, because she'd been too busy spending time with Devan.

'So why are there photos of you and Devan all over the internet, covered in what looks like confetti, and kissing in a bush?'

'What?' Alyssa grabbed her phone and jabbed the screen. 'Where am I looking?'

It only took a moment to locate the photos, all over social media – because she'd been tagged in them. They'd been posted by what looked like a new and probably fake account called @whoami23456, which had a close-up of a dog's nose as its profile picture. She read the comments.

*@lovedupbuttercup* – *Please tell me you're IN LOVE??!!! This is amazing! Is the love app working? (Weddings bells?!)*

*@garypratt* – *The app is a load of shite. She's doing it for the money. And what do you call a woman who gets dirty for cash?*

*@tinatinyharris* – *Shut up, Pratt Face. She's happy – look at her. Sounds like you don't know how that feels if you've got nothing better to do than troll people. Go Alyssa! We're rooting for you and Devan.*

At least her disgruntled ex-coaching client Gary Pratt and his pathetic messages had been drowned out by the noise of positive comments. *But still.* What a scumbag. And though she should have been grateful for the tide of good wishes for her and Devan, she was *not* ready for this news to be out yet. Why had she even invited Devan to meet her that day at Apple Blossom Lane, when she knew how tough it was not to kiss him in public?

'And that's apple blossom – *not* confetti,' Alyssa clarified.

She flopped down onto a kitchen chair, the legs scraping against the hard tiles. This could add pressure their tentative new relationship didn't need. They'd been broken by each other before, and even though they both now knew the truth about the past, their cracks were still healing. Having been sworn off true feelings for so long, she barely trusted herself to navigate whatever was growing inside her, and she had no clue if she'd bolt at the first sign of pressure – like she always did.

Not to mention this news would sabotage her mission to prove 'Appy Together couldn't make two people fall for each other. Maybe her point made less sense as their relationship progressed, but publicly admitting she was wrong felt like choosing her heart over her head. Eight days of incredibly good shagging should not make her drop her principles like a pair of cheap knickers. People needed time. And she did care about Devan and the town's causes, but she still believed there was a more human-connection-inspired way – and she'd been working on it.

'Argh.' She pushed herself to standing, rubbing her pounding temples.

These bloody photos. Who had taken them? Her mind raced back to that rustle in the nearby bushes yesterday, and someone who might have been pointing a phone screen. But seriously? This wasn't a James Bond film. Couldn't she even squeeze a nice bum in a rose bush without people wanting high-definition footage?

'It's amazing news about you and Devan, so ... Can you give me something exclusive, for promotions?' Teijo's voice broke through her blur of thoughts, reminding her he was still on the line. 'Not to nag, but you did promise.'

'We're not together,' she lied, thinking on her feet. 'The kiss was just a dare. A bit of blossom-infused clickbait, to bring more buzz on social media and keep people guessing. Definitely not falling for each other.' She gave a cheesy smile, even though he couldn't actually see. 'So there's no relationship exclusive. But we're willing to give a brief story about our past – if you could help us spread the news about something in return? Because this would make a great story too.'

Alyssa filled him in on the idea she'd run past Devan at the love gardens. Devan had been full of his usual enthusiasm, and although the idea still made her quake, it was something she wanted to try. It would hopefully bring more 'love' to Hartglove – even if she still thought of that word in inverted commas. And she could just imagine Mrs Halfpenny giving her top marks for pushing through her fears instead of skating around the roundabout like a dizzy doughnut. In fact, Mrs H would probably be right there, serving the chintzy-cupped tea.

'I like it,' Teijo said slowly. 'Even if I'm surprised you're suggesting it.'

'Well, we can't leave everything in the hands of a love app algorithm. Any idea what our next task will be, by the way?'

'Miss Heart, you know I can't tell you that. But let's just say it could tie in nicely. This app is cleverer than you think.'

***Private messages between @alyssaheart_thelovecoach and @garypratt:***

***@alyssaheart_thelovecoach*** – *Are you behind @whoami23456? Seriously, stop it. Butt out of my business.*

***@garypratt*** – *I have better things to do than hide in bushes, spying on you. Get over yourself.*

***Private message from @agent_rufusdiamond to @alyssaheart_thelovecoach:***

***@agent_rufusdiamond*** – *Loving the pics of you and Devan with the secret bush snogging. Scandal sells. (Tell him to) keep it up!*

## Chapter 34

Alyssa turned the corner into Apple Blossom Lane, nearly jumping out of her skin when she saw the impressive crowd that had amassed outside Hartglove Hall.

'Oh.' She paused to lean against an apple tree, unable to take it all in.

When the idea to bring the old town hall back to life had first sparked in her mind, she'd dismissed it as foolish, bordering on reckless. As much as the space had once been alive and buzzing with everything from spring balls to summer fetes, and cosy Christmas markets – it had also been the scene of her humiliating demise. The place where she'd stood on a stage, in front of everyone, and sang her heart out in a slightly drunken grand gesture of love – to the tune of a certain annoying song, wearing a frankly preposterous costume. It might as well be stamped with the words *rejection, public humiliation* and *wow, that was dumb.*

Why would she want to open up the dusty doors on something that was easier left padlocked?

And yet as she stood with the keys in her clammy, slightly shaking hands, she knew it was something she had to conquer. So much of her past had left ugly scrapes on her present. Since she'd been back, she'd learned the gut-wrenching truth that if she'd faced things instead of fled, if she'd talked instead of blocking people out, things may have been different. She might have saved herself – and others – twelve years of hurt.

Perhaps this gesture was a small way to do something good. And if there was a way to help bring more togetherness and sense of community back to Hartglove, she wasn't going to hide in her Cow Shed and avoid it, like a big baby calf.

'Well, this is a snazzy idea,' said Mrs Halfpenny, barging to the front of the crowd and flashing her *Save Hartglove – Everything's Gonna Be Hall-Right* T-shirt from under her coat. 'I love a good project. You've even got me started on a quest of my own.' She winked.

Alyssa dreaded to think.

'She's just here for my butties,' Sausage Sandra mock-whispered, pointing at Mrs H.

In the couple of weeks since Alyssa had come up with the hall-themed brainwave, she'd shouted about it on social media, popped her head in at local shops and businesses, and had even handed out flyers – even though she hadn't made a poster since she'd been approximately nine years old. Though she hadn't dared to believe many people would come.

But this. This was like an extreme version of that day the locals had turned up at The Cow Shed with everything from teabags to a clothes horse. Only today, there were people with ladders and paint pots, buckets of cleaning items, great swathes of material, a sewing machine … and of course, food. Because you could always rely on the residents of Hartglove to feed people.

'I think it's brilliant,' said Anna, who was clutching a large box of what looked like *torta di mele*, which Alyssa had come to learn was Italian apple cake, made from the town's own apples, with a fresh lemon twist.

Horace was standing next to her with two large terracotta pots on his other side. They contained what Alyssa guessed were small apple trees, though their blossom was a much brighter pink than the blossom trees in the lane – almost the shade of her hair.

'I bought these to go either side of the hall's doors.' Horace tipped his head in a small bow. 'As a thank you for this magnificent idea. They bloom a bit later than the town's early-flowering hybrids. But who doesn't love a late bloomer?'

He beamed at Alyssa. It took all of her inner strength not to start blubbing before she'd begun.

'Thank you,' she managed to whisper. 'Although I don't deserve so much credit.' Too choked to say much more, she nodded her own thanks to the group of residents.

Anna came to the rescue with a few more words. 'I didn't live here when the hall was the beating heart of things, but I've heard great stories.'

Alyssa remembered that many of the town's older couples had met and dated at the hall – including her own parents. Not that she would rate their free-for-all love story, even if her mum swore they were better now.

'So many good times,' said a familiar voice through the crowd.

And there Alyssa had been, trying to hold it together.

It was Devan's mum, Dawn. Alyssa felt tears spring to her eyes. With Devan's parents' long romantic trip, she hadn't seen Dawn since she'd been back in Hartglove. Dawn had always exuded love and warmth in a way that not even Alyssa could deny, and growing up, she'd always felt so close to her.

'Come here, love.' Dawn opened her arms and Alyssa gravitated into them.

Devan's mum smelt of rose tea and shea butter, like she always had, and her jumper felt soft against Alyssa's cheek, even though she hadn't meant to nestle into her quite so weirdly.

Dawn stroked the back of Alyssa's hair. 'We've missed you around here. Welcome home.'

Alyssa tried to stifle a sob, because she hadn't come here to blubber into her boyfriend's mum's mohair. And *home*? That word was nearly as terror-inducing as *love*.

'Where do you want us with these ladders?' somebody shouted. 'And who's letting us in?'

*Right, yes.* Alyssa had been grateful for the distraction, but it was time to stop procrastinating.

She jangled the keys to signify she was on it. Which she sort of, probably was. It was strange she hadn't yet spied Devan, but she could surely brave this herself. Turning to the flaking doors, she took a deep breath and inserted the largest rusty key.

She allowed her exhalation to be a long one, imagining she was breathing out her doubts and fears, and the jumble of painful memories. She was about to do a positive thing. To bring people together. Perhaps even help the town to shake off the stigma of their loveless award and grab themselves a future winning spot. And how fantastic that would be for her own reputation as a love coach. Making things happen. Proving her worth. Showing what her skills could do.

Yes, she was a goal-setting, people-motivating, problem-solving ninja. With new clients and fresh ideas, Alyssa Heart was making a comeback.

She swung open the doors and stepped in. *Oh.* Or maybe not.

She'd been expecting a bit of disarray and dust. Perhaps a few floorboards and curtains to mend. But she hadn't been expecting *this.* The hall looked like a cross between a building site and a much larger version of the World's Grottiest Flat that she and Pikachu had once escaped from. Who did all this junk belong to, and did anyone own a skip? Alyssa hoped someone had decent DIY skills. She clapped a hand over her eyes and let out a long *urgh.*

'Where's Devan when you need him?' she asked nobody in particular.

*Reasons to be cheerful.* At least with all this rubble, she could barely see the stage of doom.

'He came to ours for a cuppa this morning,' Dawn replied. 'Then he got distracted by his phone and said he had something to sort out. I'm not sure what his plans are.'

'Right,' said Alyssa. Well, she'd encouraged him not to feel typecast as *Good Old Devan* – though he could have picked a less busy day.

'It's fine,' said Alyssa's mum, Pearl, arriving behind her, with Alyssa's dad in tow. 'We've got this. More Love in Hartglove!'

Alyssa's skin prickled. She knew she'd had that chat with her mum, where they'd eaten quinoa cake and her mum had insisted their marriage was now committed and happier – especially with the help of a certain app, and a second honeymoon in Gran Canaria. But so many lies had come before that she wasn't sure what to believe. And she still hadn't heard her dad's version. Did she want to?

'It's jolly fun that you're bringing us all together,' Pearl enthused. 'What are you planning?' She pointed at the devastation.

She had no clue what she was planning anymore, other than it ought to involve a massive plate of that Italian apple cake.

Alyssa noticed her dad looking at her in a way that seemed almost encouraging, for a man who'd spent the last fifteen years telling her to get a job in a bank. In hindsight, that might have been easier. Though she resolved to avoid hearing it today.

'Shall we do selfies for Insta?' asked Pearl.

'I can do pics and logistics,' said Teijo, finally joining them.

Alyssa wouldn't leave Teijo in charge of a raffle, but she was grateful he'd agreed to create some online buzz about Alyssa's project to bring the hall back to life, as part of 'Appy Together's Save Hartglove mission. She'd promised him all the best stories, even though she now doubted there would be much to cover, unless their followers enjoyed DIY disasters.

'And I'm here for the nutritious quinoa bars,' Pearl added.

'Not today, thank you,' Alyssa sing-songed. Although Alyssa had been letting some parts of her façade drop, she was still clinging on to some things out of habit, and perhaps to protect herself – because burning *all* bridges was simply reckless. She and

Devan had recently let Teijo have some 'exclusive' info on limited parts of their past together in Hartglove, so at least she didn't have to keep pretending she'd never been Beryl and had no ties to the town. Though Devan had seemed surprised when Alyssa insisted on holding the interview in a smart hotel, to keep up her image.

And as far as the outside world knew, she and Devan were not a couple. Her reputation in trying to prove a love coach was a safer bet than an algorithm was too important to her. At least Devan was good enough to respect her wishes, even if it clashed with his desire to show his app worked. She only felt a *teensy* bit guilty.

Her eyes scanned the room, watching folk scratch their heads, wondering where to start. Some were drinking tea and leaning on ladders. Mel from the Splash 'n' Dash launderette had roped in her non-romantic husband. Hedgehog and her fiancé were trying to look busy with a tape measure. Horace was eating *torta di mele*, even though it was barely past breakfast time. There were people of all generations, including plenty she didn't recognise. But still no Devan.

'Pining over your bloke?'

Mrs Halfpenny's voice made Alyssa jump. Oh bleurgh, she had been pining – in a panicky sort of way.

'He's not my bloke,' she said on autopilot.

Mrs Halfpenny rolled her eyes. 'Anyway, it's dandy that you're trying to bring more love to the town. But as one of those coach people, I shouldn't have to remind you that loving *you* comes first. Take it from me, you can't be mooning over folk who aren't here. Get out there and paddle your own steamer.'

Alyssa couldn't believe she was taking advice from a septuagenarian sporting a '*Self-Love Is My Superpower*' badge and what looked like a knitted cape – but perhaps she had a point.

'My new quest,' she explained, as she saw Alyssa eyeing the ensemble. 'Because love is love, even if it's only with yourself.' She gave Alyssa a wink. 'Thanks for inspiring me to get up off my wingback chair and do something worthwhile. I think you've breathed life into us all.'

She rubbed Mrs H on the back, even if she wasn't usually one for too much touching. 'You're a wise and wonderful woman. Let's paddle.'

Buoyed by Mrs Halfpenny's unexpected pep talk, Alyssa moved around the hall, discussing what needed to be done and making plans. With her coaching hat on, she knew how to communicate, adapt and flipping well crack on. A couple of the locals were builders, and there was a surveyor, a painter and decorator, an electrician, and plenty of people who were handy with mops, buckets, sewing machines and a kettle. Alyssa was soon in her element, organising the slackers, making lists, tramping up and down ladders, moving rubbish and scrubbing. If nothing else, it was a more appealing workout than pretending to like yoga in a sweaty pair of leggings.

Time flew so effortlessly that she forgot to look at her phone or worry about sharing photos. She briefly considered calling Devan, but she'd got roped into learning how to change a floorboard, and it helped to have space to process her tricky memories of the hall. He was a grown man, and it was a small enough town that if there had been a catastrophe, they'd know about it.

Alyssa took a moment to assess the scene, as she sneaked one of Sausage Sandra's butties with a cup of her mum's cold tea. Was her aim to bring people together actually working? Of course, it would take more than one day and a bucket of Mr Muscle. But she could hear laughter and see people of all ages pulling together. Was that a strange sense of pride she was feeling? She'd be wearing a knitted cape and a self-love badge, at this rate.

'Thanks for suggesting this,' said Sylvie, tentatively coming over.

Alyssa had seen her across the room at various points throughout the day but had felt awkward and strangely nervous about approaching her, even though she'd pinged a last-minute text to Sylvie the evening before to say she hoped to see her here today. It had been the first time she'd used the number Sylvie had given her. Other than that, Alyssa hadn't been in touch with her since their chat in the retirement home ladies' toilets. Maybe it was stupid, but she felt guilty and foolish for running out on Sylvie all those years ago – even though she'd thought she had good reason. Could she trust herself to be a decent friend now? What experience had she had, and what if she was leaving again anyway? *And what about Emmalina?*

Sylvie had brought some of the residents from Clucky Ducks Retirement, who were busy cutting out triangles for bunting.

'I know the past was a mess,' said Sylvie, looking at Alyssa with those big brown eyes, a pencil tucked behind her ear and her apron on backwards to try and hide some of the tea stains. 'But can we ...'

'Start again?' they both said, at the same time. Alyssa resisted the urge to say '*jinx*' like they used to. She could tell from Sylvie's smile that she was thinking the same.

They both nodded and Sylvie linked arms with Alyssa's and gave it a squeeze, as though a lot of weird years hadn't passed.

'I can definitely see more love in the town today.' Sylvie lowered her voice. 'And feel it.' She nodded towards Jess Halfpenny from the shop. 'Did you know 'Appy Together has paired us? I didn't realise we had so much in common. She's such a cutie.'

'Wow, that's incredible,' said Alyssa, feeling the good vibes inside her swell. 'She *is* a cutie. And a genuine sweetheart too.'

'Yep. Can't wait to check out her tango moves.' Sylvie giggled, like they were both still teenagers.

It had worked out well that Alyssa and Devan's current love task was to learn to dance the tango because it had inspired the first event they would hold at the hall – a tango night. She and Devan had started their lessons already, even though she felt nervous about doing a demonstration on the big night, and she wasn't sure she'd be getting on that stage. The app wanted them to experience fun and closeness, although getting close to Devan with the intensity of the dance and all eyes on them would be *a lot*, when she was pretending to the world that the app wasn't making her fall for him.

'Emmalina really wants to meet you,' Sylvie said gently. 'She wanted to come today, but she had football practice. She wants to be a coach. Football, not love.'

'That's amazing. Though I'm really not sure ...'

'Devan told her you weren't ready to get too comfortable here, because you weren't sure if you were staying. She said to tell you she's not sure she'll be sticking around either, when her coaching career takes off – unless this place perks up and gets a decent football team.' Sylvie laughed. 'In her own words, she'd love to check out that ice-cream place in Taybury with you and Devan, followed by a shopping trip with me and you. Apparently, she wants advice on tango night outfits, and I only ever wear boring jeans. But seriously – no pressure.'

'Wow. They say what they think, these pre-teens,' said Alyssa, adding a quick reassurance that her friend's jeans and jumper combo looked great. 'And Emmalina sounds like quite the organiser. She could probably teach me a thing or two about being a coach. I ... I'll think about it.' It was a big step, and Alyssa didn't want to mess people around while her emotions were still so new.

'Whatever you decide, I trust you,' said Sylvie, echoing Devan's sentiments. 'Even if you don't yet trust yourself. Fresh start, OK?'

How did her old friend see right into her, like she barely had to say a word? Though trusting and being trusted were two huge weights.

Sylvie pulled her into the biggest hug, which almost made a sob shoot up her throat. Because one hug from a real-life friend was worth a million virtual ones from total strangers.

*Then the door swung open.*

## Chapter 35

'The look on everyone's faces earlier, when you strode into the ramshackle hall wearing a tight black sequined tango suit with a rose between your teeth. And it wasn't even tango night.' Alyssa's laugh came right from the depths of her stomach and rolled across Devan's bare chest.

They were lounging on his sofa watching another romcom, draped in blankets, a plate of peanut butter and jam sandwiches balanced on Devan's stomach as they hadn't fancied cooking.

'I knew it wasn't tango night,' said Devan. 'I was just trying to make it up to you for not being there. I had a message I needed to look into, then I got *a bit* carried away with outfit shopping.'

'Nooooo,' Alyssa joked. 'Anyway, thank you for not outing us as a couple, just yet. I need more time.'

Alyssa was still feeling guilty that she was relying on his good nature not to declare their relationship, when most people in their situation would be happily sharing the news. Was it rude of her to still be pretending she was devoid of feelings for him and that his software creation couldn't work?

'I guess a tiny part of me was trying to rebel against being dependable Devan today too – but I couldn't stick it. I must like my nice-guy persona.' He shrugged. 'Maybe it's a role I've fallen into, or maybe it's part of who I am. But as long as that's not *all* I am to people, then I'm comfortable with it.'

She gave him a squeeze, trying to ignore the creep of her conscience. '*Dependable* sounds better than *Good Old*. As long as I sometimes get a glimpse at *Very Bad* Devan.' Her fingers traced down towards his belly button, making their plate of sandwiches wobble.

'Oh, he'll be here.'

She heard the hitch in his voice.

'And how about you?' he asked gently, placing a hand on top of hers to slow its trajectory. 'Are you happy with the role you're still playing?'

'How do you mean?'

He looked like he was choosing his words carefully. 'I know you've been a lot more yourself around Hartglove recently. But with your Instagram image, your latest photos are still about curly kale salads and running up hills in designer Lycra. Both worthy pastimes, but I'm not sure I've ever seen you do either on purpose.' He pointed to their various snack packets. 'People would still accept you if they knew you watched cheesy movies and were partial to a crinkle-cut crisp. And if they don't, are they worth bothering about?'

'Would they though?' She picked at the corner of her sandwich. 'When you build your business and reputation online, people have to choose you. I need to look like I have my life together, so I can help others do the same. Who would pick a coach who's so undisciplined that she lives on junk food and trash TV? Nobody wants a *Beryl*. As Alyssa Heart, balanced, successful woman with an array of uplifting quotes and firm beliefs, people take notice. They *choose* to follow me.'

Even as she said it, she knew it sounded a bit pathetic. Likes and shares on social media didn't hold much meaning, but she needed them if she wanted to cling on to her respectable love coach status.

'Whoa.' Devan broke through her thoughts. 'Plenty of people chose *you* as Beryl Bagnor – and still do. The people who know you in real life and who flipping love hanging around with you, whether it's digging over a field with a tiny trowel and a shit wheelbarrow, eating dry crackers in a tent or getting to do this.'

He cupped her face and leaned down towards her, giving her a kiss that sent shockwaves to her toes.

'Well, if nothing else, your app has given me some interesting new pastimes I could post about,' Alyssa said with a smile, when she came up for air. 'I'm not boring Beryl anymore, and I don't have to pretend to have hobbies when I have all these new ones – from obsessing over hardy vegetables to cuddling stray cats.'

'That's all you're giving my app credit for?' He raised his eyebrows.

'Oh, and throwing me together with this *really* hot guy, who looks adorable in a Save Hartglove top and is no longer just the stuff of dreams.'

And to break with tradition, he wasn't a man she'd chosen for convenience.

They watched as the closing montage of happy-together romcom moments appeared on the TV screen, filling the room with light and laughing faces.

'It's getting tough, pretending we're not together in front of people, when all I want to do is hold you,' said Devan. 'How long are we going to keep this up? I'm not sure I can get through tango night and our dance, without the urge to kiss you like I mean it.'

*Hmm.* Getting up close and personal with Devan on tango night, pretending she didn't want to tear off his tight sequin outfit with her teeth and that her heart wasn't falling for him *would* be a struggle.

'You just want your app to win the bet,' she joked.

'I care more about us, than any of this mission. We could stop the tasks, if you want. Just be together, without winners or losers.'

She pondered it – but she was not a quitter. 'We'll see it through.'

'Even if we're faking it? Pretending we don't care about each other?'

He had an endearing way of asking things without loading them with guilt, which made the pretence feel so much worse.

'Who's going to employ my services as a love coach if a free phone app can fix them? And it's not about winning or losing. It's about me not ballsing up my career. It's a lot to think about.'

That was the point when he could have said *it's my career too, you bloody mean-arse.* Or all manner of things she wouldn't have blamed him for. But he didn't, because he was kind like that. It made her feelings for him swell even more.

'If it helps, I haven't felt like anyone's first choice for a long time. Sylvie needed someone trustworthy. You went out with all the popular guys before you'd look twice at me, when we were younger.'

'I did have a brief bad-boys phase,' she said guiltily. 'But it didn't last. I was immature and just wanted to look cool. All the girls on TV liked guys with a motorbike and a shady reputation. I *honestly* thought you were too good for me. And too cute.'

He looked sceptical. 'My brothers have genuine, happy marriages with women who adore them. But the only woman I ever fell in love with left for London and had her pick of impressive guys and didn't look back.'

'But I ...' She lifted her hand to his face and uncreased his brow. 'I didn't know things then.'

*But she knew better now.* She could tell the world how she felt about him and take some of those hurts away. Couldn't she? Or maybe she could just make it up to him in private, for a short while longer.

He nodded, leaning down to kiss the tip of her nose. 'And I know that. I'm not sharing any of this for the sympathy vote.' There was a twinkle in his eyes. 'But to let you know sometimes we all feel like we might not be good enough, or we're nobody's first choice, or we'll never get our own ridiculously romantic love story.' He nodded at the TV. 'But if Billy Crystal can bag Meg Ryan, there's hope for us all.'

'That's true.' She laughed.

'Do you think you'll stick around after our seven tasks are done?' he asked, looking suddenly unsure of himself. His eyes darted to his phone.

Where had that come from?

'Has someone said something?'

'Of course not. Well, sort of. I did get a couple of social media messages, but it was just a lame attempt at trolling and nothing that bothers me.'

'Devan?'

'Seriously. In my line of work, I experience it all the time, and I'm sure you get things too.'

She nodded. 'And it's early days, in terms of me deciding what I want to do after these tasks are over. I just don't know. We've only been seeing each other for a few weeks. I was with my last boyfriend for nearly two years, and I was packing my suitcase as soon as he started to look smitten. The thought of staying is *nice* – on a good day. But relationships aren't always a bed of geraniums. What if we're still in our honeymoon period and it's less easy when real life and commitments kick in? What if my ingrained instinct is to run when things get tricky or emotions run deep? What if I'm just a big old, frightened wimp?'

And she was acutely aware that if she was going to spend more time in Hartglove, she would have to stop dodging her father and the final handful of history that still troubled her. As well as things were going, there was still an *L-word* she was struggling with, and if she was ever going to ace a relationship, she ought to find the root of that too.

'It sounds like you need ice cream and a pep talk from a certain eleven-year-old. You do know Emmalina will be knocking on your Cow Shed door if you don't agree to that date soon? And meeting her doesn't mean marrying me and buying a three-bed semi in Hartglove. I've told her we're just *"friends"*.'

Well, she didn't want the poor girl getting a complex. Or banging down her door with insightful life advice.

'Then I guess it's Peanut Butter Triple Beasts, with extra whipped cream, all round.'

Maybe meeting this young force of nature was just the brave next step she needed.

## Chapter 36

'We might as well lay all our cards on the table,' said Emmalina, flopping her pink sparkly handbag onto the table and climbing onto a chair opposite Alyssa, Devan grabbing a seat next to her. 'I know you're secretly snogging my dad.'

Alyssa's eyes widened, taking in Devan's daughter for the first time as they assembled for the date for three in I Scream for Ice Cream in the neighbouring town of Taybury. Emmalina looked just like her mum Sylvie had at that age – huge brown eyes with natural lashes to die for, and brunette hair for days. Though she was definitely bolshier.

'Told you she was forward, for her eleven and a half years,' said Devan, with a low whistle.

'We're just good friends,' Alyssa said kindly. She was just about used to the idea of meeting Emmalina, even though it seemed like a tentative step towards being the sort of person who stuck around. But Alyssa wasn't ready to let the young girl get her heart set on her and Devan having a committed *thing*.

Emmalina broke into a grin. 'Hey, whatever you're up to, I'm cool with it. I know how being an adult works.'

'I wish I did.' Alyssa smiled. 'Want to give me some tips?'

'Sure.' Emmalina shrugged. 'If you're buying the ice cream.

Although I'm not having that weird thing with the peanut butter. I'm strictly a strawberry sundae kinda girl.'

'Whatever you fancy is good with me,' said Alyssa, handing out the menus.

They took a moment to choose, talking through the options before going with what they'd all originally been drawn to.

'Your first instinct is usually the right one,' Emmalina said breezily, like a person who'd seen it all.

When the waiter had brought their orders – two Peanut Butter Triple Beasts and a Strawberry Fields Forever – the three of them chatted about all sorts, from Emmalina's love of football to her aversion to green jelly, to her favourite singer, Doja Cat – whom she adored, apart from the swearing. It was sweet how Devan fussed over his daughter, making sure she had the right spoon for her sundae and that her chair wasn't too wobbly. It was equally cute how Emmalina told him to stop being a dork because she knew how to ask for cutlery. Alyssa was relieved that the conversation seemed to flow and found herself genuinely interested to hear Emmalina's quirky take on things. Though as the random chat and their light-hearted banter tailed off, Alyssa sensed her new young friend was building up to something. She could also tell she wouldn't beat around the bush.

'If you *do* happen to be sucking face with my dad at any point, there is one condition. *Hypothetically* of course.'

Alyssa raised her eyebrows.

'You have to be nice to him.'

*No pressure.*

'I mean, I know he can be annoying at times. Like, he's super keen on stuff being tidy, and he gets a bit geeky about computer coding. I get it if things don't work out and you decide to dump him. *Hypothetically.*'

'Hey thanks,' Devan added, with a hint of sarcasm.

'What I mean is, if you *do* decide to give the poor guy a chance and it doesn't work out, let him down gently, OK? Don't just run off or ghost him. That happened to my older friend Jade when she went out with a boy from Taybury High. It was *so* not cool. I had to spend a whole week of the summer holidays handing her tissues. Communication is kinder.'

'I agree.' Alyssa reached out a hand and squeezed Emmalina's, trying not to feel the guilt of the last time she'd run out on Devan, which hadn't exactly been her fault. '*Hypothetically.*'

Emmalina eyeballed her for a long moment before grinning and turning the squeeze into a handshake. 'Sounds like a deal.'

It did? Alyssa swallowed hard, sensing it wasn't one to be taken lightly. She stole a glance at Devan, who looked apologetic.

'Don't think I'm picking on you,' Emmalina bounced on. 'I know Mum's going out with Jess from the shop – for real – and I've said the same to her. I do approve of Jess, but I'm going to have a word about her bringing back the penny sweets display. How do they want kids to stick around and love Hartglove, if they're not fully catered for? I'm not *all* about the treats,' she clarified, digging out the last spoonful of her syrupy sundae. 'I've been trying to promote girls' football, because we need a better team and more prospects, if we want the town buzzing again. Sweets, strawberries, sport. That's balance, right?'

This kid could take over the world.

'And I like what you and Dad are doing to bring more love to Hartglove,' Emmalina added. 'The app is getting more people dating. I'm excited about the hall reopening, with more clubs and parties. And in Design and Technology, I've been making a suggestions box so we can collect more ideas for improvements. It's my hometown and I don't want it to be called loveless again.'

Alyssa gave her a high five, sure this young woman was already adding fuel to her own small fire.

As they gathered their coats, with Alyssa and Emmalina due to meet Sylvie for tango night dress shopping, Emmalina grabbed Alyssa's arm.

'I saw your parents in The Rat and Raspberry last week, when

Mum took me for steak pie night. Your dad wouldn't stop going on about you. He's so proud of you.'

He was?

Emmalina rolled her eyes. 'Embarrassing dads, hey?'

'Hmm,' Alyssa replied.

'I heard you don't always get on with them. Small-town gossip. But if you want some friendly advice ...'

Alyssa guessed she was going to get it anyway. Though in fairness, she was yet to hear the youngster say anything that wasn't surprisingly sensible.

Emmalina pinned her with a serious look. 'My biological dad doesn't want to know me. I mean, his loss. *Loser*. I've got this goon, and he's the absolute best.' She gave Devan a quick beam. 'But if your dad does want to get to know you again, why not give him a shot? He always seems nice when I speak to him, and he's sweet to your mum. I like them. I wouldn't say it if I thought they were creeps.'

Alyssa felt her eyes well up. 'Thank you,' she said quietly. 'I'll bear that in mind.'

Devan pulled his daughter into a bear hug.

If Alyssa had known Emmalina was going to be quite so deep, she'd have worn waterproof mascara.

Thankfully, Alyssa was granted a break from the meaningful life advice as they said goodbye to Devan and joined Sylvie for dress shopping.

'I broke with tradition and wore a skirt,' said Sylvie, giving them a shy twirl as she met them in the town square, which had always been their place for people-spotting over a Zinger Burger when they were teenagers. 'I didn't want to be typecast as the one with *boring mum jeans*, and Alyssa always looks so put together.'

Alyssa looked down at her fitted black trousers, pink army-style boots and rainbow knitted jumper. 'Pre-loved,' she whispered. 'With social media photos, I'm embarrassed if I keep wearing the same old thing. So I grab designer cast-offs online. It's amazing what you can find.' She tapped her nose, conspiratorially.

'Thanks for the idea,' said Sylvie, pulling them into a three-way hug.

'You look hot, Mum,' said Emmalina, as the three of them rocked and giggled in a way Alyssa would usually have found awkward but just seemed to work.

'Your mum has always been a hottie,' Alyssa confirmed as they pulled away from each other, Alyssa straightening out Sylvie's wayward fringe and Sylvie inspecting Alyssa's knitwear.

'If you two would stop preening each other like a pair of monkeys maybe we can shop?' said Emmalina.

Sylvie laughed. 'Did you meet my daughter? Beauty, brains and a whole lot of cheek.'

Emmalina gave a small bow.

'I think she's incredible.' Alyssa meant every word. 'She knows her mind and isn't afraid to speak it. I respect that. She'll go a long way.'

'We should share tips about coaching,' said Emmalina, nestling between her elders and linking arms with them both as she guided them towards the first dress shop. 'Did you hear I'm going to be a football coach one day? And I know that's not the same as a love coach, but goals are goals.'

Alyssa and Sylvie smiled at each other over Emmalina's head as she began sharing her best advice on keeping a winning mindset.

The afternoon played out nicely, Emmalina in her element as she swished around changing rooms in various styles of dresses, Sylvie vetoing anything too low-cut or leggy, Alyssa suggesting hairstyles and accessories. Emmalina then picked out several options for the two women, who squashed themselves into one changing room like they'd always done so they could mix and swap, and warn each other if they had their skirt tucked into their knickers.

'We definitely take up more room than we used to.' Sylvie giggled as she ducked away from Alyssa's elbow while she was trying to wriggle into a particularly tight dress. 'Though your joints are bonier.'

'They surely made the changing rooms smaller,' Alyssa reasoned. '*And* they've changed the clothes sizes. I mean, who added size zero? Give a girl a break.'

'*Breathe iiiiiin*,' Sylvie said with a snort of laughter, mimicking something Pearl Bagnor used to say on their shopping trips, adding a dress zipping action.

Alyssa swooshed open the dressing room curtain. 'Never wear a garment that only fits if you're breathing in,' she said to Emmalina, with a serious finger waggle. 'Not unless you're willing to hold your breath until you look like a beetroot *and* decline all offers of food. Also, you then can't sit down all night in case your zip pops. Devastating.'

'Why would anyone wear clothes that are too small?' Emmalina looked at them both like it was the most stupid thing she'd ever heard.

'That's my girl,' said Sylvie, staggering out of the changing room in a dress that kept riding up like it was defying gravity. 'I wish we'd been that wise. Anyone for tango-night trousers? Or maybe a jumpsuit.'

'You have to get naked every time you need a wee, when you wear a jumpsuit.' Emmalina rolled her eyes. 'Totally bad design.'

'Agreed,' said Alyssa. 'Shall we go for food, and see what clothes we can scrounge online? If I have to look at my bare bum cheeks in a changing room mirror for much longer, I might lose the will to shop.'

And with that, they abandoned the glaring lights of the changing rooms and made their way to Pepperoni Franco's pizza place, hoping for a subtly lit booth. Alyssa gave a quick glance over her shoulder before she entered, so accustomed to checking who might see what she was up to it had become a habit – even though she didn't feel the need to do it as much lately. Though perhaps she should, with the potential bush photo lurker on the prowl. She still hadn't got to the bottom of that.

They settled themselves into the comfy bench seats, breathing in the gorgeous cheesy aromas and spreading out menus.

'I like you, Alyssa,' Emmalina said, the words seeming to come so easily to her.

Alyssa looked up, her heart feeling warm.

'Though can I give you one last piece of advice, coach to coach? Then I promise I'll shut up and let you choose your food. I recommend the pesto and mozzarella deep dish, by the way.'

Alyssa nodded for her to continue.

'You worry a lot about what people might think. Like, you're bothered about what strangers would say if you *were* snogging Dad, or if they knew where you *actually* buy your clothes, or if they spotted you wolfing down a pizza.'

Alyssa's eyes widened, but she kept slowly nodding. Sylvie looked curious too.

'What other people think of you is none of your business. You should just be you.'

Alyssa blinked a few times, letting the thought settle. It was the sort of thing she'd read on Instagram many times but usually brushed off. To her, what other people thought of her *had* always been her business. Quite literally. The opinions of strangers could make or break her career. She was no health guru or fashion icon, but she'd always strived to be seen as inspirational, on top of life, good at making wise choices. She'd got a lot of social media love as that person, and for a long time, that had brought her clients and opportunities. People wanted to work with her because they wanted to be like her. It was a simple equation.

She'd been getting better at shaking some of that off since she'd returned to Hartglove. But if an eleven-year-old could spot it, clearly, she had more work to do. And what kind of example was she setting to the next generation if she was on social media, putting on a front? Maybe too much '*feel good*' could make others '*feel bad*'. The thought made her stomach drop.

'You make a great point, Emmalina,' Alyssa said earnestly. 'And I'm working things through. Are you hiring yourself out as a coach yet? I should get your card.' She gave her a wink.

'Jeez, you guys. Can't we just eat some pizza?' Sylvie groaned.

Alyssa laughed. Friendship felt good again, after all this time. And now it was like having two sweet friends for the price of one. Although that gave her a quiet, creeping fear that the more good things she gathered, the more she stood to lose if things didn't work out for her. It had hurt like hell the last time she'd lost her best people, and she had no idea if she could survive that again. She would just have to channel some of Emmalina's fighting spirit.

And while Alyssa wasn't ready to let a minor railroad her into announcing her relationship with Devan before she was ready, Emmalina had inspired her to work on at least *one* of her other problems.

# Chapter 37

'So you think you can get through tonight resisting my temptations and pretending to everyone you're not hot for me, Miss Heart?' asked Devan, his voice a delicious whisper against her skin, his hand skimming down the bare flesh of her back where her deep red dress dipped low.

His fingertips were warm, and every time he touched her it was as though he left a trail of fireworks.

'Mmm hmm,' she managed, her voice quite possibly a helpless whimper.

Locals busied around them in the hall, putting up final decorations for the town's tango night. Everything looked red and romantic, and a local band were beginning the first twangs of sultry guitar music. Luckily, people seemed too busy to focus on Alyssa and Devan. *For now.*

His lips were perilously close to her neck, making *everything* tingle.

'When are you going to come clean and tell these lovely people how you feel about me?' He put his hands on her hips and spun her around to face him, the delicate silk of her dress swishing.

His eyes flickered briefly to the exposed flesh of her cleavage, his mouth parting slightly. *Wow*, how was he doing that? She was aching for him. Everywhere his gaze landed came alive with tingling goosebumps. And it was wildly unfair that he was wearing the tightest trousers and a sheer black shirt that was unbuttoned to the waist, to show off abs that could outdo a washboard. Abs that she *really* wanted to touch right now.

Well, two could play the tease.

'I have no intention of coming clean, Mr Shaw, when you're so intent on playing dirty.'

He looked at her, his eyes a display of feigned innocence. Admittedly, they were gorgeous – but she hadn't come to assess his irises.

'I'm here to help Hartglove shake off its "loveless" title, and to give people a way to meet naturally, without having to undergo a series of daunting love tasks. And perhaps to network in my capacity as a love coach.' She winked at him. 'We can't have folk thinking a love app is the best way to fix their romantic troubles.'

'Though is 'Appy Together making *you* fall in love?' He spoke the words gently against the soft skin behind her ear, before moving his gaze to lock with hers.

The room seemed to swirl around them, his eyes like deep pools, pulling her in. She hadn't said the words to him yet – well, not since the turtle costume night – and she was still struggling with them, even if she was falling in a way she could barely control. She cleared her throat and stepped back, breaking the trance.

If she was falling for him, it had nothing to do with a piece of technology, and so it was surely fair game to avoid any public declarations. Her eyes flitted to the stage, which had been the scene of her last one – and that couldn't happen again.

'No comment, Mr Shaw,' she whispered back. 'I'll let you enjoy the thrill of the chase. And then maybe ... later at yours?' She rearranged the straps of her dress, letting one slide to expose her shoulder, before slowly placing it back.

She felt a wave of satisfaction as she saw him gulp, an interesting thought or two appearing to flit across his mind.

'Mmm hmm.' Now he was the one trying not to whimper.

She hurried off to help with preparations, before she could get pulled back into Devan's orbit, where it was almost impossible not to want to stroke a firm bicep.

And though Alyssa's time with Emmalina may have convinced her to be more open about *some* things, it had made her even more cautious about publicly admitting her relationship with Devan – because there would be more people to disappoint if things went up in smoke.

As she mingled and helped with buffet and heart-bunting-related jobs, Alyssa took the chance to talk to people about her love coaching. Since things had started going well with Devan, so many dormant feelings were reawakening – and if her energy had once repelled potential clients like a rotting frog, the opposite now seemed to be true. Perhaps she was no longer feeling like a big dating faker, and instead, was beginning to believe in herself and her work again.

She'd once helped her clients to reclaim *love* using strategies and common sense. But now she was *feeling things* maybe her coaching would be even better. She could add true empathy to her mix of skills, and that was surely better than trusting the roulette wheel of a love app.

Or if all else failed, she'd had some snazzy flyers printed, and who didn't love a shiny leaflet with uplifting words?

She did still feel a twinge of guilt that she was almost pitting herself against Devan's creation, but it was just a bunch of coding, and it would do well with or without her cheerleading. Devan could probably make a dozen other apps in his sleep, but she only had one love coach business. One thing she'd ever been good at or respected for. And she couldn't go admitting an app could do a better job.

She took a quick selfie and shared it to social media, to promote what she was up to. The tango night was separate from the love tasks, although she and Devan would be showing off their Love

Task Five dancing skills by doing a routine later on. Teijo would be along soon too, as he was always keen on more social media stories.

Alyssa smiled to see her inbox was filling up with more enquiries from couples who needed her coaching support.

And then her jaw clenched – because there was another message from @whoami23456. The same unknown profile who'd shared the photo of her kissing Devan. Her wide eyes scanned quickly. They were threatening to expose her as a liar hiding behind a fake persona – again – and there was a warning of more photos. *Of what*? She remembered Devan saying he often ignored weird messages, and Rufus telling her scandal sells. She had no clue, but she had enough to deal with right then, and random trolls were not on the list. With a frustrated huff, she deleted the message and threw her phone back into her clutch bag.

'Teijo!' she called, relieved to see him arriving at the doorway of the hall, camera around his neck.

Yes, this was the perfect distraction. He'd even brought a polling box so people could vote on whether they were feeling more love in Hartglove. It would bring a bit of buzz and would help them to assess how their efforts were going. From what Alyssa had seen, the shared allotment gardens had attracted more couples as a place to relax and chat, and more people were volunteering and meeting through the animal rescue centre. And now Hartglove Hall was sparkling again, there would be more events, clubs and togetherness in the town.

Teijo waved at her. Maybe she could persuade him to put in a good word for her love coaching in his promo material. She went to greet him, linking her arm through his and walking him to the table of weak sangria and questionable nibbles. Precisely no sparks flew between them, though the rest of the room didn't know that. Perhaps he'd make a useful decoy. She threw in a feigned laugh at whatever he was saying, like when she'd been dating men like Arnaud. Though now it just seemed empty – unlike the addictive electricity whenever Devan was near. Her errant eyes looked up. And there he was, watching her from across the room, with deep, brooding gaze, even if she didn't have him down as the moody type.

But wow. Being brooded over was intense. Subconsciously, she dropped Teijo's arm. Was Devan undressing her from across the room, *with his eyes*? She took a deep, shuddery breath, suddenly feeling hot.

'Are you OK?' Teijo asked, looking concerned.

Well, she *was* fanning her burning cheeks with an Alyssa Heart, The Love Coach flyer.

She saw the edges of Devan's mouth twitch into the smallest smile. He was tall and confident, not fazed that he was a hot-blooded man in sequins, or that old ladies were swooning over him. And yet the way his hand ruffled his hair when he looked at her, his mane always a bit dishevelled in a young Hugh Grant kind of way, told her he was nervous under the bravado too.

Urgh, she was falling *hard*. Being in the same room but not being near him was torture – but if she got too close, people would see the sparks coming off her.

'Not worried about your dance, I hope,' Teijo continued. 'Maybe you two could get up on the stage? I could film it? You could both say a few words about how you're feeling ...'

*Not* the stage of doom.

'I need a drink!' said Alyssa quickly. But *not* an alcoholic one – she'd never get drunk in this hall again. 'Got to go.'

This night was getting trickier by the moment, and it wasn't even the brainchild of that algorithm. She'd planned this one herself.

It was time to escape to the kitchen, which was surely the only bearable place at any party. She needed to stick her head near a fridge.

'Thank goodness,' she said, as she pushed through the door of the quiet kitchen. She filled a paper cup with iced water and sat up on the worktop. The hall's kitchen was now clean and well stocked, after she and the locals had worked on it. She didn't mind admitting she felt good seeing it come together. It still surprised her that she cared, and that now and again she pondered sticking around – but there was no chance of that if she couldn't brave a certain excruciating conversation. Later. *Maybe.*

Several people bustled through as she sat there cooling off. Mrs Halfpenny marched in wearing an '*It Takes Two to Mango – Be a Banana*' T-shirt, which from the knitted cape she was once again wearing, Alyssa assumed was part of her new self-love quest. She raided the cupboard for biscuits for the Clucky Ducks gang, because they apparently couldn't stomach the '*tiny spicy olives*'.

Sylvie and Emmalina came to grab their coats, as Emmalina had to be up early for football practice. Emmalina gave Alyssa her usual '*I still think you're snogging my dad*' wink and hugged her fiercely. Even Alyssa's mum shimmied in to chop more apples for the sangria, wiggling her hips to the guitar music and telling Alyssa, a little tipsily, what brilliant work she was doing. Her instinct was to bristle, and then the pep talk from Emmalina jumped back into her head. '*I wouldn't mention it if I thought they were creeps.*'

Was it time to find out for herself? She jumped down from the worktop, gave her mum an awkward wave, and then darted back in the direction of the buffet table, where she could almost bet her dad would be hovering, not one to miss out on free nibbles.

## Chapter 38

Percy Bagnor jumped at the sight of his daughter striding purposefully towards him. Alyssa noticed his head twitch as though he was seeking out his wife, but Alyssa knew she was still in the kitchen with Anna, debating the best way to core an apple.

'Alyssa,' he said, straightening himself as she approached and pulling his face into a nervous-looking smile.

It was one of the rare times he hadn't gone to call her Beryl, so she had to give him that.

'Dad.'

He put down his plate of spicy nibbles, looking not unlike a rabbit caught in the headlights of his own sensible Volvo estate.

She couldn't pretend she was dying to have a cringey heart-to-heart with him either – but she wondered if avoiding this was keeping her own emotions stuck. Discovering her parents' apparent lack of love and fidelity just before she'd fled her hometown, and spending years believing they'd chosen shagging colleagues in stationery cupboards above a family life with *her* had smashed her last hope that true love was real.

But if she'd learned anything since she'd been back here, it was that she needed to hide from her problems less and communicate more. So she *had* to give this conversation a shot, come what may.

'Well, you've done an impressive job,' he waffled, waving a hand around them. The dancing and music were in full swing, voices sounding animated and drinks flowing. 'It's been a long time since the town has seen anything this lively.'

'Thanks,' she muttered. She sensed the compliment hadn't been easy for him, but his past behaviour hadn't made her life easy either.

'Your mother says, I ... erm. I don't praise you enough.'

Alyssa shrugged. 'Until recent attempts, I'm going to say *never*.' And that had hurt. 'Though maybe you didn't see anything worthy of your pompoms, however hard I tried to be good at things.'

Oh, for the kind of dad who'd showered her in gold stars, even when she'd been a bit rubbish.

'That's just it,' he said, stepping forward and taking her hands – which was weird, because he'd never been one for much affection. She felt herself tense. 'I *am* proud of you. Look at you, paving the way, in a profession I'd never even heard of. Bringing people together. Helping folk when they're struggling with love.'

Her gaze moved off to the distance. It was hard to look at him just then. 'I didn't know you believed in it,' she finally managed. A wave of past emotions was rising up inside her. Thoughts of the time when she'd believed they were the happy Bagnors and her parents were in love. When she'd thought, without question, that she'd find her own true love one day too – or that she already had. 'You and Mum were both having affairs. Probably lots of them. Wasn't our little family enough?' She stopped short of yelling *wasn't I enough*, even though her teenage self undoubtedly would have.

'Oh, Alyssa.' He was squeezing her hands now. Still weird, but she wasn't *yet* hellbent on flinging him off. 'Your mother and I were both young and giddy back then. Greedy for a bit of fun. We cared for each other, and both knew what the other was up to. Sometimes we even ...'

Alyssa thrust up a hand. 'If this has got anything to do with putting car keys in a bowl to wife-swap with the neighbours, I do not want to know.'

Her dad chuckled, which at least broke some of the tension. 'Don't be silly, love. Your mum wouldn't bed a man who drove a Morris Minor. She's more a luxury Cadillac kind of girl.'

'That's gross.' Alyssa pulled a *yuck* face.

'In all seriousness, it's great to have you back here and to see the impressive woman you've grown into. Your mum's got me following your Instagram. It's very inspiring.'

Her heart deflated a touch, realising he was probably impressed with the feigned version of her who ate quinoa salads and had unshakeable beliefs about love apps.

Her dad seemed to be reading her. 'And I know how it works.' He lowered his voice. 'The things people share online are just *the best bits*. We put on a good show. But I want you to know I accept you, whoever you decide to be. If I've ever been tough on you, it's because I wanted you to turn out better than your old dad. And you have. I love you, Alyssa. And I love your mother too. Always did and always will.'

She was looking at him again now, though it was becoming more difficult to see him, with the tears that were swamping her eyes. The respectable version of Percival Bagnor always had a clean cotton hanky in his top pocket. He pulled it out and gave it to her, and she blew her nose loudly. A peace offering. It wouldn't solve everything, but they were off to an admittedly snotty start. And she was an adult now. She'd made plenty of mistakes of her own. She was learning to forgive.

Alyssa wasn't sure whether she was sobbing because her dad seemed to believe in love, or that he might accept her even if she didn't like quinoa, or because her mum still ironed his hankies – which was annoyingly cute, even if it wouldn't fix *everything*. But instead of being mortified that she was publicly shedding tears, she just felt relief. Like she'd begun to let go of a ginormous fake Lulu Guinness suitcase, and the weight of expectations was lightening.

And now he was pointing to her love coaching flyers and saying he'd been proudly handing them out all evening. And did he just say her special blend of coaching was probably even better than Devan's marvellous love app? Well, make room on that pedestal.

If Alyssa thought things couldn't get any more surreal, Mrs Halfpenny began rounding up people to dance to the band's impromptu version of 'I Touch Myself' by The Divinyls, although thank *goodness*, she was singing *I love myself*, or Alyssa's poor head might explode.

'Come on, dearie,' Mrs H called out to her. 'You've got to love yourself before you can let anyone else into your love garden.' She winked. 'And you did want more love in Hartglove without people needing a phone didgeridoo to show them the way. This town has got an award to win.'

Alyssa couldn't argue with that. So before she could think better of it, she was up and dancing in a big line, with everyone from Hedgehog to Horace, Jess Halfpenny to her mum Pearl – who was clearly not about to miss out on some hip jiggling. Then her mum was dragging her dad up, and the people from Clucky Ducks were Zimmer-framing over. And Devan was soon next to Alyssa, bumping hips and grinning at her. She played along, in a way that looked friendly for the photos rather than like a woman falling dangerously in … *love*?

As the song came to an end, Teijo gathered everyone around, ready for Devan and Alyssa's tango demonstration. Teijo was keen for shots of them with eyes locked, limbs entwined, to show the app was bringing them closer. Alyssa still wanted to portray the opposite. She could only pray Devan was onside with her.

He bounded up the small steps to the wooden stage, then turned and held out his hand for her to follow. Alyssa halted, her heart rate increasing as her mind did somersaults. It was enough that they had to do this excruciatingly intimate dance, in front of everyone. But up there? She hadn't been on that stage since the night of her stupid grand gesture. And although it was nothing more than a collection of wooden planks, and things were different now, somehow her brain had not got the memo. Maybe she was being absurd, but her feet simply wouldn't move. It was as though her high heels had reached their limit of brave things for one night.

Seeming to read her, Devan nodded discreetly and jumped down from the stage with a flourish, landing in front of her as though it was part of their act. The crowd clapped and he beamed at her. Her feet might have refused to get back onto that stage, but she was not going to completely reject Devan and his hopeful eyes.

So she took a deep breath, plastered on her show face, and held out her hand for the dance.

The strum of guitars began, filling her ears with the familiar tune she'd been dancing to with Devan during their tango lessons. Sometimes Teijo had been there, snapping photos. And other times, they'd practised alone at Devan's house, lights dimmed, curtains closed. She would have to stop thinking about *those* times, if she was going to get through this without melting.

Alyssa swallowed hard, knowing what was ahead. A dance that was sensual and beautiful. In that moment, she wished the app had chosen Morris dancing, or something entirely non-sexy. Devan took up his position, making her breath catch. The dance would intensify, their bodies would get closer. How on earth was she going to get through it, pretending her soul wasn't on fire for this man?

His breath soft against her face, he spun her gently, encouraging her hips to sway and her body to find the beat. She tried to think of it as a series of steps, a routine to pace out. Though as his arm encircled her, his hand landing on the soft flesh of her stomach and radiating warmth through the silky material of her dress, it was becoming more difficult by the second.

He turned her away from him, his front snug against her back, his pelvis against her bum. She heard his almost inaudible groan as he rocked gently against her, certain parts of him almost definitely warming up. As the routine demanded, he lifted her, spinning around with her against him, before gently lowering her, her body sliding down his. She felt her eyes flicker closed with the joy of it. Being against him, feeling his heartbeat, the hitch in his breath.

A few gentle claps from the audience in response to the lift made her eyes pop open. She shook herself and exhaled sharply, trying to break free from her trance. She spun back towards him, and they paced the floor together, their feet knowing the way. She just about managed the leg flinging bit, and the part where she had to do a snake-like tease in front of him, running her hands up and down her body.

And before she knew it, he was pacing towards her, taking her in his arms for one final spin before dipping her low, so she was bent backwards in an arch. His nose pressed against the flesh just above her belly button, moving up towards her chest as he pulled her body in.

*Oh God.*

His face moved slowly against her front, his warm mouth skimming between her breasts, stopping for a tantalising moment before finding her neck and breathing against it. Every nerve ending in her body felt like it might explode. She gasped and pulled herself back to standing, their cheeks now against each other, his lips hot against her ear. Blood whooshed around her head, her thoughts racing, her body barely in control.

He cupped a hand around his mouth, so the watching public couldn't catch his words.

'*Whoa, Alyssa.* I'm so in love with you,' he breathed against her, their bodies sticking together from the dampness of their flesh. 'And I'm not saying that to sabotage you.' He pulled away and looked at her. Those deep blue eyes, both loaded with truth.

She nodded, her eyes wide, her lips parting. 'Same,' was what tumbled out, in the least romantic way ever. *Same?* What was wrong with her? Why hadn't she just said the L-word? But she couldn't. Not *here*, not with everyone looking – even if she was coming to see that hell yes, she L-worded him too.

Her heart was melting. Was it time for this pretending to stop?

**Social media post by 'Appy Together:**

**@appytogether** – We're excited to report that there is officially more love in Hartglove! The results of the poll taken at the town's recent Tango Extravaganza – supported by funding from us – showed 73% of people were feeling more love. But is it the trial run of the new 'Appy Together love app, the presence of @alyssaheart_thelovecoach, or the surprise upsurge of self-love that is winning the day? We've got to say – who cares! Love is love, isn't it, folks? Let's keep it up!

**Private message from @agent_rufusdiamond to @alyssaheart_thelovecoach:**

**@agent_rufusdiamond** – Sorry I didn't make it to your dance night thing. Was planning to, but I couldn't get my roots done in time. My grey patch was fit to scare Cruella de Vil.

## Chapter 39

*Just get on with it.* That had been the advice from everyone Alyssa had dared to confide in about whether it was time she publicly admitted her relationship with Devan.

Over coffee with Sylvie, her newly re-established best friend had rolled her eyes and told her to stop dragging her feet like a sloth. When Alyssa had whispered about the possibility with Jess in the corner shop, Jess had clapped with glee and offered her a loudspeaker and a crocheted banner. Then Mrs Halfpenny had popped up from behind the new penny sweets display to suggest they get T-shirts printed. At least she hadn't tried to haul her to the truth chair. Small-town life was nothing if not quirky.

So as Alyssa walked up the stone steps of the huge countryside hotel, the spring sunshine warming her face, she was beaming to herself. Because she was a woman with a secret she was preparing to spill – only this time, the secret was a good one.

Love Task Six had arrived, and she wasn't sure what it was, other than the app had told her to pack for the weekend – clothes for gentle exercise, luxurious lounging, and dinner. And judging by where her car had arrived, the venue was an exclusive spa hotel. In her old life, places like these had brought her out in hives. At times, she'd been gifted mini breaks in exchange for promoting them. Though despite her usual radiant photos, she hadn't enjoyed having the happy lives of lovey couples and giggling friends shoved under her nose when her own life had been distinctly lacking.

A young man and woman passed, arm in arm, and she smiled genuinely at them. Things were different for her this time. Now she was arriving as a contented person too, even if she was more than a little jittery about her mission. Though this place would be perfect. Devan would be expecting her to *pretend* she was all about Pilates and namastes, and sipping chamomile tea with her lima beans. But she was about to surprise him – in more ways than one. Since the night of the tango dancing, and after finally facing her dad, she'd decided it was time.

She hadn't yet seen Devan, who'd apparently arrived earlier with Teijo, as he'd had a morning work meeting. She'd been so busy with her deluge of new love coaching clients that she'd barely seen him since the tango event. He'd been tied up with working on his next app idea too, as inspired by Mrs Halfpenny, who would no doubt be the T-shirt and poster girl. It would be a self-love version of 'Appy Together – although goodness knew what they could call it. *'Appy if Everyone Else Would Just Sod Off*? Not that that was *exactly* what loving yourself was about.

Standing at the top of the steps, Alyssa turned for a moment, to take it all in. The majestic Cotswold stone building, with its honeyed hues and deep green ivy that trailed like bunting. The manicured hedges, shaped perfectly like chickens. The spacious striped lawn, dotted with bistro tables and those hanging cocoon chairs that were big enough for two people to cosy inside, if you didn't mind a bit of motion sickness.

Yes, this time she could allow herself to enjoy this, without having to fake it.

In truth, she almost couldn't fault Devan's love app, which gobbled up her questionnaire feedback and gave her exactly what she needed – even when she didn't know it. Devan was incredible at his work, and she'd been selfishly blind to that as she'd clung to her goal of disproving his app. A pang of guilt shot through her at having counted on Good Old Devan to take her side instead of fighting for his own. She needed to make amends for that.

'Alyssa.'

She heard the upbeat tones of Devan's voice behind her in the doorway, and instinctively, she turned to him. His face was animated and his smile full. The sun caught the flecks of auburn in his hair as he pushed it back, like he wasn't quite sure what to do with his hands when they were pretending not to be a couple. She wanted to fling hers around him and blurt out how much she'd missed him – and quite honestly, how she wanted to nibble him like a biscuit in that tight black jumper and muscle-hugging jeans.

But Teijo appeared behind him brandishing his camera and notebook, and suddenly she didn't know what the etiquette was for two people who'd been secretly falling for each other, when one of them was about to confess things. So instead, she scratched her head – which in hindsight was not a good look, unless you wanted people to suspect you had lice.

'You look beautiful,' he breathed, taking in her long orange floaty dress and summery straw hat, none of which matched her branding or usual black and pink trendy casuals, but nonetheless felt swishy.

She didn't mind that her pink waves clashed or that her nails, still a bit grubby from working in the shared garden but painted glittery rainbow shades by Emmalina, didn't tie in.

Devan cleared his throat, seeming to remember Teijo was behind him. 'I mean, you're looking well. Shall we get some tea and sit on the lawn? Then Teijo can take photos. I'll find someone to look after your bags.'

Alyssa nodded, reaching for her suitcase at the same time as Devan, their hands brushing, the warmth of his accidental touch filling her. Every part of her still tingled when she was near him, and she felt the overwhelming urge to end the charade and tell everyone she was wild about him right here and now. But it affected Devan's life too, so she wanted to clear things with him first – even though they'd recently told Emmalina. And then Teijo was there with his camera, snapping her uncertainty and the flush of her cheeks, and she recoiled, remembering public declarations could be mortifying. *Stay cool.*

Doubt fluttered inside her as she wondered for the umpteenth time what people would say when she more or less admitted her online persona was no better than a glorified cardboard cut-out, and she'd been fibbing about everything from quinoa to her keenness on Devan. What would her agent say? Would she lose a chunk of followers? If she did, would it truly matter?

As Devan chatted to staff about her luggage, she took a moment to step away. She was coaching clients again now, and it would be foolish not to use her skills on herself. What would she advise people when their mind monkeys were having a jungle party? She closed her eyes. Deep breaths in, long breaths out. Repeat a mantra. *You're not a chimp.*

Teijo rounded them up again and they made their way across the lawn to a sunny bistro table. Alyssa focused on the birdsong and the feel of the sun on her face, letting her mind clear and her busy thoughts float away. Maybe she should coach herself more often.

As they walked, Devan talked animatedly about his morning meeting and the new app he was creating, pushing his glasses back up his chiselled cheeks every time they slipped a little. She had no idea what half of the tech jargon meant, but she was reminded again about his unapologetically geekish passion for what he did. He cared fiercely about the positive impact his work could make – more so than she had, until he crashed back into her life and made her *feel* again.

They arrived at a table, Devan repeating his suggestion of tranquil tea, no doubt to help her keep up her image.

Alyssa took a deep breath, remembering the right people would accept the real version of her, and those who didn't could get stuffed. 'Actually, I could kill for a bacon butty and a nap in one of those swingy chairs. And maybe a dirty great ice-cream milkshake with chocolate sprinkles.' She gave Devan a cheeky smile as she registered the surprise on his face. It was time to let Teijo get the lowdown on who she *really* was, behind the smokescreen of fake downward-dog-loving photos. *Oh God, oh God, oh Godddd.*

No. She was going to own it.

She kicked off her pumps, hoicked up her dress and climbed into one of the egg chairs, sending it rocking. The motion made her heart race – or maybe that was just the nerves. But she was going to put an end to this charade, annihilating one lie at a time. She pulled out a stash of trashy magazines from her cheap and cheerful tote bag.

'This is the perfect spot for reading,' she announced, barely suppressing a grin as she noticed Teijo appraising her reading material. She wouldn't usually be seen dead with anything other than the latest trending personal development books, even if she never *actually* read them.

'Get rid of your blackheads,' Teijo read from the front cover of one of her mags. 'And ten celebrities with sweat patches. Intriguing.'

'I know, isn't it? It's so freeing to read that other people are *human* too – even the famous ones. Although I feel for this one, with the damp patches around the crotch of her designer leggings. Those roving cameras get everywhere, don't they?'

She eyed Teijo's camera and he put it down on the white bistro table next to where Devan was already sitting.

'You seem …' Teijo's mouth twisted, as though he was trying to formulate the words. '*Different* today, Miss Heart. Everything OK?'

'More than OK, Teijo.' She beamed.

Devan was smiling to himself as he read the menu. 'I sense Miss Heart is feeling rebellious.'

'Are you not happy with the app's choice of venue?' Teijo's forehead crinkled. 'I thought a weekend spa break for two would be perfect, judging by your Instagram images. You're often singing the praises of spa treatments and massages, yoga and peaceful stays in the country to read and improve yourself.' He looked questionably at the harrowing article Alyssa had opened about how *not* to steam your lady parts, before quickly straightening his face. 'I mean, the app suggested this weekend for the purposes of quality time and intimacy, although please don't feel there's any pressure to …' He swept an arm towards the *disaster down below* photos on the pages of the magazine, his cheeks paling.

Alyssa laughed. 'Sit down, Teijo. Have a cuppa. And grab your notepad, because I'm about to get brutally honest.' It felt terrifying. But not as scary as a whole damned life of make-believe.

By the time their drinks arrived, Alyssa was in full, slightly nervy flow, confessing to Teijo she'd never *actually* enjoyed a massage, because they made her uncontrollably ticklish and she didn't like being poked by a stranger.

'It reminds me of *Friends*, when Ross massages that guy using wooden spoons to avoid touching his naked flesh.'

'Love that episode,' Devan added.

'Alyssa *watches sitcoms*?' Teijo asked. 'So is couples' massage out? And what about the sauna?'

'Those things are so *hot*,' said Alyssa. 'I always feel like a turkey on slow roast. Is it just me?'

'Exactly!' Devan nodded. 'And don't get me started on people breaking wind in hot tubs. We all know they're doing it.'

'Agreed,' said Alyssa, putting a hand over her nose. 'That's if I even wanted to share a communal bath with a bunch of hairy strangers.'

'Wow, you're not going to get any more free spa breaks if I share *these* views on the socials.' Teijo looked uncertain. 'I mean, it will get plenty of clicks and comments for 'Appy Together, but …'

'It's OK,' Alyssa replied, sounding more confident than she felt. 'This is me. Odd thoughts and all. I'll use the spa's facilities, if that's part of the task. But you'll get my no-frills views, even if they're not what readers are expecting.'

She could tell from Devan's face that he was intrigued to see how this would pan out.

# Chapter 40

'Well, I've ridden fourteen kilometres on a thigh-torturing spin bike. I've had goodness knows whose venom massaged into my face, and my body has been wrapped in sea dredgings, like I was one giant sushi roll.' Alyssa looked at Devan and smiled. 'And surprisingly, I've had a fantastic day.'

Teijo was still following them with his camera and notepad as they stepped out of the spin room, faces red and bodies sweating. Ordinarily she would have forbidden anyone to take photos of her without make-up on, especially when she was looking not unlike a pickled beetroot. But somehow, she felt like she was glowing, from the inside out.

She'd normally avoid working out – because wrestling herself into a sports bra for an Instagram post was exercise enough. But, when she was with Devan, they always found fun. Just being with him, encouraging each other and sharing jokes made everything feel lighter. Not to mention the bonus bedroom cardio. Maybe their budding relationship would be good for her in more ways than she'd bargained for. She had no desire to become a champion spinner, or anything wild. But the more she cared for him, the more she cared for herself too. She mattered to someone, and that gave her a reason to treasure herself.

'I think it's time,' Alyssa said to Devan, turning to him and grabbing his hands. Her body was pumping with happy endorphins and the moment just felt *right*.

She'd spoken to Devan about it earlier, when they'd braved the steam room, mainly to get a quiet break from Teijo's notebook. They'd enjoyed a steamy kiss in there too, before a large man in a tiny yellow thong had burst in. They'd had to quickly exit before one of them started giggling about budgie smugglers.

'Whatever you decide, I'm with you.' Devan squeezed her hands back.

Her heart lifted. 'Teijo, do you want to do this as a live broadcast to 'Appy Together's followers, so you get that exclusive you were hoping for? And let's make sure my followers are tagged too. We want everyone to know.'

Teijo's face lit up. 'A happy announcement?'

Alyssa liked how Teijo cared about the good things – not just furthering his media agency career or getting more eyeballs for the love app's campaign. It was refreshing, and it buoyed her in her resolve to do the right thing. She'd been sharing her honest thoughts on everything today, and Teijo had been sharing all of it, like she'd said he could. She would usually have been obsessively checking her own social media to see if her followers were appreciating it or calling her a dreadful fraud. For once, she'd decided not to worry. Her mission to be happy, and to enjoy these moments of falling in love with Devan – *her person* – felt so much more important than anything that could happen online.

Teijo set up the livestream on his phone, ready to capture Alyssa and Devan's words. She would usually have ushered them somewhere more appealing, but she barely even registered the boring backdrop of the hotel corridor or that the white walls were probably making her look even more purple. Teijo began his countdown to pressing the going-live button. *Five, four, three ...*

And suddenly Alyssa felt faint. What was happening?

She snatched a spa treatment brochure from a side table and

quickly fanned herself.

'Are you OK?' Devan asked, his face a picture of concern.

'Of course!' Her voice came out like a squeak.

Teijo stopped his countdown. 'Wait, what's going on? Should I get you some water?'

'N-no,' she croaked, a wave of dizziness coming over her. 'Or maybe yes.'

Teijo nipped off towards a nearby water cooler.

'You don't have to do this,' Devan said quietly. 'You don't have to admit your feelings to the wide world, if you're not ready.'

Alyssa gulped in a mouthful of air. 'But I'm *so* ready,' she replied. And she really was keen to let people know they were together. Though the thought of publicly declaring it herself to a crowd – even though it was only an online one – was giving her turtle night déjà vu wobbles.

'Are you thinking about that night?' Devan asked softly. 'Being up on that stage?'

'I'm trying not to,' she said truthfully. 'I'm telling my brain to shut the hell up. But my body?' She wiped the perspiration off her top lip with a shaking hand. 'My b-b-body is freaking out at the thought of a grand g-gesture.' *Of love.* She felt herself slide down the wall and land on the floor with a thud. 'Or maybe I need to go easy on the workouts.'

Teijo rushed back with the water. Devan grabbed the plastic cup and began to shoo him off. 'She can't do this right now.'

Alyssa reached for the water and downed it, forcing herself back up. 'I want people to know we're together,' she argued back. 'We're d-d-doing this livestream.' Though now even her voice was failing her. This was stupid. She did livestreams all the time. *But not ones where she spilled her heart.*

'Do you want me to take the lead?' Devan asked. 'I mean, you were the one who did the grand romantic gesture all those years ago. In fairness, it's my turn.'

She nodded. And Teijo began the countdown again.

Alyssa barely heard Teijo's intro. Something about this being Love Task Six of seven on their test run of the 'Appy Together love app. She focused on the warmth of Devan's body next to hers, giving her strength. She listened as he admitted to the watching followers that the more time they spent together on the love tasks, the more they couldn't deny their feelings – that they were falling for each other.

Teijo was busy reading out the positive comments of people watching, from his screen.

And Alyssa was still spinning, perhaps from the sheer joy of it. Or from the weight of all that pretending being lifted. Setting her free. Her face gravitated to Devan's and she kissed him. Perhaps she didn't have all the words, but at some point, she *would* find them. Until then, her actions would have to be enough. Their lips moved together, Devan's hands cupping her face, like all the best movie embraces. She *loved* it when that happened. And now a small piece of it was happening for her.

Teijo gave a squeaky cheer and turned the camera back to himself, which was probably for the best.

Thankfully it wasn't long before Alyssa was back to her less dizzy self and Teijo made his red-faced excuses to leave them to it, asking them to take plenty of photos, though he didn't want to see *everything*. With their room's keycard in Alyssa's hand, they were soon making haste there.

'Only one room, Mr Shaw?' Alyssa said, as they arrived. 'What does your love app take me for?'

'Perhaps it knows I'd happily sleep on the floor, for you.'

She turned to face him as they reached the door, pulling him hard against her. 'Not a chance. I want you as close as possible for the rest of this weekend.' *And always.*

## Chapter 41

'You know, there's something extremely hot about the version of you who's comfortable to be herself,' he said, as they pushed through the hotel room door and closed it behind them.

'Like laying myself bare?' she teased, pulling at the strap of her gym top, even though she wasn't sure she looked particularly alluring after their sweaty session on a spin bike, followed by a stress-inducing livestream, where they'd announced their relationship on social media.

His answer was more of a turned-on groan.

'Strangely, I enjoyed most things more than I expected. I mean, who knew being wrapped in slushy seaweed could make your bum tingle?' Which had been her exact quote for Teijo.

'Sexiest sushi roll I've ever seen,' he replied, moving towards her for another kiss, this time against her damp neck, as she backed herself playfully against the door.

'You know what else is sexy?' His mouth moved to the soft skin behind her ear. She loved it when he kissed her there. 'You agreeing to share that you have feelings for me, instead of keeping us a secret. I'm officially getting your seal of approval.'

'If this is what honesty gets me, I'll do it more often,' she breathed, only feeling a *bit* guilty that she'd left Devan to do the announcement, because the thought of publicly declaring her own feelings still made her want to pass out. And she hadn't *quite* managed to use the 'love' word.

Though feeling something particularly welcome growing against her told her Devan wasn't put off. She pulled him firmly into her, her troubles blissfully vanishing.

She was glad they were now on the inside of the hotel room door, because what she hoped was about to happen right there against the neatly painted wood was *not* suitable for the eyes of a passing cleaner.

'Alyssa Heart, I have been *desperate* to get this close to you all day.'

She noted that gym weights were a thing to be celebrated as Devan's strong arms lifted her against the door, his muscles flexing and rippling. And *hell yes* to that thin white T-shirt that gave her a glimpse at his dark, hardening nipples. She slipped one hand under it, enjoying his flinch as her fingers found flesh. *That thing had to come off.* And so did her own damp workout clothes, that were seriously not welcome at this party.

She wrestled off his top, letting her fingers trace the tightness of his abs, loving the way every part of him trembled, as though the sensation was almost too much.

He groaned deeply and pushed his mouth back against hers, their lips opening, his tongue going deep. He cupped her butt cheek with one hand, pulling her into him, the bulge of his erection straining against his shorts and rubbing against her, firm between her legs. The room was already spinning. *More.*

He broke free, taking a second to absorb her, his pupils wide with longing as though a flustered, panting woman in too-tight sportswear was *everything*. She adored how he made her feel. *It's OK to be me.* He shot a glance over his shoulder at the four-poster bed that was strewn with pink petals, the white towels twisted into two love hearts.

The past version of Alyssa would have hated the cheesiness

of it, but now she had room in her heart for *all* the rolling in petals. But not just then.

'*Good* Devan would lay you gently on the bed.' His voice hitched. 'Or maybe run you a hot bath and wash your body, particularly thoroughly.' He gave her a wink, ever playful.

She was all for thorough – but she was in no mood for waiting.

'Then give me *Bad* Devan. Right here.'

*Good Devan*, in that roll-top bath, was a treat for later.

'As you desire,' he said, with a smile that she wanted to kiss right off.

She pushed down her leggings and underwear in one sweep, wriggling one leg free because her body might explode if she had to wait any longer. She relished the look on Devan's face as his eyes ran over her naked lower half, sliding upwards to where her boobs felt like they were bursting to be freed from her sports bra. She pulled the material upwards, exposing her soft flesh. He groaned again and his mouth was on her breasts before she had to ask, devouring them hungrily as she yanked down his shorts, impatient to touch him. Her fingers roamed, her palms finding skin. She angled him against her, hooking her naked leg around his waist to feel him more firmly. *Wow, yes.* Closing her eyes, she moved against him, satisfying her ache in what felt like the most sensuous tease. Each push of her hips brought a fresh wave of pleasure. Devan's deep, vibrating moans, from his position between her breasts, was setting her insides on fire.

'I want more,' she breathed. 'I want all of you.'

He nodded against her chest, coming up for air, his face looking adorably like he'd been woken from a dream. 'Did you take your pill?'

'Yes,' she replied, grateful they'd already had the conversation about birth control and sexual health. It was another level of commitment she was absolutely ready for. 'And before you politely ask, yes, I want to have full, indulgent sex with you, right here against this hotel room door.'

'Oh, I want that too,' he said, taking the base of his penis and moving it towards her, his eyes still on hers to be sure it was OK.

She nodded and helped to hurry him, aware he was being agonisingly slow when she was aching for him. She grabbed his bum cheeks, trying to pull him inside her. He let the tip of his penis enter her, slowly and deliciously, rocking gently in and out of her, before pulling away, a tease in his eyes.

'Devan Shaw, you are *mean*.'

He entered her again, this time deeper, turning her words into a gasp. She *liked* this level of mean, and she was letting him know it. He felt incredible. *He was made for her*. His mouth was on her neck, nibbling, sucking, making her breath ragged. He thrust himself into her, finding the spot deep inside her that longed for him. *Ohhhh*. She gripped his buttocks, encouraging him, pushing back onto him.

And then he pulled out again, his lips smiling against her neck before moving downwards. His tongue traced the outline of her nipples, each tiny bump around them rising, each nerve ending feeling like it was connected to her soul. Then his tongue trailed down the line towards her belly button. *And further*.

His mouth was hot between her legs, lustful eyes looking up at her, his tongue moving in a firm, steady rhythm that made her body hum. Her pleasure built in undulating waves.

She shuddered against him, her hands in his hair, her back hard against the door, her mind spinning, joy mounting. Then he pulled away, moving upwards, kissing, caressing, until he was standing and his penis was back against her, between her legs. She took hold of it and helped it inside her.

'This time you're not getting away.' She laughed into his ear, knowing he was teasing, but loving every heavenly minute.

'I never want to,' he breathed back, pressing himself deeper in exactly the way she wanted. The way they both wanted.

They moved together against the door, each penetration more intense, more profound, as though taking them somewhere they could never return from. Her heart raced against his, their bodies sweating. Their lips found each other, their mouths open and gasping, inhaling each other, kissing madly, deeply, desperately …

She felt her insides tighten around him as they rocked and moved in ecstasy. If she'd been capable of thought she might have hoped no one was passing, as there would be no mistaking their cries of desire or the ever-increasing rhythm they were beating against the wood.

'You OK?' he asked, as though aware of potential bum bruises.

'Don't you dare stop,' she panted.

And he didn't.

She couldn't have said how long they were there, moving together as though their bodies were one hot-blooded thing. Time disappeared, her mind swimming somewhere beyond real. He took her to the edge so many times that when they finally reached it, it was *all-consuming*.

She came against him, pulling him in deeper, shuddering uncontrollably. He came with her too. *Together*.

As her legs turned to jelly, he laughed softly, taking himself out of her when he could sense she was ready. He scooped her into his arms, carrying her to the bed and laying her down gently, pulling a sheet over her, scattering rose petals everywhere and kissing her forehead.

'I love you,' he said quietly.

'Me too,' she replied, already drowsy for sleep. And though she couldn't quite say the words properly, she meant them. With all of her.

## Chapter 42

'Damn, we've missed dinner,' was the first thing she heard him say.

How long had they been asleep for? She opened her eyes slowly and looked at him as he lay next to her, his face creased from the pillows, his hair not quite sure what to do with itself, in its usual, lollypy way. She adored him. The tiny dimple at the end of his nose. The big, accepting heart under those outrageously impressive pecs. And the way her soul felt like it was attached to his by a delicate lacework of threads, some new but growing stronger, and so many still bound tightly from growing up together and that late-teen first love that had set her heart racing.

*Love.* Because she now knew it was that. Before they'd been thrown back together, she'd stopped believing in it. But now she'd never been surer that the wave of emotion that filled her every time she thought of him had *always* been love. She'd just been too afraid to admit it.

And soon enough, she would say it properly. Not *same* or *me too*. When the moment was right, she would say *I love you*. She still feared that once she voiced the words, she might jinx things. Like a wish you weren't meant to share out loud in case you ruined the magic and stopped it becoming true.

'We could order room service?' he suggested, grabbing his

glasses from the bedside table.

She smiled. And there was another reason she loved him – for his brilliant suggestions. Her stomach was rumbling and there was a whole menu of triple-cooked chip delights to consider. This wasn't the perfect romantic moment to declare her undying love for his nose dimple.

She wriggled towards him and laid her head on his chest as they pored over the hotel's offerings.

'The steak and dauphinoise potatoes sound good,' said Devan, making her belly groan even more.

'I'll second that. Although I've got a weird hankering for extra veg. I think all the good feelings and exercise are making me wholesome.'

'I've got a craving for a pot of chocolate spread on the side.' He winked at her, and she batted him lightly, guessing his intentions had nothing to do with an innocent pudding and everything to do with Nutella memories.

After Devan had called for room service, Alyssa wrapped herself in one of the hotel's fluffy bath robes and grabbed a romance novel from a bookshelf in the corner. She made a nest of pillows and snuggled next to Devan, enjoying the sound of him gently snoozing as she disappeared into a fictional world that sounded as out of control as hers had been, just a few months ago. It had been years since she'd read a love story, but Devan had got her back into watching romcom movies like they used to, and she didn't feel nearly as afraid of love anymore.

She cuddled further into Devan, luxuriating in his warmth and listening to his sleepy murmurings. She'd had hotel stays with boyfriends before, but much like the relationships themselves, they'd been for convenience. This was different. Lounging, feeling pampered, at ease with being herself. *This* was something she could get used to.

When Devan woke, he kissed her and got up to check his phone in that reliable dad way of his. It crossed her mind that she'd barely touched hers all day, even though social media would be talking about the less polished version of herself that had been emerging and the fact they'd announced their relationship. She would have to add her own comments, conceding the love tasks had been working and that feelings could grow in many ways – with or without algorithms or coaches to guide you. She'd be endorsing both.

Though right then, she was happiest being in the present with Devan. She hadn't felt compelled to check how her followers were reacting or to let anyone burst her bubble. All of that could be so fickle, and at last she had something real to call her own.

A flicker of worry danced briefly across Devan's face as he looked at his phone screen.

She propped herself up on her elbows. 'Everything OK?'

He exhaled sharply and closed whatever he'd been looking at, flinging his phone on top of a pile of discarded clothes. 'Yes, absolutely. All good. Just work stuff.'

He flopped onto the bed next to her and she used a hand to gently uncrease the frown lines that weren't quite disappearing.

'Are you sure? You can talk to me.' She'd treasured the way she could open up to him, and she wanted him to feel that too.

'I do talk to you.' He rolled to face her. 'Though right now, we're on a romantic spa break for two, as expertly chosen by a very clever app. So I won't kill the mood with talk of wireframing and UX design.'

He reached for his glasses and put them on, eyeing her with mock seriousness. Which was simply cruel, because he knew she found his tech-guy look even more irresistible. She reached out and let her fingers trace his jawline and that cute, cute nose.

His eyelids fluttered softly. Those beautiful, twilight eyes, one slightly darker than the other, that he'd often felt self-conscious about but that she thought made him even more perfect. She curled into him, his arms wrapped around her, his lips pressing into her forehead.

'Everything's great just like this, isn't it?' he said, though it was more of a contented statement than a question.

'Yes. Yes, it is.'

Was that an actual, happy tear trying to escape onto her pillow? Was she becoming the sort of person who blubbed at the sheer loveliness of things? She'd have to start carrying tissues.

Against everything she'd once thought possible, she was having an incredible weekend. Being with Devan made everything feel like an adventure, rather than a thing to be endured for the photos. She was actually looking forward to couples' yoga tomorrow, and the sound bath in nature, and even that side of extra veg that would soon be winging its way to them, complete with juicy steaks and a cheeky pot of chocolate spread.

This was turning out to be her favourite love task. After this, there would only be one more to complete. What could it possibly be? If it was half as much fun as this, she almost couldn't wait. Yet, when all of this was over, there would be big decisions and so much change. She wanted to be with Devan, but was she ready for real life to get in the way, just yet …?

## Chapter 43

Alyssa and Devan took separate cars from the spa hotel. Devan was whizzing off to an app developer event in Liverpool, and Alyssa was keen to get back to the little barn and bask in her bubble of love. There would be social media followers to respond to and coaching clients to check in with. At last, she was feeling more excited about her work, as though helping couples held a whole new level of meaning now her own relationship was a true one.

She pressed her phone screen, the quiet journey back to The Cow Shed giving her chance to fill in her post-love task questionnaire. And the quicker she filled it in, the sooner 'Appy Together would concoct the seventh and final task. As much as their last mission felt like the end of a journey, she was keen for more quality time with Devan and to know what the app would come up with. And then, they'd need to work out what was next for them, in the real world. They hadn't set anything in stone, but she hoped they were moving towards ongoing commitment and her sticking around. She might even get the sign fixed on the barn, so it didn't read The 'ow 'hed. Yes, she could see herself getting that wild.

Devan had already filled out his questionnaire after breakfast that morning, where she'd fancied a cinnamon quinoa breakfast bowl – not even for the photographs – and had genuinely enjoyed it. Her lips curved gently upwards at the thought of Devan, who'd ordered the same, to avoid anyone getting food envy.

The lush green fields of the Cotswolds slid by beyond the window, rising up into distant hills dotted with yet more apple trees, old stone cottages and grazing sheep. It was a backdrop that was quickly seeping back into her soul. In truth, she hadn't missed the busyness of London, the sometimes-smoggy streets and the crowded rush of the underground. To her surprise, she'd barely even missed the city's impersonal nature, even though she'd once told herself that was her favourite part. In hindsight, she could see it had made her lonely. All those people. All the online followers. Yet not a single person to stop and grab coffee and caramel apple tiramisu with, nor to bail her out at midnight if she'd broken a heel and got drenched in a downpour. *Just grab an Uber*. But that wasn't the same.

She closed her eyes for a moment, wondering who she'd call now in a ruined-heel emergency. She could already imagine Sylvie rocking up in her tiny blue Renault, no doubt with Emmalina and a bag full of alternative footwear. Or Mrs Halfpenny rounding up folk like she was on an impromptu 'love your neighbour' crusade, probably stopping off to get T-shirts printed. And somebody would no doubt bring cake. She wouldn't even feel averse to calling her parents to help these days, as long as they could stop with the snogging. Then there was Devan. Reliable even when she told him not to be. Gorgeous, clever, capable …

'We're here, miss.'

The driver interrupted her thoughts. It was just as well, because her list of Devan's good bits might have been longer than Rapunzel's locks.

'Thank you.'

She helped the driver with her bags and then made her way into the barn, which felt cold after a weekend of being uninhabited.

Pikachu and his girlfriend were being mouse-sat by Jess from the shop, which happened a lot these days. Though things would soon settle with just one more task to go. Then she could be more present. She could look at renewing her lease and maybe getting more cheerful paint on the walls. Buy real plants instead of fake ones. Perhaps in the longer term, she and Devan would even live together. But it was early days, and it was enough that she was serious about leaving her London life behind. One step at a time and they could enjoy things as they naturally progressed.

Alyssa filled the kettle and switched it on, then made her way to the living room, flopping down on a beanbag. She should probably invest in a sofa if she was staying on. One of those big, L-shaped ones that you could lounge on with friends, or snuggle up on with your boyfriend, watching movies and eating crinkle-cut crisps.

The polystyrene beans wriggled underneath her as she tried to get comfortable, phone in hand. She was ready to navigate whatever had been happening online since she'd last checked in, which – now she'd shaken off her phone addiction and was less worried what strangers thought of her – had been some point the day before. She clicked onto Instagram, coolly noting that she hadn't lost any followers after her weekend of being more honest. In fact, she'd gained quite a few. Perhaps the universe liked it when she took the right path.

Though her stomach twisted a little at the notification that she had direct messages to catch up with. They might be nice words from coaching clients or kind followers. But not all messages were good ones.

Her heart sank when she spied another private message from @whoami23456 – the unknown troll. She must have accidentally accepted a follow request from them at some point, if they were right there in her main inbox. *Urgh.*

**@whoami23456** – *Saw the announcement about you and big biceps Devan. Cute that you've decided to be all 'honest'.*

*Shame that guy wouldn't know the truth if it bit him on the butt cheek. Did you know he created 'Appy Together with the ONE intention of trying to get back with you, then he fixed it so you two would 100% be matched together? Signs of a stalker, much? Or probably just wanted to shag you. (Clearly, THAT plan worked.)*

Bile rose up Alyssa's throat. How dare this person throw accusations around about Devan and her relationship with him? Of course Devan hadn't spent months, or even years, creating an app on the off chance she'd take him back. And he'd assured her he hadn't engineered things to pair them. Who was this *whoami* loser? She thrashed her arms and legs, struggling to get up from the beanbag, which was now threatening to swallow her.

'What a load of bullshit,' she barked at her screen, marching to the kitchen.

Would it even matter if Devan had pressed a few buttons to pair them together? If she'd have discovered that at the beginning of this journey, she would have been infuriated. And though she didn't love the idea he hadn't confessed this when she'd asked – if it was even true – at this point in their relationship it was unlikely to be a deal breaker.

She was tempted to reply: '*Get back under your troll bridge, you absolute douchnozzle.*' But it was best not to engage. So she grabbed the teabags and started making a strong, sweet cuppa.

Though annoyingly, the online hobgoblin could see she'd opened the message – and they were typing a reply.

*@whoami23456 – I've got you thinking, haven't I? Ever wonder why he put up with you lying to everyone that you weren't together? It was because he knew he had even more lies of his own. Unluckily for him, I know them too.*

Even more lies? Alyssa felt her mind spiralling. But no. She was not going there. And she was not about to start believing an anonymous keyboard warrior over the people she had come to love and trust again – when loving and trusting had been such a fight.

Her fingers twitched, the temptation to type an evil essay overwhelming. She took a few deep breaths. *Stay classy.* This was nonsense, and it had no place in her real life. Common sense told her this was her disgruntled ex-client Gary Pratt trying to stir up trouble, because he had nothing going on for him outside of itching his scabies. Or perhaps it was someone she'd never even met and never would. She'd had trolls before – it was part of being online. And they usually ran out of steam. *Eventually.*

She swigged her tea and stormed to her bedroom, dragging her suitcase to unpack. Her phone was still in her hand as she reached her bed, vowing to block this outrageous person and their messages. But then a series of photos pinged through. Photos of parts of her life she'd still been hiding, even if she'd promised to be more honest, going forward.

Her stomach clenched at images of herself coming out of the World's Grottiest Flat building in Hackney, pulling her suitcase. And a picture of her in mismatched old pyjamas accepting *a lot* of greasy takeaway, the broken sign outside her current home, The 'ow 'hed, looming above her. It was unfortunate she'd been carrying three empty wine bottles for the recycling, because she'd only drank hot chocolate, leaving the wine to Sylvie, Jess and a few of the others who'd popped round. *Terrible timing.*

What was scarier was that someone had been following her. Someone had been that close to her, and she hadn't known. Taking a freakish interest in her movements. She squeezed her eyes shut as she thought. If this person shared these photos publicly, as the message threatened, then so what? She'd already begun admitting her life was sometimes messier than her perfectly curated Instagram grid – even if this intrusion felt like a shove too far.

Her hand moved to the zip on her suitcase, but her screen

lit up again. She *should* have pressed the 'block' button – yet something told her to keep her friends close and her enemies closer. Wasn't it safer to stay in the know? And if she blocked them, they could trick her through another new profile. So she tapped to open the message.

Alyssa took a sharp inhalation of breath as the images appeared on her screen. They were pictures taken *inside* The Cow Shed. In her actual home. She felt sick. This person had access to where she *slept*. Photos of her general disorganised chaos, which looked a world away from the orderly, on-top-of-life love coach image she needed to portray. And she was usually tidy-*ish*, but life had been busy, and she still hadn't got her head around storage solutions or the fact the dishwasher rarely worked. And who had time for dusting? Her eyes darted around, her flesh turning cold as she tried to fathom when this vile person had infiltrated her sanctuary.

More words were appearing on her screen. Threats to expose her for being a screw-up of a love coach who'd been scraping by with no work, no stable love life and a sniping belief that true love was a farce. A woman who sold services she didn't believe in. A failure who'd been publicly dumped by Devan years ago, and who was only playing along now for the money, pretending to be falling for Devan, when in truth, she had a heart of stone.

She wasn't sure why her shocked eyes were still reading. But the venom of the words was so strong, it was like a morbid curiosity. Why did this stranger hate her so much? She couldn't *not* know what she was up against, even though some of it wasn't true. How did this person know about her past? How had they got inside her kitchen, her bedroom?

*Who the hell was this?*

She dropped onto her bed, her legs giving way beneath her. Panicked sobs rose up her throat, coming out as gasping breaths. She'd tidied and done the dishes before she'd gone on the spa weekend, so the photos weren't that recent. But had this person been in here again this weekend? How were they gaining access?

Not that it was anybody's business how often she cleared up her cereal bowls, because she was only human. But what if they'd tampered with something? Poisoned her strawberry yoghurt or set a woman-sized trap in her shower? Or installed some kind of pervy camera system to catch her dancing in her underwear to The Spice Girls?

Alyssa racked her brains, trying to work out who could or would do this. She wasn't stupid enough to keep a spare key under a plant pot, though she did sometimes leave one behind the sign outside the barn, for Jess to collect Pikachu. She rubbed her creased forehead. No, not Jess. Surely? She was sweet and honest and wore her heart on her sleeve – and she was going out with her best friend. There was nothing sneaky about her, although she wasn't always great at keeping secrets. She worked in the shop and loved to natter. It was possible she'd inadvertently mentioned it to someone. But Jess couldn't have gone leaking details of her past.

Sylvie? Her parents? *Devan?* Her heart was sinking further with every possible name. Surely none of those people, whom she'd come to know and trust again. Why would they? Why would anyone? Her insides squirmed at the fact she was doubting these people, and that this horrible, sneaky keyboard-wielding idiot had pushed her to. What did this person even want?

Alyssa looked at her suitcase again. She should just unpack it. She could thoroughly search the place. Check for dodgy traps and weird-smelling yoghurt. Get the locks changed. Be more cautious. This monster should not get to dictate how she felt. Her chest was tight with the unease of knowing that they seemed hellbent on exposing her past secrets, even if she'd changed so much since she'd been here. She hadn't been planning to lay *every* awkward part of her history bare.

But now her hand was being forced.

Whatever this person wanted to spill, she could get past it. Couldn't she? When she'd first arrived back in Hartglove, she would have died of humiliation at those truths coming out. But she'd been on such a journey since then. Yes, it was embarrassing that someone had photos of her unmade bed, and her followers might hear she'd once drunkenly declared her love to Devan, only to find out he was marrying her best mate. But she'd promised herself she was going to be more honest about who she was – and if people were only there for the polished version, they weren't her people.

She pushed herself up from the bed, willing her legs to support her. 'Do your worst, keyboard troll,' she said to her phone screen, even though nobody could hear.

Or could they? Because just as she threw her suitcase onto the bed and began unzipping it, the next download of photos began.

## Chapter 44

Alyssa's mouth dropped as she looked at the next batch of photos and the threatening words that followed. Her eyes darted around, fearing again that someone might have bugged the place or hidden a nanny cam inside the abstract painting that looked like a dog's bottom.

She'd uttered the words '*do your worst*' and the online troll promptly had, and she could only pray that was unfortunate timing. The pictures in front of her were of Sylvie and Devan, Devan and Emmalina, and even Emmalina leaving school with friends. There was nothing incriminating, in terms of what Alyssa already knew about their lives. What was ugly was this deadbeat's threat to disclose what they'd outrageously and quite wrongly named 'Devan's shotgun wedding' with Alyssa's impregnated best friend Sylvie.

Alyssa gasped at the next callous words.

**@whoami23456** – *And don't think I won't drop the bomb that the kid isn't even Devan's.*

Alyssa felt herself slump onto the bed. It was a low and pathetic blow, because it made *no* difference who Devan had or hadn't married, and the biological ins and outs of anyone's family was nobody's goddammed business. And yet she *could not* let innocent and adorable Emmalina get dragged into a social media circus or have her parents shouted about by small-minded bullies. Alyssa had been just about willing to let this troll spurt whatever crap they wanted to about her own life. But *not* Emmalina's. Nor Sylvie's, nor Devan's.

How could she stop this? What did this person want?

Should she ask them, or would engaging with them add fuel to their fire? God, she wished Devan was there. He was away for a work thing, and this did not seem like the kind of bombshell to drop over a phone chat. Who else could she turn to? In that moment, it wasn't clear who she could trust.

Alyssa raked a hand through her hair. This couldn't be Sylvie, so in theory, she could turn to her. But how on earth would she explain that some freak had photos of her daughter, because they wanted to punish Alyssa for her previous shallowness? And that if Alyssa made the wrong move, Emmalina's world would come crashing down? Even though Emmalina knew Devan wasn't her biological dad, they hadn't made it public knowledge because Emmalina liked things as they were, and why should they be forced to?

She closed her eyes, willing her brain to think. Could this be one of her exes? Or twatty Gary Pratt? Who had had access to so many parts of her life?

Before she could stop herself, she opened her eyes and tapped out a reply.

**@alyssaheart_thelovecoach** – *Who are you? And what exactly do you want?*

If her hands weren't shaking so much, she would have added '*you spineless, tit-wombling BELLEND*' – and a whole lot more. But she was just about holding it together to type that much.

When she worked out who this was – and she vowed she *would* – there would be no mercy.

As she waited for a response, a notification popped onto her screen from 'Appy Together. She guessed it was in response to her questionnaire, though it had arrived surprisingly quickly. At least reading it would give her respite from this emerging hell.

> *Dear Miss Heart*
> *Thank you for completing your questionnaire so promptly.*
> *We're excited to hear you had so much fun with your BUM (Budding Ultimate Match). In fact, from the feelings that appear to be brewing, it seems Devan Shaw is well on the way to being your DUM (Definite Ultimate Match). Congratulations! We're thrilled everything is working out for you.*
> *As you know, there is just one more Love Task to go. Are you ready for it? Because this final task is completely on you (and your match won't have a clue).*
> *The task – should you choose to accept it – is to throw a grand, romantic public gesture to announce your feelings to your BUM.*
> *Good luck! You've got this.*

Her stomach twisted. A grand, public gesture? Her mind raced back to *that night*. That stage. That humiliating costume. At nineteen, that had been her first and only grand gesture – and it had gone so badly it had scarred her for more than a decade. Even trying to say the words in a social media livestream yesterday had left her dizzily sliding down the wall into a collapsed, jittering heap. If the app had suggested this before her day had started rotting like a sardine sandwich, she might have had the breathing space to consider it. But right then, it was one fish bone too many.

*Everything was working out for her?* Fat chance of that.

And then finally, the troll's reply came through.

**@whoami23456** – *Pull out of the final love task. Stir up trouble. Make a scene. Or I'll share everything I know and make a scene for you.*

'Argh.' She jumped up and threw a pillow across the room, for want of a better plan.

What was anyone meant to do in this situation? She had no idea. Should she go back to London and confront her main suspect, Gary Pratt? Or tell the police? They probably couldn't track down fake profiles in a hurry, and would this be high on their priority list when they had murders to solve and nice cats to rescue from trees? And reporting it to the social media platforms could only do so much.

Her phone screen lit up again. Another private message.

**@agent_rufusdiamond** – *Did I make it in time for your latest love task thing? I'm in your neck of the woods picking up a drunken internet purchase. (Who knew the Butt Clench Master Machine was a thing? I'm about to enter the world of extremely toned buttocks.)*

Her agent. At bloody last. She never thought she'd be so pleased to see a message from him. He'd set her up with this job, so it was about time he pulled his wobbly-bottomed weight and helped her.

If nothing else, she could trust him. Rufus definitely hadn't been loitering around Hartglove taking photos from behind bushes, because he was always too busy in London, *getting his neighbour's dog's nails painted*. And quite frankly, Rufus was too much of a doofus to concoct anything so underhand.

So much like he'd got her into this mess, he could temporarily extricate her from it. She wasn't running, exactly. And she wasn't about to pull out of the love tasks or make a huge scene on the say-so of a moustache-twiddling nobody. But she did need to get away from there and think. Somewhere she'd be safe from cameras or threats, however empty they may be. Somewhere to hide while she worked out what the hell she should do about this shambles, and who she could trust to help her.

So she tapped out a reply to Rufus.

**@alyssaheart_thelovecoach** – *I'm at The Cow Shed. Please come and get me.*

## Chapter 45

Perhaps the best medicine, when panic hit, was to be in the company of someone so self-absorbed that your own worries felt a touch trifling. Alyssa was huddled in the passenger seat of Rufus's car which, as usual, was gleaming on the outside but full of stinky old takeaway wrappers on the inside. The smell of stale chicken was making her want to gag.

'I mean, who would do this?' she huffed for at least the seventh time on their journey back to London, having already filled Rufus in on what was happening, other than the specifics about Devan's daughter Emmalina. 'It's just plain nasty.'

'Perks of being a Z-list vaguely minor celebrity,' yawned Rufus, checking his fingernails when his eyes should have been on the road. 'Though maybe a bit of scandal could help you scrape up to at least V-list.'

She narrowed her eyes at him. 'You think this is a good thing?'

'Hell no,' he said, pulling a packet of battered-looking triple chocolate cookies out of the compartment in the driver's side door and thrusting them at her. Well, beggars couldn't be choosers. 'I have to share my car *and* cookies with you, put up with your whinging all the way back to London, and let you hide in my spare room, when I was about to dedicate it to my new Butt Clench

Master Machine. Now where am I going to do my Buttathon workouts? And no doubt you'll want to hog my machine, between sobbing into your quinoa salads and posting photos of yourself wearing way too tight yoga pants.'

'I haven't posted about quinoa for ages. Do you even follow my stuff?'

'Not on purpose.' He shrugged.

Hanging out at Rufus's apartment was one of the very last things she would ordinarily choose to do. But she wasn't ordinarily being spied on and trolled by an unknown, possibly unhinged person. If nothing else, Rufus's building had good security – because oddly, he considered himself important and stalk-worthy. And apart from Devan, who was busy in Liverpool, Rufus seemed like the least likely person to be sending her these *twatograms*.

Her phone buzzed with another message. She quickly checked it.

*@whoami23456 – I see you've left Hartglove. Glad you're finally taking notice.*

Her heart hammered in her chest, fear mixing with anger and a whole heap of outrage. She did not want this person to think they were pulling the strings. She was *not* leaving because they'd told her to, nor was she decided on pulling out of the tasks, even if the thought of a final gesture of love was filling her with dread. She was getting away for her own safety, and to think. At least she could see both of Rufus's hands and knew his phone was in his jacket, so he couldn't be the troll.

And she did feel a wriggle of guilt in the pit of her stomach that she was leaving town without letting anyone know. She had a 'deal' with Emmalina that she'd let her dad know if she was running out, because '*communication is kinder*'. But the fewer people who knew her predicament right then, the better.

'This @whoami person knows I've just left town,' she barked

at Rufus, anxiety taking over. 'Did you see anyone hanging about when you arrived, or when we were leaving?'

Rufus scratched his head, which was covered by his usual backwards baseball cap. 'Might have spotted a rustling in the bushes as I was checking my hair in the rear-view mirror. Difficult to tell. Could have been a dog taking a piss. Still find it hard to believe anyone's into taking photos of your unmade bed. You're hardly Tracey Emin.'

The rest of the trip back to London was quiet enough, other than Rufus bragging about his latest 'clients', who Alyssa was pretty sure were too close to A-list to ever consider him as an agent. Between his tales of doing brunch with 'that guy from *Love Island*', Alyssa had time to start processing her thoughts. Had she brought this trollish turmoil onto herself, by living behind a smokescreen of half-truths for so long? If she hadn't pretended her life was so polished, nobody would be bothered about bringing her down.

Though it was only her feelings of inadequacy that had led her to hide behind a guise. She'd just wanted to be liked and accepted, and to build her career as a love coach. She hadn't set out to deceive people. She was *just human*. Surely, she wasn't the only person who was measured about what they shared online?

And when she'd done things that way, her soul hadn't been on display. If people didn't *like* her on social media, then it wasn't truly her. She'd been protecting her heart.

She *had* been beginning to drop the mask and share a less filtered version of herself – but this was making her feel out of control. Should she share the photos of her unmade bed and dirty dishes, to take back power from this bully? It would be freeing, and the online space needed more honesty. Sharing life's chaos would give others a sense of relief that it was OK to be perfectly imperfect.

But if she did that, would the troll retaliate by posting things about Devan and Emmalina? She couldn't risk it.

'If I'm going to stop this troll, I need to find out who they are and confront them. How can I do that?' she asked Rufus, who'd been busy droning on about his future toned bum cheeks.

'What?' he asked, as though her woes had already escaped his goldfish memory. 'Oh right, that. Erm. I do know a few private investigators.' He tapped his nose. 'It's part of the territory, in my job. I'll see what I can do.'

'Thanks.'

It sounded helpful, although there was precisely no way she was putting all her precious eggs in Rufus's shoddy basket. When they got to London, she'd do some private investigating of her own.

## Chapter 46

'I can't believe it,' said Alyssa, as she stomped through the door of Rufus's flat after her first morning of private investigating, disguised in a slightly dodgy wig and wearing one of Rufus's ginormous fake designer tracksuits. 'I'm pretty sure the troll wasn't any of the people I've hounded or snooped on this morning. Now I feel stupid as well as exceedingly cross. What the hell am I meant to do?'

'Give my tracksuit back and make me a cup of tea?' Rufus suggested. 'Seeing as I'm not charging you rent. Did you bring my Maccy D's?'

She threw the now-greasy paper bag at him, still confused at how he thought he was going to tone up his bum cheeks if he was still eating three Quarter Pounder meals as a mid-afternoon snack.

'It can't be Gary Pratt,' she said, flopping down on the sofa next to Rufus and grabbing a carton of fries. 'I turned up at his place and his new girlfriend was *really* nice. They're actually quite sweet together. She said he recently dropped his phone down the toilet and hasn't bothered with social media since. And in any case, she's been keeping him "*far too busy*" in the boudoir. I mean, I've no idea if that's true, but I haven't had any crap from his usual profile for at least a week, and I can't see why he'd bother trolling me if he's found his own happiness. What would be the point?'

'Maybe she's in on it?' Rufus asked, through a mouthful of beef patty. 'Like a dastardly duo.'

Alyssa shrugged. 'It's possible, but instinct tells me they were being truthful, and they did show me his ruined phone and the live parcel tracking for the replacement that hasn't yet arrived.'

'And that latest ex of yours? Arnold?'

'*Arnaud*. Nope. I didn't get stalkerish vibes when I quizzed him either. Anyway, he's been out of the country for a month so he can't have been hiding in Hartglove's bushes, and he was on a plane without Wi-Fi yesterday when those messages came through. He showed me his tickets. He's moving to LA with work soon, and he's just got a promotion. Arnaud's in such a good place. Again, I can't see why he'd make trouble for me after all this time.'

'Lover boy Devan?'

'No way!' Alyssa bit back. Even the sound of Devan's name reminded her how desperately she'd been missing him. She'd been in touch through messages, but she hadn't wanted to ruin his work trip, so she'd kept her words light. And she certainly hadn't dropped any bombshells.

'Well, something's not right with him and his obsession to be around you. You know, when I racked my brains, I recalled something. I didn't want to freak you out after you'd started the Love Tasks. But I remembered he came to London trying to hunt you down, when you first got popular as The Love Coach. Wanted your address and everything. Married man, he was, according to his Facebook status. I told him to get lost. Potential lurker vibes right there. Just saying.' He held up his hands, in a *don't shoot the messenger* pose.

'He came to London looking for me?' Wow. Now that she hadn't known. But that didn't make Devan lurker-ish, did it? Even if he hadn't mentioned it.

Rufus scribbled Devan's name onto the list of suspects she'd left on his mug-stained coffee table. She glared at it and promptly crossed it off. She still hadn't confessed to Devan that she'd disappeared from Hartglove, but it *wasn't* because he was a suspected crook.

'The waitress?' Rufus asked, pointing to the next person on her list.

'Princess Trudy? Well, she does have form,' said Alyssa, remembering how the bored-looking, plastic-tiara-wearing waitress from the grim café where she used to meet Rufus had once posted to her forty-three followers that Alyssa Heart was full of *'bullshit'*. 'But I got a message from the troll while I was questioning her. And in fairness, she did look genuinely confused by my allegations.'

'A new troll message? What did it say?' Rufus was already on his second burger, red relish dripping down the side of his goatee, making him look like a sports-gear-donning werewolf.

'It asked when I'm going to declare that I'm pulling out of the love tasks and the 'Appy Together g-g.'

'When are you doing that? Is this going to affect my cut?'

'I'm not, Rufus! Have you been listening to me since you picked me up yesterday?'

'Not so much.' He pulled a face, like that was obvious.

She couldn't fault his honesty.

'I'm not going to be pushed around by this loser. It suits me that they think I'm playing ball, in the short term. It buys me time to search them out and bloody well destroy them.'

Rufus started choking. 'Steady on,' he mumbled, after pulling a half-chewed piece of gherkin out of his mouth. 'You're no good to me in jail.'

'That's true. And I'm not going to physically annihilate them.' Alyssa pondered it. 'Though I'll probably give them a good telling-off.'

'Petrifying,' Rufus joked.

'And maybe some well-deserved payback.'

By the same time the next day, Alyssa had joined Rufus on his three takeaways on the sofa plan. Only this time she was lying down and sulking as she shovelled fast food into her mouth, and she'd opted for added bacon and cheese.

'You do know you're at serious risk of spots and cellulite,' said Rufus, who was a fine one to talk. 'You might be annoying, but I do need you half decent, if I'm going to get you more work.'

'Who's going to offer me work now?' she asked incredulously, wriggling to get comfortable in another of Rufus's old tracksuits, which were remarkably well-suited to her new pastime of wallowing.

He shrugged. 'Might happen.'

She didn't know how, because she wouldn't be putting herself out there anytime soon, and she hadn't seen Rufus do anything that looked like agenting since she'd arrived, nearly two days ago. Oh, that heady time when she'd been powered by fury and full of fight, ready to confront her culprits, make one of them crumble and do something heroic to rectify things. Then she would have had the headspace to work out what to do about this terrifying final love task. The task in which she was expected to miraculously let go of her fears and perform a grand gesture of love, like something from a cheesy romcom. Such gestures usually involved shouting from balconies or declarations in stadiums or running through the snow in your underwear. Well, she'd eaten too many chips for that last one.

The problem was that none of her suspected trolls had seemed that guilty-looking. And now she was out of ideas and her thoughts were spiralling. What if she could never find this person? What if she did find them, and another one popped up in their place, like a giant game of whack-a-mole? Would things always be like this?

'Maybe I should withdraw from living my life so publicly. I'm bringing danger to myself and the people I care about.'

'Calm down, love,' said Rufus, snatching away her bag of fries. 'You're not exactly Cameron Diaz. Though if we're ever going to drag you up the ranks a bit, you should probably brush your hair.' He nodded in the direction of the spare room where she'd been sleeping, amid various dusty fitness contraptions and a weird collection of plastic celebrity dolls.

'Maybe I should take myself and my coaching business offline and advertise in the old-fashioned way. Did you know I got flyers printed? It didn't go so badly.'

'You have a face for TV.' He squinted at her. 'Or at least radio. And how are you going to make me any moolah if you aren't out and about, taking on new gigs?'

'I just don't think I'm cut out for—'

'Are you going to let an internet troll ruin your career? One that I've just resurrected! It might be about to take off. But not if you keep wearing that lousy tracksuit.' He shuddered. 'It's so last year.'

She covered her face with her hands. 'Oh *God*.'

Now she was taking pep talks from Rufus the bloody doofus. As much as it was sweet of him to put her up like this when she was down on her luck, he was hardly anyone's life role model.

And worse than everything she'd dared to say out loud was the thing that was truly eating her.

What if it was *love* she wasn't cut out for?

Maybe she was no good at this heart-on-your-sleeve stuff. She'd tried to put herself out there as a more open version of herself and look what it had caused. Somebody *hated* her for it and was determined to wreck her life and the lives of the people she cherished. She was a disaster. Her trying to love and be loved was a catastrophe. The people of Hartglove were better off without her. She let out a huge sob, snotty tears dribbling onto Rufus's sofa. He threw a box of tissues at her.

'This is beneath my paygrade. And not to sound like your mum, but you could probably do with a scrub.' He pulled another face.

'So are you going to bin off the rest of this love app gig? Should I let them know, and see if we can still salvage our last payment?'

She blew her nose loudly and sat up. 'Undecided. But I am going to use the bathroom.'

Wasn't it when you showered that the best ideas came?

## Chapter 47

A grand total of zero useful ideas came to Alyssa while she was in Rufus's shower. On the plus side, at least she was clean and vaguely presentable when the video call came in from Devan.

Her heart soared at the sight of his name ... but how was she going to explain this mess? She'd been longing to talk to him, though since she'd last seen him, she'd kept her messages breezy – and she definitely hadn't mentioned trolls or fleeing to London. *Again.* None of this felt like the kind of thing to be discussed over a jolly phone conversation while he was on an important work thing, but she couldn't keep pretending all was well – and a video call was almost face to face.

She took a deep breath, adjusted the towel wrapped around her hair, and pressed to answer.

'Alyssa, where are you?' He squinted at the screen. 'I'm back from the conference and you're not at The Cow Shed. I'd wanted to surprise you. The spare key's not behind the sign and Jess said you didn't collect Pikachu and Minnie. Is everything OK?'

The look on his face seemed like genuine worry rather than stalkerish-ness, and she hated that she was even assessing him in that way.

'I hadn't planned to let myself in,' he said quickly. 'I was just worried that you weren't answering the phone or your door, and nobody had heard from you. I panicked that you might have had an accident.'

'I've been in the shower,' she explained.

He cocked his head, his forehead creasing. She could tell he was wondering whose shower, and why it wasn't her own, but that he was too polite and trusting to question her. Desperate to stop his heart from sinking, she decided it was time to fill him in.

'I'm in London, with my agent.' And as calmly as she could, she began recounting everything that had happened since she'd last seen him.

She hadn't been sure if she was going to share all of that, until she'd seen his concern. His deep blue eyes, magnified in size and loveliness by his thick-framed glasses that slid down his nose every time his forehead creased a little more. She winced as she told him about the photos of Emmalina and the threats to declare Devan wasn't her biological dad. His jaw tightened, and she could tell the fist of his free hand was probably doing the same, in defence of the child who was so precious to him and who was his pride and joy of a daughter in every way that mattered. She was expecting him to shout or get cross, because she'd brought this mayhem to their door. She wouldn't blame him for letting rip or telling her never to come back to Hartglove with her circus of problems and fake news. But he did none of those things.

Instead, he looked hurt. Which was *worse*.

'So you escaped to London,' he said quietly, as though still trying to process it. 'You didn't feel you could turn to me?'

His confused eyes seemed to say: *And you thought your dimwit agent was a safer bet?* Although he wasn't catty enough to voice it. She bit her lip, remembering what Devan had once confided in her. *I'm nobody's first choice.* She couldn't let him feel that way.

'It's not like that. It's just you were busy with work, and—'

'Alyssa, my work is *never* more important than you.'

A pang of guilt hit her chest, because she *had* sometimes

put her love coach reputation before being honest about their relationship. On the scale of great conversations, this was at the rotten tomatoes end.

'Will you be ... coming back?' he asked.

He was trying not to be pushy, which broke her heart even more. What she wouldn't give to be wrapped in his arms and feel safe again. But she'd come to London for a reason.

'I hope so. Though I have a lot to think about right now, and I want to somehow fix this. If I've brought this about with my stupid false pretences, I need to sort it out.'

'Whatever this is, you have *not* brought it about,' he said more firmly. 'That's not how trolling works. It's on them, not you. *Always.*'

'OK,' she replied, unsure how the hell anything worked anymore.

'Wait. Do you suspect me?' His face fell.

'No, of course not.'

Despite what both Rufus and the unknown keyboard maniac had suggested, she really didn't. But she did have questions.

'Did you come to London looking for me, a while after I left Hartglove?'

Devan's eyes widened. In hindsight, maybe this wasn't the best time to ask him about what Rufus had suggested, as now it looked accusatory.

'Who told you that?' he asked. Then he sighed. 'Rufus.'

Though where most people might have ranted about Rufus stirring the poo with a massive stick, Devan remained civilised. How she loved that about him.

'Yes, I did go to London,' he admitted. 'I hadn't been able to trace you as Beryl. But when I happened to notice you online as Alyssa Heart, I did come after you to try and talk. I told you that Sylvie and I were worried about you, and I hated how we'd left things. The only way I could think to get in touch was through your agent. But he told me you were settling down with some rich bloke, and a married man like me shouldn't be sniffing around you. He kind of had a point, even though I wasn't truthfully married, and I felt embarrassed and foolish about the whole thing. So I backed off and stopped trying to find you.'

Her heart felt heavy as she tried to take it in. He had come after her, just like Rufus had said. He'd wanted to explain things. What if he'd been able to? Would the past ten years or so have been different? Chances are, she would have been in one of her superficial relationships. But might she have listened? She guessed Rufus had only been trying to protect her blossoming love coach status and perhaps any money he stood to make from it.

'Hang on. Are you wondering if I display the hallmarks of a stalker?' He blinked a few times, as though he wasn't quite sure.

'No! I'm just trying to get my head straight, and nothing I'm asking you has got anything to do with this trolling.'

Well, apart from her next question, which was something mentioned by @whoami23456 – but only because she couldn't stop wondering.

'Did you … create 'Appy Together with any particular purpose in mind?'

His mouth dropped open. 'Are you trying to ask if I created the whole thing just to suck you into it, in the hope we could get back together?'

'I don't mind if you did,' she said quickly. 'I mean, I might have once, but …' Wow, she was digging herself a hole. 'It's just that you sort of named it after our song …'

'Alyssa, I have always held a torch for you. I'm not going to lie about that. And maybe that song was on my mind, and I may have entertained a few romantic ideas. But I would not doctor my own piece of software to try and force you to spend time with me. Call it coincidence or fate, or the fact I'm not too bloody bad at inventing an algorithm that works in matching the right people together. But please do not suggest I'm some sort of stalker or troll.'

'I'm honestly not, I just—'

'I'd thought we were a couple now. That we would deal with this sort of thing together.' He raked a hand through his hair. 'I had similar threats from this @whoami profile. One before the tango night, and another during our spa weekend. I didn't want to worry you with it. But if push came to shove, I would have spoken to you rather than legging it to a different county.'

The unsaid word *again* hung between them. How could she make him understand he was taking this all wrong?

'I'm not leaving you, or mistrusting you, and you *know* Rufus is just a colleague and a very odd friend?'

He held up a hand. 'If you want to back out of whatever the last task might be while you think about things, I won't be a dick about it. In fact, maybe you should, if you have that many concerns about me I'd just be grateful if you'd keep me in the loop.'

Keep him in the loop? Now he was moving from civilised to professional. She didn't want to become just his colleague, or to take a break from things. How was she meant to fix this?

'Maybe it was my fault for tagging you in the social media conversation in the first place,' he continued. 'Perhaps I was hoping for something to come of it. I can see why you might not trust me. If I hadn't made this mission so public, we wouldn't be in this trouble.'

'Stop, Devan. It's really not you. It's not either of us, it's just …' She scratched her head. For someone who coached others through their relationship tangles, she had limited experience of sorting out her own. When things got tough, she generally moved out and found someone more accommodating. 'I need time to sort things out.'

She wanted to reach out and touch him. To tell him everything would be all right, even though she didn't know if that was true, unless she could find this online troll. It would be so much easier if they were within hand-holding distance.

'Are you happier being back in London?' he asked. 'Perhaps

Hartglove isn't many people's first choice either, beyond the pretty blossom and occasional bunting.' He was trying to make light of it, but she could sense his tension.

'Erm, no, actually. I'm not happier here.'

She missed Hartglove, and the sense of community, and the people sticking their kindly noses into her business, and real-life connection, instead of friends who only existed on her phone screen – and the caramel apple *everything*. Though she was terrified that if she didn't get to the bottom of this mystery, she may never be able to trust and let down her barriers again – in Hartglove or anywhere. She had thought being in London, where people were too busy with their own lives or minding their own business, would be easier. But it just felt lonely, and she wasn't sure who she could trust outside the walls of Rufus's apartment. She'd lived in the city for over a decade and still had no one to turn to. She thought about how Sylvie and Jess were always ready with advice, nice biscuits and macramé – she'd never get that here.

But as she opened her mouth to try and explain that without adding to Devan's suspicions it was him she didn't trust, he changed the subject, as though he couldn't face hearing her polite excuses.

'Is that a plastic Miley Cyrus doll behind you?' Devan screwed up his face, getting closer to the screen. 'And wait. Harry Styles?'

Alyssa checked over her shoulder. 'They're part of Rufus's extensive collection. Although don't get me started on the bizarre gym equipment I'm sharing a room with. If you've never topped and tailed with a Fab Abs & Flab Massager, you're missing out.'

'And you're sure you're safe there?'

'Rufus is harmless. And he needs me in one piece, with an untarnished reputation, so he can make his *moolah*. He's the last person who'd be out to break me. In fact, most days, he's too lazy to drag himself from the couch.'

Devan let out a tense breath, as though frustrated she would choose to be somewhere quite so odd rather than with him.

'Honestly, I'll be OK.'

'Right. Look, Emmalina's trying to get through. I'd better take this.'

'Of course.'

And then he rang off.

Alyssa dropped her phone onto the bed, her face falling into her hands.

'Urrrrrrrgggghhh.'

On the *reasons to be cheerful* side, Devan didn't seem to know about 'Appy Together's final love task for them – her grand gesture of love. Though the idea of it had been filling her with dread, even before that stunted, confusing conversation. Now she wasn't *at all* confident he'd be open to any attempt at a romantic gesture from her. And she wasn't sure she blamed him.

# Chapter 48

'You sure you can trust that Devan?' asked Rufus, from his usual spot on the sofa.

He waved his phone in Alyssa's direction. She was cowering in an armchair as she scrolled through the breaking news on hers.

It was less than two hours since she'd had the painful video call with Devan, and fresh gossip had just broken online. One news group was reporting the *'latest 'Appy Together scandal'* was that she and Devan had had a gigantic falling-out and she'd fled Hartglove, refusing to complete the final, unknown love task and calling Devan's app *'a load of fake turd'*.

It didn't even sound like something she would say. Did that at least mean the troll couldn't know her well? Because she assumed this was the evil handiwork of whoever that was.

'Of course I trust him,' said Alyssa, sinking further into her pink hoodie as she read. 'The timing is just a coincidence. It's not like this reflects our actual conversation.'

Her soul was sinking at the fact that, if Devan saw this, it would add to his fears that she didn't trust him, and that she'd legged it for good. She'd tried to message him, but he hadn't opened it.

She did trust Devan, implicitly. But this situation had shaken her – made her question everything. And she couldn't help wondering who else Devan might have spoken to about what was going on, however innocently. He wasn't as used to this online life as she was. And she wasn't used to opening up to people and how vulnerable that made her feel. She hated having to doubt anyone, but her mind needed to work things through logically if she wanted to find answers. And there was a limited number of people who knew enough to make trouble.

Teijo had been messaging both her and Rufus to find out what on earth was going on. He was *not* over the moon about things, so presumably he wasn't behind this – although all sense of reason was beginning to evade her. Her head was a jungle.

'I'm going to lie down.'

'Hey, we'll get through this.' The look of almost genuine concern on Rufus's face touched her. *Almost genuine* were as deep as his feelings got, and she understood that. She used to be the same. 'Every cloud, right?'

'Right,' she said feebly. She was struggling to see any silver linings to this shit show, and she simply wanted to sleep.

She didn't know how long she'd been sleeping when she heard the banging on her bedroom door, but it was light outside, so in her misery she must have slept through the night.

'It's me, and I think I've found your silver lining.'

She sat up and straightened herself, pulling the duvet around her even though she was still fully clothed.

'Come in.'

Rufus flapped into the room like an excited chicken, reeling off what he called '*the best news since Khloé Kardashian tried copper tones*'.

And perhaps she should have been more excited. She should have jumped out of bed and danced the Macarena, insisting on celebratory apple-themed cake. But as he regaled her with the offers of work that were apparently flooding in now she was a '*fallen angel*' with a healthy bit of scandal brewing, she just felt sick.

Since the incorrect reports that she'd blown off 'Appy Together and caused outrage, she was being headhunted for various celebrity reality TV gigs.

Rufus was seeing the pound signs, and if this had happened a few months ago she would have been bouncing off the walls on a pogo stick. This had been exactly the thing she'd wanted, hadn't it? Being well known for what she did. Being sought out. Creating an impact, building her reputation.

She looked around at Rufus's spare room. If she dragged herself to the window, she would see life outside. Canary Wharf, with its tall, sparkling buildings, the waterside with its luxurious boats. People busying by with their impressive lives or stopping to shop or dine. There was a time she would have loved to live somewhere like this. If she took up these offers, she could probably afford to – without having to resort to a wealthy bloke.

But as she looked at Rufus's array of freakish celebrity dolls and discarded butt-lift machines, it was like a weird reflection of the superficiality of it all. She couldn't think of anything worse than spending her time doing TV shows in jungles, being forced to eat witchetty grubs with the latest fallen politician, or prancing around an island in some dreadful bikini.

She didn't want any of that. She craved the quiet but quirky town life she'd been beginning to become a part of. Cosy nights in with Devan, watching romcoms and giving them ratings for their glorious cheesiness. Morning strolls in Hartglove, bumping into Jess for a chat about the weather, or popping to the shared garden to check on her broad beans and have an al fresco cuppa with Mrs H and Horace. Discovering Anna Farina's latest flavour of tiramisu, always served with a *buon appetito*. Or treating herself to pie and chips with Sylvie at The Rat and Raspberry, reminiscing on the days when they'd worn crop tops and worshipped Katy Perry. Simple, happy pleasures, with no desire to make a false impression and no one to judge you if your nails looked ugly.

Rufus was rubbing his hands together, which brought her

annoyingly back to the present.

'Which offers are we interested in? All of them? Shall I play them off against each other?'

Was that plastic doll of Ryan Gosling winking at her? She rubbed her forehead. Not even the thought of a gorgeous Gosling could cheer her up.

'No! Thank you. I need time to think.'

Rufus's face dropped. 'You are into these deals though? I mean, that lowly life in the arse end of nowhere, living in a pig pen and pretending to go out with an ex who once dumped you, isn't your style.' He rearranged the curly plastic hair of an Alicia Keys doll, smiling a little too fondly, his jaw beginning to tighten. 'You were made for so much more.'

He said the last words through gritted teeth, and a strange, cold feeling crept across Alyssa's skin. Had she been missing something? An odd new suspicion was starting to percolate.

'It's a converted barn, not a pig pen.' Alyssa pushed herself out of bed. Maybe she'd believed Rufus had been kind in putting her up, but she didn't have to listen to his drivel. 'And that life was my style. I just have to find a way to get back to it. Now, if you'll excuse me, I need to get ready.'

She ushered her agent out of the room, resisting his protestations. She needed space to think. Because even when the universe had just thrown her what looked like a sparkly bone, she didn't want one bite. All that glittered was absolutely not gold.

'Why don't you meet me at our usual café in half an hour?' she suggested. 'The one with Princess Trudy and the *crappucinos*? We'll look through the best of the offers. Go and order the bacon butties.'

She didn't have to ask him twice. With the promise of lucrative deals and meat, he was soon scurrying out of the apartment. Though this time, from behind the privacy of the almost closed blinds, she was watching him. Keeping him in view as he walked along the wharf, Alyssa tapped out a message to @whoami23456:

*@alyssaheart_thelovecoach – This is the last chance I'll give you to come clean. Who are you and why are you doing this? I'm guessing it was you who leaked the false rumours about me walking out on the 'Appy Together gig in a blaze of fury.*

As she sent the message, her stomach was in knots. She couldn't tell whether she was desperate for her suspicions to be right – or wrong. If they were right, she could bloody well fix this. She could put this person in their place, once and for all, and she could take back control of her life. But that would also mean that someone she had trusted had cruelly tricked her. She'd confided in them, taken shelter under their conniving little wing, and had allowed herself to be completely duped. It nearly didn't bear thinking about.

Yet if she was wrong, then she was back to being a desperate woman without a plan.

Her eyes were trained on Rufus, and as he stopped and put a hand on his pocket, she felt like her heart had stopped too. He pulled out his phone and checked the screen. His back was to her, so she couldn't see the look on his face.

But she could see from her own phone screen that her message had been *opened*.

Then Rufus gave a quick glance up towards the apartment windows. She ducked back slightly, even though she was sure he wouldn't be able to see her through the slightest crack in the blinds. Then he looked back at his screen and began tapping. Three dots appeared on her screen to show her that *whoami* was typing. *Urgh.* She held her breath. Sure enough, a message came through to her. Rufus gave a shifty look around, then continued on his walk.

Steeling herself, she checked the message. Just as she'd suspected, it was from the troll – at the exact same time she'd seen Rufus on his phone. Having spent the last few days with him, she hadn't seen him receive many messages. And when he did, he usually looked gloaty rather than secretive.

**@whoami23456** – As Bryan Adams would say – Everything I Do, I Do It For You. If you knew who I was, you might even thank me.

Worse luck for him, she did now know who he was. And it was foolish of him to make Bryan Adams references when she'd seen his scratched CDs and that collection of creepy celebrity dolls. Now she knew who it was, she knew what she had to do.

# Chapter 49

Alyssa was glad Rufus's favourite crappy café was as deathly quiet as usual, and that Princess Trudy was behind the counter looking bored. The waitress may only have had forty-three Instagram followers, but with a quick whispered explanation, Alyssa discreetly handed Trudy her phone. Because what was about to happen was not a thing to be missed.

Alyssa plonked herself down at Rufus's table, having stashed her suitcase behind the counter. He was engrossed in his phone.

'I don't mind a bit of Bryan Adams,' she said, casually. 'Good song that one.'

As she'd been hoping, she caught him off guard. 'Yeah,' he said, grinning and looking up, as though they'd not long had a conversation about him. 'Good album, in fact.'

Then his face faltered – because he'd sent that message as Alyssa's troll, and he knew it.

He ran a hand over his face. 'Urgh, I'm tired. Bryan Adams?'

'You may know him from such other songs as "All For Love" and "Please Forgive Me".' She smiled sweetly, enjoying that he looked unsure how to take her.

She slid a hand across the table and grabbed one of his, squeezing it as though she was grateful for his wise, shrewd nature.

What she actually wanted to do was kick his highly untoned arse.

'It's OK, Rufus. I get it.'

'You do? I mean, you get what?'

'Why you sent a private investigator to follow me and take photos of me and the people I feel strongly about. Why you set up a bogus social media account and used it to threaten to expose secrets – not all of which hold an ounce of truth. Why you scheduled messages to arrive in my inbox when I was with you, to throw me off the scent.'

Alyssa was using some guesswork, but from the look of shock in his eyes, she was right. In the corner of her vision, she could sense Trudy was doing a good job of pretending to be staring at her phone, still bored. Rufus hadn't cottoned on.

'I didn't. I wouldn't!' He scratched his nose and cleared his throat, his eye contact shifty. He might as well be running through what *not* to do if you didn't want to look like a flaming liar.

In any other circumstances, it might have been comical. But there was nothing funny about trolling someone and threatening to blow people's lives apart. He'd put her one chance of happiness at serious risk and she would not let him get away with it. In fact, once she'd secured his confession, she'd be sharing what she knew with the police, and the minuscule list of his clients that she'd grabbed from his desk drawer. But first, she had to win his confidence.

She slid a second hand over the table, now using both of hers to squeeze his. He was shaking. A tiny part of her wanted to feel sorry for him. This sad, lonely excuse for a man, with nothing better to do than interfere with other people's lives, no doubt with the sole aim of earning more money. He'd probably envisaged some of the celebrities he obsessed over finally lining up to work with him, once he'd got her on TV. He was delusional, and she wasn't going to waste perfectly good pity on him.

'It's OK,' she repeated. For someone who'd spent so many years pretending, she was finding it a struggle. 'It's worked out well for us, you trolling me as @whoami23456 and fibbing to the media about me walking out on the 'Appy Together love tasks. It was a stroke of genius, really. Clever you.' She gave him her best smile, even though the words were leaving the taste of bile in her throat. 'Now we've got offers of *much* more lucrative work. We'll be raking it in.'

She'd massaged his dumb ego, and it was working. The shake in his hands was lessening and he was starting to smile, almost smugly.

'I knew you'd see the benefit, in the long run,' he replied. 'Whoami – good, hey? I wouldn't call it trolling, exactly. Just a nudge in the right direction. But yes. It was a stroke of genius.'

His idiotic, self-contented face was enough to make her blood boil. She pulled her hands away from his and stood up sharply.

'Rufus Diamond, you're a *troll*. A cowardly, sneaking internet bully. You've brought misery and fear into what should have been the happiest moments of my life. The moments when I was finally allowing myself to believe in something deeper, and to let myself feel it. You're right that I was a love coach who, for many years, did *not* believe in love. You're right that I hid behind an overly polished persona, pretending my life was rosy, healthy, wholesome and bloody wonderful, even though on the inside I was lonely and desperately in need of other people's acceptance. I was wrong to pretend to be someone I wasn't, even if I did so from a good place, hoping to inspire others. To help people with their relationship troubles, even if I didn't believe in the love part of that equation. But at the same time, I was frightened. Frightened that if anyone got a glimpse of the real me, they wouldn't like or accept me. I thought the real me wasn't good enough. And you were *wrong* to take advantage of my self-doubt and to use it to bribe me. And you were *all kinds* of wrong to threaten to spread malicious rumours about the people I hold dear. That was one step too far.'

As Princess Trudy moved towards them, making it clear the phone she was holding was angled at them and she'd been recording his confession, the look on Rufus's face was priceless.

But Alyssa didn't have time to hang around, gawping at looks on faces. She had a final love task to arrange. And as agonising as the grand gesture of love felt, she was ready to give it a shot – even if she had precisely no idea if she could get through without collapsing with the stress of it, nor if Devan would want to receive it.

## Chapter 50

Alyssa arrived back at The Cow Shed feeling even more nervous than when she'd first come back to Hartglove, all those weeks ago. On that first day, she'd been quaking at the thought of seeing Devan and bumping into old faces. She'd been trying to pretend, quite ridiculously, that she was the shiny, new Alyssa Heart – pink hair, a ton of followers and a snazzy career – and not unlucky-in-love, boring Beryl Bagnor. Well, that plan had spectacularly failed. And in truth, she was glad. She was now comfortable with the fact she was someone in between. She'd grown, as all people do – but she was far from glossy or perfect. And she was done pretending.

This time, as she pulled the key from her pocket, her nerves fluttered because she was desperate for this to work out. She *wanted* to see these people. She *wanted* this. To be exactly here, in this town where she'd grown up, with these slightly inquisitive but fiercely good friends and their wild quirks that made her own feel quite normal. And most of all, she longed to be with Devan – if, after all the chaos, he wanted that too. So this time the stakes were higher than ever, because her heart was *all in*, like an apple in a crumble.

During the train journey back, her plan for the final love

task had slotted into place in her mind. She knew what was needed. She just had to hope she could round up helpers. That people would even want to help, after the rumours on social media about her doing a dump and run – like she'd promised Emmalina she wouldn't – even if it wasn't quite true. And she had to hope she could pull it all together discreetly, without Devan finding out about the grand gesture of love.

Alyssa exhaled and gave her body a quick shake, still a tight knot of nerves that Devan might not want her declaration of commitment. She was about to prepare for a gesture that would involve her finally saying *the L-word* – in front of everyone. And he might tell her to bugger right off. She'd run from Hartglove twice, and who would blame him if he'd prefer a woman who was less likely to leg it? He deserved certainty and stability, a partner he could trust. She had to make him see she could be that person.

As she bent to pick up the handle of her suitcase, a small parcel near the front door caught her eye. It had been stashed, not that inconspicuously, behind the large plant pot, where she'd been trying to grow runner beans. She noticed with a thrill that a few small pods were emerging. When had she become the sort of person who got excited about vegetables? She smiled to herself. It wasn't a bad thing, and they went nicely with a decent pie.

She pushed her suitcase through the door and grabbed the parcel, her forehead wrinkling. It wasn't her birthday, and she hadn't done any online shopping. Kicking the door shut behind her, she took the parcel to the kitchen and placed it on the table, then filled the kettle. Not that she had milk, or even cake. Cautiously, she began opening the wrapped box, trying not to think about trolls. She'd shared Rufus's confession with the police and his handful of clients, and she wasn't averse to posting a few juicy clips on social media, once her next secret love task was through. With the police asking him questions, he'd be far too spineless to make trouble again.

'Oh!' Alyssa put a hand over her mouth in surprise as she took in the contents of the parcel. It was a new sign for the front of her barn, made of wood, and painted a reddish pink. She wasn't sure if it was meant to look like a heart or an apple – though now she came to think of it, they were the same shape. Perhaps apples and love were intertwined, after all. Yes, she liked that thought.

The words *The Cow Shed* had been etched onto it with a word-burning pen, in large, swirly letters. It had a note inside.

*To Alyssa*

*Mum said you'd gone somewhere, and she wasn't sure what your plans were, but I KNOW you'll be back. (We had our deal! Totally trust you.) I made this in my Design and Technology lessons. It's not quite straight, but you once told me that perfect doesn't exist and wonky is much better.*

*Hope you like the other sign on the back, in case you move one day. (Like, if you move in with my dad, I mean. Don't leave Hartglove. We REALLY like it when you're here. Missing you.)*

*Oh, and if you ever change your surname, I can make you a new sign. (Shaw is a REALLY nice surname. Just saying. But, like, no pressure.)*

*Love Emmalina. XxXxXx*

Alyssa beamed. Emmalina was the sweetest, and she was so relieved Rufus hadn't had chance to cause her turmoil. And the young girl trusted her – perhaps more than she trusted herself. That felt huge.

Alyssa turned over the wooden sign, to read the back. *Home is Where Miss Heart is.* Tears pooled in her eyes as she looked around her. This place was definitely on the wonky side, but with the items that kind locals had lent her, and small things she'd been adding, it did feel like home. She might even get some macramé plant hangers. Yet more than any of that, this town felt like home again too, even if she'd never thought it would. These people had become her people. The ones she couldn't wait to return to. She'd missed them – and one in particular.

The knock at the door made her jump. It couldn't be him. Could it? She'd updated him on the news with Rufus, but she'd said she was staying in London for a while to think things through. She hadn't liked misleading him, but this time, it was for the best kind of reason. It wouldn't be a very grand gesture if Devan knew she was back in town. This was her last clandestine mission. Though she knew keeping a secret in Hartglove might be her biggest challenge yet.

Perhaps it would be Jess at the door. Alyssa had told her she was on her way back, because she'd been stuck with mouse-sitting duties for longer than was fair. And Alyssa had mentioned she may need help with an important project – though not to tell Devan *any* of this.

When Alyssa opened the door a crack, it was clear that Jess was keen to be more than helpful. And so was half of Hartglove. Alyssa pulled the door fully open to take in the sight. There was Jess, carrying a basket of random supplies that seemed to include milk, iced gingerbread people and luxury quilted loo roll. Her arm was linked with Sylvie's, who was clutching a huge bag of pick 'n' mix as though they were still kids. On Jess's other side was Emmalina, bobbing up and down like she was desperate to hug Alyssa, but couldn't, on account of the mouse cage she was carrying. Alyssa was so thrilled to see them, she didn't even tell Emmalina she was worried Pikachu might be experiencing an earthquake with all that bouncing.

Behind them was pretty much everyone. Alyssa couldn't miss Mrs Halfpenny, who was doing a spin in what looked like a newly printed, bright pink T-shirt. The front said: '*He's Shaw Won Her Heart*' and the back asking: '*Will They Be 'Appy Together (or Two Lonely Old Ducks)?*' Alyssa couldn't help a wry smile, especially when she noticed the pile of T-shirts she was holding, which apparently read the same. Anna Farina was there, with a box of what Alyssa hoped were calorific Italian desserts. Everyone seemed to be carrying something, from her parents with a tub of frozen stewed apples – in case a girl could possibly run out in this town, to Horace in his bumblebee wellies, brandishing a bottle of alcohol-free fizz and some Vimto. Though she had no idea what they were celebrating.

'Jess said there was a project you needed help with?' said Sylvie, her eyes shining brightly.

'We love a project,' Mrs H piped up.

'And we're glad to have you home,' said Alyssa's dad, stepping forward and pulling her into a bear hug, which felt unusual, but kind of nice. 'I hope you've got the kettle on.'

*Home.* It felt good to hear that word. She hoped it could stay that way – and this final task would tell.

'You've got too many friends now for a cordless five-cup,' said Sausage Sandra, wearing a ketchup-stained apron and smelling deliciously like an onion-topped hotdog. 'I've brought the urn.'

Alyssa took a moment to thank them all.

When she'd explained her idea and got everyone to work on their tasks, Jess pulled her to one side.

'Erm. I've got something to tell you.'

Those were never great words.

Though as Jess spilled her story of not properly securing the mouse cage, meaning Pikachu and Minnie had escaped to a new life in the nearby fields, Alyssa found herself strangely smiling. Their brave escape felt symbolic, somehow. In a way, she was finally freeing herself from her own cage too. A place where she'd kept her heart locked, through so much fear and self-doubt. She'd been desperately lonely when she'd rescued Pikachu in an old shoebox – but she wasn't lonely anymore, and nor was he.

'It's fine,' she reassured Jess, passing her a cuppa and a biscuit. 'He'll be happier now. And I have everyone I need, right here.'

Well, apart from one person. That would be her next and ultimate task.

## Chapter 51

Even though the whole of Hartglove was glammed up in their Spring Ball finery, there was no dressing *this* up. Alyssa's final love task was set to be the most terrifying thing she'd ever attempted. Surviving the death-defying hot air balloon and helping Nicole Pigman to give birth without squashing her piglets had nothing on this.

Alyssa looked around Apple Blossom Lane's treasured hall. The community had done an incredible job helping her to bring this together, and all without Devan hearing a peep. She was proud of them, and enormously grateful. But somewhere in the busyness of it all, she'd managed to ignore her fears of history repeating itself. Until now. Seeing everything in place for her grand gesture of love to Devan made her heart-pounding, palm-sweaty dread come out to play.

Or maybe that was the fact she was dressed as a gigantic green sea turtle.

The idea for the big gesture had come to her, as clear as a flash, on the train back from London. It might not be as swoony as those films where they decorated a dream house or bought all the daffodils in five states, but in terms of putting her heart on the line, this was everything. And from the many rom-coms she'd devoured with Devan, there was nothing more meaningful than making a fool of yourself for love. Especially when you'd spent the last twelve years doing your damnedest to never look foolish, like she had.

With the town's help, she'd recreated the night when she'd declared her love to Devan as a carefree nineteen-year-old. The time when he hadn't reciprocated, and her heart had been shattered. She knew now he'd been called away in the middle of her love song to help Sylvie with chronic pregnancy sickness, and he hadn't known Sylvie's dad would drunkenly spout lies that he and Sylvie would later acquiesce to, for Emmalina's sake.

But knowing the truth had simply got twisted back then didn't make this evening less nerve-racking.

Alyssa had spent a huge chunk of her life avoiding her emotions and resolutely rejecting the notion of love. And she'd certainly never imagined herself publicly declaring it again. She'd hidden so much of herself behind a façade. She'd kept her guard up. And now here she was, preparing to get on *that stage* and say *that word*, wearing the most embarrassing fancy dress costume and about to sing karaoke. The same song as that night. The tune that had since made her squirm.

She paced up and down, repeating affirmations and trying not to trip over her flippers. It was just a stage. Just a song. *Just the absolute love of her life.* She tried not to think about their last awkward video call and the fact that her escaping to London might have ruined everything.

But what was a grand gesture if it wasn't shrouded in enough uncertainty to give a girl palpitations and make her head swirl?

The Spring Ball used to happen every year in Hartglove, to mark the mid-point of spring. Just like tonight, it had involved everyone dressing up in their finest. There would be dancing and revelry, and a whole lot of sausage rolls. That one ill-fated night had been her first year of attending. She'd misinterpreted Mrs Halfpenny's questionable posters, not realising that *fancy dress* had meant come in a tux or ball gown. Alyssa had taken it literally.

Of course, she'd had good reason for going dressed as a water-dwelling reptile. 'Happy Together' by The Turtles had been her and Devan's song. It was a song about loving just that person for the rest of your life. On that night, when she'd seen Devan appear at the back of the room, dressed in a smart tuxedo, having apparently understood the memo on *fancy dress*, she'd meant it. Perhaps she always had. She'd stood up on that stage and had sung her heart out, albeit with the courage from one glass of cheap wine too many.

Only by the end of the song, he hadn't been there, and she'd been completely humiliated. She'd mistakenly thought Devan had heard her words and bolted. And then the whispers had started, and Sylvie's perpetually drunk dad had shouted that Devan wouldn't be hooking up with an idiot called Beryl who dressed as a turtle and couldn't sing for seaweed, because he'd got his daughter pregnant and would be sodding well marrying her.

Alyssa put a hand over her stomach, its contents churning. The music from the band was now belting out around her and a faint tang of wine and cooked crustaceans filled the air. She gulped in a breath. And then there was a warm hand on her back, rubbing her shoulder, trying to soothe her.

'Tonight will be different,' said Sylvie, her voice reassuring. 'And I'm *so* sorry for my part in how it ended last time.'

Alyssa turned to her, waving away her apology. They'd talked about it a lot, and Alyssa didn't blame anyone for the way things had worked out, other than perhaps herself for letting that night haunt her for far too long.

'Will it be different though?' Alyssa asked her best friend. She couldn't put into words how glad she was to be able to call Sylvie a friend again, after all these years. But that wasn't taking away her jitters. 'I mean, Devan doesn't even know this is happening. He might be horrified. Maybe he's already dumped me.'

'He'd be a fool to,' said Sylvie.

Sylvie had done a brilliant job of arranging for Emmalina to distract Devan all day, while they prepared for the ball. As far as he knew, they were having a daddy and daughter day in Taybury, and he needed to wear a decent suit to take his daughter to a football dance this evening. Emmalina was more excited about the secretive plans than any of them and would hopefully keep things on track.

Sylvie grabbed a glass of fizz from a tray Jess was carrying, giving her girlfriend a peck on the cheek and passing the glass to Alyssa.

'No, thank you. I'm doing it sober, this time. Whatever happens, I want to put my full self into this. It would be too easy to dull the pain with fizz.'

'I can vouch that the wine is of a particularly good quality,' said Alyssa's mum, chinking her glass against her husband's as they arrived to give Alyssa a good-luck hug.

Maybe she should have considered that embracing in a bulky padded costume was kind of tricky. She'd spent years avoiding too much human contact, and now, when she was quite partial to a nice hug, she'd inadvertently scuppered herself with a green foam costume. Perhaps *not* ideal for the ultimate romantic gesture.

'We're proud of you for facing your fears, love,' her dad said, his pleased-father smile filling a small part of Alyssa's quivering heart.

'Proud as punch!' Mrs Halfpenny added.

Unlike the others, Mrs H wasn't dressed in a smart suit or ball gown. She was wearing a T-shirt that said '*Team Turtle*' on the front. Alyssa chose to ignore the back, which read '*Turtles don't typically mate for life, but we believe in you. And there's always self-love.*' Not for the first time, Alyssa wondered what on earth the people at the T-shirt printers thought about Mrs H's peculiar orders.

Alyssa allowed her nervous eyes to wander around the room, taking everything in. The residents from Clucky Ducks Retirement had been thrilled about Alyssa bringing back the mid-spring ball and had made heart decorations from sparkly paper, which Sylvie had hung from the ceiling, earlier that day. Horace had brought the outdoors in, with more of his potted apple trees now dotted around the room, their bright pink blossom looking pompom-like and ready to cheer them on.

Now the town had the newly renovated hall as a meeting place, Jess had set up her own macramé crafting group – The Macramé Army – and her members had been busy making bunting for tonight. And knowing Jess, she'd probably get them all dating, soon enough.

As Alyssa's gaze settled on the various groups of people, she got the overwhelming feeling there *was* a whole lot more love in Hartglove than when she'd arrived. Against everything she'd once believed, Devan's app had brought people together and so had her own efforts in coaching more locals and bringing this hall back to life.

She had to admit 'Appy Together had set an impressive final task, in terms of stretching her. If she'd been coaching a couple at this stage, she might have suggested a quiet meal for two. But where was the life-changing experience in that? At least she would always remember this – she just prayed it would be for good reasons.

Checking the clock again, she guessed she was about to find out.

## Chapter 52

Alyssa stood on the stage, her heart pounding to the beat of the band's music, the microphone slipping between her flipper fingers. She hadn't had the courage to even get on this stage since that night, nor to listen to their song, shutting off the radio if it ever came on. Yet here she was, throwing herself in like some kind of gruelling immersion therapy.

People's phones were trained on her, waiting to take photos or record. Teijo was ready to livestream the whole thing to 'Appy Together's social media, come what may. Never had Alyssa been willing to make herself a *love fool* quite so publicly. But she had to prove to Devan that she was all in on their relationship. That she loved him unconditionally. That she wasn't backing out again, without a fight. She only hoped he wouldn't be the one running when he entered the hall and realised what the hell was going on. He apparently had no clue the app had set this final love task, and he was under no obligation to accept her marine-themed advances.

Though for once, it wasn't the potential public humiliation that was eating her. Devan was worth all of that, and more. The real fear was wondering how on earth she'd deal with the heartbreak if Devan genuinely didn't want to be with her. How would she even begin to piece her heart back together?

Just when Alyssa thought she couldn't bear the uncertainty for a moment longer, the main door of the hall opened.

Alyssa's mouth dropped. In all her wild imaginings, none had involved *this*. Were her eyes deceiving her? She shook her head. Because there was Devan, arriving at the ball in a turtle outfit that perfectly matched her own. From the look on Emmalina's grinning face as it peeked out from behind him, she guessed his daughter had a lot to do with it.

And though Alyssa felt like she'd loved this man for a lifetime, nothing had prepared her for the way she would feel when she saw him standing in the doorway. Even dressed as polyester sea life, he took her breath away. This was the moment she was meant to sing. To lift the microphone to her lips and belt her heart out. To declare her deepest, most soul-shattering feelings to a quirky tune. But she needed a moment to take him in. To be sure he was real, and not some perfectly formed figment of her wayward imagination.

The waves of his badly behaved hair glistened under the disco lights, his natural wisps of auburn being joined by vibrant flickers of green and blue. Strobe lights flashed around him, streaking across his face and illuminating its intense look. He wasn't wearing his glasses tonight, though he looked serious about something. Was he serious in a good way? Whatever was going on, he was making her legs wobble.

And though she could have done with a few more moments to gather her thoughts, and her heart was in her mouth, the plucking notes of the song began. Though The Turtles, who did not to her knowledge dress as turtles, though at some point in her lovestruck teens she'd decided she would. And then far too quickly, the drums kicked in, and there was no further time to waste.

Pushing through her internal anxious blizzard, she lifted the microphone and began to sing. The words came shakily at first. She wasn't used to singing, having avoided it as much as possible since the last time. She hadn't practised, because raw emotions were better than polished ones, even if she was now cursing herself for not being prepared. She knew the words by heart, even after all this time. She always had, since that night. Though as Devan stepped towards her across the dance floor, the crowds already parting, she could barely remember her own name, let alone a string of 1960s lyrics.

Alyssa heard words about day, night and holding tight swirling around her, and she could only assume they were coming from her. With the dizzy mix of nerves, fear and a sprinkling of hope, it was like the strangest out-of-body experience. She gave her arm a discreet pinch. She was definitely here. With the movement of darkness and flashing lights, it was hard to read Devan's face, until he was in front of the stage, looking up at her. And at last, she saw those eyes that she could disappear into, like deep pools under a midnight sky. As she looked into them, it was clear they were smiling, and that his lips were moving in tune with hers. He was singing the words too. Her heart leapt.

And so did he, right up onto the stage, making easy work of the steps, even dressed in his costume. He had one flipper on backwards, and the material was so tight across his chest that he looked like the kind of sea creature that worked out a lot. But from the look of profound determination on his face, he was *her* sea creature. And she was his.

Someone from the band passed Devan a microphone, and soon his words came through to her as clearly as hers were to him, and to everyone. As they gazed at each other, both singing unashamedly in a key that would make dogs howl, the lyrics passed between them like declarations to each other and whoever cared to listen. *They meant this.* They were words about a love that would endure, about happiness and blue skies and being each other's only one. Alyssa was more than ready for all of it, whatever the skies would bring. As Devan took one of her flipper hands in his and pulled her close, she felt like she might burst with happiness.

As the song reached its crescendo, the whole room seemed swept along in the joy of it. Arms waved, and there was a chorus of *ba-bam-booming*, as though nobody was quite sure what the words were, but they were all in for the sentiment. Before she knew what was happening, Devan was twirling her around on the stage, microphone wires tangling around and flipper slippers getting all in a knot. And they were laughing and clinging to each other as though none of that mattered.

She almost didn't want the moment to end. When the song reached its final bars, she wondered what was next. She hadn't prepared for anything beyond the song, barely daring to think about whether Devan would stay to hear it through. But he was here, and he was holding her, their faces close, his sweet, warm breath against her cheek. She was vaguely aware of someone from the band taking the microphones and unravelling them, and the next tune was something softer. With a glance around, she could see family and friends watching on. Her mum was swatting away camera phones, including Teijo's, because she had made it through the final love task – the dread-inducing romantic gesture. The world had seen enough, and the rest would be just for them. Alyssa would thank her mum for that later, because she'd learned she wanted her life to be a lot less public. Her heart was not for sale.

Devan's mum Dawn was in the front row too, her eyes brimming with happy tears, Devan's dad's arm wrapped around her shoulders. Emmalina was bouncing with excitement, and if she wasn't mistaken, Mrs Halfpenny was waving a banner that said '*He's Turtley into You*'. She hoped that much was true.

Devan cleared his throat, and her gaze was drawn back to him. He removed his flipper arms and took her face gently in his hands. His eyes roamed her features, as though he was drinking her in. Once again, it was the sort of moment they'd watched together in so many films, and now it was happening for them – if she dared to believe it.

'I thought you didn't like that song?' he asked softly.

'I didn't like what happened the last time I sang it. But I was ready to risk singing it again.'

'I'm sorry for—'

She put a finger to his lips. 'Don't be. Life has a funny way of unscrambling itself in the end. And if that night had ended differently, you wouldn't have such a great daughter to show for it.'

'I've got to tell you, she struggles to keep a secret.' He looked down at his turtle costume.

'And here was me thinking you always dressed like that for a shell-ebration.'

His face lifted. 'I'm giving your romantic gesture and accompanying jokes the full ten in the cheesiness ratings.'

'Well, I'm honoured.' She moved her face closer to his. 'But in all seriousness, I don't want you to think this is any kind of gimmick, or a stunt for social media likes. In fact, I would have much preferred for people *not* to see me dressed like a big green salad bowl while singing my love for you, particularly badly.'

He gave a gentle nod. 'I know. I'm touched you were willing to put your heart on the line for me.'

'Because I love you, Devan. I'm an absolute love fool for you. Somewhere deep inside me, I always have been.' It was one thing singing her feelings, but finally saying *I love you* properly ought to have been huge. And yet, the words had come so naturally, like an *of course*. Because she'd never been so sure of them. As she spoke, it was as though her heart was opening, and a million heart-shaped butterflies were fluttering out – even if she was definitely imagining that last bit.

His eyes widened a touch, as though he understood how much courage it must have taken her to say the words.

'I love you too,' he said softly.

Although it seemed like the crowd could lip-read.

Cheers rose up around them as he drew her face to his, their mouths finally touching, setting off confetti cannons in her soul.

Time almost slipped away as they spun gently together, dancing to the music, and kissing as though nothing else mattered. The spotlights faded, and with a bit of whispering from somewhere below, the red velvet curtains closed on them, shielding them from view. But unlike the last time she'd been up on this stage, the swish of drapes didn't signify the end of things.

This was just their beginning.

## Eight Months Later

It was a crisp winter's day when the community of Hartglove gathered in the hall on Apple Blossom Lane to hear the results of The Love Awards. Just one year before, they'd been voted Most Loveless Town of the Year. Since then, the residents had been on a mission to turn their fate around. They'd used 'Appy Together and the love tasks to bring about more budding relationships, and the promotion from Alyssa and Devan's own love tasks had gone down a storm.

Alyssa had been building up her love coaching business in the area, rather than living online – and when clients were tricky, Mrs Halfpenny let her use the purple wingback truth chairs outside her allotment shed. They worked. Mrs Halfpenny herself had been the poster girl for Devan's new self-love app, complete with as many printed slogan T-shirts as she could possibly wish for. They'd had more community events and dances, and everyone had been working on the shared gardens as a place to sit or for love to grow.

Following the abundance of spring blossom, the town's apple trees had had a bumper autumn harvest. Some said that the extra romance that had been blooming had brought the trees good fortune. Alyssa was just thrilled there would be plenty of apple-inspired baking for another year to come.

She gave Devan a nudge as Teijo stood on the stage in front of them, fiddling with the projector screen. They didn't see him as often now their official tasks were over, though he'd brought along his new love interest, Cerys, tonight. They'd been matched by 'Appy Together and were well into their series of love tasks. Alyssa was confident the app had matched them well, and she hoped they'd get their very own *one sleeping bag* moment.

Devan nudged her back and slipped his arm around her waist. She didn't think the butterflies would ever stop fluttering when he did that. She leaned her head on his shoulder.

'Do you think everyone's hard work will have paid off?' she asked.

He turned and kissed her forehead gently. 'I think it already has. Whatever happens, there will be a massive celebration in this room tonight. There's one hundred per cent more love in Hartglove, whatever a tongue-in-cheek award decides.'

The official award ceremony was in London, and they knew Hartglove had been shortlisted for something, as they'd been asked to send two representatives to collect any potential award. Alyssa had been enjoying life in her quiet bubble of love lately and was doing far less in the public eye, so they'd put it to a vote, and her parents had been chosen to go. Her mum loved the limelight and was growing an Instagram following of her own. Her dad was just happy to go wherever his wife was, and no doubt he'd be over the moon with the free hot curry buffet. Alyssa employed Princess Trudy to do most of her social media tasks these days, and as for her celeb-hungry ex-agent, she'd heard he'd got a new job unblocking lavatories while the police looked into what a terrible shit he'd been. It pleased her that he no longer ran his agency and nobody would touch him with a toilet plunger.

'I'm glad we only have to watch this on a screen,' Devan whispered. 'Because I'd like to get you home early tonight.'

'Oh yes?' she replied innocently. 'Your place or mine?'

His lips twitched into a smile. 'Wouldn't you like to know?'

It wasn't long before Teijo got the projector working and the winner of the Most Loveless Town award grumpily accepted their trophy. The whole room cheered that it wasn't Hartglove. So what had their little Cotswold town been shortlisted for?

As the compere on the screen began to announce the places shortlisted for Lovey-Dovey Town of the Year, the camera swept to Alyssa's parents. Their faces lit up, and the room gave a collective whoop.

'Do you think we'll win?' asked Emmalina, bounding over with her usual puppy-like energy. Her mum and Jess followed behind, arm in arm and smiling. 'I mean, I'd never seen my dad being lovey with anyone until you came along,' she said to Alyssa. 'No offence, Mum.' Her eyes moved to Sylvie who simply shrugged.

'None taken. You wouldn't have seen me giving him heart eyes either,' she said gently, ruffling Emmalina's hair.

Of course, Emmalina knew why Sylvie and Devan had never been that way with each other. Now she was thrilled to have three mum figures to choose from, and that Devan would always be her real dad, even if she didn't have his unruly waves or his bad taste in romcoms.

'And the winner is …'

'Wait for the world's longest drumroll.' Emmalina rolled her eyes. 'Shall I make a cuppa?'

'Hartglove! Congratulations to the town for pulling together and showing us all a thing or two about love blossoming,' said the compere, all cheesy smiles and sparkly formal wear.

The whole room erupted with applause and delighted yells as Pearl Bagnor made her way to the stage to collect their award, even though she couldn't hear them through the screen. And as she accepted it, Emmalina pulled something out from behind her back and gave it to Devan.

'Are you going to ask Alyssa if she's willing to accept her award?' Emmalina asked.

Devan nodded sagely and turned Alyssa to face him, holding the wooden sign out towards her. 'Alyssa Heart, would you do me the honour of hanging this by my front door, this evening?'

Her forehead creased as she read the familiar sign, that usually lived by her own front door. 'The Cow Shed?'

Devan turned the sign over to show the alternative wording that had been burned into the back of the wood by Emmalina's own hand. Alyssa had almost forgotten about it.

'*Home is Where Miss Heart is*,' she read, the implication slowly dawning. 'You're asking me to move in with you?' She looked up at him slowly, praying she hadn't got that embarrassingly wrong.

'Only if you want to.'

She could see the hope in his eyes and sensed he was holding his breath.

'Is that why you were smiling when I mentioned *your place or mine*?' Checking Emmalina couldn't see, she winked at him.

'Get a room, you guys,' said Emmalina, holding out her arms to shoo the crowds away. 'And you lot can stop being so nosy.'

But Alyssa didn't care who heard her answer. 'Unequivocally yes!' She flung her arms around him, and he wrapped his around her.

She was already imagining their first Christmas together, surrounded by friends and family. They'd probably be scoffing caramel apple tiramisu and chocolate quinoa cake after a belly-busting roast dinner, a potted apple tree decorated with baubles and fairy lights glittering in the corner. It would be a far cry from her last festive season, which had been all about boring parties, fake smiley photos and a boyfriend she'd chosen for his swanky bathroom rather than for her sheer, soul-stirring love for him. And she already knew that this time, she'd be starting the new year with a happy heart and a genuine smile, rather than dragging her well-worn fake Lulu Guinness suitcase to a dodgy flat in Hackney. Or anywhere. She couldn't wait.

~ The End ~

# A Letter From Anita Faulkner

Dear Gorgeous Reader

Thank you for choosing to read Meet Me at Apple Blossom Lane (and for making it this far)! Your support means the world.

I feel like part of my heart will forever live in Apple Blossom Lane, with its flowering trees and its cast of quirky characters. I had a whole lot of fun hanging out with everyone, from Mrs Halfpenny and her never-ending supply of outlandish T-shirts and no-nonsense advice, to Horace in his bumblebee wellies, and Anna Farina with the delicious tiramisu.

Though of course, my favourite part will always be the one big love story. Alyssa had created an imaginary world for herself, but inside she was lonely. My heart was breaking for her. She so deserved a second chance at her teenage sweetheart romance, and to rediscover the joy of small-town life in Hartglove where the hugs are real and the caramel apple *everything* is sweeter. I'm so proud of her for taking a wild leap towards her happy ever after.

And an extra cheer for *Good Old Devan*, who deserved his chance to explain his story and fight for the love he'd lost. (Yes – she's *turtle-y* into you – even when you wear too-small T-shirts and strip off in allotments when you really don't need to! Bless you.) I adored writing Devan, with his big heart, geek chic glasses and nervous bravado.

All of my romcom novels so far are set in the Cotswolds (though Apple Blossom Lane and Hartglove are figments of my imagination). If you've enjoyed this one, do have a nosy at *A Colourful Country Escape* (with Lexie and those naughty peacocks), *You Had Me at Pumpkin Patch* (with Rosie and her pumpkin farm retreats), and *The Gingerbread Café* (with Gretel and her dodgy yet delicious baking). If you want the gossip on what's coming next, jump onto my mailing list! We can stay in touch.

And when you love a book, authors love YOU when you leave a review! Your kind words mean so much and help us to keep writing. So if you have a few moments, please do pop over and leave a quick review in the usual online places. Thank you for being fabulous.

Finally, do come and find me on social media! If you're a reader, author, budding writer (woo hoo!) or a generally lovely person, let's hang out.

Love

Anita Xx

**Here are my favourite places to share good fun and gossip with you ...**

My Facebook group, Chick Lit and Prosecco:
https://www.facebook.com/groups/chicklitandprosecco/

My author mailing list:
https://bit.ly/anitafaulknerhotnews

My Instagram:
https://www.instagram.com/anita_faulkner_writer/

# Acknowledgements

Writing the acknowledgments is always the hardest part – because there are SO many people to thank. I could not do this without you all! So grab a moment to congratulate yourselves. Take a bow. Give us a twirl!

If you're reading this and you've taken time to immerse yourself in the spring joys of *Meet Me at Apple Blossom Lane* – THANK YOU. I had so much fun creating this world and I'm so grateful that you're right here, embracing the magic.

I'm beyond grateful to the powerhouse teams at HQ Digital and HarperCollins. Thank you to fabulous, clever and patient editors Georgina Green, Sophia Allistone and Ellie Jardine. Your ideas, support and cheerleading are SO appreciated.

It was also a treat to work with Dushi Horti on structural edits and Sarah Bauer on line edits. Your insights helped to shape this story – so thank you. (And there will be more edits and proofreads after I type this – so huge thanks to those wonderful word polishers as well!)

Thank you to the fantastic marketing, PR and cover design teams too. You do such incredible work.

My agent, Kate Nash, has been brilliant – as always. Thank you for your valuable advice, winning title ideas and story tweaks, and for being on the other end of a call or message whenever I need you. Love having you in my corner.

On a more personal note, my husband, Neil, ROCKS! There is no way I could write books (or feel inspired to create stories about true love) without this guy. Quiet, dependable, gorgeous. Thank you for choosing me to be one half of team Faulkner!

Talking of teams, let's give my small person, Luca, a big cheer. Thank you for being the best little man and taking everything in your stride. I'm proud of you in all the ways. Keep writing your stories about fierce spider snakes.

Yaaaaay to my mum for always being so excited about my books. If it wasn't for you, taking me to libraries when I was little and reading me the best stories – from *The Velveteen Rabbit* to *Matilda* – I wouldn't be such a book geek! (And I LOVE being one of those.)

Huge thanks to my friends and family for always rocking up to yet another book thing! I am truly blessed to have you. It would take too long to name you all, but you know who you are. (Extra shout out to Vic Buchan who travels the farthest, cheers me on most days and magics up special book-themed gifts!)

To my online book friends – thank you for making this journey so worthwhile. Your kindness, cheerleading, reviews and fun photos make my soul sing. Extra thanks to all of the gorgeous Facebook groups, like The Friendly Book Nook, The Friendly Book Community, Riveting Reads and Vintage Vibes – and of course, my own beautiful Facebook group, Chick Lit and Prosecco. (If you're reading this and you haven't joined us yet, come and find us!)

And enormous thanks to the people who are right there with their social media pompoms, supporting us authors and celebrating books and stories. There will never be enough room to thank you all, but let me sneak in a word for Meena Kumari (gift-aholic!), Grace Power, Rosie Owen (bunting queen), Sue Baker, Barbara Wilkie, Chrissie Taylor, Vikkie Wakeham, Ceri

Evans – to name a few!

Bonus joy and sparkles for the world of Bookstagram (where I've met so many incredible readers). Extra excited waves to the readers, bloggers and authors who travel many miles to come to my live events too. (Just wow.)

Thank you to all who follow HQ Stories on Insta and Facebook. (Give them a follow for the best giveaways and fun!)

Sending an extra big thank-you hug to the authors and budding authors in my fiction writers' membership, Writers' Dream House. It's wonderful to have your good vibes and daily accountability, and to support you too!

And a lovely shout-out to Christina and Gloucester Book Club – you're all fabulous.

Massive thanks to the bookshops and libraries that support authors and stock our books. A special wave to Gloucestershire Libraries, Waterstones, The Cleeve Bookshop in Cheltenham and Alison's Bookshop in Tewkesbury. People who celebrate books are my kind of people.

Thank you to the Romantic Novelists' Association and their New Writers' Scheme, for being the springboard for my writing career. (If you write love stories or you aspire to, please check them out.)

To my author friends – you're the best! Thank you for inspiring me with your page-turning stories, kind words, positive reviews and boundless, beautiful energy. There's not enough ink to shout out to all of you – but I feel honoured to know you.

And if you've read this far, thank you again! Do come and join us in the Chick Lit and Prosecco Facebook group for readers and writers – where more fun and friendship awaits …

https://www.facebook.com/groups/chicklitandprosecco/